Fractured Series

Book Two

Conspiracy Theory

John Morris

Charlotte Greene

Dorset, England

Also by John Morris

Fractured Series
Inner Sanctum
Conspiracy Theory

Star Gazer Trilogy
The Gatekeeper and the Guardian
The Twelve Tribes
The Wrath of Gaia

Stand Alone Novels
Islamic State: England
Domicile

Printed in the United Kingdom (or country of purchase)

Published by Charlotte Greene, Dorset, England

Editor in Chief: Susan Dewey beeberrywoods.com/FiberEtc/

Cover: L. Fabry lfabry.com
Additional Graphics: Boris Junkovic
http://www.charlotte-greene.co.uk/Agents_BorisJunkovic.htm

Cover girl left by: african_fi (Belovodchenko Anton)
shutterstock.com/g/belovodchenko
Cover model left: Alekseenko Oksana
Cover girl right by: geloo www.freeimages.com/gallery/geloo
Cover model right: Name unknown.

Acknowledgements: Terry Dickerson, Monica San Nicolas

Dedicated to my wife, Siu Ying, & every woman who believes they
do not live in a man's world

Language: Fractured series, unlike all other work, is written in
American English.

Official author website: www.john-morris-author.com

ISBN Print: 978-1-910711-01-9
ISBN eBook: 978-1-910711-03-3

Table of Contents

Chapter 1 – Crazy Man Michael

April

The girls walked for ages until they finally found the road. Their feet hurt and they were way past tired. Annaliese quipped, piqued with frustration, "I'm pissed. There's gotta be a room for rent somewhere in Aztec. We've been walking forever. Zilch!"

She threw her bag down on the sidewalk and slumped her butt on the curb. "I suppose we could commute from Rosa's. But without transport, or even with, it's a long chunk out of each day."

April humored her best friend, "Here, have some of my isotonic juice, it'll help keep you going. That ad on the info-wall said there was a place down this road, we just gotta find it, Hon."

They sat in silence, their thoughts lost within the drudgery of trudgery. April had been staring at the house for … she didn't know how long. There was a sign in the window she couldn't read from so far away. It seemed to call to her. She was drawn to it, walked towards it, and found a scribbled note in joined-up writing. It was almost illegible until she was very close. It read, "HELP WANTED. Apply within. Michael."

April drew her fingernails across the sign from the other side of the grimy glass pane, knowing they had found their destiny; intuitively, she rang the bell.

The pair waited and April banged on the grained door of peeling paint and solid hardwood loudly. A noise came from within. They both stood down a step to wait and wonder.

The door snapped open as far as the chain would allow and a voice spat, "Wadderyouwant?"

"Sir, pardon the intrusion, but I saw the sign in your window, and well, we thought to offer our help."

"Wassat?"

April spoke slowly and loudly, "'HELP WANTED'. It says so on your window. We are here to apply. Can we help you?"

The door slammed shut.

Annaliese turned to go, muttering about his rudeness. April heard the unmistakable sounds of metallic fractures in the lock, and put a restraining hand on Annaliese's shoulder to still her escape. A stream of curses came from inside, followed by more metallic scrapings, as the man proceeded to unlock the door he had just locked. There was nothing happening. Annaliese shouted loudly, "Remove the chain."

"Huh? Damn-fangled modern contraptions, I hate the lot of you." They knew the guy must be quite old, as was the place; dated, and dilapidated.

The chain finally slipped from the safety and the door was thrown open wide. The owner beaked down at them. He changed his seeing eye and moved his glasses around his ancient skull, trying to get the girls in focus. After his examination he stood tall, thumbs resting in his top waistcoat pockets, and proudly stated, "You better come in."

He stood back, but stopped April as she put her foot inside his home and leaning down furtively, asked, "You weren't followed were you?" Solemnly she shook her head.

The crazy man ushered them quickly inside, poking his head out of the door to check everything was as it should be. He seemed satisfied, and, after locking the entrance, asked to see their credentials. April offered her SDSU ID card. The man gawked at it, and then did the same with Annaliese's ID. Satisfied, he said conspiratorially, "I didn't think you were CIA, but I had to check just to be sure. You do understand?"

He led them through to one of the most extraordinary rooms April had ever witnessed. It seemed to have been lifted straight out of the 1920's, and even had a wind-up gramophone with a huge horn coming out the top. "I've left the place more or less as Mammy and Pappy liked it, but did add that modern television over there."

He pointed at a 1950's screen that had to be black and white. It was almost buried under a mountain of debris and objet d'art. April whispered to Annaliese, "He doesn't need help in here, he needs an archae-effing-ologist."

They had stepped into a different world. He offered the girls drinks, setting down before them china teacups and saucers. He poured cold water from a teapot asking them if they would like milk, and holding silver tongs in a shaky hand, how many sugar cubes. They quickly declined.

He cursed the tea swearing, "This modern stuff is never as strong as it used to be back in the good ol' days." He glanced at the girls, seeming to remember why they were there, and stated, "You will need to fill out these forms, and afterwards, I will select one of you, or not, for the position."

April asked, "What does the job entail?"

"Why, to help of course. Isn't it obvious?"

With subtle probing, this turned out to be cooking, cleaning, shopping, and help with his medication. Once resolved, he put a couple of ancient, blank consumer questionnaires before each girl. It was clear he knew what he wanted to be doing, but had some form of mental problem. That was not to say he was insane, he was simply too old in a world that had moved on too quickly. As the sign said, he needed help.

The girls scribbled their names, qualifications, and interests quickly and handed them over for inspection. His eyebrows twitched a lot, and they were very furry, hawkish even.

Taking the forms in his hand, he paraded around the room, ruminating on his thoughts. He stood before an old oil painting of Thomas Jefferson and bowed. Turning he said, "I have deliberated over your applications, and cannot choose between them. You both have excellent credentials. So tell me, which of you can start today?"

Under the gruff exterior of a once proud man, April found him to be quite cute, in an ancient, crusty sort of way. April rose and spoke, "We come as a pair, but charge as one. We do not want money. We will look after you in exchange for food and lodgings."

Somewhere within the miasma of disassociated thought, April struck a deal that suited all of them. Annaliese was giving April looks to get out of the door fast, but April thought this might turn out all right, and may even be fun. He said, "The servants quarters are here. I will show you to your rooms, but only if you begin working right now."

The girls followed him upstairs and passed several bedrooms in the large and sprawling house, before he stopped and opened the doors to the last two. They were musty, dusty, and each had its own bathroom, being larger than their previous shared apartment. Annaliese walked into her new room, checking her Smartphone, "This place has Wi-Fi. Brilliant connection too."

April acknowledged that The Universe According to Michael was a very crazy place. She also admitted they all got along very well after a few teething problems. Michael's dementia appeared to recede at times, and he told them much about his life, which was

3

far more riveting than the crap on TV. All three of their lives settled after that night, Michael coming back to the real world in many small, but important ways, and the girls being able to devote time to college studies once more, and train for their fourth Dan Black Belt in Kung Fu.

As trust and mutual understanding grew, Michael started to mention odd things. "Tomorrow at three o'clock the New York Subway will fail, up near Baychester."

The girls thought little of it, but the next evening Michael said, "I was right about the Subway, points failure near Gun Hill Road. They say it was component failure, but I knew beforehand. How about that?"

The girls were a little perturbed, but wrote the incident off as one of those things. Two days later Michael came whistling into the kitchen, his face beaming with the delight of prescience. He called the girls to him and whispered, "On Tuesday a bridge will collapse over in Orange County. It has stood for years, but will be gone by ten a.m. Trust me, I know these things."

Annaliese brushed the remark aside, but April kept an open mind. She checked and discovered the bridge did fail, and pressed Michael for more information that evening. He told them about a cabal to blow up the Presidency. The girls laughed at first, but in time came comprehension, some of his meanderings, they realized, were facts that began to stick. Their nominal duties to cook and clean, were supplanted by what they learned, it was astonishing. The girls were learning about a different America from the one they thought they knew.

One morning Michael came through to the dining room for breakfast, and he was whistling, a sure sign he had received another of his mysterious warnings. As he ate the girls pressed him to say what was about to happen, but he smiled cheekily, and enjoyed his moment of prior knowledge.

Once replete, he looked at them and said, "Today, just after 1230 hours, Port Arthur Refinery will be hacked, and they will lose control of all their systems for three minutes. There will be a discharge of processed product into the bay. What do you make of that?"

The girls chuckled, but he had been right before, so they kept a watchful eye on the media. Nothing was reported that day and they concluded it was a false lead. They talked about it the next day, beginning to lose all interest in Michael and his crazy predictions. There was nothing on the news at all.

That evening they challenged him, wanting an end to his lunacy. He nonchalantly replied through a mouthful of food, "You don't think they would let the press get hold of it, do you? That would be why the hackers made the minor oil spill, so they could independently verify it. What's for dessert?"

Slightly chastened, the girls surfed at once for other news, April taking local media, and Annaliese activist groups. Their searches immediately revealed a leak of oil, which began at 1231 hours, and lasted for exactly three minutes, as Michael predicted. Authorities were blaming operator error for the relatively insignificant oil-spill. April read out local reports, and Michael pumped the air in delight. They had confirmed he was correct.

That was the last time they doubted him, but he would never tell them where his information came from. All he would say was, "It comes to me sometimes. Often I get it before the President does."

He winked at them, and delved into his apple pie, his face a picture of culinary inspired bliss, as he added both custard and cream.

Both girls knew there would be nothing rational coming from him again that night. They had learned not to doubt Michael, however ridiculous whatever he predicted might sound.

They had come to believe, there was a real and deadly threat, to blow up the President of The United States of America.

Chapter 2 – The Running Man

During the Easter break, April went to stay with Rosa and her Mexican family for a few days. Rosa was her espoused new mother, the one who had rescued her former runaway self, given her a new language, a new identity, and a new life. The break was excellent therapy, and she was already on the bus back to San Diego, when Annaliese called her cell and told her not to go to the shopping center as planned. "Michael has had another of his warnings, 'North entrance, running man'."

Annaliese should have known better. April went regardless, not because she didn't trust Michael, but because she needed to begin to understand his world of predictions. All she had to go on was the time, and the words Annaliese had relayed from Michael.

With fifty minutes to go, April sat across from the north entrance of the shopping center, simply watching. Later she entered and walked in search of anything to do with a man running, either in real life, as video, or advertisement. There were several posters in a sports store, but those were too far inside the complex. Everything was as it should be with her view of the mall.

Having bought what she needed, she returned to the north entrance, and hadn't walked far when she saw Usain Bolt posters advertizing one of the latest sports vehicle lines. The Auto City was one of the most popular in San Diego, and was diagonally across from the north entrance of the mall. It was very busy. She looked across and saw her least favorite fast food place ever, well, since she had grown up to know better.

She ordered the weekly special, and got a window seat on the third floor. Setting her Smartphone to the glass, she recorded the lot directly across from her in video mode. One minute later, the Star Coupe exploded and rose into the air. Her hands were a mess of seeping dressing, as she grabbed the cell and panned, then zoomed, with sticky tomato and mayonnaise fingers.

Suddenly, she was bashed in the small of her back as others tried to cram next to the window and observe the carnage. Two more explosions greeted the imminent arrival of the Fire Department, cars lifting like airplanes into the wind, before crashing down on top of other brand new models. People started running as soon as they smelled gas fumes, the river coming from an opened fuel tanker outlet set at the top end of the lot.

Someone rushed to turn off the faucet. They must have heard a click, as the person froze, then dove for cover, just before the transporter blew. The explosion showered the yard with burning gasoline that also took root in the structure of the building. The burning liquid inferno rained down upon the dealership next door. Cops hurried to seal off the access road and surrounding areas. April wiped her fingers and phone, and began to pan and zoom in earnest, moving her focus away from the scene of the attack.

She caught sight of movement way behind the commercial area and zoomed, but the distance was too great for detail. The man disappeared from the fields behind the lot into a ravine. The crowd behind her diminished, but April waited and watched. She spotted the distant figure again, as he headed toward a dark SUV, which drove off seconds later.

April knew this was very well planned, rehearsed even. She followed the vehicle for as long as she could before it disappeared from view. Police sirens approached from the distance, and one cop was already checking the crowd. She knew they would soon have extra cops on hand to stop and frisk. She quickly finished what food was edible, grabbed the ice cream, and left before she could be caught in their interrogation net.

Appearing disinterested, April caught the local bus home, eager to tell her story. Michael and Annaliese were both amazed by the video, which was soon copied to their tablet and laptop for Michael to see it properly. He became animated and spent ages examining the video repeatedly. He noticed things they had missed, and said, "I need a bigger picture."

They ended up taking him down to the superstore, where he bought the largest laptop they had in stock. Michael was delighted with the purchase once they got back and set it up for him.

Michael was preoccupied with it, and later asked to go to the library for research. Instead, April and Annaliese introduced him to browsing the internet. It became hard to eat because he had taken over the dining room table. The girls ganged up on him and forced him to use the study. He complained, "The study belongs to my Pappy."

"Michael, it is time you take your father's place as head of the family."

"But he would never approve."

"He passed over a decade ago, and would be delighted to have his son take his place. As the new head of the family you must swear an oath of allegiance before the oil painting of Thomas Jefferson."

Michael confided, "I am the last of my family line remaining. My parents remain the strongest link to my remaining reality."

Once the girls understood this, his bizarre behavior became a lot more understandable. He was not only preserving their memory, but also his meager grip on sanity.

After his vow and confession, Michael unlocked the room, which was old and musty. It had a large oak desk with leather chair centered, in front of an enormous fireplace. To one side were two matching leather recliners framing a sofa and large coffee table. On the opposite side was a study area, set with antique bureau, writing chair, and cabinets to either side.

Otherwise the walls were lined with shelves of old books, many of them leather bound and no doubt of great value. Dust lay everywhere; April doubted the room had been entered for centuries, millennia even. The girls got to work spending several hours bringing the place back to life. Michael mainly hovered outside the entrance, either lost with his internal dialogue, or talking to the portrait of the Founding Father.

They cleared the desktop of all but the banker's lamp, Bakelite rotary dial telephone, and inkwell, before starting to empty the drawers into cardboard boxes. Once cleared, they brought in all of Michael's stuff from the dining room and set the desk up for his personal use.

Michael was clearly thrilled to be officially taking his father's place as head of the family. In the days and weeks that followed, he spent virtually all of his waking time in the study. This in turn left the girls free to get on with their own studies. April was ahead of the clock, with most of her projects nearing completion, and course work well on track.

Her only problem at school was a soliloquy that each student had to perform from a noted theatrical play. She also needed to submit an additional written interpretation of what it actually meant. April knew what to say and do. That was easy with her photographic memory. She could get nowhere in trying to divine any deeper meanings. No one she talked to about it at college was any the wiser, or at least not letting on.

Chapter 2

April asked the instructor and he was, at best, ambiguous, and at worst oblique. One night she mentioned her problem in passing to Annaliese during the evening meal, and Michael appeared to ignore her. They were about to clear the table and bring in dessert, when Michael asked April to speak the opening line.

She was reciting the first verse, when suddenly Michael stood and grabbed her urgently by the hand. He went directly to a bookshelf within the study and, hardly glancing at the many shelves, handed her the original version of the play and a book of notes. "These are my grandmother's notes on the play. Use them wisely."

April glanced through the latter, and found the part, the soliloquy, but said, "This is cheating."

Michael smiled tapping his temple, "Consider it coaching from beyond the grave, that is all it is. You still have to work your own magic to perform."

April thought him done, but he added, "She should have made Broadway, but was Mexican by birth. Such a shame how deluded our preconceptions and prejudices can become."

Later, back finishing their meal, Michael waxed lyrical about her memory, and the great Mexican food she used to serve. The next night April cooked real Mexican food, as Rosa had taught her, and their relationship deepened.

When the time came, April performed the part unlike anybody else, leaving the stage with hunched shoulders. Her peers laughed and even jeered. She wanted to hide in a hole and never come out again. When the results were finally out, April scored 97%. No one else got over 80%. Regarding that particular examination, 80% represented 100% of expected score. The additional marks were awarded for personal understanding way beyond normal perception.

Soon school was out and they were free for the summer. Michael still locked himself away in his study for days on end, but he was lucid most of the time, and appeared many years younger. He was still an oldster, but now sprightly, quick-witted, and fun. April and Annaliese had the idea they may have been responsible.

Chapter 3 – Mine of Information

Rosa

Rosa sat with Tepin on a part-built terrace, seated at one of the outdoor tables that fronted the road. They had watched the sun set, and were talking quietly into the night about how the hotel would eventually become a tourist attraction.

As they chatted, they became aware of the sound of an engine approaching. The twin pots fired into the darkness, and disturbed the silence of the night. Conversation slowed as the Harley went past, and they heard it stop a few seconds later.

Tepin looked at Rosa and said, "Now why would a stranger be going to your store at this late hour?"

Rosa looked back at him, and shook her head. She was about to say more, when the distinctive engine fired. Moments later a large man drew his Super Glide to a halt outside the hotel. The Hells Angel went into reception, and shortly the serving girl rushed up and said, "He's just booked the very best room we have. He's such a hunk, even for a Gringo."

Heavy boots thudded into the bar. The stranger's voice said, "I'll take a large bottle of cold Bud and two packs of smokes."

Rosa knew instinctively who the stranger was, even though she had never laid eyes on him before. He walked out, looked around the terrace, and seeing the one he sought, he went over. "Rosa, my pleasure to finally meet you, heard a lot of great things about you."

Rosa smiled and stood up to shake his hand, "It has been a long time coming Bill, and we are delighted you finally made it. This is my dearest friend Tepin, and know there are no secrets between us, we can talk freely here."

Bill sat down and took a large gulp of his beer. He looked intently at Rosa and said, "Tell me about my daughter."

Teves

Some time later, Teves pulled up in his Sheriff's cruiser. He greeted the owner warmly. "Congratulations Rosa, I hear you finally got the kitchen plans approved. Please accept this finest bottle of Mexican red to assist your celebrations."

Rosa called for a girl to open it and said, "Thank you Manny. It has been so hard, but I finally got approval. I never realized it would be so complicated, all that red-tape and bureaucracy. I never could have gotten this far without your help, that of the Town Manager and Tourist Board. Thank you."

Teves nodded to Tepin, and looked at Bill. The stranger looked out of place, and his gut was churning with curiosity. Rosa broke the moment, "Undersheriff Teves, allow me to introduce my cousin Bill."

Teves shook hands with Bill, as he rose in lukewarm greeting. Their grip was firm, and lasted too long as their eyes narrowed. Teves looked at Bill, and then back at Rosa, failing to see the slightest family resemblance. Rose interrupted his thoughts by pouring the wine. Teves let go of Bill's hand, and put a hand over his glass, saying, "Not tonight Rosa, I am on duty. Next time, OK. I'll take a coffee if there is one going begging."

Bill clinked glasses with Rosa and Tepin, and drank the wine down in one go. He congratulated Rosa, nodded at Tepin and Teves, and moved away to the makeshift bar.

Teves watched Bill leave, and decided to find out more about this "cousin" of Rosa's, who had shown up out of the blue. Rosa said very little in response to his gentle probing, and changed the subject to the hotel. Teves stayed to enjoy his coffee, and said his goodbyes.

He returned to his cruiser, where he ruminated. Rosa was a good person, a pillar of their community. Bill seemed anything but, and Teves noted down the bike's plate. He was about to call in a check, when he received a call to attend a fatal stabbing.

Bill

Bill sat at the bar and ordered a large glass of Rebel Yell. He was thinking about Teves, when he received a call from his daughter. "Dad, I will try to leave ROTC in twenty minutes and catch the last bus back. I've missed you so much. I can't believe you finally made it."

Bill could hear the party in the background, and someone asking her to dance interrupted her call. It was a girl, which calmed Bill's fears. He also remembered being young once, and knew April thrived off experience, and a little personal indulgence. He also understood that by the time she returned, it would be bedtime.

Bill knew she would be safe, if pretty wrecked the next morning. He said, "Enjoy the party, sip water with the wine, and keep your legs closed, d'you hear me girl? I'll see you in the a.m."

April enthused, "Thanks Dad. I didn't think today would turn out like this, but we're having a great time. Love you, see you soon."

Disappointed, Bill went through to reception, intending to get on his bike and ride out of town for a bar he had noticed a little way down the road. While crossing the foyer, he was distracted into helping a migrant Mexican patron nuke his fast food. Because the device was in English, a language they did not understand, Bill found himself giving class on how to use a microwave.

As he finished, Pepe rushed up with a bottle of complimentary Rebel Yell. "They do not understand the 'Ingerlish' Señor. Thank you. Rosa has sent this for your enjoyment, and would ask you to stay a while, as she will join you a little later."

Bill looked at Pepe, wondering if he stayed where this night would lead. The free bottle was welcome, but he was seeking to lose his mind that night, not have it bombarded with another's life-trivia. Pepe said, "I go. I return with beautiful girls. One, Señor, you will very enjoy, I know it."

"Can she cook?" asked Bill.

"She cooks the very best fajitas and tacos, Señor Bill."

The bear of a man resigned himself to his fate, tore off the cork from the proffered bottle with his teeth, spat it aside, and drank deeply. He fixed Pepe in the eye and stated, "Tell her to make them with meat, not fruit, use far too much salt, and zero sugar. You understand? Can she cook burritos?"

Bill found himself surrounded by people he did not know, asking all sorts of personal questions. He knew it was their way, but it was not his. Once he had suffered enough, he stopped them dead and said, "Tell me about your lives, or I am gone."

The tales of the poor illegals were woeful, and dismally repetitive, they all shared a depressingly common thread. Despite the Rebel Yell, Bill was losing interest fast. Manuel, the one that first accosted him that night, reached forward to top off his glass.

Glancing down, thinking to make it his last drink, he saw rose-red marks on Manuel's forearm. He grabbed the man's sleeve, yanking it up to reveal more of the most evil burn marks. "How did you get these?" barked Bill.

"Señor, it is the mark of the work we do. It is no problema."

Bill forgot about his drink, "What exactly do you do at work?"

José was first to speak, "Señor Gringo, we are simple miners for the silver and the gold."

Bill was about to reply, before he thought a little deeper. Instead of asking the obvious, he asked, "What does the ore you are mining for look like?"

José was again first to speak, "Señor, we mine the silver and the golden balls. I have a small silver stone here."

He removed his pendant, and Bill noticed the livid red mark where it lay against his skin. Bill took the pendant, but held it at arm's length, instinctively sensing a rattler before his eyes.

José added, "We know it is not the silver, as it is wrong. We think it is the titanium, because the bosses always lie to us."

Bill was pretty sure he was staring at a lump of uranium 238, mildly radioactive. He suspected that the yellow ore was probably uranium 235, yellow cake, and fissile. He knew that could be enriched to make atomic weapons.

Pepe arrived at that moment, bringing several "beautiful girls," with him. One distracted Bill and presented him with a fajita, a taco, and a large burrito, which were very good. Musical instruments appeared out of nowhere, as Latin rhythms beguiled boys and girls to promenade, swing, and sashay in dance.

Bill was dragged protesting to his feet, but did enjoy himself, becoming the center of attention for several young women. In time, his eyes strayed for the first time in many years, as his inherent libido was gently coaxed from its protective shell. The girl was young, yet womanly, and definitely attractive.

He knew he must leave before she broached his masculine defenses. He took his bottle and headed out back to watch the stars, alone, and to think. His mind replayed the girl's laughter, and her touch, as he tried to dismiss the distraction, and failed. However, the burrito she had cooked for him was mighty fine, and one of the best he had ever tasted.

Bill muttered distractedly, "Everything is fine in a man's life, until a woman comes along." He raised the bottle to the light of the moon, and in turn to his lips, as if toasting in admission of mortal frailty. He drank deeply and settled, knowing the past, his past life, had moved on. Bill realized his sanity demanded a woman to share life with once more. He knew he must choose wisely, and spoke a single word into the night. "Shit!"

The moon became fuller as Bill sipped from the bottle. He was not quite ready to leave the security of bachelorhood just yet, but that time was approaching fast. Within the gathering storm clouds of frustration, he threw a stone at a rat, but noticed a metallic roll a few yards away from his target. Getting up to check, he found it was soft, pliable, and quite heavy. He worked two large squares free and had a plan.

Bill went back inside and spoke privately to José, "I'll take your pendant, how much do you want for it?"

"It is not for sale, unless you have fifty dollars American?"

"I'll pay you thirty-five now, and one hundred more for some of the yellow ore."

"It is impossible. The yellow balls are kept under high security."

Bill looked knowingly at him until he broke, "If I am discovered I will be fired, or shot dead. My family needs the money I earn for medicine Señor. My mother, she is very ill. Three hundred dollars American, and it will be here late tomorrow evening. No haggling or no deal."

Bill knew the price was too high, and that the mother was probably fine. Still, he could afford to indulge this man, one time. He gave the miner a one hundred dollar bill up front, and one of the lead squares. He took the pendant and showed him how to meld the lead into a large ball. Once done, he went up to his room.

The next morning Bill greeted his daughter and took her to buy a Harley. She was over the moon, and afterwards, they spent hours alone catching up, each of them overjoyed to be with the other again. Bill reminded her about his big win in Vegas, and how he had paid off the house, and still had more money left than he knew what to do with. She had to remind him her name was no longer Shona Waverley but April Bekkons.

Later, they went for a hike in the nearby mountains, where April told Bill about Michael and the string of curious predictions. She showed the explosions at the car lot using her Smartphone, and Bill was immediately curious. However, he could not get his head around the plot to assassinate the President.

She said, "Dad, I know you think this is absurd. Both Annaliese and I thought the same at first. Trust me, something much bigger is going down. I will have to show you. Everything is detailed at Michael's house, and I can run through all the evidence.

Let's go there tonight. Michael is looking forward to meeting you."

She called Annaliese, and made plans to meet at Michael's home for dinner. Their pact sealed, they made their way back to town.

Teves

Officer Teves watched from a window across the road. They parted the trailhead with a very familiar kiss and cuddle. Bill returned to the hotel, while April went into Rosa's store, and never came out. Teves had grown attached to April, and he knew Rosa treated the girl like her own daughter. He was concerned, because spending hours alone in the woods with a Hells Angel was not what he considered appropriate behavior.

Yet, she had just kissed a much older man, one old enough to be her father. He laughed for a split-second, admiring the bear's tenacity, when another tangential thought struck him. He spoke aloud, "What if—she is his daughter?"

He thought to confront them, but waiting to learn the whole of the truth was his natural game. Teves called in the motorcycle plate, and got a load more information than he bargained for. He started putting a new case file together as he waited and watched. He expected either Bill to go to the store, or April Bekkons—if that was her real name—to go to the hotel. Neither happened.

Teves was about to give up for the night when he heard the Harley roar to life. Bill passed by his lookout on the way out of town, and the only thing in that direction was the reopened mine. He wanted to follow, but was far too late to pick up the trail. Cursing in Mexican, he gave himself another hour on watch.

Ten minutes later, Bill came back with a passenger. It was one of the mineworkers, and that was very strange. Teves deduced that even on a motorcycle, there was not enough time to reach the mine and return. Therefore, Bill had to have known in advance the man would work late for some reason, and be walking back to town.

Try as he might, the deputy could not figure out the link between them, but it had to be important. He watched the Mexican hand over a small, but extremely heavy carrier. Bill held it at arm's length and dropped it into a rear pannier, before handing over a couple of large bills. Teves was already running for his vehicle, as the Harley sped off into the night toward San Diego.

Chapter 4 – Wrong Side of the Law

Bill

Bill saw the lights in his mirrors, and knew instinctively who it was. He powered the engine to outrun the idiot, before easing the throttle back. He knew he would have to deal with the man. He let the cop catch up with him on the freeway, and pulled into an all night diner.

He ordered a dog, took a table near the back, and ate. The Deputy came in and made him as he surveyed the joint. Teves headed for a nearby table, but Bill called him over with a flick of his eyes. They sat opposite one another and ate in silence, each ignoring the other's presence.

Bill finished his food and looked everywhere around. Teves spoke, "Mister William Wenceslas Waverly, child missing for two years, ran away from her mother by all accounts. As her father, I would expect you to know of her whereabouts?"

Teves looked Bill directly in the eye. Bill stared back at him, unmoved. He spoke to heighten the tension between them, "You got any more absurd detective theories, or is this simply a 'social call', Undersheriff?"

Teves smiled and rocked back in his chair, baiting Bill, and using the chair as a prop to project his personal comfort zone. "I won't ask you to explain, because you obviously got some dumb-fuck story past LA's finest. However, I would like to know exactly where your daughter, Shona Waverley, is right now?"

Bill roused from his casual manner, and dropped all pretence. He leaned forward menacingly, and locked Teves deep in the eye, "My daughter is fine, and she is no concern of yours. You got that asshole?"

He took out his Colt, waving with the other hand for the officer to relax. He opened the cylinder, spinning it before he selected one bullet, setting it down before the Deputy. "I need you gone from my life, so here's the deal. This slug has your name on it, Undersheriff Teves."

Teves fingered the bullet tentatively, before pocketing it, and said, "Hmmm. A three fifty-seven Magnum. Seven chambers, and the shorter barrel version. Nice weapon. Usually used by the hoods and pretend modern cowboys."

Chapter 4

Teves glared at Bill, who glared back and added, "And cops. That's why they call it 'The Police Special'."

Teves quickly realized he would get nowhere with his current line of enquiry, nor his projected attitude. He leaned forward for the first time and said, "Bill, I respect Rosa immensely, and she speaks highly of you. I do not like Hells Angels. They have caused me many problems in the past. Which chapter do you belong to?"

Bill chuckled, "Teves, I do not belong to any chapter, and never did. I was in the U.S. Marines if you must know, Nicaragua. I just like to dress this way. That's all there is to it. Sort of fits with the bike, you know."

Teves nodded his head, confirming this was the correct approach to elicit information from the large man. He took a moment to arrange his thoughts and said, "I have a problem, one I will share with you. You will be aware an old mine reopened last year, and it is a highly secretive place. I do not like secrets.

"I make community visits, but without a warrant I cannot search the place properly, or find out what is really going on there. I have asked around, including Rosa and that goth girl that works there sometimes, what's her name?" Teves clicked his fingers in the air, and stared at the ceiling.

Bill didn't miss a beat, "April Bekkons."

Teves was quick to pursue, "Yes that's the one. She seems really nice, and clever too. I gather you know her quite well?"

Bill realized Teves must have been watching them earlier in the day. He needed to discover what the deputy knew. "Yes, we are good friends from way back. I used to know her mother quite well. What of it?"

Teves smiled. For to him the words sounded as close to an admission of fatherhood as he was likely to get. He considered that Bill was toying with him, and if his suspicions were confirmed, he also realized Bill had not actually lied, apart from the name of course. He found himself drawn to admit a begrudging respect for the man, which surprised him.

Teves said disarmingly, "That's no concern of mine, Bill. Del Fuego mine is. Nobody seems to know very much about it, and when I make enquiries through normal channels, I meet a wall of bureaucratic nonsense that has to originate from a very high and powerful authority. I do not, as yet, know who or what that source is, but I believe this goes as far as Washington, D.C.

"My other leads end with Coulson Conglomerates, and again, the trail goes cold."

Bill looked at him and said, "Why don't you ask the mine workers?"

Teves laughed, "Look at me, what I am wearing? A Sheriff's uniform. They would all run a mile as soon as I got within sight. They all know my face, even if I wore plain clothes. They will think I am going to run them in and ship them back to Mexico. I need information from somebody that knows exactly what is going on there. What can you tell me?"

Bill looked at him. Their eyes remaining locked as they judged one another other as men. Bill realized Teves must also have been watching as he went to collect José, and later witnessed their exchange. That would be why the Deputy had followed him so quickly when he left town.

As if it were a poker game, Bill judged the odds, and knew he was being called. The only wise thing to do on this hand was raise and call. His fingers reached into his backpack, bringing out the heavy carrier Teves had witnessed exchange hands earlier.

Bill said, "I do not trust you Teves, simply because you are a cop. Nevertheless, I do need help. Do you trust me? If not, I say no more."

Teves nodded his head, but Bill pressed him to say the words and make a vow. Once satisfied, Bill drew out another carrier also holding it at arm's length and set it down in front of the Officer.

Bill stated, "I need to know what this shit is. Inside each lead ball is a substance. I believe the unmarked one to be uranium two thirty-eight, and the one with a cross on it to be uranium two thirty-five. Now are you paying due attention, Undersheriff?"

Teves gingerly picked up the carriers and peered inside. Bill chuckled to himself, and rose to leave, "Do not follow me ever again. I am one of the very few good guys, you got that Teves? Cross me and you are already a dead man."

Teves laughed in Bill's face, adding, "Uranium, you are pulling my chain, sunshine. I ought to run you in right now. Where did you get this shit, from your imagination, or your asshole, huh?"

Bill rose to his full height and looked down at Teves, "No asshole, they came from that reopened mine you are beholden to."

Teves came alert and ran with the evidence outside, dumping it in the trunk of his cruiser. He stared at the carriers, his thoughts drifting to the poor Mexican migrants who had actually mined it. He said, "I wonder what level of health and safety they are working under. I doubt it is a lot."

Nearby, Bill replied, "You bet. They mine it with their bare hands."

Bill walked out of earshot, before Teves could say more, and called April. Minutes later he caught up with the only other Harley on the road that night, and settled in behind. His daughter rode the steed well. As prearranged, at her signal, he turned left onto the other side of the block, checking for anything out of place. April was already parked in Michael's garage with the lights out as Bill turned right, and right again. He cruised passed a nondescript dark vehicle with a man inside. Bill barely saw the observer and wondered who was being watched.

He rode by and made a left at the main road, following it for a quarter mile, before mounting the curb near the big oak, turning off his lights, and flicking the hidden switch to kill his brake light. The small trail was hard to follow, but became easier as his eyes adjusted to the darkness. He leaned well back where the trail forked, one path leading on, and the other down into a small gully. The Harley rode the drop well, and sprung up the other side headed through the gateway April held open for him.

Immediately, April retraced his tire tracks and wiped the trail clean. Moments later, Bill was introduced to Annaliese, and he took her proffered handshake, and turning his wrist, brought the back of her hand to his lips. He lightly kissed it in quaint and courteous fashion, before saying, "My pleasure to finally meet you Annaliese. I have heard many good things about you."

Bill had expected the young girl to blush, but instead she quipped, "And I of you, kind sir."

She turned at once to her friend, and with overly ponderous eyes, said loudly, "April, you never told me your father was such a gentleman, nor such a hunk."

Bill was having none of her youthful flirtations, and turned away, asking gruffly, "You got any Rebel Yell hereabouts?"

Annaliese replied, "Of course, Mister Waverly, I bought a bottle especially for you a few hours ago. Go sit down and I will bring it to you."

Bill took an armchair and shook his head. Annaliese continued to flirt mildly with him, until he said, "Annaliese. Please stop it.

You are very attractive, but way too young for me. You can call me Bill, but only on condition, the flirting stops right now. You got that?"

Annaliese, clearly shaken, apologized immediately. Bill realized the girl's hormones were surging, probably for the first time in her life. He wrote the incident off. She did not know how to deal with the way she suddenly felt.

Annaliese cooked Mexican for four, but only three ate, Michael being locked away within his study and mystical mind, except for one brief restroom dash. He took a moment to welcome Bill, and told the girls to give the man their best guest room, and he would speak to them later.

Bill chose a room at the other end of the house from the girls. With the lights out, he settled into a chair in the towered bay window. He had been watching the man in the vehicle parked down the street, until he nodded off. He had left the window open on purpose, and came instinctively awake when a car door closed.

A dark shape hurried and got into the passenger side of the sedan Bill had been watching. The two men worked quickly, both attending to the front of the automobile, before one man did something in the trunk. Both rushed to a second vehicle, and disappeared into the night.

After the incident, Bill went to bed but could not sleep. His best guess was they had fitted some sort of surveillance equipment, as the sedan's only occupant had left. A car bomb in this neighborhood made no sense. Somewhat reassured, he chuckled at Annaliese's obvious flirting, and feeling good, finally slept.

Chapter 5 – Conspiracy Theory

Bill awoke the next morning to the wonderful smell of bacon and eggs. He dressed quickly and went down to the kitchen. There he found a fresh pot of coffee on the stove, and a full breakfast being prepared just the way he liked it.

Bill complimented Annaliese on her culinary skills, but she made light of it with an unaffected air. "April told me how you like breakfast cooked, it's nothing." She turned away from him at once, and went back to work the stove.

Bill had expected her to flirt, but instead he felt mildly rebuffed. He took a moment to watch her work, before hunger got the better of him, and he eagerly awaited his breakfast.

Once cooking duty was completed, Annaliese brought through the breakfast tray, as April was serving strong coffee. All four residents sat down and ate together, Michael having at last resolved the problem that had preoccupied him for most of yesterday. Once they finished eating, Michael told them what he had discovered.

"I got the lead from the Auto City incident. As you know I studied that over and over again until I was certain. I can confirm an organization is behind the string of recent disasters, and I am sure it extends throughout the U.S."

Bill queried playfully, "You gotta name for this supposed organization?"

Michael quipped back, "ADF, they are some quasi departmental corporate dimension of the government machine."

Bill smirked at the implied conspiracy theory. He had heard them all before, and wondered which version this was. Meanwhile Michael continued. "I have evidence that suggests the New York Metro was brought to a halt deliberately, and not because of a component failure as stated in the media. There are hundreds of other incidents, all seemingly unrelated. They are all different. What do you make of that?"

"Tell me what you have so far," said Bill as he refreshed his coffee.

"You know about Auto City, although I do not understand why they did that. The rural bridge collapsing over in Orange County was more interesting, as it had recently been inspected. The concrete where the main supports were embedded gave way. That is highly unlikely for a bridge that has stood for so many years. I need a sample of that concrete. I suspect a concrete weakening agent was used."

Bill asked, "Michael, can we go back to New York for a moment. What exactly happened that indicates this was sabotage and not component failure?"

Michael replied chirpily, "The New York Subway shut down is well documented. The points safety device that failed had been checked by a contractor just two days before, and had been certified fit for service. What interests me is that a most competent contractor carried out this work around ten in the morning. A passing jogger stated there were workers in the vicinity at eleven o'clock, forty minutes after the original contractors had left. Investigators never followed it up.

"There have been reports of intermittent short wave radio interference at local toy boat and flying clubs in Tulane. A few days later, there was the outbreak of a super bug at a hospital in Illinois. The contagion was easily contained, but the hospital concerned was closed to admissions for over a week."

Bill interjected with a wave of his hand, "But all this seems word of mouth. What proof have you got? As far as I see it, the only thing you can say is that you knew about these events before they happened."

April immediately rounded on her father. "Shit Dad! This is serious. Now either listen-up or butt out. Michael please, we believe in you. What else happened?"

Michael was hardly fazed, and continued as if nothing had been said, "Across in Milwaukee, a suspected computer hack into the emergency services main control center resulted in the operators being unable to process emergency calls for eight minutes. The glitch simply stopped and full service resumed at once. Something similar happened to a main cell phone relay station in Nebraska, this time people could not communicate over a large area for almost thirteen minutes.

"There is much, much more I have documented over the last few years. They all appear to be unrelated. Yet, every single one of the physical attacks has either a report of a black SUV in the vicinity, or a white van with the markings ADF. Usually, they both appear on the day of the attack, but not at the same time. I can confirm it is the same SUV in the Auto City attack, from the footage April shot."

April was quick to respond, "They are targeting communications, in all of their forms. The others are first responders, emergency, and critical services. It is clear to see they are practicing for a concerted attack."

Bill rose to pace the room. The suggestion had merit, but without knowing the targets and diversionary tactics, he was at a loss. He refilled his coffee and sat down to speak once more; "I am not convinced by any of this. Yet."

April grabbed her father's arm and tugged him to his feet, "Well, you better come and see everything we have. It is all in the study. Michael, if we may?"

Bill looked through the evidence, but it was all circumstantial, and most of it, conjecture. He spoke into the round, "I can see why you are worried, and I see the logic in your deductions. However, as I asked earlier, where is the physical proof?

"Now, if you were to show me say, concrete samples, ones that I could touch and feel, I would have physical evidence. Were you to have them analyzed for confirmation, then I could begin to believe some of what you are telling me. As it stands, there is nothing that a court of law would entertain, and neither do I.

"Nevertheless, I do believe in you, and by extraction, what you are trying to expose. However, there is nothing here that amounts to solid evidence. So far, all you got is 'a hill of beans'."

He left the words to hang in the air before he continued, "Yesterday I had a very interesting meeting, a couple in fact. I believe a local mine that is stated as producing silver, is in fact turning out uranium. I believe that most of it is uranium two thirty-eight, but some is weapons-grade two thirty-five. I have two samples being analyzed right now."

April exclaimed, "How? What happened last night?"

Bill smirked and said, "Let's just say that Officer Teves and I had a heart-to-heart. He followed me when I left town, and had been watching us all day as far as I can tell. I decided to call him out. He seems honest, for a cop at least.

"April, you will know that I got one sample of uranium earlier from a mine worker, and that I was waiting for a second to arrive before I left to come here. Teves and I appear to be on the same side, at least as far as the mine goes, so I gave him the samples for official analysis. How else can we get bona fide proof?

"This is what you need to do, send samples for testing in official laboratories, equals proof. Until that happens, you have nothing, except a load more conspiracy theories. Make them real, or give it up and stop wasting your time."

April rose to her feet and shouted, "Why are you pulling us down? We are trying to do what is right. Isn't that what you always taught me?"

Michael spoke before anyone else could, "Bill, you are entirely correct. We need what we have gathered, analyzed, and we do not know how to do it. Perhaps this Teves can help us also, like testing what we have already collected."

A hush fell over the table, and people nodded in agreement. April apologized to her father, but he shrugged it off. Bill knew their minds were converging, and having said his piece, was pleased by the response. He deduced they really did believe in this plot, and he made a decision to support them as best he could.

Bill waited for conversation to die before he broached his own worry. "There is a dark sedan parked down the road. Yesterday it was occupied, but just before dawn, another man with a duffle bag arrived. They worked for a few minutes inside the vehicle, did something in the trunk, and shortly after, both men left. I need to know what they did, and especially if they have placed a bomb, or have cameras focused on this house."

Michael blanched, but April rose, "That won't be a problem. We'll go now and play with our Smartphone's. I'll use old Powell's dog across the road as cover. Come on Liese."

The girls left at once, talked to the old man across the road, and took Patch for an unexpected walk. Annaliese posed with the mongrel several times, April snapping away. They took several shots near the front of the suspicious vehicle catching the number plate. Both of them noticed the camera hidden under a duster on the dash, and got good pictures of it. They took photos of the side and rear, before they moved on their way, and later, returned to the house.

Meanwhile, Michael and Bill talked candidly. The latter viewed all of the man's research. He could see there was a pattern to most of it, as his daughter had pointed out. Put this all together and you had a whole region under attack, and incapable of forming any coherent response. It reminded him of what he had done in Nicaragua, running covert interference before the main strike.

They had each become lost in their thoughts by the time the girls returned. The photographs they took showed quite clearly the house and road were being monitored. Bill noted the number on the plate, and stared for a long time at the close-up pictures of the camera.

In time he said, "This is military hardware. Look at the shadow just here, that is a second lens, and it is a night vision camera. I used an earlier version of this same thing in Nicaragua. It was manufactured by …, now let me think …no, I forget. It will come to me in time.

"Annaliese, can I have a look at the rest of the photos you took?" The girl brought the pictures up on his screen, and he was momentarily distracted by her delicate perfume. He thought of complimenting her, but she had already gone.

Bill shrugged and waved the smell away. He leaned forward to examine the screen more closely. He pointed and said, "Here. This shot from the rear of the sedan is almost in line with the camera angle. See how it appears to target this house. I need to go buy some stuff. I also need to see somebody. I may be gone for a while. Is there any way I can contact you, that people can't eavesdrop on?"

Both girls started to speak, but Michael cut them off. "In this digital age there is only one secure way, but if it was ever monitored, know it is the easiest of all to break. However, it is so ancient, that like me, nobody even bothers to consider it. The system is mechanical and analogue." He patted the antique, Bakelite, rotary dial telephone and enquired, "How do you think I get my information delivered?

"This is a pulse dial telephone, and there are very few telephones still connected to the underlying network, but those that do, work perfectly. It is exactly the same principle as the telegraph, if you understand me? You will find connections in the maintenance department of the oldest telephone exchanges; try the basement first. Any connected telephone with a dial is the only type to use to avoid detection."

Bill queried, "Surely anybody could monitor the line if they wanted to?"

Michael chuckled, wrote his number on a piece of paper, and pushed it toward Bill. "Yes they could, very easily. However, they would need to record the call using ancient analogue technology. Today, everything is digital, which will not record analogue without an expensive converter. It is a bit like shellac records versus a CD, my Pappy's phonograph for instance."

Bill understood and nodded at the man, taking him a little more seriously than before, and pocketed the number left on the desk. He still did not accept the plan to blow up the President, but he knew something of a large scale was afoot.

Before he left, Bill spent quality time with April. They talked openly and he thanked her for telling Annaliese how to cook his favorite breakfast. April replied, "She is a great girl Dad, and much too good for you!"

The skies prematurely darkened at 4 p.m. and Bill wandered into the garage where he spotted an odd thing. He examined the ancient specimen under a dustsheet before returning to speak to Michael. "I see you have an old Indian mothballed in the garage. Nineteen twenty-five if I'm not mistaken."

"She's a nineteen twenty-six Special actually, one of the last of that model ever made. It belonged to my Grand-pappy…"

They settled to talk about old motorcycles for a while, Michael even offering him a ride on the old bike once he finished preparing it for its annual run. Bill offered to help service it.

By 5 p.m., Bill was gone, riding out during the heaviest of thunderstorms. April decided that they also had to leave. They looked for Michael, but he appeared to be missing. He was last seen in the study. April scribbled a note for him, stating that they would be back tomorrow.

April knew that sometimes Michael disappeared, as if he was not in the building at all, but later he would reappear in his study. She imagined secret passages, hidden within the walls and stairs leading above or below. She presumed they were accessed from a secret panel in his study.

Michael

Michael watched them leave, and wondered if the cameras were actually targeting his own home, or that of half-crazy Mr. Rogers, who lived next door. They were on agreeable and neighborly terms, but Michael could never consider being friends with the man. He was eccentric, and an inventor. And anyway, his house was a trash heap of scribbled writings, and unfinished projects.

His thoughts returned to the cameras, and something Bill had said. He wondered if these ramshackled misfits would, could, change his long-acknowledged destiny. His eyes watered. He remembered looking through a night-vision headset, and once more descended into his living nightmare-hell.

All alone within his madding mind, once more he witnessed the lightning strikes, and heard bombs falling, exploding, the ground shuddering nearby. He fell and hunkered down, but that night came back to haunt him, became his reality, myriad fractures of modern warfare. Ten thousand scenes of destruction flashed by in the blink of his eye, before the one scene, as forever, became manifest. His unseeing eyes settled upon those of a young girl.

Again, he watched his mind replay the scene, as past circumstance reclaimed his reality. He watched himself try to save her, sweeping her up into his caring arms and running through a hail of hostile gunfire in his effort to keep her alive. They were almost there, safety yards away, when yet another explosion ripped her already torn body to pieces, and by doing so, saved his own life.

Michael could not live with the fact that he survived, and the child he tried so desperately to save, died in his arms. She was innocent. It was anathema to his psyche, mere repetition of his eternal, internal dance macabre.

He looked over at where his meds were hidden, the ones the two girls did not know about.

Sinking to his knees, Michael cried out, head upraised and arms lofted in supplication, seeking The Good Lord's mercy…

As usual, there was no reply.

Chapter 6 – Queen of Diamonds

April

April and Annaliese spent the night with Rosa, free from surveillance and hoped, like Bill, the heavy rain had covered their getaway. The next day they were in Orange County, but to their dismay found a dismantling crew working. It was clear there would be no evidence left on the collapsed side, but the other end of the bridge was still attached.

They headed back towards a small town. Annaliese bought a map, and asked directions at the general store. An hour later they arrived at the far side of the bridge, waiting out of sight. The men worked until almost six before heading off towards the local town.

The girls wasted no time. Using small press-seal plastic bags and a Leatherman, they collected samples from near the four main attachment points. The concrete came away easily, like lumps of old cement. As they worked, the bridge began to give way, and they realised it was only remained in position because the other end had dropped, foreshortening the angle of decent.

They heard a vehicle and ran for cover, hiding in bushes near the forest's edge. A black SUV pulled up and a man in a dark suit got out. April was recording immediately. Annaliese copied her, taking pictures and video.

The man went down to inspect their side of the bridge. April saw her chance and ran, hunkered over, to film the inside of the vehicle. The driver's door had been left open, and there was a briefcase on the passenger seat, which was not locked. She pulled out the documents and quickly turned the pages, taking a camera shot of each one.

She heard the man come back and still had one file to check. A rock landed near her, Annaliese warning her no doubt. April continued to take pictures. The information was extremely important, and would serve to convince Bill they were right to be suspicious. The man stopped by the passenger door, and was reaching to open it, when he received a message via his headset. April caught his East coast accent and deduced he had been ordered back to film the demolition work.

She barely had time to finish and put everything back as it had been, before the man returned to the vehicle. April watched his footfalls to see which way he would come to the driver's side. He went around the rear and she eased around the front, to the passenger side. With excellent timing, she dove over the embankment hoping for a soft landing. She rolled and came to her feet, hiding under the bridge until the SUV pulled away.

When the coast was clear, April clambered back up to Annaliese. They ran to where the bike was hidden, and left in hot pursuit. They caught sight of the SUV turning onto Highway 60, and keeping well back, followed it onto I-10, and later, H-62. They were surprised when the SUV disappeared into Twentynine Palms military base.

They were stymied, but had their first real clue. April headed back for Yucca Valley, where she topped off with gas. Annaliese paid, and came back with fast food and colas. April was trying to decide the best route back to SD, when Annaliese said, "A Humvee has just turned onto Highway 247, and stopped. It is waiting for somebody. We better move girl, the chase is still on."

April spun the engine, and took H-247 as a white ADF van followed by another Humvee pulled over and swung onto the road. Annaliese got the waiting Humvee's military plate as they went past. In her rearview, April noticed the parked vehicle pull into the road and the three vehicles drove in convoy.

The new game commenced with the prey following the hound. Annaliese wanted April to drop back and follow. April insisted there was only one place to go from where they were. "What better way to follow someone than from in front."

Once through Barstow, April slightly increased her speed, putting a little distance between them and the vehicles they were monitoring. They were out of sight sometimes, occasional glimpses of three sets of headlights in convoy confirmed their tail.

Reaching the outskirts of Vegas, April pulled off onto Saint Rosa Parkway. She topped off with gas again, unsure of the destination. Again, Annaliese paid and again brought back cola and snacks. They waited for the three vehicles to continue down the main highway, but were surprised when they pulled off and took the same road they were on.

They followed the convoy to Henderson, and onwards through Boulder City. They both knew there could only be one destination, Hoover Dam. They crossed from Nevada into Arizona, but the expected excursion to the dam never materialized. Unexpectedly, the vehicles turned left, back the long way towards Hoover Dam.

They were following a long way back to avoid detection. Cresting one of the most magnificent dawn views either girl had ever seen, they knew immediately something was very wrong. There was not a vehicle in sight.

April spun the back wheel and they retraced their steps, finding a side road, and diverging from it was a well-worn earthen track. The road forked and they took the trail as it dipped toward the valley below, revealing an isolated farmstead surrounded by mining equipment. April glimpsed a 6-wheeler headed their way. She eased the Harley to the side and slid down a short slope, coming to rest as several dump trucks went past on the gravel road above. The girls scrambled up far enough to see the trucks were hauling rock.

Hiding the bike, the girls made their way toward the valley at a slightly lower level. They soon spotted the two Humvees and white van, parked outside the strangest ranch they had ever seen. It simply did not make any sense. There was a homestead and typical barn, but a massive complex rose behind, and another to one side that looked very strange, a long, low shed on wheels. They took pictures and shot video of the main complex, from which extended a conveyor belt that was pouring rock into a silo. Trucks lined up below to take cargo away.

Annaliese stated, "They are planning to destroy the diversion tunnel caps."

April stared at her and said, "Liese, how on earth have you figured that out?"

Annaliese replied, "It's obvious. There's an awful lot of rock coming out of the ground. ADF are involved, and by the looks of the road and the building, this has been going on for some time. There must be a pretty deep hole in the ground under that roof."

April could see the point of her logic, since it was obvious a lot of rock had been removed. It still didn't make sense to her. April continued her thoughts by asking, "OK, say that is what they are planning. Why would they want to blow the tunnel caps?"

Annaliese proudly informed her, "This area has been near drought conditions for decades. There's barely enough water left in the reservoir to service basic human requirements. The diversion tunnels are what they used to build the dam in the first place, allowing the Colorado River to pass by the construction of the dam, until they were sealed.

"Girl, you unblock just one of those diversion channels, and the whole thing is empty. It may take days, Good Lord, but to empty the Hoover Dam is their intention. With no water, and no electricity, Las Vegas is dead within days."

April responded, "Buy why? What do they really want? Say they knock out all modern communications also, then what. Bank and Casino heists—and I mean all of them. This is way-too big for us girl. We are out of here, now! Let's get back and see what Michael knows about all of this."

It took them five hours to get back to Michael's, and they found him in his study. He was delighted with their work, immediately checking the concrete samples the girls had obtained, finding them as he had suspected. April copied the rest of their research onto his laptop, explaining briefly what they had done, and what they suspected. Michael was visibly shocked by the news from Hoover Dam, but the video was compelling evidence. They were able to pinpoint the smallholding location using an online map, just inside Arizona.

April worked on the photographed documents from the briefcase, and with time made good readable copies of each. They detailed past projects and what resulted. Present ones, excluding Hoover Dam, and two that were scheduled for next week. They continued to appear unrelated in purpose. Michael started placing colored pins in his newly fitted map of the U.S. up on the wall, and muttered, "Pattern. There is no pattern here."

Meanwhile, Annaliese had not been idle, managing to isolate several quality photographs of the man who drove the SUV, and these were filed together with the vehicle details. They knew they needed the plate checked, and thought they could get Teves to do that for them.

They slept, then talked for many hours. There were two major targets for the coming week, one day apart, at either end of the country. There was also a third from the new information gathered from the SUV, the other being a duplicate. It appeared impossible for the girls to monitor all of them.

At dinner, April made a decision, "Annaliese, can you handle the toxin attack in Miami yourself? We now know the precise location thanks to the information from the SUV, so it should be easy."

Annaliese agreed, and April continued, "I will follow-up the new information from the documents in the SUV. This is important, because it is the first information we have that did not come from Michael. Michael, who do you get your information from?"

Michael grinned at said, "Why, it is simple. Someone I know sends it to me every week."

Both girls wanted to press him further, but Michael crossed his arms and sat back, clearly indicating he would say nothing more on the subject. "I believe I'm ready for dessert," he said. "Who else is interested in ice cream?"

April shook her head, she knew food was his ruse of self-protection, and continued. "I will go to Detroit and see where this new lead takes us. Tampering with a city water main shut off valve doesn't sound like much to me, but it needs following up.

"Liese, can you cover the third target if you get back in time? Perhaps you can hitch a ride with my father?"

The plan was set, and, as they all felt drained, they went to bed, the girls a little later than usual.

The new day brought with it a little clarity. Their aim was to identify who was responsible, and not get caught up in the fall-out. By midday, Annaliese was on an express bus headed for Miami, and April was settled in a similar seat bound for Detroit. The trips would take three and four days respectively, but the girls would arrive in good time to observe their targets.

Chapter 7 – Reconnaissance

Annaliese

Annaliese was dressed in hot pants and tee shirt, with a blonde wig and green eye-lenses to mask her own auburn hair and brown irises. She found the Miami mall with ease, and quickly identified the garbage can where they believed the biological weapon would be released.

She complained to one of the cleaning staff that a trashcan was full and asked how often they were emptied. The reply was defensive and abrupt; "All trashcans are emptied every two hours. If you have a complaint, go see the management."

With four hours to spare, Annaliese wandered around, finding herself at a similar garbage can on the floor above. This one was also labeled W30. She checked her information, and made out the target number, W30–C. The one she was at was W30-B. She found the one she wanted on the floor above.

With time to kill, she ate and window-shopped, being nearby to notice the trash was emptied at 4:20 p.m. Her target time was 6:30, meaning there was one empty before the evening rush began.

Time dragged, but by 6:10, she was on the floor above with a clear view of the garbage can concerned. She waited until it was emptied, and began recording. Her escape was already planned in detail. There was nothing at all unusual for the first eight minutes, until a suited man put a package like a small shoebox in the trash. She did not manage to get a close-up of his face, but knew he did not fit in, if simply because his manner was all-wrong. He was outwardly attentive and businesslike, challenging, not furtive.

Annaliese focused immediately on the canister. Almost at once, a student came by and tried to place a large plastic carrier inside. He had great difficulty forcing it through, but was about to win the battle, when the suited man collared him and started bawling him out. The student took back his trash and went looking for another disposal unit. The man glanced at his watch and hurried away as fast as he could. This time, Annaliese got excellent shots of the man, and disliked him immediately. He had no facial expressions, even when yelling at the student.

Annaliese followed him down the stairs, and saw him enter into the gents' restroom on level two. She waited nearby, apparently engaged in a telephone conversation, but she had the video on and pointed at the door. No one went in, but thirty seconds later, one man in the same suit came out and rushed off in a hurry. He had a completely different face, but his body was identical.

There were no mall cameras nearby. Annaliese entered the men's room and discovered an expensive mask inside a carrier in the trashcan. She took it and turned her own bag inside out, showing a different color and doubling its size in the process. She stayed to remove her wig and throw on a floral summer dress, and ran for the stairs.

At 6:31, people on the third floor started to keel over, gasping for air. It had happened. Annaliese was heading down the stairs as fast as her legs would carry her. She was already out on the street by the time the alarm sounded. There was no sign of the mystery man. She boarded an intercity bus bound for Houston, just to cover her trail.

April

April felt uneasy in Detroit, dangerous as it was. However, her destination was Farmington Hills, a well-established and respected suburb. The target was a water main shut off valve. She was searching for a specific manhole cover, on a street where there appeared to be hundreds of them. She perched her butt on the outside of a store window half way down the block. "Son of a bitch!"

April kept her eyes on the street. She had expected to find a typical, temporary worker's hut, fenced off from the traffic flow by cones and warning signs. There was nothing. She tried to find a reference via her cell and the internet, but the records she needed appeared to be privy to the Farmington Public Works Department.

Distracted, she noticed a white van pull up in a no waiting zone. Everything about the truck seemed familiar, except there was no "ADF" on the side. Her intuition was roused as it was parked illegally, especially when no one had got in or out. She was on her feet at once, her eyes not particularly focused, scanning. As she reached the rear of the truck, her pace slowed. And then she saw it, the small fracture of dark against white on the truck's side.

She stopped short and grabbed her cell to take video. She pretended to be having a rage on the cell, and caught the angle perfectly; there was a plastic, stick-on cover, and the painted letters

"ADF" showed beneath the white from her present angle. "Sneaky Bastards!" she exclaimed.

She knew at once it must be parked over the manhole cover she had vainly been searching for, but how to make sure? She pretended to quarrel into her cell as she stopped directly behind the truck, and ducked down to check underneath, getting a clear shot of the plate.

She was in time to witness the manhole cover being lifted and set to one side, and knew the covered back must have a false floor. This was confirmed when a pair of legs appeared and a flashlight was shone into the hole. A male voice said, "It is deep like we expected, better get the ladder down here."

Realizing she would be seen, April dropped her bag on the ground and propped her cell against it, concerned if the camera angle was right. Both Smartphone and bag were black, so she hoped they would be ignored. However, she was ready to run if the alarm was raised.

The man worked in the hole for several minutes, and she could hear him asking his accomplice to hold the top of the ladder as he made his way backup. She heard the scrape as the ladder was hauled back inside, and knew her ruse had worked. April returned to direct filming, hoping she had caught everything. The manhole cover was quickly replaced, and she strode casually onto the sidewalk, the video still running, as she slowly wandered past the cab, hoping to record a glimpse of those inside, before it pulled off.

She reasoned the water supply was now turned off, and saw no reason in hanging around. She wanted to know if the recording was useable, so rewound until the point she placed the camera on the ground. The angle was a little off, but she had caught everything, including the man's face. He went into the hole with an obviously heavy bag on his shoulder. When he resurfaced, the bag appeared empty, and he casually threw it up and inside the back of the truck. April could think of nothing, except that he had planted a bomb. She immediately started filming again, and moved away upwind, still pretending to talk into her cell. One minute later the manhole cover blew, taking out the front of an approaching sedan. A geyser erupted from the hole, before settling into a flowing mother of a river, which had already started to undermine the roadway's sub-structure.

She rushed forward to get a brief video of inside the hole, which had by then formed a small crater that was being filled with automobiles that could not stop in time. They had not shut off the valve, they had blown a water main. The ground beneath her trembled slightly, and she ran, clearing just in time, as another section of road gave way. She wasted no time in getting the hell out of there.

April took several days to return home, breaking her journey in LA to visit John, her father's closest ex-Marine Corps buddy. He opened the door, and welcomed her inside. Satan, her favorite pit bull took one sniff and was all over her, bowling her backwards as she bent down to fuss him, and slobbered on her with great enthusiasm. He had been her savior when she had run away from her mother, hiding out in his outdoor kennel, before John had driven her to freedom.

They settled to catch up, before April told him about Michael and his weird predictions, the conspiracy theory, and what they had discovered: The plot to blow-up the President. John was riveted by her words and wanted to know more.

John wrote crime novels, and the information they had gathered, galvanized his curiosity in a meaningful and real-life way. He instantly wanted to check all the facts and see their evidence. April called Michael, to prepare him for visitors. John treated her to a restaurant meal, and offered to take her back to San Diego, hoping to meet Michael and learn more about the mysterious world the girl inhabited.

They were on the road by 5:30 a.m. Once clear of the city, they pulled into a roadside diner for breakfast. April had slept for the first part of the journey, but came alive with food and coffee. Satan was let off for a run, but hurtled back to the pickup when the engine fired. He loved rides in the auto, especially with his two favorite people.

As soon as Michael saw April, he rushed up and hugged her. It was the first time he had ever touched her, and she was very happy. She tried to introduce John, but Satan took one sniff of the new human, and immediately liked him, a very rare occurrence. They played 'kill the towel' on the carpet until John intervened. Satan gave Michael a big lick as some semblance of normality was restored.

Conversely, Michael was wary of John at first, but this changed when he was told the man was Bill's best friend, and also an ex Marine. Their exchanges passed into sharing as they got to know one other better. This was made easier because they were both unconventional people, each regularly thinking outside of the box, each wary of the world as it had become.

As they talked, John became aware of the mounting array of information and physical evidence. He was impressed, and labored the point, suggesting, "You should consider implementing a dedicated filing system to keep track of all this. I'd actually get as much as possible on computer, I mean a real big desktop one with full capability. If you don't mind me staying a day or so, I can help sort this out for you. Is there a hotel nearby? Nothing posh, but secure and dog-friendly would be nice?"

Michael answered, "Ridiculous John. We thank you for your support. You are both most welcome. You've already shown us you have a keen eye for detail, and believe in us. April, please prepare the blue bedroom. I'm sure you will find that particular room most comfortable, John."

April left to take John upstairs, while Michael raided a cookie from the jar. "Now Satan, where would you like to sleep? No cookie for you until you show me, let's try outside, no. How about in the kitchen. Yes, the kitchen I think. Let's make you up a bed right now."

Michael's home took on a new air of purpose, as the newcomers settled in. They devoted more and more time to rationalizing the evidence and potential threat, as Satan and Michael got on very well together.

April asked about her father and Annaliese. Michael said, "Annaliese decided to go directly to the next target, and stayed overnight in Tucson. Whatever the truck did next day, caused major problems for Amtrak—something to do with electricity, but then they did take out a major sub-stanchion, whatever, suburb station, that's the word, isn't it? You will need to ask her … Annaliese about the rest of it. Can I eat tortillas tonight?"

It was clear Michael's mind was beginning to fracture, and with a glance towards John, April tried to change the subject at once. However, with his last coherent words Michael added, "The girl left with the big guy … and they went off to do something…"

41

Chapter 7

April knew Michael had already lost it. He had tried too hard, and once he reached his limit, the only way was down.

She wanted to give him a big hug, and tell him it was OK. She was surprised when John rushed to his side, and spoke softly to him. He cajoled Michael to go onto the rear stoop with him, and mouthed to her silently with labored syllables as he passed.

April was confused. In time she rationalized, "It must be something about a forces buddy named 'Petey Esdy'."

Chapter 8 – Disregarding The Box

Tucson made absolutely no sense, but then again, neither did any of the other catalogued targets. April knew instinctively they were all missing the bigger picture. She had no idea what that was, but she realized it was time to take a step back, and look at what was going on from a different perspective.

Perhaps because of her mother, April had learned to interpret the world around her without the help of adults. Who could she rely on except for her father, and most times, he wasn't there.

One time at SDSU April had questioned, quite rhetorically in class, what a greater world awaited to be discovered, and why the masses were shielded from all knowledge. Her lecturer in that class, Susan, took her to one side afterward and said, "April, you are bright, intelligent, and ask questions nobody else does. I won't ask about your life, simply because I already know that today, you will say nothing, or lie.

"However, I will pull you up about one thing. Seeing inside, or outside the box. Is that it? Everything? What you need to get your head around is thinking 'disregarding the box'. Whatever appears, feels, seems wrong, will steer you in the right direction."

Within the moment, April came back to the present, and applied what Susan had explained to her months ago, to her present predicament. She grabbed a beer from the fridge, and opened it without thinking. John and Michael were out back in their own world, and she needed to solve the problem, the real question: "What the fuck is really going down?"

April knew she needed to step back, away from the daily intrigues, and warp her mind to a higher level. Everyone around her was working bottom up, trying to place pieces within what appeared to be a three dimensional jigsaw puzzle. She set her mind to look at the information and headlines, top-down.

Michael had stated from the very beginning, this was a plot to "blow up the President." April was getting nowhere until she recalled his very first words on the subject, precisely. "This is a cabal to blow up 'The Presidency'."

Her mind began going round in circles, but was distracted when she heard her father's bike arrive, and seconds later he appeared with Annaliese. She asked her friend, "How did Dad know where and when to pick you up?"

Annaliese replied, "Great to see you too, Hon. We arranged it when I decided to go straight to Tucson. He was very concerned about me." She grinned at April and added suggestively, "He gave me his private number, you know?"

Annaliese threw back her hair, and licked her lips suggestively. They burst out in fits of giggles and walked out arm in arm, to join the others out back. The newcomers had collected a bucket of fast food on the way back, and everybody dove in, Satan ensuring every scrap and bone was eaten. Annaliese was dead on her feet, and said, "It went great, but I'll tell you tomorrow. I need my bed."

Bill talked late into the night with John, as they caught up properly with times passed and present.

After breakfast the next day, Annaliese watched the breaking news, until she had the confirmation she needed. The girls assembled their presentations; before meeting in the study. Annaliese told the story of the mall in Miami, and April followed with what went down in Detroit. After they had spoken, both girls presented their evidence, and answered any queries.

The turn came back to Annaliese, who said, "The hit in Tucson was anticipated for early yesterday morning, so I found a cheap hotel nearby and got little sleep. I was at the target site, waiting an hour before time. It was just as well, for ten minutes later an ADF truck pulled up and two workers got out. They went behind the main electricity substation and were out of sight for almost thirteen minutes.

"I tried to get eyes on what they were doing, but it was impossible without giving myself away. I recognized the license plate, and guess what, it was the same plate as the one we followed to Hoover Dam. I have no idea what could possibly link blowing diversion channel caps, and disabling a voltage reduction station over five hundred miles south, but there has to be one."

The revelation was greeted by muted by talk and consternation. Bill spoke up, "Power supplies. Perhaps we are onto something after all?"

Annaliese continued her tale, "As soon as the van left I went to investigate. There were still thirty-five minutes left before the hit was supposed to take place. But I was wary, careful. I had already had defined a hiding place for if they came early. It took me a while to spot what they had done, until I examined the metal fence in detail.

"As you can see from the photographs, the fence is composed of three sturdy cross members, with uprights placed four inches apart, and being two inches across, that equals six inches. They were about eight feet high, and shaped into a point at the top. To stop people from getting inside, razor wire had been added above, making the compound secure.

"The ADF men had removed the bottom and middle fixing bolts from four uprights. I noticed drag marks in the soil, and tried pulling the uprights apart, two to each side. The gap was big enough for a person to get through.

"I put everything back as it had been, and hid in the bushes and overgrowth. A man in a suit arrived sometime later, and gave orders to his accomplice. The worker opened the railings like I had done, and dove through. He sprayed some seriously thick and heavily insulated, high voltage cables, and repeated the process a second time, using a different aerosol.

"I expected them to leave quickly, but the worker remade the fence by replacing the bolts, and repainted to hide any trace. I got good headshots of both of them, as you can see in your file. You will notice the suit is the same man I photographed in Miami days before." A hush fell over the table as people looked to their files and concurred.

"I got a good shot of the vehicle, and its plate, just before they left the scene. You will recognize both of course. I went back and took close-ups of what they had done, to both the security fence, and the power transmission cables. In 'photograph G', you will notice the outer insulation already appears to be breaking down.

"We now know what happened as a result. The insulation failed, and shorted the entire substation when it rained heavily overnight. Power to the Amtrak Tucson depot was disrupted, causing delays of mainly freight trains. There was also a critical voltage drop at the nearby Tucson High Magnet School, which according to media reports, meant several experiments had to be restarted."

Talk became animated as the wealth of evidence increased. Even Bill was now wavering, having to admit that however 'Michael knew in advance, his predictions had been proved correct.

The serious work began a short time later, John assisting the girls with the pictures and video taken, while Bill and Michael discussed what it all meant.

The girls kept track of online news, with Annaliese getting the first hit. "The attack on Miami. They are reporting it was Sarin. Wait... Yes, Sarin, but a small dose, although dozens of people were hospitalized. No one is dead yet."

Annaliese sat down abruptly. It was clear to everyone how close she had come to death. April rose to comfort her, but Bill took two giant strides and held her close. As her father comforted her best friend, April finally discovered what had transpired in Detroit.

The media had been full of a water main failure, but there was little stated apart from regions of the city being without water, and oblique references to "contamination." Obviously a lid was being kept on the news.

She had to look at the local websites to finally discover what went down. She rose from her seat and walked to the map, unconsciously drawing everybody's attention. She pointed at Detroit and said, "You will never guess what the sneaky bastard's actually did, what they got away with?"

All eyes fixed on her; she continued, "We all know it was a deliberate act, presumably a bomb, right? It appears, we are the only people in the entire U.S. to suspect this."

A hush fell, awaiting her next words. "There has been no mention of the ADF van. They simply think the valve blew due to old age, and are instigating a Farmington Town wide series of checks. The crater is now twice the size it was when I shot the video, and the whole street has been closed to traffic, including pedestrians.

"Local businesses have been closed in the vicinity, and special crews, with the aid of private contractors, are racing against time to prevent the loss of buildings, by underpinning the substructures. They are appealing for volunteers, and considering asking the National Guard for assistance.

"Like in the San Diego case of 2006, most of the major shut-off valves don't actually work, so millions of gallons of drinking water are being lost.

"One consequence is that the sewer system is badly overloaded and cannot cope. Raw sewage is backing up and overflowing onto the streets, compromising businesses, homes, and precipitating a critical medical emergency. There is more, but those are the most interesting facts as of right now. The implications are clear, Farmington, Detroit even, could be facing a major crisis."

Michael spoke into the general discussion that followed, "I remember when the San Diego main blew. It took them weeks to stop the leak, and longer to repair the damage. It was a wake-up call for the city fathers."

April stayed with them at first, but her mind wandered back to her thoughts of the previous evening. She walked around the room, her eyes focused one moment, unfocused the next. She heard snatches of conversation, but all was conjecture, there was nothing moving their greater understanding forward.

Needing to think, she wandered outside and, unknowingly, stood beside the old oil painting of Thomas Jefferson. Abstractly patting Satan's head, she looked up at the Founding Father, and repeated her words from last night, "What the fuck is really going down?"

Inspiration seemed to come from above, as she marched into the study and said to Michael, "What is this plot about?"

Without a flicker, Michael replied, "April you know already, a cabal is plotting to blow up the Presidency."

Within that nanosecond, her focus switched from the target being a man, to an institution. She extrapolated, and realized the entirety of Capitol Hill was under threat. She gazed at Michael's map up on the wall. It seemed to taunt her—there was hardly a State or city untouched by marker pin or reference.

April had no need of a box. She looked at all the targets on the map, and focused on Washington, D.C. The abstract thought came into her mind, as if speaking to her on an entirely different plane.

There was only one answer that fitted, the enemy was practicing to gauge response times and destabilize infrastructure. The odd thing was, they had done this everywhere of any note, across the entire U.S., except for one extremely important city.

April cursed aloud, finally unlocking the apparent paradox. She rounded on everyone and shouted, "What if, 'all of this', were to happen in one place at the same time?

"The location is conspicuous only by its absence. The only city they have not hit so far is Washington, D.C."

Chapter 9 – Clued Up

Bill

Bill got a call from Deputy Teves. The rendezvous was a rundown bar on the bad side of town. Doughnuts were the first item on the menu. Bill knew it was a police haunt. Teves was waiting for him. Bill strode over with two beers and no doughnuts.

Bill opened as soon as they had clinked glasses, "You got the results back yet, Undersheriff?"

"Nope," came the bluff reply. "They will be a few more days yet. I wanted to know which of the miners got you those samples?"

Bill was immediately defensive, protective, until Teves added, "There has been a cave-in at the mine. I simply want to join the dots. Who was it, Bill?"

Bill thought back, initially saying, "His name was Manuel… No, he was the first, it was José Santos who gave me the nugget, and the next night got the yellow ore."

Deputy Teves leaned back in his seat and rolled an ancient silver Dollar between his fingers for a moment, clearly deliberating on what to say next. Bill watched him like he would an adversary at a poker table, and tried to discern his tell.

"Bill, it is now your turn to indulge me. Both of those men were caught in the rock fall, a supposed mining disaster. They are now in City General, unable to pay their medical bills. They are alive, but the hospital has virtually stopped treatment because they have no insurance, no money either. So they will eventually die, or live out their lives as cripples."

Bill fixed his gaze on his adversary and stated bluntly, "No they will not. They are good people. You got anything else for me?"

Teves was surprised by Bill's reaction, and said, "Most people do not value itinerant Mexican workers lives. What makes you so different?"

Bill retaliated to the implied jibe, "Good people are good people, bad people are bad people. That's all there is to it, Undersheriff. I thought you would know that."

They eyed each other for a moment, neither giving anything away, yet sharing communion at some deeper, animal level. They drank and Bill opened, "You remember that bridge collapse over in Orange County some weeks back? This is a sample of the concrete

49

around the four main supports on the other side. It is all the same, and crumbles like old cement. A concrete weakening agent was used to destroy that bridge deliberately.

"Trust me on this, that it is a genuine sample. You can check and get more yourself. That and several other incidents, like the recent explosions in the vehicle lot opposite the mall here in SD, have one thing in common. This SUV, this registration plate, and this man." Bill deliberately punctuated his sentence as he laid photographs on the table between them.

Teves did not like this line of information, and said, "This is outside my jurisdiction. Well, Auto City could be mine for the right reason, but not Orange County, unless I opened a case file specifically."

Teves picked up the bag containing samples of concrete and it flaked under the pressure of his middle finger and thumb. He toyed with it as his mind worked, unsure how this related to the man opposite him, or the connections, except for the SUV and its driver.

The deputy was still ruminating when Bill pressed several more photographs on the table. "This white van is also deep in all this shit. But the Army Humvees are special. Get what you can on them without drawing attention to your enquiry."

Bill slid over more photographs. "This is the man who placed the device at the mall in Miami, the one where they released Sarin, although I believe it was, in reality, a small dose to check the delivery system. This next is from a video of him placing the device, and this next without the mask on, which we also have for forensic examination. That is, if you are even vaguely interested?

"We believe all these events are practice demonstrations for hits on, as yet, one or more unspecified targets, sometime in the future. There are dozens of them. The same people, the same vehicles, the same plates. The SUV and ADF truck are associated with them all."

Bill drank as Deputy Teves wavered, his mind working. Bill had used the word "we." He wondered if April, and perhaps others were involved. He needed to remain alert and pick up on any more clues Bill let slip.

Bill broke his train of his thoughts by saying, "I know you don't believe me. That's fine, twist. Please do me the courtesy of leaving your mind open and simply conduct a few follow-up checks. You will not be disappointed, I assure you."

Teves responded at once, "Damn right I do not believe you. Next you will be telling me of some plot to kill the President."

Bill did not react at all. Teves looked at him, judging his response. Eventually he picked up the beer and they clinked bottles before drinking. "I will do as you ask, but I believe very little of what you say. Is there anything else you have for me? My family is waiting."

Bill played his next card, "Undersheriff." He slid over a hand written slip of paper. "Indulge me one more time. I need to know who really owns this vehicle, and I do not mean the name on the registration documents. That will be false. It has been parked for far too long in a place it has no right to be. Understand?"

Deputy Teves took the paper, and recognized the number immediately. They had already received numerous complaints about it. He said, "That vehicle will be gone tomorrow morning. The Sheriff's Office signed the recovery slip a couple of hours ago."

Bill said, "Shit!" and rushed out of the joint. He glanced back from the doorway, noticing Teves deep in thought. "Good," Bill thought to himself, "Knock yourself out."

Bill rode his Harley to City General and did not waste any time. He found the cashier and demanded to pay the full costs for patients, José Santos, and Manuel Figuera. The bill was a lot more than he had expected, but his roll covered it easily. The clerk processed the payment, and for once, Bill felt good inside.

His duty done, Bill headed at speed to his favorite gun store. It was owned by Hilcott, an ex-Marine buddy, and would have what he needed. It was almost closing time, but the place was still busy, and what he wanted to buy was marginally legal. After a quick word with Hilcott, Bill checked out the displays, waiting for the last customers to leave.

Having checked out the handguns and rifles, Bill moved on to the shotguns. He had never been a shotgun person, but one intrigued him. The barrel was shorter than most, but not too short. He asked to have a look at it, not intending to buy, but to pass the time while Hilcott, got rid of the last persistent customer.

The gun fell flawlessly into his giant hand and seemed to sit just right. It was perfectly balanced within the guard on his trigger finger. It felt like an extension of his arm. He hefted it and noticed the pump action moved an inch. He tried again with force, and the weapon slid the next imaginary cartridge into the barrel. Bill really liked the gun.

He took it with him to the counter and spoke with menace to the idiot. "You do not have the right paperwork. Leave now!"

The guy looked at him, then at the shotgun and fled. "Thank you Bill. He is harmless, but can be a pain in the ass when he's had a few. You know what I mean."

Bill nodded and placed the unusual shotgun on the counter. "How much?"

Hilcott said, "I call this the Terminator Special. You know, after that scene in the movie. It is a lovely weapon, if you have very strong wrists."

He looked down and patted Bills, "Which you have. It will be a marriage made in heaven."

Bill glared at him, "What have you got in night vision, and make it quick."

Hilcott pulled the outside shutters down and locked up. He led Bill through to one of his secure display rooms, going straight for the headsets. Bill walked away from him, headed toward more serious equipment. "I need zoom on a vehicle at 120 yards, and good enough to make out a zit on a person's face, and record it. What you got?"

Bill took his time, but found what he wanted. The equipment was higher-level than the Town Car he wanted eyes on, but manufactured by the same people who made the scope in the sedan, and his night sight from Nicaragua: Coulson Tactical.

Bill haggled the price, but added, "I'll take the shotgun on the counter, with ten boxes of Bear-shot cartridges. I need a revolver and a pistol, both nine-millimeter, and ammo. What you got?"

Chapter 10 – Counter Surveillance

Bill arrived back at Michael's home and perfunctorily said hello, before making his way up to his room. He opened the window with the lights out, and set the new equipment well back. When he had finished assembling everything, he checked out the car down the road, and focusing on the dash, saw the camera was still in place.

He set record mode and real-time monitoring, before he sat and watched for a few minutes, checking to make sure the system worked. It did admirably. The movement sensor was highly sensitive, and even at the range he was using it, clocked the night acrobatics of moths and bats. He dialed it down a few pegs, and once satisfied, left to talk to the others below.

The meeting was short and intense. Bill laid out all that had happened between him and Teves, holding nothing back. They all knew they needed inside help, and if Teves came through, they agreed it would resolve many of their problems.

Afterwards, Bill spoke to the girls, offering them a handgun each, and their names matched the certificates. He gave April the revolver, knowing she preferred 'old school'. It was a special like his Magnum, and carried extra rounds. It also came with a couple of quick reload clips.

He gave Annaliese a pistol, a couple of clips, and a few boxes of the same 9mm bullets. Annaliese was thrilled, and leapt up to hug and kiss him, something he was not used to. He blushed, and April giggled. Reasserting his manliness, Bill showed them how to use and maintain the guns. The girls were overjoyed, and spent time playing with their gifts.

April

April woke abruptly. The clock read 4:32. She had been asleep for just a few hours and knew something was happening. She shook Annaliese awake, before donning a bathrobe and heading directly for the front bedroom her father had been working in earlier.

She understood what the equipment was doing, but not how to use it. Annaliese staggered through in her wake, just the conscious side of asleep on her feet. April feasted her alert eyes on the screen, as two men approached the surveillance vehicle. She realized she must have heard the bleep of the sedan's doors unlocking.

Before he opened the trunk, she got her first real glimpse of one of them. She thrust Annaliese's head to the screen immediately. It was the same guy from Miami. Suddenly, Annaliese was wide-awake and concurred, leaving at once to wake the others.

April ran to the man who had instigated it all, but Bill was fast asleep on the downstairs sofa. Even if he woke, he would be useless after finishing the bottle of Rebel Yell that lay empty and discarded on the floor.

By the time April got back to the observation bedroom, John was monitoring the two men strip out the vehicle, and trying to enhance camera footage. Michael watched John work, before peeking, and suddenly became animated, as if a shield had dropped and he was now part of the present.

Michael tactfully ushered John out of the way, and quickly set the device to zoom, and operated the controls for maximum gain, and streetlight reduction. The result was extremely good footage. He continued to tweak controls, until his enthusiasm waned. They got good shots of both men, and the other vehicle's plate before John took over once more.

April asked, " Michael, how did you know what to do?"

Michael, eyes seeming to lose focus, his mind awhirl and beginning to wander. He blustered, "I've done it a few times. Don't know where, don't know when. It was very dark… and very loud. There were bright flashes that shocked the ground. I remember it was the same weird green as this one. But most of all, I remember the girl…"

April had noticed Michael's periods of intense lucidity, were often followed by mental withdrawal, as if his mind needed to recuperate from being normal—in this case, highly skilled. Her insight was confirmed when Michael added, fidgety and distracted, "It is an old hat—have you ever eaten one? I think I did once, or it could have been something else…"

Mumbling to himself, Michael rushed out of the room immediately, as if panic-stricken. John stayed to watch the men at the sedan leave, before going in search of their host. The girls watched the recording several times, adding comments that led to a short discussion, before tiring to bed.

The next morning John was able to transfer the recording to a memory stick and load it into Michael's laptop. "We desperately needed some serious computing power in here guys!"

Michael's study was slowly evolving into an operations center; tables and chairs had been added as needed, and people began working on individual parts of the project. Satan had taken over the couch, since nobody ever used it, and kept a watchful eye out for his new family.

That morning they ordered a top of the line color printer, a state of the art desktop computer with massive storage capabilities, and software to match their specific needs. Michael insisted on having the largest plasma monitor available. There was additional storage media so everything could be backed-up outside the main computer. John set it up for them and ensured the whole thing worked correctly. He added a highly secure access Wi-Fi hub, turning the desktop PC into a residential server.

Bill woke for lunch and ate his fill, soon coming back to life. He was very satisfied with the recordings from the night before, and apologized for sleeping through the action. He praised John and Michael for their camera skills, stating he could not have done better. He asked for prints of the two men, and registration plate of the second vehicle, which Annaliese processed and gave to him a short time later. April told him off for drinking too much liquor and made him promise to drink less.

He said, "OK Hon, I won't, 'cept for them special occasions," without the slightest conviction behind his words.

April knew it, and knew it was against his rebel 'One Star' Texan heart. Later, in her room, she concluded she had used the words her mother would have said, and had spoken in the past. She needed to rethink the whole thing, her whole relationship with her father.

Chapter 11 – Phoenix

Teves

Across town, Teves was headed for the County Sheriff's Office with a mind full of worries and pieces of a puzzle that did not fit together. He resented the feelings of mounting frustration.

He was returning from the Official Lab and had answers to all of Bill's questions, ones that only presented unanswerable questions of his own. He needed to see Bill, and confront the rest of them, but wanted to wait until he finished running a few secondary enquiries of his own.

He pulled over. Something was not right, but he could not put his finger on what it was. He wound down the window, and looked out afresh at the world, smelling the stench of deception all around.

Over his years in the Force, Teves had come to value his gut feelings, and this one was settling heavier than a thirty-two ounce steak. For some illogical reason, Teves did not want to return to his office. He checked in, and turned his cruiser around, heading out to Del Fuego mine.

Teves knew the receptionist and manager from previous visits, asking routine questions and offering the usual support. He was about to leave when a dark SUV pulled up and the man from Bill's photo of the Orange County Bridge got out. The stranger was obviously well known to the manager, and feared by him. The new arrival turned to the deputy and said, "I don't think I know you."

Teves replied at once, "U.S. County Undersheriff Teves at your service. And you are, Sir…?"

"John Smith, Regional Head of Mining Operations West Coast. I was not expecting to find the U.S. Sheriff's Office interested in our small operation out here. I hope there is not a problem, Officer. If there is, know I will sort it instantly."

Teves knew this type of city slime ball well, and answered, "Nothing at all, just a regular community visit. We are supposed to come out once every month, but things happen and it's not always possible. I hope you will forgive us, but sometimes our service becomes very stretched. Today I was in the area for another reason, and just dropped in for a couple of minutes to say 'Hi'. Everything appears to be fine, and I have been assured new safety precautions have been initiated since the unfortunate cave in."

John Smith replied too quickly, "Yes they have. I came down from head office today, especially to check progress of modifications, and ensure this tragedy can never happen again."

"That is most reassuring to hear. I have since discovered that both mineworkers will make a full recovery."

"That is excellent news, and a great relief to us all. Please excuse me, Undersheriff. I am a very busy man. My pleasure to meet you."

They shook hands perfunctorily, John Smith turning at once for the office, the manager a whirl of bustling subservience at his side.

Teves probed the receptionist, "Seems like a nice guy."

The girl froze, and her frown covered the clouding of her eyes. He had his answer, but covered smoothly, saying, "Excuse me, but I must be off. I have several more calls to make before I finish for today."

As he departed, Teves noticed the blinds in the office move, and knew he was being observed. He reversed and in the rearview saw a small truck, heavily overloaded. The front end was up, and the twin rear tires were under great pressure. He used the mic, pretending to receive a call, as his eyes remained glued on the vehicle coming from a very secure section of the site, one he had never been allowed to visit without a warrant.

He noted the registration and replaced the mic. For distraction, he flicked on his lights, blipped the siren as he spun the rear wheels, as if off on an emergency call. He knew the truck would only take the road to San Diego and not the one to Rosa's small town. He hit the gas and went as fast as the unpaved road would allow. He reasoned that the overloaded truck would be several times slower, and that might just be enough time for him to dump the cruiser and return in his own vehicle.

Teves swapped vehicles at his home, and donned a normal jacket to hide his uniform. He headed back to the main intersection, and caught sight of it in the distance. He closed the gap and dropped in a dozen cars behind. He was not surprised when the SUV he had seen at the mine, cruised past ten minutes later. It dropped in front of the truck and they had a convoy.

He followed them for hours as they headed east. Teves dropped a long ways back on the country haul into Casa Grande, but quickly closed the distance as they came into Phoenix.

He almost lost them when they diverted to Scottsville, just recognizing the distinctive twin rear lights of the truck in time.

Five hours after leaving the mine, they pulled into an old warehouse district, and headed toward what appeared to be a disused factory. There was security on the gate that waved them through with a salute. Teves thought that was very strange. He parked in a side alley and scrambled onto the roof, putting in a dent that he hoped would easily pop out.

With the binoculars from his emergency pack, the one his wife always moaned about, he was able to see into the building. There were two men by the truck sweeping water into a drain. The vehicle was no longer overloaded. He could not locate John Smith until a door opened and he came out in the company of an odd looking man, who was wearing a white lab coat.

Smith spoke quickly, but Teves could not hear the words. The men finished sweeping and went into the room, appearing moments later with a black box that looked like a heavy safe. Although it was relatively small, the two heavy-set men had obvious difficulty carrying it using a handle each. They put it in the trunk of the SUV, which dropped down significantly on its suspension.

The SUV departed a few minutes later, followed by the scientist in his own sedan. Teves followed them back into Phoenix, and a five star hotel. He parked and watched as the men entered the hotel. Teves moved instinctively toward the foyer, being sure to remain out of sight in the semi dark parking lot. A limousine pulled up and out stepped someone who was obviously a Director of a senior company.

Teves watched and saw Smith greet the youngish CEO warmly, the scientist hovering innocuously in the background, Smith's men likewise to the other side. Teves started filming on his old style cell phone. He knew the quality would be bad, but it was better than nothing.

He waited until they were in the elevator and noted the floor number. When the clerk was distracted, Teves took a snapshot of the register. The name John Smith was the last entry for a Parlor Suite. Most notably, the one before it was Anton DeMellor, who took the Presidential Suite on the top floor. The entry above these was for a Dr. Black of Coulson Systems.

Teves sidled away and waited. Nothing was happening, so he left, wondering if his time had been wasted. The road home was long and lonesome. He pulled over at opportune places to stretch his legs and clear his growing tiredness. His understanding of what was really going on, remained as black as the moonless night that surrounded him, and he felt like it engulfed him.

For the first time in a month, Deputy Teves had a long weekend off. He arrived home just in time for breakfast, and needing his bed. Instead, he was told he was going shopping with the family. The day dragged a little because of his lack of sleep, but family time was always the best time of his life. He survived until late sunset, and picking his moment carefully, offered a trip to the family's favorite restaurant, just on condition he could drive home afterwards and go to sleep immediately.

Teves woke before his usual time feeling refreshed and ready to face the world once more. He set about the to do list and yard chores, before devoting the rest of the day to his wife and children.

The next day, he insisted they all attend church, and he took Confession, which was rare. Afterward, they played in the local park and splashed about in the nearby lake. It was good to share normal things with his family. He knew it might be the last time they could do this for some while. They ate lunch at a fast food place the kids loved, and he detested.

When they were alone he spoke to his wife. "I must do something today. I may be an hour, or several days. It is not dangerous. I must solve several mysteries. Xochitl, take care of our babies and know that I will come back strong. If this works out, I will become the next County Sheriff."

Teves leaned over and kissed his wife, before looking at their children enjoying the games area. He waved and they reluctantly came running. Xochitl dropped him home to pick up his cruiser. He stopped by his office, finding the last pieces of information waiting for him. He did not hang around, but headed directly for what he called, "The Hideout."

Chapter 12 – The Hideout

Teves had already put his reasons for the visit in order, and a threat if he needed to use it. He parked at the curb and looked over at an old, rambling house that needed some restoration work doing. He sighed in resignation of what was to come, and got out.

Annaliese answered the door and froze. "Annaliese, how nice to see you again. I trust you and April are well."

The girl replied too quickly, "We're fine, but this is most inconvenient. What do you want?"

"I would very much like to come in and have a little chat with everyone inside," he smiled magnanimously.

"You cannot, we're very busy Undersheriff. It's not a good time, why don't we make an appointment?"

The Deputy laughed. "I will enter with your permission, now, or I will enter chasing a runaway I know to be living here. Her name is Shona Waverley, and I especially want to speak to her father, Bill."

With his words just spoken, Bill appeared behind Annaliese and stated, "If you enter for the first reason, we can talk. I have several things to tell you." He opened the door and waved a welcoming hand.

Bill continued speaking as he showed Teves to a seat in the living room, "How did you know we were here?"

"That is elementary, dear William. You asked me about the vehicle that was towed away. This was the only residence in the entire street not to report it. You yourself gave me photographs of it. You had to be here. It was simple deduction. Now I would like to speak to all the residents if you don't mind, it saves having to repeat things."

Bill was unmoved. "What were the test results?"

Teves was playing the game, but replied truthfully, "Uranium two thirty-eight; and the yellow ball, uranium two thirty-five."

Bill clenched his fist and punched the air in victory. "I knew it. That's a damn mighty fine result Teves. You on or off duty?"

"Social call."

Bill left to get them both a beer. He knew they would need it and several others. He asked April to get Michael and John. After introductions, they settled round the large dining room table.

Deputy Teves recapped, "I am off duty and this is a personal visit. I hope you will trust me and be as open with me, as I will be with you. The samples I tested were uranium two thirty-eight, and uranium two thirty-five, yellow cake, and potentially weapons-grade. Thank you, because I did not believe you at first."

The Deputy went on to tell them about his recent visit to the mine and the resultant journey to Phoenix. He had also tested the concrete sample, and it had been treated with a state of the art weakening agent. Michael was jubilant. Once again, his evidence had been independently analyzed and confirmed his hypothesis.

April disappeared for a moment and came back with four large cans of beer. Bill thanked her, but said, "Make mine a Rebel Yell, Hon."

"But Dad, you promised." She froze, realizing what she had just admitted.

"I'm my own man."

Teves smiled gratuitously and looked at April for a little too long, before saying, "Make that two shots please, April Bekkons."

The release of tension was palpable, and everyone began to talk openly. They discovered the military vehicles were out of Twentynine Palms Marine Corps, and both the ADL truck and SUV were untraceable, at least as regarded real ownership. The mug shots were similar, several names associated with each one, but nothing definitive for a real identity.

Teves assured them, "I made all these checks unsupervised and personally. Now if we understand one other, please level with me and show me what you got."

There was a short break while Michael discussed their options. Trusting a cop was a very big step for all of them. Deputy Teves became frustrated as time passed and nothing was resolved. He downed a measure of Rebel Yell and rising, slammed the glass down hard on the table. Everyone stopped to stare at him.

"I do not like my intentions to be called into question. I can easily change sides from supporting you, to wrecking whatever intrigues you are plotting. In this room, there could be a runaway called Shona Waverly, but I do not intend to pursue the matter. At least not yet."

Teves sat down and filled his glass at once, and topped off Bill's as an afterthought.

Bill took the glass, clinked the Deputy's, and downed the measure, before standing and leading him upstairs. In the front bedroom, the Deputy saw the surveillance equipment and whistled. He became focused when Bill ran the recording. "The mystery man from Miami" was all Teves said.

Michael entered the room and wandered around, apparently disinterested. He spotted something, and said animatedly, "I see someone has just moved into the old Mathers place down the road. That's been empty for several years."

Both Bill and Teves stopped instantly, taking just a moment to lock eyes in understanding. Michael pinpointed the building and seemed happy to have new neighbors. April was the first to voice everyone else's concerns, "With the vehicle gone they've now taken over one of the houses. We'll take Satan for a walk."

Meanwhile, Teves watched as April and Annaliese played Frisbee. As the girls neared the old Mathers home, Annaliese threw a Frisbee a long way for Satan to chase. April immediately sent another deftly into the open and brightly lit garage.

A goon rose up and appeared to bawl her out for being so stupid. April reacted instinctively by giving teenage lip back, and the man threw the Frisbee with venom at her throat. She only just ducked in time.

Annaliese was closest, and got to the second Frisbee just before Satan did. She threw the usual one for him to chase, carefully putting the one the man had touched in a plastic carrier. They played around nearby for a while, managing to take a few photographs, before heading home the back way.

Teves met them downstairs and Annaliese said, "On this Frisbee are the fingerprints of a very nasty man. He is working on the Mathers old house. There is a vehicle in the driveway, and a pickup truck reversed into the garage. I will download this into the computer and let you have snapshots in a few minutes. You should know we also saw men setting up equipment in the front bedroom, you better check it out."

Teves turned for the stairs, but dallied for a moment and saw the girls enter Michael's study. He surmised this was the hub of their operation.

Returning upstairs, Teves discovered Bill had reset his surveillance equipment, and called them to look. Inside the bedroom was the man from Miami, setting up both video and voice recording equipment, the latter via a strange sort of dish.

Teves left them to use the bathroom, and they found him some minutes later, agog in Michael's study, chaperoned by Satan. Gone were all pretenses. Now he was genuinely aware of what was going on. In return, he offered the full support of the Law.

Chapter 13 – On the Take

The deputy stayed overnight and all of the next day. Over time He gained their deeper trust and understanding. He came to embrace the notion that something far bigger was afoot, although he never accepted any of their suspicions without indisputable proof. As far as it being a plot to execute the President went, he could only move his position so far without hard evidence.

That afternoon a knock came to the side door. By chance, Teves was in the kitchen, making a pot of coffee the way he liked it. A voice shouted from inside, "Get that will you."

Although he knew it was not intended for him, Teves opened the door. Before him was a strange looking man. His graying, shoulder-length hair was awry, and his face looked haunted. His eyes darted around with flyaway looks, and at first Teves though he had escaped from an asylum.

The odd man spoke, "Erm, is er, Michael…. Yes, is Michael at home? I need to speak to him urgently."

Teves said, "That depends upon who you are, Sir?"

The man replied hesitantly, "Rogers. Bob Rogers. I live next door. Michael, is he about?"

Teves began to close the door, without inviting the stranger inside, but the man said, "Oh. Can I come in? I am not sure if they are following me. Please."

Teves focused on Rogers' use of the word 'they', and wondered if all the residents of the street were unhinged. Perhaps there was something in the water? He glanced back at the fresh coffee pot on the stove, and said to himself, "Damn. Next time I'm bringing bottled water."

Roger's situation eased when April rushed through and, recognizing their neighbor, invited him into the living room. Michael greeted him moments later, and they exchanged brief words. It turned out the cop cruiser parked outside had freaked Rogers out. Between them, they settled Rogers' concerns, and he left moments later, a very relieved man.

Michael returned from seeing the man out, and tapping his temple said, "That man is not all there you know."

He winked conspiratorially and added, "Rogers has always been a bit strange, but he is harmless. I guess a lot of very clever people are like that. Used to be a professor of science at a college, I remember. Chemistry, physics, something like that.

"Is your Mexican coffee ready yet Teves? I'm looking forward to remembering it."

Teves left them the next morning, having considered his situation, and all the people he could trust with his life. There were not enough to count on one hand, if he excluded family.

Begrudgingly, he admitted the people he had just stayed with, perhaps. He knew what to do, and pulled out his rarely used emergency cell phone. The text he sent read: "Red, been a long time coming. You hot for a ticket to the A game? Aztec coffee on my mind. I got a heap of moles under the pitch, and they're running deep and wild."

At the FBI offices in San Francisco, a Supervisory Special Agent took out his cell phone when it beeped. SSA Nigel Redmond read the message and instantly texted back, "I'll see you 2 in St. Louis, for Louis. The Cappuccino is on me."

Deputy Teves chuckled at the reply. He knew that in two day's time, Redmond would be at a specific café in San Diego at four p.m. That had always been Cappuccino time from way back when.

It had been several years since Teves had seen his old friend. He remembered how he first met Redmond, who was an FBI probationary officer at the time. They had been working a joint case and went into a building to make arrests, but their intel was flawed. It turned out to be a trap.

They came under heavy gunfire at once, before grenades where thrown at them. Teves reacted immediately, football-tackling Redmond through the nearest window. They were the only members of the team to survive, and had since become very good friends.

After reliving happier memories, Teves headed back to the office directly. A strange thought filtered up from his subconscious, as he realized his number two, Deputy Rodriguez, had been acting a little strangely of late.

There was nothing substantial, yet the Deputy had developed a habit of speaking on his mobile in deserted corridors, or finishing telephone conversations as soon as anyone entered the room. What worried Teves was the man was unusually dismissive when pressed about the calls. He decided to find out what Rodriguez was up to.

At first, Teves thought to follow the man and check his contacts, but soon realized that would be a wasted effort. Instead, he inserted a tracking chip into his cell when Rodriguez went to the restroom. It looked like a typical banner on the battery cover, and was one that was not authorized by the department, yet. He personally tracked it, and later that evening found it located at Del Fuego mine.

He knew the officer had no reason to go there, and that he was off duty. The tumblers rolled inside Teves' mind. There was only one conclusion he could come up with. The deputy was on the take.

Two days later, Teves greeted Redmond in a coffee bar. Redmond was already seated with his favorite coffee, eagerly waiting to catch up his old friend. In due course, Teves told Redmond what was worrying him, and a short time later they left for Michael's home.

Teves introduced Redmond as his most trusted friend, adding he was FBI. Before they had time to consider, Teves said, "Michael, may we please adjourn to your study? If we want to get anywhere with what we are about, then we need Redmond on board. He can access information even I do not know exists."

Redmond added, "From what Manny tells me, we are both working on the same case. It was only recently handed to me, and I do not have much as yet, but will share with you everything I have. Let's work together and preserve America."

Redmond was amazed at the facts they had collected, collated, and complimented on them on obtaining and verifying physical evidence. He was visibly shocked when they gave him details about the local uranium mine, and he wanted to call in Special Forces immediately.

Teves countered at once, "Nigel, although this seems like an entirely separate issue, I could get nowhere with finding out who actually runs the place. All my enquiries end up blocked by either Washington, D.C. Government departments, Agency, or Coulson databases. It is as if the whole thing is politically, or financially, ring fenced. Instead of reporting it, why don't you try and find out as much as you can about it first?"

"Don't give the game away in the first quarter. OK, work with me here. Explain what you got. These targets are senseless.

Talk returned to focus on what the team had achieved so far. However, the random targets remained senseless, unless there was another objective. He listened as April explained their thoughts, and he nodded his head in agreement. Practice runs for a major hit was one of his own theories.

He made a snap decision, followed by a private telephone call made out of earshot. When he returned, he stated, "I will fly back to Frisco in the morning. Manny, please request FBI assistance as soon as you hear from me. Here is the number to call.

"I'll see the Assistant Director as soon as I get back, and text you as soon as our meeting is concluded. Call as soon as you can after this, and I will return promptly to set up in the San Diego field office. I'll return with the full file, everything I have I will share with you.

"Manny, are you still allowed to make people temporary Deputies, or has that been abandoned nowadays?"

Teves thought for a moment before replying, "Temporary deputies are common, and a great asset to us at many community levels. They are called 'Reserve Deputies' in San Diego, and undergo formal induction and training.

"To answer your real question, as far as I am aware, it is still possible for an acting Sheriff to appoint anyone as a deputy to serve as backup should the needs of the moment warrant it. One of the stated duties of a Reserve Deputy is, and I quote; 'to assist Deputy Sheriffs in the execution of their duty,' and that works for me.

"The sort of temporary deputy you are alluding to has been uncommon since cowboy days, but I can deputize anybody if the situation warrants it. I foresee no problem. Why do you ask?"

Redmond responded, "I would normally work with Angie Fallon, as her Spanish is excellent, but not local to here. She is on maternity leave, and I know we are already very stretched for manpower. Therefore, I will request a small team from the local office here. I hardly know them, so I cannot trust any of them. You may, or may not know, the FBI is a departmentally fragmented organization, and trusting other teams is not our forte.

"I would like to keep this venue completely secret," He nodded to Michael and the others. "So I would have somebody we trust to liaise with your office and mine. Somebody present here today."

Bill simply shook his head and headed for the Rebel Yell. Michael was not going to volunteer, so that left the two girls. April had transport, so it fell on her shoulders. She liked the idea and said, "U.S. Deputy Sheriff April Bekkons. Has a nice ring to it, don't you think?"

She giggled, as Teves reacted by clutching his face in his hands, and shaking his head at the absurdity of the situation. Redmond slapped Teves' shoulder and stated, "She would also be my choice, as it must be somebody who can melt away into the crowd as needs be."

Teves looked at Nigel and knew he was deadly serious. He looked across at April and grimaced. "I will deal with it myself, but know that the County Sheriff must approve it personally."

Teves went back to shaking his head as every other person's mood lightened. Bill put a shot glass down heavily on the table. Teves looked at it and asked, "Ain't you got any bigger glasses?"

Michael responded at once by looking in a cupboard. He brought out several lead crystal whiskey glasses and, after dusting them out, gave one to each man. Teves passed his shot glass to Redmond. Annaliese got a beer for April and herself, and they both lit cigarettes.

It was clear to all, the world of order, which Emmanuel Teves had dedicated his life to preserving, had suddenly shattered. It went from being turned upside down, to becoming perverse, surreal. He drank deeply, accompanied by Bill.

Chapter 14 – Housebreaking

Teves

The following day Teves received the message from Redmond and requested FBI assistance, which was immediately granted. Teves had already spoken at length to the "Chief," as everybody called the County Sheriff, and had his full support.

Teves asked for a "temporary" Special Reserve Deputy. At first, the Chief laughed, but Teves explained his reasons, and mentioned that one of their deputies was working for their quarry. At this, the Chief's laughter turned to alarm. Teves stated he already knew it was Rodriguez. He added that he was about to spring a trap and catch the officer in the act, but first he needed the appointment of the Temporary Reserve Deputy.

The Chief reluctantly agreed, asking him to call the man to attend. Teves smiled and stated it was a girl, but one he trusted with his life. Noticing unease in the Chief's eyes, Teves added, "She is a second year ROTC Cadet, and she will be in this office at 6:15 p.m. I need to wait for a certain member of 'our own' to go off duty first." The Chief nodded and Teves was dismissed.

Teves called April, and then spoke briefly with Bill. The trap was set. Teves planned to expose Rodriguez by forcing him to go to the Mathers house on Sacramento Drive.

Teves waited until near the end of the day, before inviting Rodriguez into his office, speaking candidly with him, and luring the deputy into a web of intrigue. Teves got up and paced the room as if fixing his thoughts, allowing Rodriguez to feast his eyes on the photographs and report he had laid out on his desk. The deputy took the bait, as Teves knew he would.

Teves confided in his understudy, and asked him to conduct the raid on the Mathers house, Sacramento Drive, at first light. Rodriguez, tried to mask his internal conflict, but Teves saw right through him, and sat down as if to work at his desk. Teves did not want to draw any attention to the trap he was setting, until it was sprung.

Rodriguez left immediately, and as soon as he was alone, picked up his cell to call the occupants of the house concerned. There was no connection. Teves was surreptitiously watching his every move, and monitoring his cell in real-time with the service provider.

Chapter 14

Rodriguez tried several other numbers, but the result was the same, network failure. All deputies were aware landlines were monitored, and the call could be traced back to the originator, and was recorded. Rodriguez cursed and headed immediately for his vehicle, only to find it boxed in. Teves called Redmond and said, "Sting is live," and hung up.

April was early and waiting for Teves outside the Sheriff's office. She showed her ROTC credentials, was printed, processed, sworn in, and issued with a Deputy Sheriff's Badge within a few minutes. The Chief looked at Teves as she left and stated, "I hope you are right on this one Teves, otherwise your highly promising career just ended."

Teves offered a magnanimous grin and replied, "Chief, you will be promoted because of this. Thank you. Please excuse me. I still have several hours' work to do tonight."

April

New U.S. Deputy Sheriff April Bekkons caught up with Rodriguez's cruiser. The cop pulled into a store and used the landline for thirty-seconds. April waited out of sight until he drove off, and moments later, pressed redial: "Del Fuego Mine, how may I help you."

April made a brief call on her cell, and sped off in hot pursuit. She turned off the highway and used the Harley's agility and power to take a shortcut. She filled the gas tank near Michael's home and waited.

Redmond pulled up and parked across the courtyard, out of sight. April kick started the Harley for effect, although it was difficult for her, and idled on tick over in first gear toward the road. She pulled over and appeared to check her cell, hearing Redmond start his engine. She called Bill, and the plan was in action.

April's eyes were fixed on the passing cars, not the cell her fingers played with absentmindedly. Within moments a dark SUV hurtled by in a great hurry, as if trying to get somewhere on time. April knew the plate, and that it could not have come from the mine, so must have been nearby. She held up one finger into the night, knowing only Redmond would be able to see it. Several minutes passed until Rodriguez cruised past. April held up two fingers, pocketed her cell, and headed onto the highway.

One block from Michael's home, she pointed left. She already knew Redmond would take the road in a pincer movement.

April turned into Sacramento Drive, knowing the vehicle behind her was Deputy Teves. He flicked his headlights once and roared passed her. April blipped the throttle and they motored down Sacramento Drive in convoy.

Mendez

As they did, Special Agent Maria Mendez jumped out of the FBI SUV. She ran to make cover at the rear of the Mathers house, and rendezvoused with Bill and Annaliese, who were waiting for her.

Redmond's voice came comm., "Go!"

Mendez said, "Bill, give me a leg up so I can get over this wall and into the back yard."

Bill smiled and replied, "Won't you use the rear gate like us?"

She tried the handle and the door was locked. Bill told Mendez to stand back and cover her eyes and ears. From within his coat he produced a shotgun, and from a foot away, blasted the lock. He smiled and kicked the remains in. Doffing his cowboy hat, he ventured, "Ladies, I would always allow you both to go first, except on this occasion. I would rather take the first bullet headed our way myself, if you will forgive me."

Bill replaced his hat, and strode boldly through the now defunct rear access. Annaliese hid in the yard to catch any potential escapees. He walked straight towards the back door of the house, and repeated his actions. This time, he stood with the barrel three feet back and fired. The result was a lot better, leaving the lock still in place, but the remains of the door swung open. He winked at Mendez and said, "Better, this is my first time at housebreaking."

Bill punched the shotgun in the air with his right fist. It loaded the next cartridge, ejecting the used. Mendez became seriously aware of the man's innate strength.

SA Maria Mendez was confused. The guy must be shooting dinosaur shot, and he had just done it twice, with one hand. One wrist. She thought it was impossible, yet she had just witnessed it. Her respect and admiration turned on that moment, and again when he walked first into the unknown, shielding her. This was not in the FBI training manual, but it worked for her, out on the streets of the hostile unknown.

She tapped him on the shoulder to take the lead, but he simply nodded for her to check the darkened rooms downstairs, as he confidently stepped through from the kitchen into the hallway, his finger flicking like a gleeful butterfly upon the nectar of a hair-trigger. C'mon!

Mendez's cursory checks took moments, and she was behind Bill as they saw the thug slam the front door closed and slide the deadbolt across. He must have felt the ominous presence behind him as he instinctively dove for the stairs. Once safe upstairs, he fired to try to buy time, calling out to his colleagues in the front bedroom.

With all downstairs lights now on, the main living room window was shot out. Moments later Teves rushed through to take the lead. He was filled with battle lust and followed by Redmond.

Taking the stairs immediately, they met gunfire as soon as they gained the upper level. A gunshot sounded from the front bedroom, and the henchman momentarily distracted, was shot in the arm by Teves, and quickly arrested. They rushed into the room to find a nerd cowering, and a body bleeding out on the floor.

Redmond

Redmond heard a noise from outside the open front bedroom window, followed by April's cry, "He's escaping down the drainpipe. He dropped something. I am moving to intercept him."

She confronted the man stating, "Deputy Sheriff Bekkons, you are under arrest." Hearing this, Redmond reacted at once by calling out, "I'm on my way April."

The perp pulled out his pistol and fired, April reacting just in time. She feared a tendon in her arm must be ripped, and blood dripped to the ground. From his posture she inferred his style was the flamboyant and theatrical Wushu, which had become very popular. She knew without the gun in his hand, she could take him easily, even with her damaged arm. He fired again and diving once more, April was hit in the foot.

They both heard the click, as a Glock's slider was pulled back. Ignoring the wounded girl, the hoodlum displayed his weapon with an extended arm, and let it fall. He turned toward Redmond as if to offer his hands in surrender, but the position of them was for a striking blow. April rose and chopped his neck from behind.

Redmond cuffed him, as an FBI sedan screeched to a halt and two men came running over. Redmond stated flatly, "You are late Grainger, don't bother me with excuses. Just arrive before time in future."

April looked back and saw a shape running across the front of the house. "He's stealing the evidence," she cried in alarm. Redmond wheeled and fired instinctively. The man was near the bag, but rapid fire from the front lawn saw him break away and dive through the destroyed front window.

Redmond shouted, "Mendez, grab the evidence bag and put the computer tech in the back of my SUV. Grainger, check the garage, then take this suspect into custody. There is an SUV missing."

Redmond ran after the man who had entered the house. He popped a fresh clip into his Glock as he followed and dove through after his quarry. Redmond rolled and came to a kneeling position with gun cocked and ready to fire. The light had been shot out. He was alone.

Teves appeared in the hallway, a frightened Deputy Sheriff Rodriguez at the end of his grip. Bill was following them. Redmond relaxed and said, "You caught him at last. What about the other guy, you see anyone come through here?"

Teves replied, "Nope. Nothing. No one. We are the only people in this house."

Redmond stated, "I just followed someone in here, are you sure?"

Teves confirmed, and Bill added, "Yeah, Annaliese caught this scum ball trying to sneak out back a minute ago."

Redmond instructed, "I'm going to check the house. Give Rodriguez to the next FBI Agents that turn up, and tell them to take him back to Aero Drive for questioning."

Turning his gaze to the deputy, Teves spat, "Rodriguez, I am looking forward to a long chat with you, tomorrow. Sleep well, and know your promising career just ended." Rodriguez shrank visibly under Teves' withering look. Teves escorted the deputy to meet his fate, as Redmond and Bill began a thorough inspection of the house.

Chapter 14

They checked downstairs, finding one door locked, presumably the door to the garage, which Grainger should be checking outside. Out back, Annaliese was fine, but unhappy at missing all the action. Redmond rechecked upstairs, confirming the man in the front bedroom was a dead. He heard Mendez and Grainger arguing outside, and from the window, watched as the henchman was loaded into the back of the federal sedan. Grainger grabbed the evidence bag, and the vehicle pulled out.

Redmond hollered, "Mendez, I need that evidence here at the crime scene."

Mendez rushed to Redmond's SUV and used the radio to order Grainger back. Moments later she slammed the door shut and called to Redmond, "Grainger said to me, 'With all due respect Mendez, I have no intention of letting some two-bit Special Agent from San Fran bloody Cisco upstage our Office and steal our glory,' then the radio went dead, Sir."

Mendez cursed in Spanish. April understood her and laughed, adding a thought of her own in the local Mexican dialect. Maria Mendez chuckled and said, "You are very good, girl. You should join the Bureau." April merely smiled and shook her head. Redmond stayed by the window to catch the exchange, and knew he could probably trust Mendez, but not the rest of her office, yet. Grainger was an asshole.

The search of the house complete, Bill and Redmond returned to the locked door downstairs. Redmond asked enquiringly, "You got a key for that door?"

Bill smiled and pumped his fist in the air. Another cartridge slid into the 12 bore and he said, "Stand back." This time he fired from two and half feet. The lock stayed put as the rest of the door swung inwards. He turned to smile as they heard the screech of tires from inside.

They rushed through and fired after the disappearing vehicle that had smashed through the unlocked, wooden garage doors. It was already veering and crashed through the old wooden fence onto the driveway next door. They cursed in unison, as the SUV got clean away. They saw April running for her bike as best she could, bouncing on her right heel and leaping with her left foot. It was an impossible gait, but she was doing it.

April jumped on her trusty steed and fired the engine, but could not get a gear. Through the pain, she cupped the fingers of her left hand, but could not pull the clutch lever against either the heel of her hand or thumb. She leaned her whole body back and pulled the lever to the handlebars. She stamped the foot changer to second gear, revved the engine, and leaned forward.

The bike almost did a wheelie as she set off in pursuit. Bill turned to run for his own bike, parked in Michael's garage, but Redmond stopped him by saying, "They will be long gone before you even get there. Anyway, I need you here with me. I need people with me I can trust."

Bill stopped and acknowledged he was correct, although he went to the sidewalk and watched his only child disappear left at the end of the street. He prayed for her safety, before he looked back, knowing his duty.

Minutes later the sound of sirens grew closer, as the disparate team settled the crime scene, and called for specialized FBI CSI. Within moments, they were swarmed by all emergency services, all intent on gaining access to the scene of the firefight.

Redmond held station out front, letting no one past. Mendez took the rear yard access. They told SDPD, Ambulance, and Fire this was an FBI Scenes of Crime investigation, and they were not permitted entry. Teves initiated a Sheriff's Office cordon, selecting his best officers for the task.

Word came through that FBI CSI were extremely stretched, but someone would be with them "in a while." Darren Yates, the lead CSI, arrived two hours later, and after a quick word with Redmond, got straight to work.

§

SA Grainger was driving up Interstate 15, headed back for the old FBI Field Office on Aero Drive. He said, "George, have a look in that bag and see what they're so wound-up about."

SA George Hackenridge replied, "You know we ain't supposed to do that Grainger, this is scenes of crime evidence, by rights it should be processed on site."

Grainger looked over and stated disdainfully, "If you want your own team after I am promoted for breaking this case, you will do as I say."

Hackenridge opened the bag. "It's mainly memory sticks and audio/visual surveillance recordings. All state of the art."

"Show me."

Chapter 14

Hackenridge pulled out a box of tissues to avoid touching anything personally, and laid the contents out on the dashboard.

Grainger began interrogating the suspect while driving, but his questions were stonewalled, and he was getting pissed. He used the rearview mirror to look at the man, trying to intimidate him, and not looking at the traffic behind. He asked, "George, what have we got in total from these assholes?"

Hackenridge replied, "One tablet computer, a couple boxes that I do not know what they do, ten Blu-Ray disc's, and nine assorted solid state memory devices."

Grainger glanced at the road ahead, before swiveling his head to the rear and opening his mouth to speak.

As he turned, the driver's side window imploded and a bullet lodged in his chest. Before he could turn his head back, a large SUV slammed into the side of the vehicle, pushing it deliberately off the road. Grainger instinctively yanked the steering wheel away from the source, slamming his foot down on the brake. He forgot to move his right foot, and hit the gas pedal instead.

Hackenridge dove to yank the steering wheel back, but was too late as Grainger slumped at the wheel unconscious. They mounted a short ramp and sailed over a gorge into the night. The driver of the SUV watched as the vehicle landed on its front bumper, and careened down a steep incline. It hurtled into the opposite bank of a dry streambed, before rolling nose over tail across flat and rocky terrain. The vehicle landed upside down with the engine compartment on fire. The SUV drove off.

Chapter 15 – Accidental Investigations

April

April was in hot pursuit of the SUV, and had found fourth gear was the best to avoid unnecessary gear changes. She gunned the machine and soon caught sight of the SUV, dropping back as far as she could to avoid being marked as a tail. She also remembered her father's instructions, and managed to make several clutch-less gear changes, although changing down was a lot more difficult. She found the key was low revs, and getting the throttle just right for the new gear.

She could not understand where the SUV was headed. As she followed, she felt her left hand tingling, and a little more use came to it. She continued to flex her fingers, and by the time they hit Interstate 15 and headed north, she was able to use the clutch. She realized a main nerve must have only been numbed, and she felt greatly relieved. The SUV was speeding and she followed, pulling in behind a sedan when her prey finally slowed, as if the driver ahead were waiting for something.

They were closing on the Mission Road turnpike when the SUV suddenly took off. April gunned the engine to follow, but dropped back behind her cover as soon as she saw the agents' car sideswiped. Instinctively she slowed, switched off her lights, and pulled over to the side to watch, pretending to look at her bike. Thinking quickly, she pulled out a roll of duct tape from her saddlebag, and wound it around her foot, to stem the bleeding and give her a lot more support.

April felt the eyes of the SUV's driver sweep over her as he departed. She was close enough to read the license plate, and licking her finger, wrote it down on the tank. She waited until the SUV disappeared before switching on her lights and cruising up the small embankment, still keeping to the shadows. She crested the rise, and looked down into the darkness of a ravine. She saw a small fire in the distance beyond, on the other side of the gap, and she knew she had to get there immediately.

The agents' vehicle traveling at speed had somehow made a jump of thirty yards. She knew there was no way she could make the gap, but she had to be there.

She reacted instinctively, her eyes cleared, and she threw her head back, accepting the challenge. April headed back down the short ramp, and with little traffic around, she swung the Harley freely onto the interstate. She was heading in a large curve in the wrong direction. She got a blast from a trucker, but he was nowhere near her.

Coming around, she lined up, and accelerated back up the ramp in third gear. The bike flew across the gap, but too far and downwards. April leaned as far back as she could, and waited for the bad landing to come. The jolt almost threw her out of her seat, but with Kung Fu balance of mind, she kept control and miraculously fired the big machine forwards.

The rear wheel was all over the place at first, but the front stayed true. She picked up an animal trail in her headlights and followed it toward her objective. It saw her safely across the dry riverbed, and to the vehicle that was alight. She parked a good distance away and hobbled to rescue any survivors, and what evidence was left. She slowed as she closed. Gasoline was leaking from the tank.

The suspect was groaning in the rear, but everybody else appeared to be unconscious. Grainger, the driver had been shot. She grabbed for the mic, before noticing the fire extinguisher. Flames were snaking underneath the dash. She put them out, buying time for her call. She grabbed the mic and started speaking, only to realize the radio had been turned off. "Idiot!" was all she said before turning it on again.

"Officers down, road traffic accident, Interstate 15 and junction, just south of Mission Road turnpike headed north. C'mon?"

The radio came to life, "Who is this?"

April spoke quickly, knowing her time was limited. "Deputy Sheriff April Bekkons. Undersheriff Teves will confirm. I have Agent Grainger in the driver's seat, and a driver fleeing a crime scene driving a dark SUV on the highway northbound, APB dark SUV. Grainger has been shot in the chest. His partner is unconscious on the front seat. One suspect in the back, taken for questioning re incident at Sacramento Drive. SSA Redmond refers. Evidence bag from scene of crime Sacramento Drive has been opened and compromised by said FBI Agents. I will try to recover evidence of national importance. Engine compartment on fire, gas leaking from rear tank, the glow in the sky will guide you here. April Bekkons OUT."

April dragged Hackenridge out first, followed by the suspect. She reasoned the shot driver was least likely to live so she left him until last. She pulled Grainger out in time, and simply rolled his body down a small but locally significant dip. Next, she focused on the evidence, collecting nineteen items using the tissue paper she found, and throwing them in Hackenridge's general direction, before flames entering the cabin forced her back.

She turned to find the suspect attempting to escape, and Hackenridge trying to pull out his pistol to stop him. April rushed to the oaf and chopped his neck, rendering him unconscious. Returning to Hackenridge she found him barely holding a grip on reality.

April demanded, "What was in the bag? I have nineteen items."

Hackenridge mouthed something, before saying softly, "Two: Two". He tried to hold fingers up, but got confused. Finally, she heard the words, "twen-T two."

April bolted for the vehicle that was now beginning to burn fiercely, as sirens wailed their lonesome call far away. She grabbed the fire extinguisher, and emptied it, before she dove in the back, finding two more memory sticks; her hair began to singe. She pulled out, throwing them clear as she cursed the damage to her beautiful hair. She knew that there was one more item to be found before she was done.

April did not know what she was looking for, but a weak voice behind her said, "Tablet."

She dove back into the now burning wreck, looking for drugs. She saw a flame catch under the driver's upturned seat, and spied a screen-glow. Tablet computer, she realized. She had to react, but took a second to center her energy deep within Qi Gong philosophy. In the still part of her mind she focused on the thought, "There is no pain."

She returned to the present, knowing the seat was alight and the tablet smoldering. It would be useless, but the hard drive might be recoverable. Focused on just one action, she reached into the burning mass and held fast to the plastic case, drawing it out and hastily thrusting backwards to escape the flames. Her head crashed into the sharp metal of the door opening, causing her to stagger backwards and away from the inferno. All twenty-two items of evidence were recovered.

The screen was now a part of her body, but due to her kung fu training, she felt nothing. Instead, she staggered a few more steps before keeling over and becoming a part of her own protective nebula.

Agent Hackenridge tried to drag her away from the wreck, but he was too weak and still completely disorientated. The wreckage blew and he simply dove on top of the girl to shield her from the worst of the blast. His clothes began to smolder and the skin on his back blistered. The worst of the blast over he rolled on his back and his world went black once more.

April came alert as hands reached for her, thinking at last help had arrived. This was replaced by waves of pain as a sharp knife cut the prints of her fingers away from the tablet. Her hand was roughly turned over to cut her thumb from the casing. The pain focused her, and she reacted by twisting her body away and ripping herself free from her oppressor. Her mind was still confused, but her body instinctively, was fluid in motion. April came to her feet glaring at the enraged man.

No sooner was she erect than he thrust at her with knife outstretched, intent on plunging the blade into her heart. April collapsed to her right, the knife cutting her already wounded left arm as she tumbled aside. Again, she rolled and came to stand once more as the man landed badly.

He cursed and began to rise as April closed the distance between them, her mind clearing quickly as adrenalin powered her to action. She was aware of flashlights in the distance, but still too far away to be of any assistance. She needed time and a distraction. The fingertips of her hand now dripped a steady flow of blood down the tablet and onto the rock and sandy earth below. She had hoped to land a telling blow before the man rose, but was hampered by her injuries. Her adversary rose and took guard, as moments later they faced-off once more.

He glared at her and stated, "I am going to kill you now."

She laughed back into his face, hoping to enrage him further, saying in prophetic tones, "Which is mightier, the Tablet or the Sword. The Girl or the Dumb Ass she has already bested?"

April spat at him and he rushed her. She knew her reactions were slowing and she was quickly weakening as her blood, the vital fluid of her young life, dripped wasted onto the ground. To stem the flow, she willed her fingers to push hard onto the surface of the tablet, which instinctively became a weapon.

April transferred her weight onto her damaged right foot, and with the adrenaline rush taking over, time slowed. She no longer saw a man before her, but a wooden dummy. Her first parry was to block the arc of the knife into her heart. A split-second later the tablet computer crashed into the man's temple.

He faltered to a halt, as her mind became a punching machine, like back in the academy. She used both arms and legs, now oblivious to her pain. The tablet was gone somehow as she concentrated her blows on the head and chest of the bulk before her, offering dead-leg kicks to augment her rhythm. In one instant, she knew instinctively the secret of The Killing Blow, a deadly punch to the heart as known by but a few Kung Fu Masters such as Bruce Lee.

April pulled back to unleash the blow, but the wooden dummy was gone. Confused, her movements slowed, she became aware of flashlights circling, one shone into her face. A gentling voice from the darkness said, "Deputy Bekkons? You are safe now. We are from the FBI and have come to rescue you."

April knew that name, but couldn't place it, her mind awry. The voice came again, closer this time. Still she wondered who Bekkons could be. Moments later there was a man in a suit in front of her, and he cried out, "Oh my God! Come here child, I mean you no harm. Let's get you safe, and treatment."

Large arms engulfed her and she wailed on a giant intake of breath. The sound was ghostly and haunting. Her whole body shook, as tears ran like streams from her eyes. Her weight was gone in an instant, and people were shouting. She caught fleeting glimpses of flashlights, faces, and words, but could make no sense of anything. She knew she was quickly losing consciousness.

From the depths of her being, she began a mantra, shouting it to her saviors: "Two Feds, one prisoner, and twenty-two evidence. Repeat. Two Feds..."

London

SSA Niall London, Head of Field Operations, FBI San Diego, was holding her and shouting for silence. He bent to listen to her whispers. On the third repeat he understood, and joined with her, shouting to his men, "Two Feds, one prisoner, and twenty-two items of evidence. Find them all. We only have two men here and evidence missing."

She was passed to a man whose size and gentleness brought her father to her foggy mind, SA Solomon Walker. He was about to take her on his broad shoulders, when the man in charge told him to wait. The ground around where she had stood was covered in blood. The leader immediately jerked off his tie and used it as a tourniquet to slow the bleeding from her fingers. He took Walker's tie and did the same with her arm.

Satisfied he ordered, "Walker, go. Save her. Run as quickly as you can."

Walker took her in a fireman's lift, and ran as fast as he could for the main road. He ignored paramedics on their way down to the scene. He believed the girl's only chance of life lay with an immediate blood transfusion and proper hospital treatment.

SSA London watched the girl being carried away and stood to salute her. "I'm not religious, but I wish I could be. The horrors of this job make that impossible. If I were, I would send a prayer, for your safety and total recovery."

At his side a medic responded in awe, "This man should live, although it looks like he just went fifty rounds with Mike Tyson. I think every rib is broken, and so are most of the other bones in his body. It appears she did not kick him in the genitals, but the rest of him is more like jello, than a human being. Sir, I've never seen anything like this before."

London replied as he glanced once more toward the main road, "Get him to hospital ASAP, and you better make that one across town from the girl that just did this to him."

"Are we protecting him or her, sir?" the medic asked.

London shook his head. "Frankly, I have no idea."

Sergeant MacCaber of the SDPD spoke next, "Supervisory Special Agent, I have Agent Hackenridge plus the jello-man over there. Agent Grainger is missing."

London said, "Widen the search area. He has to be here somewhere. He was shot in the chest according to reports. What about the evidence?"

The sergeant replied, "I have Officer Vickery working on that Sir. You sure there are twenty-two pieces, 'cause we only got seventeen?"

London looked at the sergeant, and then at the ground nearby. "Sergeant, with all due respect, I would think it extremely likely that the tablet computer over there is evidence. Now you got eighteen. Tell your men to use their eyes and initiative. I don't care if they collect two hundred twenty-two samples, just as long as we get everything from the crime scene on Sacramento Drive."

Under his breath he swore, "I cannot believe SSA Redmond allowed that evidence to leave the crime scene, but maybe that's San Fran? I will need to have a serious word with him."

London tried his radio, but he was out of range. His cell did not work in the valley either. He glanced at the wreckage of the auto, knowing it had a much more powerful transmitter, one that was now useless. He could not afford the time to go back to his vehicle on the main road, so instead replayed presumed events in his mind, rebuilding the probable scene Deputy Bekkons confronted.

He mused, "Deputy Bekkons reported the driver shot, presumably on the main road. It was almost certainly shunted off I-15 by a larger vehicle, the mysterious SUV mentioned perhaps."

He examined the smoldering wreckage of the sedan, and there was little left of use. His examination revealed a possible dark paint mark in one location, set low on the offside. The paint on most of the wreck had been burned off.

He retraced his steps, beginning from scratch to understand the crime scene anew, talking to himself. "The cruiser ends up here, and somehow Deputy Bekkons followed."

He looked up at the trail and knew she must have jumped the gap. His eyes came to rest upon the Harley everybody was ignoring. He walked over to it, noticing a license number written on the tank. He noted it and resumed, using his eyes and his flashlight, picking up small footprints leading away from the bike, and forming an unusual pattern. There was blood on the odd steps, which matched the front footrest and rear brake pedal.

Agent London turned around and tried to imagine the scene April would have witnessed. He saw the vehicle, imagined the engine compartment on fire, and gasoline dripping from the rear tank. He asked himself, "What would she do?" He answered with what he would do, playing it out in real time.

"I have three passengers, and know one was shot in the chest, and Bekkons probably knew that before she arrived here.

Therefore, take the two passengers out ..." London found the drag marks. He would have called for assistance first, but doubted a U.S. Sheriff would do so. His next find was a used-up fire extinguisher, and he wondered.

Having worked through the probable actions so far, his next question to himself was, "Get the evidence, or the driver?" He strode around the vehicle and shone his flashlight on the driver's window. There were faint drag marks and small bloody footprints in the earth leading away.

He followed the trail for ten feet, and into some hardy scrub that surrounded stunted bushes. His light shone on a flashing tongue, but the rattle was still. He backed away very carefully, but noticed the ravine and crushed grass ahead. Once clear, he hollered, "MacCaber, medics, officer down. Location found."

Sergeant MacCaber rushed over at once, two medics and a stretcher following him. London pointed, but held his arm out stating, "There is a rattler just inside the brush there, and that one is a Mexican rattler, which is an endangered species. Do not kill it, Sergeant." He mused, "I better tell the wildlife people about this, tomorrow."

MacCaber edged forward and saw the snake coiled and waiting. He knew it was hunting something, and whipped the nearby foliage with his long baton. A small rodent leapt for safety and the snake struck, intent upon swallowing the prey whole.

MacCaber walked forward and picked up the rattler-prey combination, and ambled casually to the side where he put them down out of the way. "That do for you, London?" he stated with a cursory nod. MacCaber led Medics to the ravine, and spotted Agent Grainger at the bottom of a small defile.

SSA London turned around after he heard the shout, "He has a pulse, but it is very weak."

§

As London continued to investigate the crime scene, an ambulance sped toward the nearest hospital emergency department. Despite the plasma drip, the patient flat-lined before they screeched to a halt outside the emergency entrance.

Solomon prayed she would not die in his arms.

Chapter 16 – Gathering Acorns

Teves

As soon as news came through from Mission Turnpike, Redmond sent Bill and Annaliese to the hospital, tasking Teves to get whatever he could from the hospital staff and SA Walker.

The three left immediately to see April, Bill and Annaliese collecting his bike and following Teves. They found April was in critical care and heavily sedated. Bill immediately rushed to his daughter and hugged her urgently, Annaliese doing likewise on the other side.

Agent Walker was still at April's side, refusing to leave her alone for one second. He greeted the deputies warmly and complimented them on having such an outstanding officer. To allay their concern he assured them, "Doctors tell me that Deputy Bekkons will live and make a full recovery. It could be several days before she can be transferred to an ordinary ward, although she should be provided with a private room."

Teves said he would arrange a secure room at the department's expense, before asking for a full report. Walker began telling what he knew, and did not object to his words being recorded, asking only for a copy for his own report. He picked up at the point they arrived at the scene in response to the emergency radio message April had sent.

He dwelt on the incredible sight of this small girl beating to a pulp, a very fit and strong man twice her size. "We ran to assist her, but, even with her broken limbs, she had demolished the man before we got to her. I have never witnessed anything like it. She was like an automaton punching a dummy."

Annaliese spoke up, "She is like that sometimes when we are training for Kung Fu on the wooden dummy. I would imagine in her weakened state, all she saw in front of her was the same wooden post, and not a real person."

Walker took over, "Yes, that is exactly what I saw. How good is she?"

Annaliese smiled proudly. "You saw for yourself. We are both Fourth Dan Black Belt, Wing Chun style Kung Fu. That is Sifu Ip Man and his prodigious student, Bruce Lee. You may have heard of him?"

Teves looked long at Annaliese, unsure whether to be impressed, or very afraid. He couldn't help thinking of his own daughters.

Walker told them of her last conscious words, and how that changed the way they operated the crime scene. He moved on to tell of her collapse, and taking her to the ambulance, and again inside the hospital. At this, Bill broke away, and simply put his arms around the man in brotherly fashion, thanking him for saving her. He showed amazing emotional frailty for such a massive man, causing Walker to ask, "She is close to you, Deputy Waverley?"

Bill was lost for words, "She is ... I am ... She is like a daughter to me."

Walker nodded and said, "I can understand that. She is a very special young lady."

They were still talking when two nurses came in to check the patient. The head nurse asked them all to leave, and they refused. Teves demanded a brief medical review; the head nurse knew the deputy well enough to know it was useless trying to argue with him. She stated, "The patient was clinically dead when she was brought in. Walker's earlier actions probably saved her life, or at the very least, her higher brain functions.

"Bekkons arrived suffering from Hypovolemic shock, and before you ask, that means her heart stopped beating because there was not enough blood in her body. We set a team to work on her immediately, to keep oxygenated blood flowing throughout her body.

"We attached two drips of blood, one to each arm, since she was very low on fluid. She was intubated and later, coupled to an automatic oxygen supply diaphragm. We think she lost four pints of blood, and she is such a tiny bit of a girl. The bed was inclined slightly so more of the little blood she had left would go to her head.

"We could not try to restart her heart until the doctor was sure there was enough fluid in her bloodstream, so we maintained cardio vascular massage, later replacing this with a mechanical device known as a LUCAS.

"Before the drips were finished she displayed Return of Spontaneous Circulation, or to put that in English, her heart started beating again of its own accord. Her wounds were treated and dressed. She may appear a wee slip of a girl, but let me tell you, she is one very strong young lady.

"She should make a full recovery over time, and we do not expect any complications, but you can never be sure. There is always the slight chance of brain damage, and a greater chance of cardiac problems in the future, especially as she ages. The doctor will give you fuller details, but know it will be weeks before she is well again. I must emphasize, this is unofficial, so do not even think about trying to quote me Deputy Teves. This is all off the record, you hear me?"

After the nurses left, Teves recounted what had happened on Sacramento Drive. Walker and Teves left to interrogate Hackenridge. Bill remained at his daughter's bedside with her best friend. As time passed, Bill agreed with Annaliese they would take shifts.

The others found Hackenridge in another wing, recovering quickly. He gave a full statement to Walker and Teves, telling how Grainger insisted on keeping and examining the evidence, recalling his partner's exact words and his own objections. Walker thought this good enough to dismiss Grainger from service.

Walker and Teves went to check on Grainger, but the prognosis was not good. "He should pull through," The doctor stated, "But he may never be fully active again, and there will probably be some physical and mental impairment."

Walker called London and informed him first of the patients' conditions, before telling him about Grainger's actions. London was not impressed. He instructed Walker to meet him at the house where Redmond was overseeing the crime scene operation. Teves told Walker to follow him, as he was headed back there as well.

London was already talking privately with Redmond when Teves and Walker showed up at the Mathers place. Mendez, hovering nearby in case a buffer was required. She quietly told Teves, "Both men are SSA's and of equal rank, with similar service histories and distinctions. Redmond barely outranks London on length of service, but this is London's turf."

Teves watched, as it appeared Redmond and London were getting along quite well together. They went into the house, and Teves saw them speak to Darren Yates, the CSI shift leader. When they returned outside, Redmond called the group together. They all got into his SUV, where Redmond gave a short debrief.

"CSI has already completed the first sweep of the second floor, and should finish downstairs within an hour. Teves, I need this building locked down. SSA London, I need this entire investigation put on Highly Classified status. I want commitment. I want this done in practice, so all evidence and all agents, are those most highly trusted within your department. Not like the two goons that came to un-assist us tonight.

"The chain of evidence we wanted to keep intact and process here in first instance, has already been contaminated by your staff, and God knows who or what else. This will now have to be done in the lab, and I need that locked down as well. This is more than a Monkey Wrench Gang out for a little public mayhem. This entire investigation is of federal significance."

They were interrupted as the radio came to life, "CSI now on scene of burnt out vehicle, I-15 and Mission Drive."

Redmond responded at once, before finishing the meeting. "Teves, if you please, CSI will need DNA, fingerprints, and ID verification of all your deputies that were present here. Please add an identifiable list of all weapons deployed. Someone appears to have used an elephant gun in the house. It is simply to dot i's and cross t's, and exclude them from the investigation. That is precisely what I intend to do."

They all got out of the vehicle, Walker immediately talking with Mendez aside. They appeared to be good friends as well as colleagues. Redmond commented on this, and London agreed, "Despite his Caribbean lilt, the big guy's infectious manner and humor are most disarming and a boon to any team. Walker is an excellent agent, and can always be relied upon, as can Mendez."

London walked with Redmond as they naturally separated from the others, but Teves hovered unobtrusively within earshot. London opened by saying, "Earlier tonight I was ready to report you for gross misconduct, letting the evidence leave the scene. Instead, you have won my respect, which isn't easy. I also find myself having to discipline one of my own, if he lives.

"Redmond, Nigel, will you level with me and tell me exactly what is going on here? It makes absolutely no sense." He stopped walking and waited.

Redmond came round to stand directly in front of London and look him in the eye. "I will consider it, but not here. I am putting together a small team of people who can track this nationally.

What we have here is related to many other incidents, some going back years. I am planning a dedicated group that works from their own secure offices, and only focuses on this investigation.

"So far, I have two civilians, three Temporary Deputy Sheriffs, plus Undersheriff Teves, and perhaps Agent Mendez. I would consider Agent Walker a useful addition to the team. At the moment it feels like I am gathering acorns. I still need a building to work from, and a Number Two from the Agency. Someone I can trust with my life. Do you know of anyone that fits the description?"

London smiled and replied, "I can only recommend Supervisory Special Agent Niall London, although it has been a long time since he was anyone's Second."

Redmond shook his hand. "I'll introduce you to the pieces of the puzzle tomorrow." They exchanged personal phone numbers, and London left the scene without a backward glance. Teves fell in step with Redmond as they walked back to the Mathers house, where they remained until CSI left. Teves handpicked his team of guards and left them with precise instructions.

Chapter 17 – Bedside Manners

The following morning Teves gave the Chief a verbal report of last night's successful operation, before requesting two more Temporary Reserve Deputies.

The Chief stopped and stared at the man. His initial reaction was to say 'No'. But this was turning out to be an exceptional case, and one of the increasingly few where they had precedence over the SDPD. He was also very aware that one sensational bust would ensure him his long-dreamed of promotion, and a good pension for him and his family for life.

The Chief asked, "What of Deputy Bekkons? I heard there were … complications."

"She is my problem, Sir. She was badly injured, but still managed to save the lives of two FBI agents, one prisoner, and a bag full of evidence. Were it not for her, this case would be destined for the cold case file. She was critically injured and I need to replace her, and this time have a backup."

The Chief sighed, resigned to accepting the request, and asked the people be shown in. He took a quick look at them and asked, "Do you have any police or military experience."

Bill replied, "I am ex-Marine Corps, special operations. Spent too much time in Nicaragua, and was honorably discharged as Sergeant. Annaliese is ROTC, like Bekkons."

The Chief nodded respectfully, "OK, but I will need to see documentation for the both you. Teves, please attend to it."

The Chief quickly filled out the paperwork. Bill and Annaliese signed their names, the first grudgingly, and the second with enthusiasm. The Chief threw them each a badge, hollering for them all to leave and never come back.

They went directly to City General Hospital, where Walker was again on guard. April greeted them; she had been transferred to a private room, was chirpy, and determined to leave as soon as possible. She looked like hell, but had been very lucky. The foot had been reset with a plaster cast firmly in place. She insisted Teves sign it, before she gave her statement. Teves added to her collection, "Heal soon Brucella Lee, we miss you, Manny."

Annaliese

Chapter 17

Annaliese took her turn to stay with April, Bill leaving with Teves to meet Redmond. The girls talked for a while, but soon nurses administered a sedative, and the patient drifted off to sleep. Annaliese was also tired, having slept little the previous night. Although they were in a private room, it was cramped and the only comfortable chair was in the alcove behind the door. Annaliese got an extra cushion from a nurse, and, curling up into a ball, joined her friend in slumber.

She roused some hours later when a man in a white coat entered and banged her chair with the door. He made straight for April without looking around, and pulled back the covers. Annaliese observed sleepily until he pulled out a gun and began attaching a silencer.

Annaliese rose and with two bounds, sprang onto the bed and sailed through the air, using the mattress as a springboard. She caught the man full in the chest and sent him flying toward the window, which shattered as his head crashed into it. She punched the emergency call button, and dragged him back inside, securing him with a bandage. She called Teves and told him the situation, requesting he return immediately.

The duty nurse came in and screamed, calling for security. Annaliese finished securing the man, and made another call on her cell. She stood up and pulled out her badge just before security rushed through the door with guns drawn and aimed at her.

The girl stood her ground with her badge held high, stating, "I am Deputy Sheriff Annaliese Braun. I am unarmed. I have just arrested this man for trying to kill the patient, April Bekkons. Please lower your weapons."

The head nurse spoke up and confirmed her story, security stating they would check. One guard stayed with his pistol trained at Annaliese's head, and not the man who tried to kill April. She asked the nurse for a pair of sterilized gloves, and was quickly provided with a new pack of surgical ones.

Annaliese held up her hands as if asking for indulgence, and took photographs of the man with her Smartphone, before examining his wallet, and checking his ID. She made very clear her intentions, and flicked the intruders gun away from him and under the bed. The security guard followed her moves, his gun still trained directly at her.

She placed a second call to Teves, who told her he was only a few minutes away. The door opened and a Sheriff in uniform strode into the room, flicking his badge quickly before putting it away. He said, "Deputy Teves tasked me with taking this man into custody. Security you are dismissed."

Annaliese held her ground and placed her cell, still connected to Teves, on the nearby nightstand. She stated plainly, "Deputy, you will not because I will hand this man over to Undersheriff Teves personally."

There was a knock at the door and Annaliese relaxed, knowing it must be Security returning, a nurse, or Deputy Teves.

Instead, two orderlies came in with a gurney, and one said, "Where's the body you want us to get rid of Harris ... Oh."

Harris said, "You better get rid of the doctor instead. I'll deal with Bekkons, and the girl. You bring the backup plan?"

Annaliese attacked, despite one orderly pulling out a machine pistol. She was overpowered, the false deputy using a roll of duct tape to fasten her legs together. They manhandled her into position near the bed, and bound her hands to radiator pipes. The imposter wound an extra spiral of tape around her legs, as there was nothing handy for him to secure them to.

"Load up the doctor while I finish with this one," Harris said to the orderlies. Smiling like an alligator, he wound the duct tape around her head. He covered her mouth first, followed by her nose as he looped the sticky tape up to and over her eyes.

He pressed the tape down and stood back to admire his work. "You will soon suffocate to death, so don't fight it. You may consider this your death mask." He laughed as he walked away.

Annaliese could still breathe, but it was extremely difficult. She knew the false Deputy thought her airtight and dying, but it was just, not quite so. She slowed her breathing using Qi Gong training.

The orderlies loaded the supposed doctor onto the trolley and were leaving. Machine gun man said, "Harris, secure the door and don't let anyone inside until both girls are dead. Use this liquid on the other one, here's a syringe."

Harris locked the door and began a short monologue, "Girls, it is time you both left this world and moved on to the next. I see one of you is almost there already.

"Now it is your turn, Bekkons." The man slapped her groggy senses. Annaliese knew it must have stung, yet the sedative was still too strong within her friend for April to react.

Harris said, "You may wonder why? Well, I will tell you. Now pay attention." He hit her face again. "This is the sad tale of a nosey girl, who decided to follow somebody she should have left well alone. Her motorbike broke down supposedly, just at the time there was an inconvenient road traffic accident.

"Unfortunately for you, my client recognized you as the rider of that bike, and I tracked you down to this bed, in this hospital. He asked me to 'take care of you', and that is precisely what I am about to do. What I have here, as you may be able to see, is a very beautiful blue liquid. It is called pentobarbital, and I am now going to inject you with a large dose. Good bye."

At the side of the bed, Annaliese sagged, as if the lack of oxygen was finally becoming too much for her. Harris, playing for himself and audience, said, "Ah, first we need to swab where the needle will enter."

Annaliese heard him spit on April's inner elbow and rub his phlegm around with a grubby finger. His monologue confirmed her assumptions. He slapped the spot, but no veins appeared. April murmured. She was trying desperately to come awake, and failing. Harris continued to goad her, and said, "Your veins are not very good, are they. I better use your wrist instead."

Annaliese was clamped down within her own thoughts, very aware of the room around her, as her ears had not been fully covered. She focused on her temporal Kung Fu training, and mapped the room in her mind. She was good at fighting blindfolded, and understood that Harris would be within range of a kick, if she could pull off the extremely awkward maneuver. She crouched down, appearing to wither, the balls of her feet pumping, as she sought by sound her adversary.

In her mind's eye, Annaliese saw her upper body trapped like a mummified perversion of a crucifix. While her legs were bound, they were only bound together, remaining free to act as one. She would need to grasp the hot water pipe tightly, and swivel like a gymnast performing on the pommel horse.

She replayed her imagery, and knew from the creaking of the mattress nearby; when Harris sat down to take her friend's arm, she could feel his proximity. It would be easy for her to strike his back, but all except a kidney punch or neck kick would only exacerbate the situation. If the needle was anywhere near her dearest friend, her actions would drive it inwards and deeper, the plunger also.

A siren wailed to a stop outside, but it was a very long way away from their imminent battle of life and death. Time and Space. All Annaliese needed to do was be in the right space at the correct time.

Her mind went lateral. She opened her heart to the attack parameters, waiting, and waiting, and waiting still. She sprang.

Annaliese knew from contact she had caught Harris's jaw below his left ear, her double strike back-kick followed through to impact his trachea and jaw. The contact was not enough she already knew, but it bought them both a few more seconds of life.

She heard the hollow thunk of a melon on tile and knew that Harris banged his head quite hard on the floor when he ricocheted off the bed. He started to rant and rave at her. She smiled under her duct tape mask, as if to say, bring it on.

As recuperative adrenaline rushed through her system someone shot the door out, and suddenly there was a giant of a man in the room. The only man she had ever fallen in love with. Her second cell call had been answered in the flesh. She heard the shotgun reload, and the words, "Don't move, asshole."

Suddenly Teves appeared at the door with Agent Mendez. Annaliese was released from bondage and gave a quick verbal report. Teves was calm, cool, and very methodical. Agent Walker arrived and was tasked with taking Harris to Aero Drive for interrogation.

Moments later Walker was outside, headed for his cruiser, the captive deliberately hampering any attempts to move quickly. Walker cuffed him to a large dumpster and made for his cruiser. He had gone only thirty yards when a vehicle came toward him. At first he thought nothing of it, until he saw the passenger window slide down and a gun barrel appear.

Walker fired, shattering the rear windshield, but he was still too far away to prevent a tragedy. He emptied his clip, hoping for a lucky hit, but the passenger opened fire with a machine pistol and his captive was left dangling from the cuffs.

Teves raced outside, but the vehicle was already past him before he was able to react. He took careful aim and fired into the vehicle as it accelerated into the distance. He had the license plate and called a BOLO immediately.

Redmond

Redmond had been monitoring radio traffic as he closed on the hospital. His hand hit the steering wheel hard as the news came in. Momentarily distracted, he was slow to notice a vehicle pass him in the opposite direction. It was the same make, model, and color as described, although he could not read the plate. In the rearview he saw blackness where the rear window should have been.

He radioed back at once, confirmed the probable visual, and turned around in hot pursuit. He closed as quickly as he could, without raising an alarm. He rounded a turn and the vehicle was gone. There was only one exit close enough. Redmond took it and found it led into a private housing development. He took the first road off the main drag and saw the vehicle he was pursuing parked a short distance along.

Redmond radioed-in and went with pistol raised to investigate. The vehicle was empty and had apparently been wiped clean. Using a handkerchief, he flicked the trunk release. The only thing he found was a sports bag. Cautiously, he unzipped it and stared.

The digital display clicked down from 00:05 to 00:04.

He instinctively grabbed the handles and swung the bag like a hammer thrower to preserve the scene. Cars were approaching from both directions, and he had residential houses to either side. One house nearby had all its lights out. He let the bag fly toward the grass out front. The bag exploded in mid-air, taking out most the overlooking windows.

Agent Redmond called for FBI CSI, asking the vehicle to be towed away for examination. He stayed at the scene until Teves arrived. Both confirmed how good it was to be working on the same team again. Teves brought order to the street, his men arriving shortly to form a cordon.

Some time later, Redmond followed the FBI tow-truck back to headquarters. He was taking no chances, but also had a secondary reason to visit Aero Drive. He needed access to a secure videoconferencing suite.

Redmond spoke at length to his superior in San Francisco, who informed him someone from the higher echelons of government had been enquiring about his current investigation, and they wanted the FBI to enlarge it. The details would be known the following day, but Redmond was given the distinct impression the outcome would be favorable. Nevertheless, Redmond would need to present his case formally and in person, to The Associate Executive Assistant Director, FBI, California.

Meanwhile, Mendez and Walker investigated the hospital assault, while Darren Yates and his team processed the crime scene. Hackenridge was due for release the next day, but volunteered to assist them, he needed to make amends.

They discovered the orderlies had taken the injured Doctor through a secure corridor leading to a new extension that was being built. The odd thing was, the camera in the corridor had gone down the day before. Walker checked the passageway, finding the camera had been deliberately disabled with acid, and the fire escape into the new building had been compromised.

Mendez tracked the orderlies, one leaving site with the recovering phony doctor, and the other returning to complete his overtime shift in Medical. She got his name and home address, discovering in the process, the security supervisor had been complicit in liaising with the attackers. Yates had a lot to process, and Mendez was left staring at 'a can of worms'.

April had disappeared from her room, and after suspecting abduction, they were proved partially correct. Bill had removed his daughter to a place of real safety, and Mendez thought that fitting.

The team left the hospital late that night. Darren was pleased to see them go. Apart from working virtually a double shift, they had a week's worth of evidence to process.

Chapter 18 – New Beginnings

Redmond was waiting for Yates when he arrived for work at 7 a.m. the next morning, he stood tall and looked him in the eye. "Darren, do me a favor—submit a report, a complaint if you will, regarding the pressure our team is causing you."

Darren considered the peculiar query. It ran contrary to every other agent's wishes he had ever worked with. Usually they were afraid of being reprimanded. He looked at the man with newfound admiration, "Redmond, are you playing politics?"

With mischievous intent, they wrote the report together. Once completed and submitted, Redmond enquired, "Darren, can you spare me a moment? By the end of today, I may need someone to become Operational Head of a specialized CSI unit with federal brief. If I were to offer this to you, would you take the position?"

Darren did not hesitate, and they shook hands in anticipation. Redmond called London, "Where's the best place for breakfast? I want a word with you before I start my day."

London radioed back, "I'll be at Elsa's Bar and Grill in five, it's off Pimento and Seventeenth."

Redmond arrived twelve minutes later, and London ordered the special breakfast, and a large jug of strong coffee. He knew they were going to need it. Redmond briefly reviewed what occurred yesterday, and London told him what he had discovered.

At that moment, Mendez and Walker came to join them. Yates walked in next, holding the door open for Teves. They ordered separately, and were surprised to find themselves sitting at the same table with four others.

Redmond sketched in the details of the plan that was fermenting in his mind. "With a dedicated team of professionals from all walks of life, we can take on the syndicate opposing us on a level playing field, all across America.

"I have identified a terrorist operation within the U.S., they are very well connected. Little is known about them, although my own findings have been confirmed and augmented independently. We need to identify who these people are, and their target.

"We will need a safe location to work from. I imagine a core team of fourteen, perhaps twenty people, including us here today. I have already contacted a secondary team of foot soldiers. We need to be state of the art comm., offices, and labs. Regarding staff ..."

Chapter 18

He finished by saying, "Mr. London, please find a suitable and easily accessible, but safe place for us to conduct this investigation from. We will need very secure headquarters."

London surprised him by opening his briefcase and laying three location reports, "I consider the last to be the best."

They locked eyes, each aware he could trust the other man to anticipate the needs of the team. Redmond quickly scanned the information and turned back to London, "Niall, please see to this immediately. The third location near I-8, between La Mesa and El Cajon is just perfect. We will go there as soon as we finish. Please arrange rental at once. Providing the building is OK, I want it staffed and operational by seven tomorrow morning. I will handle our dedicated building services and security personally."

Redmond smiled, tapped his temple, and quickly moved on, "I need someone on comm. I need a secure communication channel we all share. We were compromised last night with people jamming the airwaves and using their cells as walkies."

Redmond looked at London for support, but Teves spoke up, "The best in the city is Wendy Laredo. I have been trying to recruit her for years. The only trouble is, she works for the SDPD."

Redmond looked back at London, who nodded his head. He thought for a moment before saying, "I will second her once we are through here. This may take a few days, but she will be on the team. You have my word on it."

Redmond pressed forward with his delivery, "I need everyone at this table to give me details of anyone they consider useful to this operation. I do not care if they are agency, police, military, or even civilians. What we need are people we trust implicitly to help us. I'll call for questions, but we are basically done here until our new headquarters becomes operational."

Redmond looked at London. Reading his eyes he finished, "I have an appointment with the Director at Division today. I am out of contact unless the situation is critical. Thank you everybody. Let's get to work."

The new headquarters was an old data center from the seventies, one that had more recently been used as a call center. Electronic doors guarded the large reception, and all major doorways within the structure. They could be operated by code or swipe card, and had differing levels of access.

The building was purposely built with computer upgrading in mind; it had false floors and ceilings above and below the standard concrete floor slabs. In the middle was a central core, that offered elevators, stairs, male and female restrooms, and janitors' closets. There were also storage rooms, and a PBX room, that interlinked power and telecom to adjoining floors via vertical shafts. These acted as a distribution hub for that particular floor. Redmond noted the rooms would enable easy conversion for their purposes.

They toured all floors and it seemed they had far too much floor space, but both Redmond and London agreed they had no idea how their operation would expand over the coming months. The top floor had a small restaurant with professional catering facilities. The roof had been designed as a helipad.

They traveled down to complete their appraisal. The first basement floor had a garage entrance leading to a workshop and maintenance area. The building was set on a short, but steep down slope, allowing the first basement level to open onto the tarmac.

Near the door stood a large diesel engine that was part of the old mainframe reserve power supply. Adjacent were a bank of old and seriously huge batteries. Redmond stalled to investigate, and switching to test mode, followed the simple instructions as the large engine came to life, before turning it off almost immediately. He smiled at London with a very happy look in his eyes. Below were two more basement levels, this time entirely underground, which afforded parking for eighty vehicles.

The building had not been used for several years, and London had been assured a quick rental would be available. Redmond said, "See to it Niall. I need this building today, even if I have to take it by eminent domain. We begin making this building operational as soon as I get clearance from the Director. On my word, see to it."

Redmond flew to the main LA office, where he met with his Department Head from San Francisco. The Director called them to the meeting; the only other person present was the Director's attaché, a woman Redmond knew quite well.

Redmond was well aware of his precautionary confines, but knew he either made a compelling case for his own national investigative team, or the cabal poised against them would win. He was there to sell his task force capable of neutralizing the threat.

Redmond outlined each strike they and Michael had logged, and the resultant intelligence. He made a damming case for a deadly threat against the security and infrastructure of the U.S., finishing with what he hoped was the closer line, "You may ask, if we know about these incursions, why we make no move to stop them. We suspect a larger picture and have no wish to drive the fomenters further underground.

"Imagine that all these events occurred on the same day, in the same place. These strikes go back six years, and there are hundreds of them. The group behind them is one willing to take the long view to see their project through to completion. The events occur in all parts of the U.S., every state and city. One of my people was the first to note one singular exception. Washington, D.C.

"I believe these are all test runs, either to establish control of IT, or gauge response times and emergency response capability. I repeat, what if, all of these attacks were to happen on the same day, say in New York, Silicon Valley, or Washington, D.C.?

"I believe this threat represents the gravest danger our great nation has ever faced. I am speaking about the total disruption of national governance, widespread public outrage, and the breakdown of law and order resulting in a state of emergency."

As Redmond sat down, a hush fell over everyone present. He had made a compelling case for the dedicated office, staff, and equipment he needed. He did not mention the uranium mine, since that would immediately bring in others. He would tell them about that in good time, after his team was established.

The meeting concluded quickly. Redmond and his line manager left for a private chat over lunch. Later he cleared his desk and closed down his home for an extended stay in San Diego. With his affairs in order, he received a call from the Director.

"Redmond. You have your new assignment. Know this comes from the very top. You also have the staff you requested, including the computer geek. I was amazed when the Pentagon released him. He will be with you tomorrow, as will Officer Laredo. You better not screw this up Redmond, or you are finished, d'you hear me!" The line went dead and Redmond pumped the air in triumph. Now he could start making constructive plans.

SSA Redmond was temporarily promoted to Operations Manager, with a provisional FBI status of Section Chief. This ranked him higher than his normal line manager, and made him very aware of the potential of the operation, if he succeeded. His was an extraordinary brief, and reported directly to Division.

Chapter 19 – Home From Home

Once back in San Diego, Redmond headed directly to the new headquarters and found London and most of the team working to make their new center operational.

He took a brief tour, delighted to find they had done an excellent job. Redmond congratulated everyone, before rolling up his sleeves and digging in.

Bill arrived with Annaliese just after 8 p.m. and they got to work immediately. Redmond knew all of them had been taking extra hours from both ends of the day to get the job done. At midnight, he called a halt, knowing that his team needed food and sleep.

Bill had done the work of three men in those few hours, and stated, "I'm pullin' off to Trucker D's all-night for some grub, before hitting the sack. Six a.m. OK for you, Redmond?"

Before he could answer, everyone stopped what they were doing and headed for their cars. The diner was rough, but the food quick and filling. Bill looked around and said, "I'm staying here tonight, anyone else need a room?"

London realized Bill did not know about the temporary bedding. "Bill, I had one dozen mattresses delivered earlier. We will all spend the night at headquarters if you don't mind."

Bill returned with the others and headed for a nightcap. He found Teves filling a glass of Rebel Yell in the restaurant. He brought over a glass for himself, and another bottle to share with his friend. Without words, they touched glasses and drank. By turns they looked at their inside hands, both wondering what a palmist would make of their futures and fortunes, yet to be written.

Teves traced his heart line and said, "If I go home now, my family will be asleep. If I wake them for no reason, they will know at once that there is a problem, one I cannot tell them about. If I go home and do not wake them, I will be gone tomorrow before they wake up. They will not even know I was with them, unless I leave a note. What is the point of going home?"

Bill put down his half empty glass and looked Teves straight in the eye. "Because they will know you were there. They will know you were present and looking out for them, like a good husband and father should. Let's go."

Chapter 19

They pulled into an all-night gas station, where Bill handed Teves some flowers and chocolates. No scholar of literature could ever consider the words Teves wrote on the card to be poetry or prose, but they were her husband's words, and that was all that mattered to Xochitl Teves when she found them in the morning. He had placed the card, flowers, and chocolates on her nightstand.

Knowing that he loved her strengthened her heart, her resolve. She knew what he was doing now was something extremely important. He had only ever done this sort of work once before, when he was last a liaison with the FBI many years ago. Moreover, although she worried about him, she took great comfort in the knowledge that he loved her.

As his wife cried with relief and despair, so her husband embraced the future, unsure of what was to come. Back at headquarters pest eradicators left the site at 2 a.m. and professional cleaning at 3:20. Company electricians and network providers followed them. The operations center began functioning when workstations came online just before 9 a.m. By that time, Teves was already interviewing Rodriguez.

§

Rudolph "Rude" Berkovitz arrived at 11:42, expecting some state of the art geek's paradise. He was rudely disappointed. Within moments, Wendy Laredo entered, and seeing what was provided, she was vilifying in her condemnation of the operation. She turned to leave at once. Rude moved to walk with her.

London blocked their exit with a large grin on his face, and stated, "Your personal work stations are over here. Tell me exactly what you need and it will be provided."

Laredo rattled off a list of items, but Rude was more circumspect, asking instead, "That depends upon what you want me to do?"

Redmond rushed over to join them and smiled, "That is the correct question."

He called everyone present to their newly furnished meeting room. The large table and chairs were still in factory wrappers, so they did the unwrapping themselves. Redmond began, "You are all now seconded to the FBI. You will continue to gather pension rights and benefits from your existing employment, and return to them once this threat is resolved. That may take weeks, but probably months, or even years."

The door opened and a wraithlike form glided into the room. Laredo screamed. The ghostly mask was of a face raised from the dead. Bill and Annaliese ran to the newcomer's side. Redmond welcomed her, "April, are you sure you're fit enough to join us? By all rights you should still be in hospital recovery."

April stated bluntly. "I'd rather be with the team. At least I will be with you from the beginning and know everything that is going on. I may not be able to do much physically, but my brain works fine and I am here to support you all."

She sat down between Annaliese and Bill. Redmond picked up where he left off, "London, please see to it that everybody in this room is employed directly by the FBI. Most will be Special Skills Operatives, but due to their ages, April and Annaliese will both become Tactical Intelligence Analysts. Please attend to their formal induction and issue appropriate identity cards, thank you."

Teves was surprised to be included, but not as much as Bill and Annaliese. April had half expected it. Laredo nodded her head and Rude said, "I'll add this badge to my collection."

Without wasting time, Redmond laid out what they faced, and the national brief of their specialist team. Laredo's eyes opened wide when she understood she would be required to provide secure channel communications for all staff members anywhere they might be in the States. What thrilled her most was she got to choose the equipment, and set it up the way she wanted. Her opinion of her new role changed dramatically.

Redmond introduced Darren Yates officially to his new role, again with the mandate that he was to choose his own hardware and software. He added, "Yates' work is to bring together all CSI evidence from crime scenes scattered across the entire U.S., and identify what is persistent, as in people, vehicles, explosives, et cetera. This information goes back six years.

"Rude, you are to identify fingerprints, DNA, and anything else the team needs. These may be held on very secure databases. I also need you to access things such as this hard drive from a couple of nights ago, and get around the encryption on these memory sticks." Redmond passed over the evidence bags and continued.

"Tomorrow we are anticipating a cyber attack on a facility in Cleveland. I need to find out where this originates and who is responsible. Can you do all this yourself, or do we need extra help?"

Rude stated, "I can do all this, but I doubt we can get all the computing I need installed before midnight. I'll need access to satellite feeds to monitor these attacks indirectly. The area you want me to cover is very wide. With your permission I would call in a favor and bring another able body to join us here."

With a nod from Redmond, Rude stood and walked away to make a private phone call. London asked, "Who are you calling?"

Rude smiled for the first time, and looking over his shoulder, said askance, "The Pentagon." He disappeared, but returned a few minutes later looking very pleased with himself.

He tried to play the expectancy, but finally told them, "Everything, including comm., will arrive this evening. Laredo, tell me specifically what you want. It will take about six hours to install the IT, and become fully functional. I need a room for the main servers and backup database. It must have full climate control. You got someone to do that, or want me to arrange it as well?"

Redmond told him to get on with it. Rude continued, "I have asked Bridger Jones to assist us, and she will arrive a little later today. Our talents overlap, although she comes from an operational background, not a coding one like my own. I am sure the pairing will be of great benefit in the longer term."

Redmond thanked him and laid out their targets for the week ahead and what they needed to do. The meeting turned into an informal discussion as people found their spaces and became familiar with each other, and their new roles. Redmond allowed it to continue for a while, before judging the moment right to call a halt and get to work.

Bridger Jones arrived in the early evening and was introduced to the team. She was tall, thin, wore black, and looked like a vampire. She acknowledged her introductions with looks, but without speaking and was shown to her station. Before looking at the equipment provided. She stood facing the wall behind her workstation and pointing with a long, delicate finger, spoke for the first time, "I need a hook in the wall right here."

She stood back and stared at the spot. Bill strode over with a coat stand and placed it where she wanted. She smiled and thanked him with overly large eyes. She removed her cloak with a flourish, hung it up with gusto, and began placing trinkets on her desk.

Annaliese was intrigued and said to her, "Isn't that an ankh?"

Bridger looked at her conspiratorially and replied, "Yes it is. You Goth?"

"No," Annaliese giggled, "Pagan."

Bridger's laugh was musical, "It's gonna be a lot of fun working around here with all these uniforms and suits. I see you already have a yummy Hells Angel, and a pet ghost."

Their conversation was interrupted when a woman entered the room and was shown directly to Redmond. She was dressed as Special Forces, but carried an FBI badge. Redmond introduced their new head of building operations as Agent Grace. He asked his old friend to introduce herself, saying, "Best get this over with."

"Listen up everyone, my name is Grace. This is my surname, and my first name. Just so there is no confusion, it is also my middle name. My parents were very special people. They hoped my life would become the embodiment of The Three Graces. If any of you has a problem remembering any of my three given names, you can call me 3G.

"I just got in from Beirut, but will have food sorted for you all within the hour. Tomorrow we can start on a menu, but tonight you will all eat what is provided, or go without. I'll also be working on rooms, and once security is fully staffed, begin building administration. You need anything in future, you come see me."

She returned to Redmond and spoke quietly. He introduced her to April, and the two left together talking quickly. In basement one, Grace introduced her new associate to a platoon of soldiers who looked a lot like SEAL's, but weren't. "Platoon, this is Intelligence Analyst Bekkons, FBI. She is my dedicated liaison on site. You will do whatever she asks of you. Dinner before the turn of the hour: 'Mark'. Security detail, full sweep of all floors, two men on the main gate, two more on patrol at all times until surveillance is up and running. Tompkins, you're on the new security system at once…"

Teves and London both went home that night to spend quality time with their families. Bill wandered around into the night, a bottle of Rebel Yell in his hand and no one to share it with. He ended up in the canteen and wondered where his life was headed. Had his freedom been revoked, or was that just a temporary casualty of trying to help others out? He eventually fell asleep slumped at a corner table.

As the father slept, so the daughter came awake. She was bored and needed to do something. She wandered around to familiarize herself, and ended up in ops. Unlike her father, she wondered if she had a place there in the future, and yearned to be a part of something bigger, much bigger.

The clock came around to 4 a.m. and April noticed Rude's workstation come to life. She had no idea what was going on, but guessed it was important. She hollered for security to go and wake the man.

Rude was deep under. Security had to shake him hard. It took moments for him to understand what was happening, before he jumped out of bed, dressed hurriedly, and fled out the door cursing, "Shit! They must be on Eastern Standard Time. Damn, Cleveland, Ohio!"

April moseyed through to the mess and found two security guards eating, and her father slumped in one corner. April asked for the largest coffee they could muster, commercial style with extra everything. The resultant concoction appeared interesting. She took it down to Rude, who hardly acknowledged her until she turned to leave. "April, sorry. Too many things on my mind here. Wake Bridger, we got some serious shit happening in Cleveland. Damn fine coffee, keep 'em coming."

April sent Security to wake Bridger and Laredo, since she knew they might need comm. also. She sat down at a desk and surveyed the room. She knew she needed to think ahead.

The building went dark.

Power was maintained to their server and specified nodes. Low-level lighting was supplied by the completely separate emergency lighting system. A radio crackled nearby, it was an awakening 3G, "We are on battery power, maybe ninety seconds until all down I need the generator working now."

April picked up the radio and ran as best she could, telling the others to preserve data anyway they could think of. She was soon in the basement and said into the mic, "I'm at the generator, what do I do?"

A waking Redmond answered her, "Turn the main switch from Test to Auto. My mistake. Open any fuel valves you see. It's like your Harley, simply follow the pipes. I think the fuel storage tank may be turned off outside. Security, turn that valve on at all costs."

April flicked the switch back to auto, but no sound came. She kicked through the fire door, finding her cast quite useful as it absorbed the shock. She came out running awkwardly. Gunshots rang out as she dove and rolled for cover, the fuel tank now clearly visible, a man working beside it. Near him, an armed guard stopped to change clips. April rose and knew she could get close, but not close enough.

She saw his gun arc to bear on her as she hurried forwards, and dove to hide behind a curb decoration with a few flowers on top. All the flowers were soon dead, but she clutched to life, and to complete her mission.

At that moment, a Harley rode out of the underground garage, but instead of buckshot, a pistol loosed several rounds. The guard reacted firing his clip empty, as the rider appeared to take a hit but continued to taunt him. April made close cover and sprang at the man working with an explosive device. She dropped him with a single blow, and he fell unconscious. April rolled and needed both hands to turn on the stopcock. She managed a few turns before the barrel of a gun came to point at her face.

She sprang up and away, marking her spot on the ground, and leapt into the unknown. She somersaulted backwards, but somehow her backward flip moved her body forwards. April's plaster cast foot drove into the man's solar plexus, her left foot taking him full under the chin. He dropped like a stone onto the hard concrete below. She twisted in mid air to land on her feet, and heard the generator fire into life.

Annaliese pulled up and high-fived her, "Care for a ride, Hon?" Her arm was weeping blood, but her eyes were alive with mischief, and sparkled with feminine intent.

The fire door burst open as a fully trained security detail came running to the rescue. 3G headed them, enquiring, "You men all right?"

Annaliese giggled, but April replied matter-of-factly, "Both intruders should live, but I think we got C4 on the tank, and a detonator over there. You may want to put Yates on that right away."

Chapter 19

April had Annaliese shuffle back on the seat. She made sure she rode her own bike back inside the complex. Grace stood to watch them leave, her mind unsure if she had yet arrived in the same ballpark as these extra-ordinary people.

Chapter 20 – Held Hostage

Redmond

At 6:55, as the new day started early, 3G gave Redmond a report. "Last night the electric substation for this entire block was destroyed. We believe it was a bomb set on a timer. They came through the rear fence where the trees are thickest and took out one of our men. He is badly wounded, but we hope he will pull through. They obviously knew about our generator. This was a deliberate attempt to take us out before we even started.

"We captured all six intruders, although four needed medical treatment. They are all now at the local field office. I have tapped extra personnel who will arrive in a few hours time. One of the men due to join us is an expert in interrogation, although you are welcome to choose your own staff of course, Sir. His name is Salamander.

"I will of course be erecting a more formidable security fence. I would like to take an area of the lower parking lot for cells and interview rooms, and install our own medical facility. I will send you a full report and recommendations within two hours, but I would like verbal approval now if possible, Sir."

Redmond considered carefully. "Having our own interrogation area is quickly becoming a major concern." He noted her enthusiastic approach to her job, then looked his controller in the eye. "3G, you better check out relevant laws first. There are strict rules concerning prisoners. Neither do we know how long we will be here. See what you can come up with regards temporary cells, I've seen some modular precast units that would be ideal and easy to install. You better convert workrooms J1 and J2 into interview rooms.

"Regards medical facilities, we do not need a field hospital, just a small room with emergency treatment capability, but maybe a gurney, and somebody qualified to administer first aid." Redmond gave provisional approval, knowing District would be extremely unhappy with the expense, unless he started bringing in solid results.

Redmond called London to his office and said, "I need our prisoners processed as quickly as possible. Find out what they know, and either charge them or let them go. Their controllers already know their mission failed, so there is little the new prisoners can share."

A knock came on his door and, with their business complete London left, passing Rude in the doorway. Redmond asked for his progress report.

"I'll save the best for last." The computer expert smirked, and continued, "I know how they operate. The attackers spent the first hour infiltrating specific systems without doing anything malicious. This allowed them to isolate and take charge of critical operating parameters, which they did at 07:22 EST precisely. They controlled the power station for seven minutes, and did just enough to demonstrate they were in complete control. Local personnel were unable to counteract their moves until the infiltrators returned control back to the plant management. It was very slick.

"From where they were, they could have done anything, including shutting the whole plant down, or causing critical failure. It was obviously a test run, and one that would be significantly difficult to protect against without knowing a future target and mission objective in advance.

"The good news is that we discovered the location where the attack originated, but not the exact source. I had tracked it back to a specific router within the complex when the attack was called off. It came from inside the Pentagon!"

"You cannot be serious."

"Deadly serious, there can be no mistake."

"This is way out of my league. I know you used to work there. Is there anyone you trust who can follow this up?"

Rude shook his head before answering, "What I am about to tell you does not leave this room. The only reason you got me so quickly, if at all, was because of what you are about. Your operation here is directly linked to a line of enquiry my current, sorry, recent employers are following."

"And they are?" Redmond probed.

"I am not at liberty to disclose that information, Chief. Know they work for the government at the highest echelons. I will try to arrange a meeting with somebody, and it is up to them whether they reveal themselves to you or not."

Redmond dismissed Rude and started making phone calls from his secure line. Mendez was studying and reevaluating security footage and evidence. They now understood what had occurred at the hospital, but pieces of the puzzle were still at large.

Teves came over the dedicated channel at 7:34 a.m. "I just had a very interesting conversation with the orderly from the hospital. Apparently, his two children have been taken hostage to ensure his compliance. They have not been returned as promised, and he is frantic. He tells me their home is also being watched. I'm sending the confirming details now, and recording."

"Excellent work Teves. I'll have someone check out the street and see if we can't compromise their operation. Please join London for the interrogations, and know a specialist called Salamander will join you shortly."

"I'm just on my way there. We made some progress yesterday, but the people we really need information from aren't talking. I have a feeling that will change today."

"Enjoy yourselves but remember which side we're on. I'll meet you back here when you are done. Redmond out."

London and Teves worked with Salamander, coming to admire the way the man operated. They each thought they knew everything about interrogation, but each learned a lot that day. They had gotten all they could without employing illegal methods, and headed back to headquarters when their long day finally concluded.

Meanwhile, Redmond sat back and checked his priorities. He called Walker and Hackenridge into his office, and primed Mendez. He told them what the orderly had told Teves, passed over Teves' information, and laid out his requirements. The execution of the plan was left down to Mendez, Redmond wanted to see how she performed in an SSA's role, and this was the perfect opportunity.

Mendez was a little stunned when Redmond also saddled her with the SSA's paperwork, which she had never done before. Daunted at first, she quickly recovered and saw this as a great opportunity to impress. There was a new confidence about her as she strode out of the office to prove herself.

Redmond's next task was to understand what that day's threat was about. It had come from Michael, and must be related in some way to their overall mission. However, a hit on a private detective agency was not on his list of anything important. Redmond wondered if whomever was sending Michael the information, was having a joke at his expense. As ever the professional, Redmond cast his personal doubts aside, and followed through diligently.

He tasked Annaliese and Bill of their roles, before they left to complete the mission. With London and others committed, Redmond informed everyone that April was in charge until he got back.

Mendez

Maria Mendez changed into a business suit and donned one of her natural disguises as a realtor. She pulled up at number 32 Casa Villa Street, and knocked on the door. She was turned away, and cursed into her cell. Mendez, as a realtor, was clearly one unhappy lady.

Mendez had one eye on two hoods parked in a nearby Town Car. They were obviously watching the orderly's home, up and across the street. She noted they observed her with little interest.

Meanwhile, Walker and Hackenridge had been progressing down the street as New Wave Christians. As they expected, all doors that opened were slammed in their faces, making for quick progress. They approached the orderly's house, as just as across the road, Mendez went into full rant on her cell.

They rang the orderly's doorbell, the wife opening the door to find Walker doubled over in apparent pain. Walker held up his FBI badge, and with a conspiratorial smile, barged through the door asking where the restroom was. The orderly's wife was horrified and screamed, but Hackenridge calmed her fears, and convinced her by saying, "We know about your situation, your missing children. Please, we are here to help."

The woman hesitated, before smiling uncertainly, and ran after Agent Walker. The owner preoccupied, Hackenridge wrapped a state of the art transponder around the DVD power supply cable and took photographs of pictures in the room. They needed visual confirmation of the children. Hearing noises he returned to the porch, departing moments later with Walker.

During the interval, Mendez had apparently received new instructions, and passed the lookout sedan on her way to number 23. She kept the doorstep conversation going for enough time, entreating the owner to add her For Sale sign to the one already out front. It became clear the owner was not interested, so she left but tarried in the driveway to update her notepad.

Her eyes were focused over the road. As soon as Walker reappeared from inside the orderly's home, she made her first real move. The occupants of the Town Car distractedly watched her approach, apparently working on her gadget. Their attention was firmly focused on what was happening at the orderly's house and they were prepared to move at once. As Mendez neared the rear of the automobile, she crashed sideways and landed with a thud against the side of their vehicle.

She howled before picking up her shoe, now missing a heel. She shouted apologies to the hoods inside, put on the remains of her shoe, and carried the heel with her, cursing as she made directly for her sedan. Not many minutes later, both Mendez and the New Wave Christians left the street.

Laredo could hear everything the orderly's minders said via the sticker Mendez placed on the rear quarter light, and had a great feed from the transponder now in the orderly's home. It was an excellent result for the team. Later that day, the results became more fruitful when the second tracking device Mendez had placed under the vehicle, began to move. Bridger traced it to a very unusual location and reported immediately to Redmond.

Chapter 21 – Friends in High Places

Redmond

As the agents worked the orderly's street, Redmond and Annaliese were getting nowhere with the receptionist at Snoopers, a private investigation agency run by two ex-cops. Redmond was being diplomatic, and being rebuffed. Annaliese put up with the bullshit for a short while, before striding into the PI's office with her FBI badge in one hand, and her gun cocked in the other.

There was another gun pointed back at her. She stated, "I can't work out why we should bother to save your worthless butts, but we have information that in a few minutes time you will be targeted by some people who want to destroy your operation, and probably kill you in the process. We want to know why? What case are you working on that is so important?"

The PI said, "I knew you would come today. Where did you get the FBI badges from, I could use one of those myself."

Questioning was stilted, all but stalled, when the glass in the window shattered and something hit the back wall. A whining sound was increasing in pitch. Annaliese flipped backwards, grabbed the device, and threw it out of the broken window. It exploded moments later. Redmond shouted, "Everybody out!"

Annaliese grabbed the receptionist and got her through the door. The PI was running as two more devices landed in the room and whined before exploding. Redmond football tackled him through the door, just before the office was enveloped in flames.

As the fire raged, Bill burst in with his shotgun gun pointed at the receptionist, who screamed. Redmond rose and cuffed her, and then secured the PI. The team heard Rude over their comm., "I need anything to do with computers from that office. Hard drives, laptops, storage media, all of it."

Redmond and Annaliese grabbed fire extinguishers and got to it, while Bill stood with shotgun in hand pointed at their captives. Redmond got as much as he could, while Annaliese poked around in drawers and found some USB drives. She added a handful of bling, and Redmond asked why. Annaliese held up the cheap and gaudy necklace, and twisting it, pulled out another USB drive. She said, "Knowledge lies within the eye of the beholder."

Redmond and Annaliese checked out the other detective's office, and shortly, Bill welcomed the second ex-cop with the barrel of his shotgun. The PI appeared to be genuinely horror-struck, but Redmond thought he recognized the man and arrested him. They cleared the building a few minutes later.

Redmond called in at the SD field office on the way back to base, to offer London three new people to interrogate. Salamander wasted no time getting started.

Teves had been interviewing the receptionist, and took Redmond aside, "Nigel, these so-called investigators were looking into a private complaint. I don't have the full story yet, but it involved a wife who worked for a company called Coulson Systems. What is more, a Dr. Black heads it, and I presume he is the same one from Phoenix. See what you can dig up about Coulson Systems, DeMellor, and ADF. My gut tells me Del Fuego mine is in the middle of all this shit. Leave the mine with me, and I'll see you when I have the full story."

Redmond spoke with the rest of his team, and left. Returning to HQ, he took a brief update from April, before Grace informed him that Darren was snowed under and needed help. She showed him through to Yates at once. Redmond wasted no time, "Yates, Darren, you need help in here. How many people do you need?"

Darren was absorbed in his work and randomly said, "Three."

"Do you have names?"

That got Yates' full attention. "I need somebody on cross-reference and admin. There's a trainee in the LA CSI office who would be ideal and would not be dramatically missed. Her name is Suzy, but spelt like that punk singer. The other is Juliet Winthrop, 'Jules' from Miami. She retired to look after her invalid mother and won't be easy to get, if at all. She is the best for what we are up against. There is no end to it. And that's without entering in six years' past data, identifying it, corroborating and correlating it."

Redmond said, "I'll see what I can do. Who is the third?"

Yates' mind went blank, "Those two will do for now, thanks."

Redmond walked into the corridor with 3G. "Pooling all our information is vital for the long-term success of our operation. Get *Suzy* A.S.A.P., and run full background checks on Jules." Grace nodded and moved away, her notepad already working.

Redmond returned to his office and started drawing all the threads together, knowing he needed a dedicated PA of his own. Grace walked in and stated, "Siouxi will be with us in the a.m. Here's the file on Jules. She ain't gonna be easy Boss."

Redmond read the file thoroughly. He understood why Yates wanted her, and knew he would have to see her in person. He spoke to 3G, "It is almost lunchtime here. I need to spend a few hours in Miami and return here today. Please organize it for me."

3G confirmed his departure in two hours. London was still interrogating suspects, so he spoke to April, asking her to keep a general eye on everyone and everything while he was away. One hour later Grace, ill at ease, sought Redmond out and asked to speak to him in private, straight way. This was most unlike her.

"Sir, I made the booking as you know. I just received a communiqué that your seat has been cancelled and that you are to leave for Gillespie Field immediately. Apparently, 'Company' transportation has been reserved for you."

"What do you mean by Company transportation?"

"That is all I have Sir. It may be a trap."

Redmond thought, and remembered someone was due a visit soon. He strode over to Rude and demanded, "I have just received word that I should take a Company plane to Miami. You wouldn't happen to know anything about this would you?"

Rude stopped what he was doing and looked up, "Chief, you have been accepted. This is excellent news. It would be very foolish of you not to take this offer, Sir."

Redmond turned and found Grace waiting for him again. "Sir, Agent Shackleton has arrived in reception to accompany you. Apparently, he is very experienced and will cover your back at all times. You need to be ready to leave within three minutes."

Redmond wasn't sure which world he had just stepped into, and carried a gun in case it was the wrong one. Shackleton drove them at speed and was waved through airport security, soon coming to a stop by a small jet. A man was waiting at the bottom of the steps and greeted the agent like an old friend.

His host came straight to the point once they were airborne. "Redmond. Heard a lot of good things about you. Your team looks like it can do the job, but it's early days yet. I work directly for the Office of the President of the United States of America."

Redmond interrupted him amazed, "You are Secret Service? POTUS?"

The Secret Agent could feel a cold shield around Redmond, so made a snap judgment, "Yes, I am. Euan Knowles at your service. We picked up on this cabal six years ago under the last Presidency.

Presidents and Parties change, but we, and this threat, remain regardless.

"It is difficult for us to follow without exposing our interest. I understand today's cyber attack originated from within the Pentagon, which we expected. You see how badly our inter-agency intelligence is compromised. I did not obtain that information from Rude by the way, although I am sure he will verify it. Knowing Rude, I would presume he confirmed it before we did."

Redmond nodded, still not quite sure what he was facing. Euan moved their understanding along. "Redmond, we have been supplying Michael with two leads per week for almost three years. This has been off the record and could never be corroborated. He has a way of pulling information together and coming up with something tangential that works. Do not ignore his input, whatever you do. Before his mind went sideways, he was one of our most highly valued operatives, so let's just say we indulge him."

Redmond butted in incredulously, "You mean Michael was Secret Service?"

Euan nodded in confirmation. "Men of Michael's skills and courage were... are few and far between. Look after him Redmond. He went into the depths of hell, and came back the way he is now. I owe that man my life, and so do many others."

Euan took a moment out to fix coffee, ushering the flight attendant out of the way. Redmond knew he needed the personal space. When Euan returned with the beverages, his formal persona was immaculate, and he launched into the next part of his delivery.

"You have already proven yourselves several times, so I am of a mind to give your team full access to our quantifiable information, which is running at three or four threats per week. We simply cannot keep the lid on it without inter-agency cooperation. If we did cooperate, we would in turn leave ourselves exposed to unknown forces. Or we use people like Michael to follow it up. You can do this for us, and you get whatever you want in return. You are already ten times over any budget you would normally be granted by your department. This will be no problem, trust me.

"We did not know about the Hoover Dam project your team discovered. We suspected the uranium mining, but could never define a location. You have already done that, and much more."

Redmond was disconcerted, "You have somebody on the inside monitoring us? I do not like that."

Euan smiled and stated, "Apologies. One of our top operatives now works for you, and it was conditional upon our level of support to know exactly what your team was all about. What we learned led us to conclude you had the skills to take over the entire operation from us, although we do expect regular reports. Redmond, in future I will expect these from you, or your appointed stand-in. We will not be using our man inside again, unless your team is compromised. You have my word of honor on that."

Redmond left the word "Rude" to hang in the ether between them. Euan shrugged and looked away. Redmond pressed the point further until his anxiety was dispelled, and Euan revealed the situation from the Secret Service point of view. Redmond was politically aware enough to realize that without Euan's support, his enterprise would quickly turn into a backwater office of little worth, and his fledgling operation would become trash. What disturbed Redmond the most was that the bad guys would probably succeed.

They were coming in to land. Redmond was still unsure how much he could trust this person, when a video call came in. Euan turned the screen toward Redmond. It was the President himself. "Redmond. Nigel, good work my boy. By now, Euan will have briefed you fully. Know you have my full support, and if you ever have need of anything, call me. Twenty-four seven. You got that? This is not just a threat against my life, or the Office of the Presidency. It is a threat to destroy the entire civilization of The United States of America. This will not happen on my watch.

"We have come a long way in six years tracking this terrorist cabal. Their aim is not just to destroy the Presidency. They want to destroy the Senate, and the Constitution. Nigel, they want to install a totalitarian government that answers to 'No One' but themselves. I believe this. Your team is now our main thrust in trying to prevent this from happening. Know, they spent the first few years compromising our integral security, and they will soon be in a position to strike. Trust no one except your core team, Euan, and myself."

The feed died instantly as someone entered the Oval Office. Redmond had the distinct impression it was the First Lady.

Euan handed Redmond a form to sign. He read it fully first, realizing it was confirmation of transfer of the aircraft he was traveling in. Euan explained, "This is an old plane and you will

need several of these before this job is done. It's a leg-up by order
of the President himself.

"I have business here in Miami and will not need this plane
again. It is now under your personal control. You will need Ms.
Winthrop, she takes an open view of the rules also. Meet her price
and do not worry about the bill. Vincent, please see Nigel to the
helicopter as soon as we land. It has been a pleasure meeting you
Redmond. Take this satellite phone, we will be in touch."

Vincent Shackleton came forward to escort Redmond off the
jet. Euan was already in a meeting with his cohort via
videoconference. Redmond patted the fuselage on his way out of
the airplane, and wondered just what was coming.

He had gained extra awareness and support, but at what cost?
He now had, perhaps, new friends in high places. What worried
him most, was the potential—knowledge lies, but on which side?
Was this the whole truth, or a ruse intended to bring him, his team,
to align with another's cause?

§

Juliet "Jules" Winthrop was not pleased to see Redmond, and
his common courtesy was taxed to the limit. Her price was a secure
home for her aged mother with full medical facilities and twenty-
four hour nursing care, at no personal expense. Redmond signed
off on that immediately and dealt with her other demands,
reinstated entitlements and pension, and one raise in pay grade.

Jules reluctantly accepted the post, and asked when they were
to leave. Redmond said, "You begin work now and have five
minutes to pack."

Vincent's local team came in to remove her mother on the
same flight. It took fifteen minutes in total, but the target was
achieved, and Redmond knew that at last his team could begin to
function properly. He let Jules stay with her mother for the night
and settle her in, knowing it would be her last visit for some time.
Jules was at her desk the next day at 7:30, half an hour before her
official start time.

Chapter 22 – United in Knowledge

Redmond could not let go of the fact that it had all been far too easy. He had been expecting battles over budgets, not being told he had a blank check, and be given a free jet. He smelled a rat, but could not place it, as Euan and the President seemed kosher.

He became thoughtful, wondering whom of his staff he could trust implicitly. The answers flowed easy, and yet changed within moments. At the end of it, he came down to only six people, plus 3G. Redmond determined to share his worries with them, first speaking in confidence with Grace. She left to action his plan, as his confused mind continued to wrestle with the thistle at the core of their operation.

Bill and Annaliese left on the Harley and prepared Michael to receive guests, the others followed in Redmond's SUV. Michael was delighted to see Annaliese and April again, plus he respected Bill and Teves, and remembered Redmond. The others disturbed him, but after commendation, he accepted Mendez and Walker as being trustworthy.

John was not with him, having left the previous day to spend time at home working on his latest novel. Michael's face broke into a Cheshire Cat smile as he said, "We email every day, and sometimes," his voice dropped and he looked around with theatrical drama his grandmother would have been proud of, "we Skype!"

To most in the room, this meant little. But April and Annaliese made a specific point of congratulating him on his newfound computer skills.

The meeting began in the study, and, after everyone was introduced to Michael officially, they got down to business. Redmond spoke briefly about his meeting with Euan, and Michael seemed genuinely happy. Next, Redmond laid out their achievements, inviting Michael to visit their new base whenever he wished. Michael politely declined.

After laying out the background, Redmond came to focus on his concerns. "What is the largest obstacle to getting things done, or anything of an official nature?" He enquired.

Several suggestions were made before he interrupted, "The biggest obstacle to getting the job done as quickly and efficiently as possible, is always budgetary constraints. We all know this. No overtime allowed, shortages of staff or equipment, repairs waiting for approval. Agreed?"

There was murmured consensus of agreement. Redmond continued, "Since we began this operation a few days ago, I have been given approval for whatever we wanted. I found out today we are already way over any normal budget. In spite of that, I get whatever staff and state of the art equipment I ask for. This is unheard of. This afternoon I was given a Cessna jet to use, and it is entirely at our team's disposal. Something is not right and I need to discover what it is."

The team talked for several minutes, and were getting nowhere, until Michael suddenly stood up as if he was in a trance. He started walking around and speaking almost abstractly, "The Cessna ... that would be SFD079A. She is a tough old bird ... the first aircraft I requisitioned. I'd like to fly in her one more time, just for old time's sake."

Michael stopped, lucid for once, and looked at Redmond, "You've had a meeting with Euan. You can trust him with your life, and whatever information he gave you. What is happening is that everyone wants to stay well clear of this operation, yet they need to prevent the worst disaster this country has ever faced. Everyone is petrified of making a mistake.

"Now the focus has been identified as this team. What will happen if you miss something, or somebody unknown to you makes a mistake? The answer is simple. You, Redmond, and this team, will be blamed for it. You are the fall-guys when this goes pear-shaped."

Redmond smiled genuinely for the first time in many hours, and clasped Michael to him in brotherly fashion. He had never, ever done that with a man before, but it felt right. When they broke apart Redmond stated, "When we are successful, a lot of people none of us know, will get a big pat on the back for what we have done. If anything goes wrong, know we are expendable. Nice people."

Michael replied, "'Peace, commerce, and honest friendship with all nations, entangling alliances with none'."

He pointed to the inscription below the oil painting and finished, "Jefferson's Admonition. What I mean is that you need to be clear of purpose, and to cover yourselves without becoming embroiled in political maneuvering, and counter-agency activity."

Clearly battling his fragmenting mind, he concluded, "Evelyn Steinbecker. She's the very best I've worked with. She outflanked the wrong person, and was persuaded to take early retirement. She returned to Pasa … Pacoima … Ahha! I think you will find her in Acapulco. I knew it had a P in it. Now April, what's for dinner? You brought any of that fine Mexican fare for me to eat?"

Some minutes later, after examining his fridge, the girls realized that he did not have many ready meals prepared. They headed off to the all-night for supplies. Redmond did not intend to exclude them, but time was the imperative. He recorded the conversation for them, but used the juncture wisely to take reports from everybody in the room.

Mendez and Walker spoke in turn, but they were waiting on CSI reports and interrogation results. They were, however, able to report the success of their work at the orderly's house, "The vehicle that was parked across from the orderly's house was relieved at dinner time. We traced it to Del Fuego Mine, but it got there by a road that doesn't exist on any map."

Redmond was quick to pick up on this, even though he had already received the full report. "You are absolutely sure there is a second way into that complex that nobody knows about?"

"Yes Sir," Mendez spoke up, and then smirked, "Well, nobody but those that use it. It leads directly to the secure compound. I have asked for satellite surveillance and we should have this the next time someone uses the way in daylight. I got Laredo to backtrack archived images, and have the route established."

Walker spoke next, "The orderly obtained a duplicate key for the disused corridor. He took out the camera with acid, and disabled the alarm on the old fire door. His contact provided the acid and the knowhow, he simply did the work. Teves and I put the pieces together."

Redmond spoke quickly, "Excellent work. Thank you. Teves, what have the interrogations uncovered?"

The Undersheriff rose and began by pacing the room. "I am very concerned for the safety of the orderly's children. You have my report of course, in which he confirmed everything we discovered from the hospital. He is almost clean, just very worried.

"However, he allowed his ID and security swipe to be used several times, and he says that a few days ago, the kidnappers forced him to let them raid a secure medical depository. The interview was long and taxing, but the orderly eventually revealed the Phenobarbital was made from a concoction of recently, discarded partially used bottles. All the orderly did was allow the perpetrators access to the secure room, and disposal bin."

Teves crossed himself and continued, "We need to recover his children, and from what I just heard, I believe a secure location to hold hostages would be Del Fuego mine. The secure compound is far bigger than I first thought. It is almost as if the standard entrance is a cover for something far larger in purpose. I would like to get eyes on it from the hills surrounding. Maybe we can learn something useful. We also need inside information. Perhaps Annaliese and Bill could investigate subtly, have a chat with the hotel staff and mine workers perhaps?"

Redmond told him to see that it was done. Teves continued, "The hospital security supervisor accepted a small bribe to see the cameras didn't pick up too much. A few days ago, his wife was threatened with a life of prostitution, if he did not assist with the kidnapping of April Bekkons. He claims no knowledge of the murder plot. Salamander is certain this is the truth of his understanding.

"This whole thing appears to have been orchestrated outside of the hospital, and with coercion. I think we should return him to duty, either with a formal report, or a duty to repay us in the future. I prefer to retain the leverage, just in case.

"The two PI's were working with and against each other, trading on their status as ex-cops. They overcharged for poor service, and were looking into a domestic dispute. A worried husband contacted them as his wife was working unscheduled overtime and he presumed she was seeing somebody. She was not.

"She was a technician at a local factory called Coulson Systems. PI Amos, the guy who was caught in the blast, interviewed the suspect after work one day, and put her in hospital. The only reason she told him what she knew, was to stop him from barraging her stomach with punches. He had discovered she was pregnant.

"I have no information why the other PI decided to go down to his vehicle at the moment of the attack, but he did and missed the blast. I would presume this was not a coincidence, and we are working on that angle. Meanwhile, someone inside Coulson Systems known only as Dr. Black had blackmailed the receptionist into giving him feedback on the inquiry. You may remember he was one of the people I identified in Phoenix. That trail is small-time and I consider it a dead end.

"The Coulson Systems factory is highly secretive, but we invited the technician the PIs in for a little chat. They checked out. With her assistance, we have established that hardly anything goes in or out, except for staff and light freight. The owners appear to be for real, yet something stinks about the whole setup.

We discovered the factory makes specific military electronics to order. We are talking about bugging devices and state of the art tracking systems. They also make digital timers and detonators. In particular, it seems they have just received an order to manufacture nuclear fissile detonators, as in bombs. I do not have a number, but it appears to be at least two. The good news there is that the order doesn't call for mass production, so we're not talking a saleable number of bombs.

"I have since traced a few of the investors, but it was very difficult to follow the money trail, even with Rude's assistance. I have one name, Godfrey DeMellor. I did see his name once on a certificate at our recently reopened local uranium mine. The title on the certificate was Coulson Conglomerates."

Teves looked up from under heavy lids and added, "The name Coulson appears at the end of many lines of enquiry, and I can get no further: Coulson Industries, Coulson Biotech, Coulson Conglomerates. And then there is nothing. The Godfrey DeMellor line of inquiry ends with Coulson Tactical Technology and Systems Support. I did see his son Anton once, that night I followed the decoy truck to Phoenix.

"The soldiers that attacked us are saying nothing of importance, except they take orders from Coulson Securitas. Salamander eventually got that from them, and that they are based locally at Twentynine Palms.

"I have taken it upon myself to approve Salamander's continued interrogation of these prisoners as he will. Both London and I have now withdrawn from that line of inquiry. Remaining prisoners were signed over to him for further interrogation. As we have withdrawn, he requested to bring in one other person skilled in advanced interrogation techniques. I approved this subject to your personal confirmation, Nigel. All I know is that the interrogation expert is known as Thresher, and is admired by Salamander.

"Finally, Deputy Rodriguez had not been blackmailed. He became embroiled in a clever plot, and went along with it because the people who contacted him were CIA. This is what he believes. From the names and other information he gave us, we believe it was either real CIA Agents, or people impersonating them extremely well. Rude is already checking them out.

"Rodriguez believed he was working undercover on a matter of national security, which is the truth. He had simply been hoodwinked to work for the wrong side. I have his full statement, and there is nothing in it to be unduly concerned about. It is my intention to return him for discipline and duty tomorrow."

Redmond nodded his consent, adding, "It is better to have him where we can keep an eye on him. See if we can use him as a double agent, although that would be doubtful given such exposure. Well done Manny."

Redmond was worried again as Teves finished his debrief. He was interrupted in his considerations as Michael arrived back with the girls at that moment. He burst into the room like a child, yelling with great enthusiasm, "You should come see the sky. It is orange and very special tonight."

Redmond raced into the back yard, where the sky was awash with flames over the docks area. The explosions in the night sky reminded him of Independence Day celebrations. The group stayed for supper, and watched the news. The explosion at a fireworks storage warehouse was the main news item of the evening.

Redmond sighed in relief. How could that have anything to do with their interests? He hoped the question was rhetorical.

Chapter 23 – A Day of Changes

The next morning Siouxi arrived and Redmond welcomed her to their theatre of operations, and led her through to CSI. Jules was already at work, and Yates had instigated an immediacy protocol; it was senseless to continue processing hospital data when they already had signed confessions of what had taken place.

The day was a long one for all operations staff. Redmond discovered Rude and Bridger had worked into the small hours, finally getting all their base information up to date. They had already passed what they had on to Yates, whose office was fully functioning, despite the late hour.

Siouxi had taken over the office next door simply to control data and administration. Evidence was stored for later corroboration if required, or when they had time to process it. Darren found her asleep at her desk at 2 a.m. and sent her to bed.

He returned and smiled at Jules, "You need to sleep as well. Take a few hours and then relieve me. OK?"

Jules leaned back and looked at him, knowing he was both right, and wrong. "Hon, we gotta do this. We both know it. Once we are current, this will become a lot easier. You know it, and I know it. So, what's one night?

"That stated, I do believe we need to be staffed twenty-four seven, and that means bringing in someone for nights. Sherry Oberhumer would be ideal, and I know she is free right now. Her world just collapsed, shall we say." She ran her fingers through her hair and waited as Darren's tired mind put the pieces together. She knew he and Sherry had possibly been lovers some years ago. At least they'd stepped right up to the brink if they hadn't fallen over the edge. But Sherry was the best, after herself of course.

Darren remained confused for too long. Jules knew she was right. She stood up and walked out to get some downtime. She took his lack of response as affirmative, and planned to ring her friend in the morning. Jules got a small bite to eat, set her alarm for 7:45 a.m., and fell asleep as soon as her head hit the pillow.

Redmond had fallen asleep on the sofa in his office, and was woken by Grace at 7:30 with a large mug of coffee. No sooner had he returned to his desk than Vincent Shackleton appeared and gave him a thumb drive containing all the information the Secret Service had gathered over the last six years. He almost called

Rude, but remembered how late they had worked and left word with Grace to send him along when he surfaced.

Redmond knew he was with close allies, so asked, "Vincent, do you know the whereabouts of someone called Evelyn Steinbecker? I believe she is down in Acapulco."

Vincent laughed, replying, "You have worked out why they are giving you free reign. I presume Michael told you about her. I'll give her a call, that is if you serve a decent breakfast here?"

Redmond nodded and was surprised when Shackleton made the call right there in front of him, from his secure phone. They spoke openly before he passed the cell across. Redmond told her why he needed her services, and Evelyn replied, "That is a part time job. To be effective I will need to be your PA, I presume you don't have one yet?"

"No, and I ..."

"Good, then I will begin in three days time." She hung up.

Redmond closed the cell, and pocketing the drive as a security measure, took Vincent for breakfast in the works canteen. No sooner had they arrived in the restaurant and ordered, than Jules came up to him and asked for a night staffer called Sherry. He approved the appointment, if she was available. Jules stated, "She will be here later this morning."

During breakfast, they agreed Shackleton would act as go-between, the Secret Service having a nearby field office, which Shackleton would work from. Vincent would ensure that secure information flowed both ways regularly. This greatly eased Redmond's worries.

As they were finishing, Rude came in. Redmond called him over. "You didn't get much sleep. Please take this drive and examine the data it contains. It should hold full information of every identified or possible threat going back six years. It is to be treated in highest confidence."

Shackleton added, "It also contains probable future threats, some of them for weeks in advance. It contains erroneous leads as well as bona fide data. Treat every entry as possibly either."

Rude looked at the drive, noting it could hold a massive amount of information. He whistled and stated, "I'll have a look Chief. Once I know what we have I'll create an algorithm to identify definitive threats. I'll call you when it is done, although it may take some time if this drive is full."

Redmond asked him, "How is the crime scene evidence coming along Rude?"

He replied, "Thanks to April, the tablet's hard drive still functions, and from it I should be able to get the encoding keys used on the peripheral devices. I had intended to begin as soon as I finish breakfast. You want me to proceed with that or this new hard drive?"

Redmond answered at once, "I need the crime scene data processing as a priority. When you come to the new drive, check data for the coming weeks first and work backwards. Let me know immediately if you find anything significant. Oh, and share all positive leads with Darren so he can pull files for events that have already occurred."

Rude went to eat breakfast as Redmond walked Shackleton down to his vehicle. On the way, Redmond asked if he had any information on Coulson Group or DeMellor.

Vincent stopped in the middle of the parking lot and, leaning close to Redmond, whispered, "We also came up with both of those names, but we were warned off by another Agency.

"Obviously the President could have overridden, but not without some kind of justifiable proof. As it stands, all the CIA will tell us is that they are involved in a discreet infiltration inquiry and undercover operation that has been ongoing for several years. We do not believe them. I'll deliver what we have ASAP.

"Nigel, know the order for us to drop the Coulson investigation came directly from the Director of National Intelligence, personally. This is one reason why you need Evelyn Steinbecker, she fully understands the politics and powers involved here."

Later that morning, Redmond was taken aback at the sight of a fringed deer-skin dress walking toward Siouxi's desk. It took him a moment to see beyond the outfit, the bead-bound, feathered hair, and the multiple hoop earrings to his new controller.

Redmond looked over at Bridger, the consummate vampire, dressed all in black with her totems spread around her desk. Nearby stood Bill, the accomplished hells angel, with pagan Annaliese, and April the goth. He thought about introducing a dress code.

Siouxi interrupted his thought. "Is there a problem, Boss?"

"Are you making some kind of statement?" Redmond enquired.

"My parents are Blackfoot, as you know, hence my nickname and my roots, Sir. I had to earn the eagle feather in my headband. It represents a rite of passage in my culture."

Redmond thought about how he would feel forced to wear jeans and a tee. He felt comfortable in a suit, buttoned up shirt, and tie. He could only do his job when dressed appropriately. It freed his mind and gave him grounding, strength. The same thing surely worked for his team. Redmond knew their worth as individuals, regardless of what they looked like. He wandered away, happy and feeling indulgent.

April was bored. With London back, she had no specific role and idled time away by keeping tabs on all progress being made. She was watching a live feed over Bridger's shoulder when a vehicle left the secure compound of the mine, and she stayed to watch her track it.

She knew they had to get close and asked if they could get some type of video devices to replay a live feed. Rude interrupted and said, "We have half a dozen in the storeroom. The transponders need to be attached to a main power cable of some description, and not high voltage power lines, or DC current either, 110 Volts only."

Bridger countered, "No problem Hon, I'll track it via satellite."

Laredo intervened, "Why don't you let me use the drone. I have one at my disposal, and a second available for emergency use."

April hobbled over to her and asked, "You have a recording of the vehicle that just left the mine?"

Laredo brought up the screen, and showed her the recording. April asked, "Can you zoom in and read the plate?"

Laredo looked at her, beginning to realize the problem. "I could zoom-in in real time, but with the recording, not that close Hon."

"What you got, Bridger, can you make out the plate?"

"What is this? A competition? Sorry Hon."

Laredo pumped the air. Bridger scowled and continued, "I would normally be able to enhance the screenshot to read the plate, but the sun is at totally the wrong angle and casts a shadow. When I have the angle, the vehicle has changed direction."

Bridger looked over at Laredo, not admitting this was a tie. April interrupted, "So, same with the satellite feed. Laredo, say you need to use the drone somewhere else, we lose coverage, right?"

Laredo agreed, but said, "Don't forget, I can use SDPD traffic cams to track the vehicle, the nearest one is half a mile from this intersection."

April said, "That could work, but it is time consuming, especially if there is no threat. This is why we need physically fixed, and dedicated recording. We need to monitor everything that goes in and out of the secure compound at Del Fuego mine, and be able to read the plate immediately. Thanks girls."

A plan to monitor all access to and from Del Fuego mine was forming in April's mind, and she took full advantage of the satellite feed when Bridger left for a restroom break. She knew that today would be a day of changes, and she would instigate the first of them. She left and spoke to her father and Annaliese, before tracking Teves down. He was preparing to take a team and go mountain climbing behind the secret area of Del Fuego mine. She asked him to wait for her.

April shambled toward Redmond's office, her mind made up and set once more on a purpose. She laid out her plan to Redmond. He questioned her, and refined her idea slightly, but it was something that needed to be done. They had to learn as much about the mine as possible.

April said, "I'll set up to monitor the workers. They are good people you know." Redmond handed the operation over to her, on the condition she provided regular feedback, and did not get up to any more mischief.

April got a wink from Redmond, before she went in search of Teves and her trusty companions. They pulled off fifteen minutes later, two Harleys and a Humvee.

Chapter 24 – El Cazador

The motorbikes arrived at the rural crossroads a few minutes before the Humvee, as planned. Annaliese had taken April's bike, but they swapped back to their usual pairing as soon as possible. There was a gas station and general store on the turn into the track they were interested in. They searched for somewhere to mount a camera, but nothing they had access to was suitable.

Bill took a ride up the track with Annaliese on back, while Teves and April looked around. Teves said he would get a crew to mount a full control camera on the streetlight straight across from where they stood. Bill returned a few minutes later and told them the track led to a farm that had tall security fences topped with razor wire. He added there was a high security presence on the only entrance, and the guards were fully armed.

Teves spoke via his headset to the six special security agents in the Humvee, who would continue and circle around from the south. Their brief was to locate and operate a suitable observation post. The motorbikes departed moments later heading north, pulling off into the road that led directly to the mine's official entrance. April pulled over and pointed across the road, "You better get a camera fixed on that streetlight also, Manny."

They had no reason to travel that way except for their ongoing interest in Del Fuego mine. In time, they passed the entrance and nothing appeared to be out of the ordinary. They did not turn in, but carried on along the road as it headed north to a small town some miles away. There was absolutely nothing beyond wilderness along that stretch of road, no farms, no houses. However, they were closing quite quickly on a small truck farther up the road.

April was first to realize it must have come from the mine, and her intuition fired. They caught up with it near the outskirts of town where the road became better made. The Harleys roared past and left it in their wake, before pulling into Rosa's store. The other two went inside immediately, but April tarried near the roadside with Teves, as if inspecting something on her bike. The truck passed them and turned left at the new hotel, headed for the highway.

April used her headset and spoke to Bridger. "We're at Rosa's. I got eyes on a maroon panel truck. I need a satellite trace on it immediately. Tell me which way it turns when it gets to the main road. If it turns left, south, track it."

Bridger replied, "I'll use the drone, Hon.." Moments later she added, "It turned left Hon, and I'm tracking it."

April replied, "Can you backtrack the feed and confirm it came from the mine?"

Her headset went dead for several moments before she got new information. "Nice one, Hon. It left the secure area of the mine about five minutes before your Harleys came along. Wait a moment—it has now just passed the other junction."

April stated, "There are probably reasons why they might take a fifteen mile detour, but I doubt it makes any sense unless they want to appear unobserved. Tell me where it goes, and see if we have anything for the last couple of days. You had better mention this to Redmond, and see if Laredo can get the plate number off a traffic cam for Rude to follow-up. Thanks Bridger."

Teves looked at her and added, "I may as well set up a camera on that junction as well while we are at it." He spoke to 3G, ordering three full-function cameras to be sited at each of the junctions as soon as possible. She passed it by Redmond for signature, who added coverage of Coulson Systems to the list.

Teves and April both spoke to Rosa, and extra food was prepared for them as lunchtime was approaching. Teves spoke candidly, "Rosa, we are not just visiting, but have work to do here today. We need feedback from the miners themselves, and any information they have about what is really going on inside that compound."

Rosa released a hearty chuckle. "They are all very grateful to Bill for paying the hospital tab for those two poor souls who were caught in the rock fall. Everybody knows it was a deliberate act by the company, and they appreciate Bill taking responsibility for what he got them into. They are both recovering well and are now back with their families in Mexico.

"Send Bill over to speak to them. He has their greatest respect, and that is extremely uncommon for a Gringo. Illegal's seldom honor anyone in this way, but Bill is the exception. I would have you all stay for dinner, but first join the men as they prepare for nightshift, and return from dayshift. I will ensure Pepito will be there also."

April looked at her enquiringly, and Rosa added, "Pepito is an endearment of the name Pepe. What is the other thing you need information about?"

Teves was surprised how well she read him, but began, "Thank you Rosa, you are certain of a place in Heaven beside our Good Lord." He crossed himself, continuing, "We need to get into the hills behind the mine overlooking the secure compound. Do you know of any trails not marked on the map? I know the general area quite well, but that region is well off the beaten track."

Rosa spoke quickly and quietly to April in local dialect, and within a few moments knew exactly what they needed. She called Tepin and asked him to join them for lunch. During the meal, April explained the problem and Tepin smiled, his sparkling eyes and broken, cheroot-stained teeth exaggerating his mask of conspiratorial complicity.

Tepin steadied his mirth, but his ancient eyes remained alive with intrigue as he said, "Christos Valdez used to have a cabin way up in the hills. He inherited it from his father Juan, who I knew slightly from schooldays. He was several years ahead of me, when this small town was much larger and had its own Mexican school.

"The old man died many years ago. The Coroner stated the cause of death was scurvy, but nobody believed that, for that place where he lived is evil. I will show you where it is, on condition that you leave as soon as your work is done. El Diablo, The Devil, lives in the mountain and stalks the lands around, bringing death to all who venture those remote parts."

Tepin crossed himself and looked to the sky, searching for absolution from on high. "We have a stop to make before the cabin, however. You will need to talk with El Cazador, The Hunter."

Unlike Tepin, April was not superstitious. She knew there would be a rational explanation for the old man's death. A little later, Tepin drove them in his jalopy, up into the hills encircling the town, hoping the person he wanted to see was at home, since El Cazador was often gone for many days at a time. Bill and Annaliese followed on the Harley.

The road degenerated into an earthen trail, before it petered out into a grass track. All the occupants, except for their driver, wondered if the struggling rattletrap would make the climb, but it survived. Like Tepin, it had stood the test of time.

At last they reached a dwelling. Tepin went in alone, the others waiting for his signal. They were lucky as the man was preparing to hunt mountain lion, which was a good seller at that time of year. They talked for a short while before Tepin beckoned the others over to join them on the stoop.

They were introduced to El Cazador. Teves greeted him in standard Spanish, but April beguiled the man by speaking the local dialect. He asked for $300, all up front. April got out a $100 bill and held it up for him to look at. She said, "I need the truth. Is the cabin habitable, or a derelict relic?"

The hunter looked her in the eye and said, "It needs some work doing, but I used it last winter and it was fine for one night. What you make of it is up to you."

April handed him the greenback, and a fifty, stating, "Let's go, you get the rest once we arrive."

The others followed El Cazador on foot, Bill idling behind in first gear with April on back. In time they ditched the bike, turning to follow a cleft upwards through the rocks, and walked beside a mountain stream. Teves bent to take water from it, but El Cazador shouted, "Stop! That is The Devil's own poison."

Shortly, they came to the spring and turned due south following the cliffs. They came to a defile in the rocks about two feet wide at the base, and passed through sideways to the west. The way was constricting, but even Bill managed to squeeze through. They came out onto a small plateau that overlooked the secret portion of the mine. Nearby was a log cabin that was still standing, although it appeared to be in dire need of repair.

They headed straight for it at once. Teves noticed a small stream south of the cabin, and asked if the water was safe to drink. El Cazador said it was, but advised them never, use the stream on the opposite edge of the plateau. Teves and April exchanged a brief look of concern.

Once they examined the old cabin properly, it turned out to be in quite good repair. The main structure had been built using seasoned wood, and only some cladding and one small spot in the roof needed repair. The view from the front porch was spectacular, and it took them several minutes to focus attention on the secret part of the mine.

They walked to the edge, and there it was laid out in front of them. They had exactly what they needed.

Teves asked about rent and ownership. El Cazador said it had been left intestate and returned to the State as far as he knew. Teves excused himself and using his headset asked Bridger for confirmation. He was simply being thorough.

April paid the hunter the full amount and thanked him, plus asked for any other advice. His eyes fixed on her, he pointed and said, "There are large fish in that lake to the South. Do not fish anywhere North." He bowed his head to her, turned, and left quickly. The others shot video before retracing their steps.

When they got back to town they stayed to talk with the miners, first the night crew assembling for shift. Later they greeted the day crew returning for evening meal, and sharing drink with them. Bill was already a celebrity to their minds, and his friends were their friends, even Teves to a certain degree, and more so when he stated categorically he was not interested in their ID's.

Later, Teves received word that the mountain cabin was for sale or lease. They talked quietly and it was decided Bill would rent it privately, so as not to leave a paper trail. Redmond would supply the money, the soldiers, and the equipment they needed for observation. April updated Redmond, who was delighted and also very proud of her.

The evening was a great success and they learned much in a few hours of open conversation. However, time was pressing and Teves knew he could spend the night with his family. April took him home early, and discovered he lived in a good residential neighborhood not far from his regular office. His home was about eight miles from Rosa's small town, the same one where Teves' wife had been born and raised.

The whole family rushed out to greet him, clearly delighted to have him home for the night. Before April left, Xochitl placed a hand on her forearm in thanks. She mentioned that she would drop her husband into work the next morning, but that he might be late. A mischievous grin played around her face, and April couldn't help but giggle in conspiracy.

§

April cruised around the streets for a while, knowing that tonight, her father, the first man in her heart, would be sleeping with her best friend. Her heart was torn; divided. The two people she loved most were about to become one whole. So what about her?

Chapter 24

Her thoughts turned inwards as there was not a single male she liked that wanted her romantically. She ended up in the works canteen, dabbing at her food and sipping from a beer.

Redmond came in and joined her. They talked of small things, of big things, and of dreams. He was like a father to her, offering his concern and wisdom. In time, she broke down and cried. He moved beside her, and held her like he would his own daughter. He remained her stalwart comforter and protector until she revived.

April recovered her sensibility when Redmond said something very strange to her. He quoted:

"The Path of Life.

There is no path in life,
Except the one we walk ourselves.
We leave behind our stepping-stones,
Those things we did, or did not do,
That mark the passage of our lives.
Some may linger throughout all time,
Some may dally for the moment's indulgence,
Most may disappear before we make time to turn around;
To witness what has already come to pass.

Each day,
Each step,
Each decision we take is but testimony;
To the human estate,
Our innate predilection,
Of strengths or weaknesses,
Of riches or drought.
Mostly, we are found wanting,
nor not nary more enough.

At the end of the day,
When life's rich tapestry unravels,
shredd'd: destiny's dearth;
'Tis then The Reaper calls us to account;
We are judged on merit,
for what we wanted to do,

for what we actually accomplished,
and what more we could have done…
For well or woe; as chance may be.'

April, you are a true survivor. This is what I admire most about you."

Something in his words sparked a fire within her. April's eyes became alive, turning her despondency around. She knocked back her drink and thanked him, leaving immediately. She was surprised to find herself pausing in the doorway to look back at him.

What made the moment special was that he was watching her leave. He gave her a large smile, and a conspiratorial wink. April knew she had to leave before she giggled like a girl.

April remembered her thoughts on "looking back" the first time she had gotten the bus to leave Rosa's; "Only look back if you are unsure, and can't hide the fact, or you fancy the guy to pieces."

Suddenly, her dreams were alive once more, as was her appetite to experience all that life had to offer. Her heart instantly erupted with unknown emotions. She wondered if she were falling in love.

Chapter 25 – Human Nature

The next morning broke with a thunderclap. Rude isolated San Diego Fireworks Import & Exposition Company, Inc. as a target. The data he had spent days and nights processing was revealing results. He re-ran sections of the Secret Service drive as he refined his algorithms. London was intent on sending a team down to the docks, but Redmond countermanded him, insisting it was more prudent for Teves to drop by in his role as Deputy Sheriff.

A few hours later, Rude was working up certifiable leads, and there was virtually one event for every day planned for the next two weeks. They were all apparently unrelated and scattered all across the States. Redmond was at first inclined to send teams to each, especially with the Cessna at his disposal, but in time, he settled with April and they talked it through.

She had a way about her of seeing the important, and not the obfuscating avalanche of reactive information he wanted to respond to. In due course, they started to profile and prioritize. They were discussing a threat for later in the week, when out of the blue April asked him, "Why don't you call in a professional profiler? I have seen it on TV, and I guess they also exist in real life."

It took Redmond five seconds to move his eyes, by small degrees, and look beyond the wild makeup at her self. His head twitched involuntarily toward her face, by increments, his eyes searching for the truth. Seeing deeply into her eyes, she became the sole focus of his irises. When they collided, the spark of energy between them was far more than electric. It was eclectic, and full of forbidden promise.

They could have stared into each other's souls for a second, or a lifetime. It was the same thing. The spell was broken when 3G rushed in and shook Redmond out of their personal gridlock. "Sir, Sherry Oberhumer is entering the underground parking lot, and I have Evelyn Steinbecker at the main gate. You need to greet them both. Next, an extreme interrogation specialist called Thresher wants to help plan our medical facilities, and finally Bill needs money for a rental on a derelict mountain shack."

Redmond broke eye contact with April, although he could feel her eyes lingering upon him. He dismissed his small male thoughts and went straight back to work. "3G, I will speak to Thresher personally, and remind him of the Geneva Convention, and the limits we impose on interrogation techniques. Bill has his blank check. As for the women, let's greet them together, let's go."

He did not say a word to April, but cast a glance back at her from the doorway as he exited. April smiled happily, beguiling him with a look of deeper intensity. Then he was gone to attend to his duty. April found she had a vacuum to fill. She wandered down to ops and occupied her station.

Redmond and Grace greeted Sherry in the parking lot, and waited for Evelyn to park. 3G made introductions between them, and apologized, hoping they did not mind being shown around together. Redmond gave them a quick tour, introducing them to the staff, before Grace showed them to their quarters. 3G said, "Apologies, I know the rooms are a bit basic at the moment, but we have only recently moved into this building, and Redmond insists everybody live-in for security reasons. Let me show you to the restaurant."

Both women started work a short time later, familiarizing themselves with their new duties and other team members. Evelyn found her bearings quickly and spoke to Redmond, "You have done an amazing job here in such a short time. However, you need someone for Human Resources and another for Accounts. Also, all these people will expect to be paid at the end of the month. You know that, don't you?"

"What do you suggest?" answered Redmond, looking somewhat alarmed.

"You have a small dedicated team here, and as long as it stays that way, I will handle it myself."

Redmond saw the sense of her remarks, and realized how a field office was normally structured. He simply had a smaller version of one. He asked her to let him know if she ever needed an assistant.

Evelyn replied, "I will, be sure of it. One more thing. I will bring myself up to speed today and tomorrow. The following morning I must leave for at least one full day. I will begin officially once I come back. Now, if you have a moment, could you explain to me how this place works and what it really does?"

§

As Redmond introduced his team's directive and role, Teves was paying a belated call to the ruins of the fireworks storage warehouse. As per their arrangement, the Fire Marshal was making an appraisal visit for his report. Teves knew him well having worked together previously on wildfires.

They walked through the utter destruction together. The Fire Marshal being brought up to date on his team's latest findings, the fire having long since been put out. The broad opinion was the blaze had started due to a faulty firework or detonator, since these were mainly fireworks for large public displays. However, specialists were still trying to establish the seat of the blaze. They remained nonspecific about cause.

His friend left the scene, but Teves stayed to speak with the specialist investigators. He talked to the most senior, and asked him to look for a detonator once they ascertained the point of origin.

The firefighter answered him, saying they would have a look when it was isolated. His reply was dismissive. Teves spoke warmly, but forcefully, "I just received confirmation, that information about this explosion was identified four-days ago. Please see to it you make a thorough investigation. I would like your preliminary and full findings sent to me at this address…"

§

Meanwhile, Bill and Annaliese negotiated the purchase of the Valdez place with Mountain Realty, Inc. The process took far longer than either expected, but they came away with the deeds, Bill buying the place outright with a cashier's check.

They again stayed the night at Rosa's hotel, and breakfasted with her in the morning. Bill led the surveillance team into the mountains on his Harley, the Humvee following farther than Annaliese thought possible. Eventually, they had to travel the last part on foot. When they got to the stream, Bill stopped to examine the water in a small backwater pool. He was not surprised to discover it was radioactive. They continued and squeezed through the gap between the rocks. What their forces found was exceptional. They took time out to congratulate Bill and Annaliese before going about their business.

The experts set up in the front room with long-range cameras and listening devices. Solar powered remote devices were placed along the cliff face, to completely monitor the mine. Everything was backed up on recording equipment, but electricity supply was a problem. There was an old generator out back, but Captain

Williams, OIC, said he would return for the night crew and bring back solar panels, and several large batteries.

§

Despite her late night, April had been one of the first in ops that morning. Her foot was troubling her from all the walking of previous days. She knew she needed to behave and take things easy for a while. The plaster cast had broken above the ankle and she simply cut the excess away with her Leatherman. The scrape of her sharp nails brought instant relief to her itching calf.

Distracted, she looked around, before realizing there was nobody acting as liaison between ops and CSI. She worried about duplication of effort, or missing something important. She spoke to Redmond when he came down and he told her to do what she thought was best. April spent the morning with ops, learning first hand all they were doing, being taught how to control some of their systems, and how to access the database.

She spent the afternoon with CSI, learning their database, and gaining a working knowledge of their cataloguing system. By dinnertime, she understood the flow of information between CSI and ops in real-time.

The next morning she spoke to Redmond. "As you know I've been learning what ops and CSI actually do, and how they pass information. There is no set protocol. Information is passed by word of mouth, or email, sometimes later rather than sooner if people get busy.

"I've already set up a database both can access, it loads basic information automatically, each time either department makes a report. Bridger says she can easily make a blog type interface, so there can be commentary on what the other department is doing. I want to implement this, and put Bridger in control of it as data management and liaison. She is the key person monitoring everything in real time."

Redmond smiled, "That is excellent work April. See to it at once."

April tasked Bridger with setting up the new information exchange, and put her in charge. Nearby, Rude finally began unlocking the crime scene evidence from Sacramento Drive that she had rescued from the burning car. Her shock was palpable. Michael had not been under surveillance at all. The observers had been monitoring the house next door. Redmond was called and examined the information together with London.

Redmond called a meeting immediately. "My concern is the appearance of coincidence. What are the odds of Michael living next door to the target of surveillance by a group we are interested in? I think that an exceedingly long shot. Mendez, please see what you can dig up in reference to houses and residents, how long each has lived there, and anything else of the slightest note."

April said, "The neighbor's name is Bob Rogers if that helps you."

Mendez left and Redmond continued, "April, I need you to pay Michael a visit and find out what he knows, I hope he is having a good day. I will send London to have a word with the man next door."

Mendez quickly completed her initial investigation online, "I discovered the house owner is named Mr. Robert Roy Rogers, a recluse, and there is minimal information about him in the system. I did find reference to him having a doctorate. There is also a patent application for some new kinds of porcelain, but checks are still ongoing regards that. He has many other accepted patents, but I will need to dig much deeper to find out what they really are. What is of interest is that he paid cash for the property four years ago, and that is all I have for the initial sweep. He looks like a kook if you ask me.

"Virtually all information regarding Michael is restricted, although I can confirm he was born in the house, and became owner of it after his parents died."

Later, when he was alone, Redmond spoke to Shackleton, who said, "I will verify all I can officially tell you about Michael, and get back to you. This will need a very high security clearance."

Chapter 26 – Discoveries

I due course, London and Hackenridge paid Rogers a visit. The inventor had a home come workshop befitting a mad scientist. At first, Rogers was protective, but with gentle persuasion, he began to open up about his work. He had designs for all sorts of things, most incomplete, or being redesigned. They were becoming lost within the man's imagination when London's headset came to life. It was Laredo.

"London, be very careful what you say. Rude has just unlocked the last of the forensic evidence from the Mathers place, we believe there are surveillance bugs in the house."

London moved quickly outside to complete the call, before working with Hackenridge to remove the bugs, one video with sound, focused on the man's computer. Once the house was cleansed, the agents showed Rogers what they had discovered, and began questioning him seriously. He broke quite quickly, and related the story, which Hackenridge recorded.

"I had been working with a special ceramic for several years and was trying to identify a use for it. I accidentally discovered it was invisible to even the most sophisticated radar surveillance. I worked with it for months, refining the surface so it was undetectable to all but the naked eye.

"Eventually I made several small rockets, and began testing. After initial experiments on just the ceramic rocket, I began comparison trials using several types of metal cased rocket, as common in amateur rocketry circles. With indulgence of time and a little luck, I found the perfect form.

"Using adapted radar, I was able to trace the metal rockets clearly. The ceramic one was undetectable, except for the motor, which I have since crafted in ceramic form. I immediately filed several patents, and started on a scope capable of detecting it. I am probably several months away from perfecting that, and so far, all I can interpret is a vague trajectory. My design is very cunning, the key is…"

From being reticent, Bob Rogers was opening up about his pet subject, and quickly lost the agents in a stream of technical theory, jargon, and scientific gobbledygook. However, they kept up apparent interest, hoping that somebody back at base would understand what the man was talking about. London asked him,

"What's so special about this rocket, this ceramic? Other than that you can't see it with radar."

Rogers replied, "This is a unique ceramic. It is aerated, you know. I hold the patent on that process as well. This is very big stuff. You have no idea how difficult it is to manufacture, virtually impossible without a very special mold, kiln, and firing parameters.

"You will remember from school art class, that a single air bubble in clay can make your masterpiece explode when it is fired, yes? I added a plasticizer and an elasticator, and I introduced a special inert gas compound into the final mixing process. These are all my patents as well."

When Rogers finished, London went back to the vehicle for a conference call with his boss. Redmond said, "Good work London, keep pressing, and see what you can find out about his move into that house, and what he did before. You'd better stick a tracking chip on his car as well, and check to see if there are any others. Something is not right about this whole thing."

London quietly entered Rogers' house through the side door. He went into the garage and set a tracking device under the sedan. He noticed one other that was not of police or agency issue. He made out a manufacturer's motif that read, "CS." He took a picture of the bug, and returned outside, where he dusted himself off, before entering the house again, loudly.

Hackenridge was trying to get samples of the ceramic, and download information concerning the rocket and special radar device. Rogers was having none of it. That was until London said to him, "I've spoken with my boss. We will be your first customer, so finish preparing the next rocket, and have the special tracking radar working as quickly as you can.

"I will arrange a display with the military, and you will receive, not only the credit as inventor, but also a lot of money. Now please, we are not here to rob you. We want to work with you. The files and sample please, otherwise the Joint Chiefs will not believe me."

Everybody knew London was not given everything, but he had the basics of the man's research. He tried to find out a little about Bob Rogers' history, but all he got was that he had been a college lecturer, before being offered a contract to develop his inventions. London pressed him, but all Rogers would say was, "They are a very big arms manufacturer. I can't even mention their name, it's part of my contract with them."

London knew they could join the dots, and left with more worries than he had expected. Later Redmond held council in ops, and asked Evelyn to attend also. The research presented was that of hobbyists, yet Redmond noted, "If the scale were upsized for military purposes, the outcome could be horrendous. It would change the face of modern warfare."

They watched the video recording of the rocket trials, which had the radar display superimposed on the screen. It was replayed several times before Redmond closed the meeting.

April remained with him and said, "We could do with another conference table here in ops, so people don't need to leave their desks, or the ops room at least, for meetings."

Redmond added, "It would also allow people to work in groups when necessary, excellent idea. 3G please make suitable arrangements."

Redmond returned to his office with April, where they went over developments. Talk turned to the mine, and they discussed ways of increasing their flow of information.

Redmond said, "We need to have cameras monitoring the inside of the hangar-like facility that can be seen from the cabin. I will mention it to 3G and see what her team can come up with. It may allow us to see what they are loading into the decoy truck."

April continued where his thoughts finished, "This is all part and parcel of our greater plan. The truck Teves followed was, and still is, regularly used as a decoy. I want to trace where it goes to each day, and get a sample of what it is carrying. I am sure it is only water—a diversion, but we need to rule it out and concentrate on the real threat.

"The team on the ridge also monitored the maroon truck. It is loaded every day, and leaves after the decoy. I will focus on those two, is Teves free to assist me?"

"This brief is already yours April, show me what you can make of it. I will ensure Teves is free to assist you."

Evelyn knocked and entered immediately, "I need to leave in a minute, and will be back the day after tomorrow. For good." She was taking her new job a lot more seriously.

Grace interrupted them and said that Profiler Nicholas Norton was in the parking lot. 3G greeted him on his way through the front door, and escorted him to Redmond's office. The man had little idea why he had been sent to them, and was slightly truculent at first. He began speaking without introduction. "Nick Norton. I am here because a mutual friend insisted. It had better be the crisis he intimated or I will be an unhappy camper."

Redmond beamed at him, rising to welcome and shake the man's hand, "I am so pleased you got here so quickly; thank you. We need your support, and are up against a nationwide threat. Their aim is to destabilize the governance of the U.S., and undermine the constitution. I have this from the President's lips, personally. The role of this team is to prevent that from happening."

It was clear Norton was taken aback. Redmond was deadly serious. April chipped in, "We need the eyes of an expert on this, and you came highly recommended."

Redmond resumed at once, "Nick, several of our team have profiling knowledge, enough to help us do our jobs in the field. I need someone who can not only deliver a full working profile of several people we are interested in, but also, somebody who can profile the teams those people work for, and various associated companies as well. Even if we had the expertise, we would be working full time on these profiles, while other things went unchecked. I need a dedicated profiler. What do you need?"

After a brief reply and attending to his requirements, Redmond showed him to a workstation. As Norton started to familiarize himself with the data, he said aside, "I feel like a freshman with a lot to prove."

§

In the late afternoon, April and Teves used Redmond's SUV to follow the decoy truck. They kept well back and let Laredo direct them. They were guided into Mission Hills where, closing fast, they found the vehicle pulling into a small factory unit. Teves drove past, not seeing any security presence.

Teves pulled around back, and April went to look over the wall, noticing lights were on inside the building. She hopped over using the hood to stand on, and ran to an open window. She saw what appeared to be water being released from an outlet, hidden behind a secret hatch on the small panel truck.

April filmed as she waited until they were done and left, switching off the lights as they went. She forced the window and went inside, waiting for her eyes to adjust to the low level light. There was a bottle nearby with a screw cap. She washed it out under a faucet and took a sample from the remains of the tank. There was not much, but it would have to do. She was securing the cock when the doors opened and the lights came on again. She finished quickly and rolled under the vehicle.

One of the guys had forgotten his bag, and the other berated him, "Why do you always forget something. C'mon! We got beers to drink and hot Latina chicks to party with."

The other replied, "What do you expect after one year of this charade, even if it is very well paid?"

"Yeah, well it's only been ten months asshole, and we only got another couple of weeks to go before your sorry butt will be looking for a new job. Hurry man, time's a-wasting."

Their banter continued, but April had a vital piece of information. As soon as the place was dark, she rolled out and cursed, soaked to the skin from a puddle she had lain in. She shook off her irritation and made good her escape. Teves asked for a look at the contents, and enquired, "You know this sample is already contaminated by the previous contents."

April said, "Sure, I washed it out under a tap, that's the best I could do. What's the problem?"

Teves said, "You need a proper field kit. Everybody does. I should have realized this sooner, Santa Madre! I'll give you one when we get back, and ensure you keep it up to date."

April put the bottle in her bag, and called Laredo, asking for CSI to be ready to identify the contents, she was sure it was just ordinary water.

"Will do, Hon. … I just received contact from the ridge. I'll patch you in."

April put the phone on speaker so Teves could hear as well. She heard her father say, "I have eyes-on the maroon truck. It just left the secure compound, are you monitoring it?"

Time passed as Laredo tracked the vehicle, first to Lemon Grove, and then headed towards El Centro. April said, "We may as well head back towards HQ. The truck is moving in our general direction. We'll try and pick it up as a tail."

A few minutes later, Laredo said, "Forget it Hon, just come home. The truck has pulled into a motel off I-8, and the guys have headed for the bar. Another decoy, this is getting me pissed."

Teves returned with April, and they presented their report. April said, "Looks like this is winding up. I was almost discovered, but one goon said they had two weeks of work left."

Redmond considered for a moment. "This could be when they take action, or not. We should not presume, but gear up to cover that eventuality. Good work April, excellent intelligence."

As evening shadows approached, information finally began to flow from Aero Drive. Redmond went down to ops and sat at the head of the new meeting table. FBI CSI had found paint transfer from the burnt out vehicle, and it matched precisely the make and model of the SUV that reportedly left the Mathers house.

Rude followed up immediately, "I have confirmed the license plate number that April had marked on her gas tank, the trail went cold when it hit CIA servers. I can hack in and discover more, but there is always a risk of backtracking involved."

Redmond shook his head. They had what they needed, for now at least. His admiration for Rude grew as his operative followed by stating, "The man from Miami and the one at the Mathers house are the same person. I have identified him as an ex-CIA operative. His DNA found a comparison on a secret NSA database. I also identified the other operative, probably his immediate boss, perhaps higher peer? He had been sequestered from Homeland Security to Opus 3, a mysterious military branch directly under the control of the Director of National Intelligence."

Redmond digested the data and moved on, "What of the bugs from Rogers' house?"

Bridger spoke up, "I followed that one up, Sir. All the bugs are listed in the Coulson Tactical Brochure, as is the tracking device London found under the sedan. The part numbers confirmed Coulson Systems made them, and are latest spec. I discovered Coulson Systems is a specialist arm of Coulson Tactical. Their catalogued products are available to anybody with enough money, so that doesn't confirm Coulson was the initiator. But we do have recordings from the Mathers house, the people who were monitoring Rogers."

Redmond said, "Good work Bridger, Rude." He returned to his office, immediately placing an extremely secure call to Euan.

Chapter 27 – Surveillance

That evening, people on the ridge were monitoring audio and visual, plus tracking all movement in and out of the secure complex, a reinforced air force hangar of World War II design, with raised roofing rows that let in light, looking similar to five raised turrets in profile from the front and rear.

The crew deployed a specially adapted, remote controlled, model helicopter. It was four feet long and could carry a payload. After they established the high roof had no inward facing cameras, they planned to deploy their own video and audio. Using special filtering equipment, they were able to select likely points for more refined eavesdropping to occur. All they needed was for someone to complete the installation once the mini-copter dropped the equipment. Shawn Cooke volunteered, he was a keen freestyle parachutist.

Making his mark, Shawn sprinted for six strides and flew into the evening air. The paraglider took wing. Cooke was invisible from the ground against the dark rocks and sky. Shawn was relieved to have such a strong eddy, and hoped it would still be there for his return flight. He gained height easily before looping out of the rising warm air current and coming to settle gently upon the roof. After unbuckling his paraglider, he identified the key points. Laredo was staying late until this operation was complete, to ensure nothing went wrong with comm.

Shawn first deployed two cameras with sound at opposite ends of the hangar internals, via a small hole he made in the glass. With a proper view of the inside revealed, the targets were adjusted, and Shawn went into action. He cut small holes in the vertical panes, and placed monitoring devices in situ, with external antennae and solar power packs placed on the top coving stone. With four special cameras left, Shawn attached one to each of the hangar roof's four corner poles, just above the existing Coulson cameras.

His work finished, his heart began to beat with worry. The strong currents from before had lightened considerably as the land cooled rapidly. There was not a moment to lose. He ran for his transport and strapped himself in. His Captain came over the headset, "Cooke, the helicopter is getting assisted lift toward the north east corner. Go for it."

Instantly, Cooke was running for safety, protecting the secrecy of the mission. He heard the miniature chopper before he saw it, and marked his place to jump. With three paces left, he put a foot on the shoulder of the ridge, jumping up onto the flat covering stone for his last stride and leapt into the unknown. He sailed into the darkness, knowing that if the wind died, he would plummet to his death below.

With a silent scream, he threw the paraglider wing high into the air and prayed the strings to go taught. They tensioned, but not enough. He was headed straight for the outer wall and safety, but dropping too quickly. A mere whiff of warmth to his left drew an instinctive reaction, as he turned to meet the rising current. He was now level with the top of the wall and holding station, but the updraft was elusive.

He spied a swirl in the sand and turned north, this time catching a decent gust that took him a lot higher. He worked with it for some time, before it petered out. He looked around and realized he was higher than the hangar, and almost over the wall a long way below. He was determined there was no way he was going to end up climbing back up the mountain to camp.

Cooke studied the terrain again, identifying one spot close to the steep sides of the mountain that looked particularly inviting. He recognized several identifying features that marked it as a probable up-thrust of power. He headed for it and after dropping height considerably, was suddenly rising into the night sky. Shawn arrived ten minutes later, having had a fantastic ride. The crew greeted him with hearty cheers and great relief.

§

Late that night Redmond wrote up his notes, not knowing how long Euan's men would need to check the information he had sent. He reasoned it would take some time and considered getting a more comfortable sofa to sleep on.

At that moment, the secure telephone rang, it was a man from Washington, D.C. who identified himself only as Agent 9. "Redmond, this is great work. I am sending you the full file now so keep the line open until I speak again."

Redmond watched as the transfers took place, and waited for the voice to come again. "Agent 2 mentioned something about ceramic missiles when he saw you. I have included what we have on that also. It is all in the folder marked Coulson Aerospace."

The line went dead. Redmond reacted to the mention of another arm of Coulson, already knowing they were big players on the global market. He examined the files and what he discovered was most disconcerting. It appeared both ex-agents were now employed directly by DeMellor Head Office, and had personal access to the CEO.

They were both listed as Board members of Coulson Securitas, and had free reign over the entire conglomerate. More importantly, it appeared John Smith was currently involved with Coulson Commodities (Mining Operations), and Coulson Tactical Technology. Johan Smidt, the man from Miami, was linked to Coulson Aerospace.

Redmond realized that John Smith and Johan Smidt were the same names, but spelled in different languages. He wondered if they were not so smart after all, since the names were obviously false. Next, he opened the file relating to Coulson Aerospace and froze. Before him was presented Rogers' missile, but it was no longer a boy-toy for use on Sunday afternoons. It was being developed as a tactical missile and there were production plans for a long-range scud version. Reading between the lines, it was obvious Coulson had already test fired the missile.

Redmond stared at the screen, his tiredness replaced by overwhelming anxiety. He ran through his options and knew which staff he would need to call on, formulating directions for the day shift. Once satisfied, he went to his room.

On the way he bumped into April, who replied to his concern, "It is nothing, honest. I had trouble sleeping, and feel a bit queasy. I have a headache coming on, it must be the time of the month."

Redmond abashed, said, "April, take a soak in the bath, and look after yourself, I am sure you will feel fine later. We need you." Redmond politely excused himself, still trying to hide his embarrassment.

After an uneventful night at headquarters, the new day started early with a bang. Regional news was running with the story of how two freight trains collided. They should have been on different tracks, but ended up headed for one another on the same one. Rude was at work as soon as he heard the news; one of the day's threats was the theft of detonators from a train.

Chapter 27

April had not slept well, but took Bridger's place beside Rude, working satellite feeds. The smash was not bad at all, the trains having virtually ground to a halt before they met.

April scanned the bogeys, and found one container near the rear of the southern train marked Coulson Group. Six men were busy offloading boxes from the rear of the container, and loading them into a nearby 4x4. She counted twelve large boxes, and nine small ones. The doors were quickly closed and the vehicle sped off, well before any local interest was shown.

Bridger joined them, but she left April to hone her skills in real time, giving her occasional tips. They tracked the vehicle into a nearby tunnel. It did not exit from either end, but simply disappeared. Bridger said, "Laredo, send a cruiser to check the route, the vehicle can't just have disappeared."

Minutes later Laredo reported, "The Deputy Sheriff just exited the other end of the tunnel. He reported the tunnel was empty and there was no secret way out."

April moved back to her own station, but continued to search, finally deducing their quarry could only be inside one six-wheeler that left in the direction from which the smaller vehicle entered, some forty seconds later.

April was slow at picking up the trail. Bridger came over at her signal, showing her how to work a grid. Once they got a registration plate, the process became semi-automated. Bridger made the call for Laredo to monitor April's work, as traffic cameras were technically under comm.

Laredo sat helping April learn how to use regular SDPD road cameras. Together, they were able to track the vehicle easily. Not surprisingly, it ended up going to Del Fuego mine.

Redmond had slept little, but returned to duty and immediately asked April how she was feeling. She said, "I'm OK, I just feel like I have a flu or something, but being busy helps. It's of no concern, you sure you had enough sleep?"

"I am fine, I need to catch up with what has happened, what's most important?"

"The railway crash up in Bakersfield, Laredo and Bridger are both on it, so it should be fun, they're really competitive. My money's on Bridger—she's a 'vamp' you know?"

April winked at him, and Redmond gave her a disconcerted look, before turning away and speaking to the team. He was as

160

perplexed as was everyone else, "Why go to all this trouble—to steal your own product? It does not make sense." The consensus was that if they wanted the equipment at the mine, they would simply have sent it there.

People were returning to routine work when April finished thinking through her idea. "I believe that only a small part of Coulson Group knows what is actually going on. I also believe that if you want to draw attention away from yourself, you stage the robbery so as it looks like a third party took the goods.

"What would you all be thinking, if this morning a truck from Coulson Tactical or Systems turned up at the mine?"

Redmond shrugged. "Go on."

"You would be thinking, 'They are putting a bomb together, maybe a nuclear bomb'."

Redmond hollered for their ridge lookouts immediately, telling the men to monitor everything that came off the truck, and record whatever speech they could. The four-wheel drive was the only thing offloaded, but they unpacked one dozen large boxes and nine smaller ones from it. The audio recording was ragged, but Rude assured them he could clean it up.

Redmond asked Nick to add this deception to his profiles, but could not shake off the feeling they were still missing the bigger picture. He called a meeting. "Listen-up everyone. This crash happened up near Bakersfield. Do we have CSI or Sheriff's Office people nearby? People we can trust to go and have a look at this supposed robbery?"

Yates spoke up, "Perry Horner was one of our very best. He retired several years back, but I'm sure he still dabbles. He has a retreat in Bear Valley Springs, a few miles south of the city, and close to the crash site."

Redmond replied at once, "Ask him to run his eye over the scene from a CSI point of view, and tell him to expect the unexpected.

"London, I want you and a small team to follow the ceramic rocket's paper trail. Obviously, Coulson Aerospace has usurped Bob Rogers' designs and are upgrading them to military specifications. I want you to go back to the day Rogers filed his first patent application, and don't stop looking until you find something. I also want everything off that guy's computer, so be there if he ever leaves the house. Rude, you will go with them; I want no mistakes on this.

"We need to understand exactly what is happening inside the secure hangar at the mine. This is top priority. Questions anyone? … Good, back to work."

London took George Hackenridge and headed off at once to the patent office. They discovered that within a few days of registration, several parties had shown great interest in Bob Rogers' designs. Official copies had been released to Johan Smidt of Coulson Aerospace.

London inspected the register and got all details relating to the copies, since these documents were not released without bona fide checks. Hackenridge said, "London, look at this patent application. There is one copy with full information, stamped 'RTA.' What does that mean?"

London did not know, so they asked the clerk. He responded matter-of-factly, "That is short for 'Released to Agency', I thought you two would know that."

London asked immediately, "Which one?"

The clerk pointed to the margin, "CIA first, and a few days later, the Secret Service. I hope there is not a problem, Sirs?"

Chapter 28 – Synchronicity

April was checking prior video feed of the maroon truck, scanning on fast forward, until she saw it leave just before sun up. She followed using traffic cam backup, eventually discovering the truck wound up near the docks. It went into a container center of some sort, and disappeared from view under a commercial awning that covered a large rear yard used by many trucks.

Bridger was occupied, so April pulled up the satellite archive, and the view was the same. The truck she was interested in drove round back, and disappeared under the yard roof. It reappeared fifteen minutes later, and looked a lot lighter.

April smelled a rat, and called Teves over to ask his advice. With a brief word to Redmond, they headed out moments later.

They arrived at what looked like a transportation hub. Teves drove around the maze of back streets to the rear of the building. The encircling brick wall was fifteen feet high, and topped with razor wire. He pulled up outside a derelict office building, overlooking the yard, and they searched for a way inside.

Stymied, April kicked in a window, and hauled Teves through. They went up the stairs and eventually found an office that overlooked the rear yard. What they saw was a typical container-loading bay, only shaded by a huge tent. It had three sections, one to offload, another to load, and a third for storage containers, or so it appeared. This did not make commercial sense, so they stayed and watched, discovering a truck pull up to one and took a storage container away. Minutes later they saw another small truck arrive, and load some things into one of the storage containers.

Teves said, "This is a private loading area. I would guess these containers are rented out. We need to be here to identify the container the mine is using. Hopefully it has not left yet. Let's find a better vantage point for next time, and get back to base."

§

While Teves returned to headquarters to follow-up, Rude had made progress with the audio, identifying several lines of inquiry, including the phrase, "Better get these ready for Homer."

No one knew if Homer was a person, a company, or a place. "D'oh" became a prolific expression in ops for the rest of the day.

Rude also isolated several distressing segments relating to prisoners. He traced these to the rear of the hangar area where a separate, secure area was located. There was a single guard on duty, and food was delivered for seven inmates. They could only presume the orderly's children were two of that number.

Once he finished his report to Redmond, Rude commented, "Chief, I am good at this, but we need a specialist soundman if you want to make progress quickly. Ronnie Spellman is the best I know of. Want me to get him here?"

"How good is he?"

Rude reluctantly admitted, "He makes me look like an amateur, but only as regards sound, that's highly specialized stuff."

"Get him here soonest. Within the hour works for me. April, I want you to focus on Del Fuego mine and tie up all the loose ends, vehicles that come and go on a regular or irregular basis. We need to identify the real threats from the red herrings, and find out what each is carrying. Teves, you are with April until this is resolved."

Rude interrupted, "Ronnie will be at Gillespie Field at 2 p.m."

Redmond said, "3G, greet him and bring him here. Thanks."

The hours passed quickly, but Redmond was conscious that certain people were putting in extended hours because they were the only ones at the post. He called Laredo to his office for a chat. He complimented her on her great work and dedication, before asking her what was wrong with the setup she had.

At first Laredo stated it was perfect, before Redmond pushed and asked, "Would your role not be a lot easier if we had a night crew to staff the station 24/7?"

Redmond knew Laredo was prickly, and could easily take his words as an affront. She was one volatile woman. She did not disappoint. "Redmond, I can handle everything. I am the best at what I do. There is no need for anybody else. I am fine!"

Redmond calmed her. "I already know you are the best, that is why I asked for you, specifically. Last night you worked very late, and today, were at your desk before 7 a.m. Your working day is too long as it is, and we are beginning to work twenty-four seven here. You, nobody can do that. I need you fresh for when the important stuff hits. I need you to find a junior partner who you can train, and will work as your apprentice. Do we have a deal?"

Begrudgingly, Laredo took his words in context, and acknowledged they needed twenty-four hour comm., something that had already occurred. To train somebody, to her mind, was a promotion, and boosted her ego.

Laredo was left to fill the position. She settled on Lonely Willowsmith, a girl she had hardly worked with at the Police Department, but one highly regarded as having great potential.

Laredo made her recommendation and Redmond approved it. The girl arrived a few hours later and was quickly brought up to speed. Laredo stayed late to ensure Lonely had the basics covered, but quickly discovered she would soon have a rival on her hands.

Redmond asked the crew on the ridge to liaise with SWAT for a full-scale invasion of the secure mine area. He made it clear the hostages were top priority, and should be evacuated at the earliest opportunity. Redmond labored the point, "This is an outline plan, not an operational brief, yet. However, you should be ready to go within ten minutes of my order."

The one thing holding Redmond back was the knowledge that they would learn a lot more, and a lot more quickly, by leaving the current surveillance in operation. However, his heart bled for the children that remained captive, and he found his emotions debilitating. He balanced this with the knowledge that if they went in too soon, their foe would simply evolve, and disappear into the ether. His job was to stop them, first time round. With a heavy heart, he knew they had to continue with the current plan, and hope the hostages were not mistreated. Obliterating the greater threat was what mattered most.

Redmond's thoughts were interrupted when Vincent Shackleton came to him. "Redmond, please see we are not disturbed. I have some very sensitive information for you. This folder contains a complete dossier on Coulson and DeMellor."

They spent a long time going over various aspects of the group's activities, and Redmond knew he would need to copy it to Nick at once, and go over it again when Evelyn returned.

Concluding, Shackleton said, "I have the latest intel on the new ceramic missile. Details are at best sketchy, but there is enough high interest to ensure top military are engaged. You will find it all in this folder."

Redmond scanned the contents, interpolating, "Vincent, what you intimate, is that top brass are aware of the ceramic missile, and are working with, or rather, monitoring the Coulson project. Your problem is that you suspect Coulson has already developed full-scale prototypes, which the military are unaware of."

"That is the essence of the game, as play stands today. Yes."

"The worry in that case is, will Coulson sell them, stockpile them, or deploy them for use in this plot against the Presidency?"

While Redmond and Shackleton were in conference, word came back from Perry Horner. He reported to Yates, "The train crash scene appeared at first sight to not be robbery. The Coulson container had a seal in place and appeared untouched. Had I not known the container had been entered, I would not have given it a second glance.

"I did find signs of human passage: dislodged gravel, flattened grass, and another seal. This one bore the same number as the one on the container, which should be impossible. It had become lodged under one of the train's wheels, and was difficult to extract.

"I did full evidence collection, fingerprint swabs of all doors and levers, seals, places people would naturally put their fingers, et cetera. I also found several cigarette butts on the adjoining track where a vehicle had obviously staged. They will have DNA samples, and were definitely fresh today. You want me to process these locally?"

Darren wanted to speak to Redmond, but he was busy with Shackleton, so he answered, "Perry, you fancy a few days fun, like old times? This is a nationwide investigation, and I have a feeling you would enjoy a working break."

His interest piqued, Perry said, "Sure Darren, it'll be good to feel useful once again. I'll drive down later today. We'll process my findings in San Diego, and I'll hang around to see where things lead." Darren knew they were short of staff, and a man of Perry's experience was very hard to find.

In the meantime, Ronnie arrived. 3G had set him up in a room with all the toys he required. He started to work at once and was soon making progress. Like Rude, he set parameters, ran algorithms, and refined them until he had eight sources isolated and could work on each one separately, before recombining them.

Once in position, he worked from the first recordings forward in time, saving most to file as being irrelevant, and identifying only certain portions as being of note.

Chapter 29 – Ceramic Missiles

April called in to see CSI, hoping for some encouraging results. Darren said, "I have tested the sample you got last night, and it was ordinary water. I am still running standard checks for toxins, biological, viral, and metallic contamination, but so far, there is nothing. I cannot check for anything more specific without more information. On the surface, all you got is water."

She accepted his finding, but was disgruntled. So much work for nothing. She wandered through to ops, her mind working overtime as she tried to find the bug that she sensed was in the works. Glued to the video on her screen, April waited, until finally, the maroon truck left the hangar. She needed to follow it. She had ignored the water dumpster, it was simply a decoy for this truck.

She limped as quickly as she could to find Teves. She smirked as Laredo exclaimed, "I have a black SUV that has just left Coulson Systems. I need four hands. Nothing for ages, and then all hell breaks loose."

Bridger tittered nearby, "Damn you Eris! Ah, 'For the Fairest,' a wedding, a–wake. It would appear 'The Golden Apple of Discord' has been cast amongst womankind once more. I'll track the SUV with satellite until Lonely gets here, you follow the truck with the drone, Hon."

Laredo spat back, "I can handle it myself, thanks Bridger, no need for you to butt-in. I got both on traffic cams also. Who's 'Eris?' your alter-ego?"

Bridger let the intended slight pass. Laredo had certainly never read the classics, nor studied Homer's Iliad, unlike herself.

Minutes later, Lonely rushed in appearing half-asleep, but eager to lend a hand. She set down a giant-size "Café a le Rude," as commercial style coffee with extra everything was now called, and took over following the SUV from Bridger.

Bridger knew something was happening when the SUV arrived at the mine. She called Redmond at once. He viewed the footage, and appeared as confused as the team.

He watched as two very large boxes were loaded into the maroon truck. They weighed the suspension down considerably. He could see the tailgate of the SUV open above the roof. It was probably being loaded with something, but the maroon truck obscured views from all cameras.

Men appeared carrying three small wooden boxes, about eight inches square. They were typical freight handling boxes, with rope carry handles on either side. These were loaded into the back of the truck, which left immediately, followed a few minutes later by the SUV.

Redmond spoke aloud, but not to anyone in particular, musing, "The three small boxes are similar to those nine from the railway heist. Perhaps they are now inside these wooden freight boxes? We should, and should not presume."

Redmond paced the room, knowing vital seconds and insight were within reach, yet being lost, despite his team's best efforts. Lonely interrupted by shouting, "The SUV is currently headed for National City."

Laredo looked at her and added with an air of foreboding, "The maroon truck is headed for Bonita, and they are right next to each other, near the docks."

Redmond whirled on reactive instinct, and took comm., "April, Teves, I need you to get to National City ASAP! Precise location of target destinations to follow, but I am sure the maroon truck is headed for the container hub you discovered yesterday. Copy?"

Teves replied, "That's where we are headed. I'll drop April off at the building we used last night, and stay with the vehicle until you have confirmed both destinations."

Redmond hovered eagerly behind the pair on comm., hoping to divine what was actually going down. The truck passed by Bonita on Highway 54, leaving only Chula Vista or National City and docks as the destination. Lonely added, "The SUV has stopped for gas—looks normal to me."

Laredo interrupted, "Truck now on I-805 Northbound, headed for National City. Less than one mile from you Teves."

Redmond made the call, "Bridger, I need satellite feed over National City harbor, now."

"I am already locked on Sir, but still have no view under the container hub's roof."

Redmond continued, "Laredo, can you find any angle with the drone to see inside?"

"Not without flying it in there, all the surrounding buildings are too tall. We need a state of the art dragonfly drone to do that, Sir. You should order some."

Moments passed; Laredo said, "Truck now entering container hub … going round to the rear yard. You will have eyes on in a moment April."

April watched as the maroon truck came into view, and pulled up beside one container. She was already shooting video, and zoomed in to get container numbers, and shots of the people.

Lonely came over comm., "SUV now entering same container hub, keep your eyes peeled. Yes, confirm. Auto is headed for the rear loading bay."

Teves was already inside the old office building. He raced up the stairs and joined April. He brought out his binoculars, notepad, and pen, as April continued to zoom in video mode. They both tracked what happened next.

The two large boxes were loaded into the container using a forklift truck. They almost filled it, but there were a few feet of space left before the tailgate. The three small freight boxes were loaded next.

The SUV parked nearby, and two men loaded five boxes into the rear of the container, the last appearing to be small, and extremely heavy. John Smith placed a seal and talked with a hub official. Some minutes later, both vehicles departed. Teves said, "Let's go check this out."

Teves flashed his badge at the gate, and asked the guard to see the list of scheduled, outgoing containers. The one they were interested in was due for departure the next day. Its reported destination was Dallas, Texas. Teves said casually, "I thought all containers went to the docks."

Security replied, "Not at all, about one third come from the docks, containers stage here to be split into delivery runs. Around half are going to the docks, plus most of our rental containers. The rest, like the one you pointed out, are completely unrelated to the docks at all."

Teves realized they had wasted their time, but did give Redmond a brief verbal report, a full written report to follow when they got back. He drove towards the Fire Department, having already made an appointment to see the Fire Marshal. He was greeted warmly, and Teves said, "This is April Bekkons, FBI. We are working this case together, we can talk freely. You wanted to see me?"

The Fire Marshal said, "I got your noted input from the senior investigator of the fireworks blaze. He found nothing related to any known detonation device. The seat of the fire appeared to be towards the middle of the warehouse, and probably started near the top of the stored boxes.

"The strange thing is, there were no internal patrols, no cigarettes. The fireworks were still packaged in large, sturdy, wooden shipping boxes, and came from Leiyang in China, as did most everything else, except for the electronic show controllers. With Chinese quality in mind, all we can assume is that a firework self-ignited. Why the interest?"

Teves looked concerned, "Nothing else? The reason I ask is, that after the event, we discovered information stating the warehouse would be targeted. It was dated four days prior to the fire."

The Fire Marshal returned, "That's why I wanted to speak to you privately. The official report is now filed. The only thing I have, is one passerby reported glimpsing a shooting star, but when she turned to look for it, it was gone. The place erupted moments later. We looked for metal casings of a rocket, just to be sure, and after your warning, but there was zilch."

Teves swore, "Santa Madre! Did anyone note any ceramic at the scene?"

The Marshal thumbed through the report and said, "Yes. There is small mention of ceramic, but it was scattered all over the place. Why? Is that important?"

April quickly interjected, "No, it is of no importance. Teves, looks like we wasted our time. My theory is a dud. Oh well. This information, like the other stuff we got from this informant, is useless."

Teves was quick to catch on to her ploy, and added, "I guess so April, back to the drawing board. Thanks Marshal, I'm sorry we wasted your time. You never know, it could have been a good lead. I'll see you at the Fireman's Ball in a few weeks…"

As soon as they were back in the SUV, Teves headed directly for the firework warehouse. The building was a wreck, and security tried to stop them entering, stating, "This place has been condemned as unsafe, and will soon be demolished. I cannot stop you from entering, with your badges, but I remind you, you do so at your own peril."

Teves thanked him, and they went inside. Using the fire report, he marked the probable seat of the blaze. They worked outwards in straight lines, finding a ring of ceramic fragments, before using this as a grid search parameter. They collected all they could find, hoping for some larger samples, but there were none.

April sat down to take a break, and Teves sidled over to her, patting her on the back as he joined her. April jerked away from his gentle touch, but said, "Sorry Manny, that was a bit sore for some reason. But thank you. I think I have a dose of the flu. I feel dead tired all the time, and bending over like this makes me want to be sick. Let me rest, and I will be fine in a moment."

Teves was about to speak, when the guard popped his head inside the door and shouted, "The demolition crew has just arrived, you will need to be out of here very soon."

Teves said, "April, one last effort and then I'll take you to see a doctor. We need to walk these inside walls. Rest a moment if you need to, I'll start right away."

April got to her feet, following Teves to one wall, and started walking in the opposite direction. She had not gone far when she called out, "Manny, over here. I have a lot of ceramic in one place, as if it hit the wall and shattered."

They collected the evidence, which looked like a ceramic jigsaw puzzle, but they knew the pieces, like shattered china, fitted together. They had what they needed, and headed off for late lunch.

Chapter 30 – Window Seat

Earlier that morning, Bob Rogers had received a telephone call, one Laredo monitored. He was summoned to a meeting against his will, and left in his vehicle. Bridger called Redmond over.

Minutes later, London left for Rogers' home with Hackenridge and Rude in support. Meanwhile, Redmond took 3G in civvies, and let Laredo guide them to the point of interception. Rogers was headed to Lemon Grove. Redmond pulled into the chic, trendy mall moments later, and watched as Rogers looked around clueless. A man came out of a restaurant and went over to greet him. Redmond and 3G were immediately on their way inside.

Redmond flashed his badge and asked, "Where was the man, who just went outside, sitting?"

He was pointed to a quiet booth facing the courtyard. Redmond turned to the waitress and said, "Interrupt us when we have just moved past the booth in question, and offer us a table across the room. Thank you."

Grace was playing the part of a woman who wanted to sit at a window on the plaza side. They were getting into a small argument by the time they reached the booth, noticing two others already present. 3G grasped the wooden privacy panels, setting one bug in place, as Redmond did likewise on the other side. They tried the next booth, which appeared to be empty, but the waitress caught up with them and said, "I'm sorry, this booth is already booked. Why don't you try a window seat on the other side, which has a view of the pool."

Grace liked the idea as soon as she learned it was stocked with Koi, and immediately dragged her partner off to check it out. They had acted completely oblivious of the people at their table of interest.

Laredo had great feed, as Redmond and Grace enjoyed a leisurely breakfast. A lot was said to the inventor, most of it threatening, but Bob Rogers was reluctant to commit to a date when his ceramic missile radar detector would become operational.

The man from Miami turned the screw, "Bob, we have been friends now for a many years, and know it hurts me to do this, but there are things you must understand. For instance, we need your radar working within one week. This is not a request. It is a fact of your continued existence in this world."

To emphasize his point, Johan Smidt made a call, and once connected passed the cell to Rogers. "Speak to your parents while they are still alive, Bob. One of them will be dead in seven-days if you do not do what we ask. A few days later, we will kill the other one, before starting on your sister and her family. Enjoy the phone call. It may be the last time you ever speak to any of them. That is, unless you give us what we want."

Laredo had Ronnie working real-time to try and narrow down options this phone call afforded. He found the channel and got great results, honing and narrowing the contact source within the mine facility. Laredo superimposed cell phone triangulation, thus defining parameters within the structure where the hostages were being held.

Bob Rogers visibly wilted in his seat. After speaking very briefly with his parents, he agreed to do whatever he could to get the device they wanted working as quickly as possible. The meeting did not last long. Bob left his food untouched, ambling out a broken man ready to commit suicide. Except for his parents' confinement, he would have done so eagerly. But to protect them, he returned to his cave.

§

As Redmond pulled into Lemon Grove, London arrived at Bob Rogers' home. They hurried to inspect the man's computer, but London knew something wasn't right, the side door was ajar. London pressed ahead, alone, and heard voices complaining about accessing the computer. London placed an audio bug on a mains wire near the corner of the kitchen, before he fell back to place a locator under the vehicle in the garage.

London placed a bug under the car and checked for other transponders, and found another that should not have been there. It had the letters 'CS' on it, and looked just like the other one he found under the orderly's car. This was pissing him off. He called back the license plate and began to make his way out. Laredo stopped him, "They are leaving. You better hide."

Moving quickly London responded, "Get Hackenridge to back the vehicle a few houses away from here and duck down inside. I will be fine. Radio silence until they leave."

London crouched behind a large, red toolbox trolley and switched off his receivers. He pulled his Glock, set his finger to squeeze the trigger, and waited.

The men passed him by, oblivious of his presence, and within thirty seconds were gone. London came out of hiding and had the others join him in the house. Laredo assured him the vehicle was being traced and a destination would be forthcoming.

Rude fired-up the computer and looked at it for a moment before asking, "London, is this the same computer you saw last time?"

London said, "All PCs look the same to me. No, wait, this is not the same one. There is a scratch here, the one we saw last time did not have that." Hackenridge was certain the front panel was different from before. He asked London to show him the clip from their last visit, and was proved correct. This was a different PC.

Rude closed the computer down and started to search. In time, he found another tower computer hidden behind the sofa in the main room, and fired that up. The password encryption was good and would take some time to get around out in the field.

To save time, Rude booted to Bios management and configuration, and made a new socket connection to his laptop. He gave his captive audience a short lecture on the benefits of Unix as he initiated a bit-level copy of the drive. He would get around the password problems easily back at the base. The copy would take forty-five minutes, regardless of how full the drive was.

London asked Rude, "Can we copy the other hard drive also? Just in case."

"No problem, I'll get it started. I thought you only wanted this one."

Minutes turned into tens of minutes. Laredo informed them Rogers was on his way back, and they had perhaps twenty minutes to get out of there.

London asked Rude, "How much longer?"

"Twenty-three minutes, perhaps less—it's just like sex, the end always comes unexpectedly quickly."

London gave him a quizzical look, before speaking rapidly into his headset. As a result, Rogers was pulled over by traffic police for a routine check. They took their time, but were also under instructions not to find anything, just delay for as long as possible without it becoming obvious.

As it turned out, one of Rogers' brake lights was faulty, which provided all the necessary means of traffic in order to make the interception. It bought them ten minutes. Rogers pulled into his garage as London and Hackenridge left by the side door. Rude had already reconnected the decoy computer, and hurried back after locking the side door when his associates left. All he had to do was put the real computer back behind the sofa, and leave by the front door.

He returned the computer to its hideaway as the outer garage door closed with a loud bang. He was missing his laptop. It was on the side near the computer desk. Rude ran and picked it up, reckless to being caught, but made it back into the living room, easing the door closed as it had been. He heard the inner garage door into the house slam shut, and slid out of the front door, which closed against the self-locking catch. Turning, he ran and rounded the corner, grateful to make the safety of London's sedan.

Michael watched them leave, and nodded his head. He filed the day's events in the part of his mind that usually worked best, before ambling over to have a leisurely chat with his very good friend, Thomas Jefferson.

Teves and April arrived back at HQ, and went to see Darren at once. He was preoccupied, but Perry, standing nearby, volunteered to assist them. He had already processed the evidence from Bakersfield, and been shown how to enter the data and cross-reference with their state of the art systems. He did not have a specific job to do, so they gave him their evidence and began to fill him in on the background. April coughed, and then wretched, but nothing came up. She said, "Excuse me, but my headache has come back. I need to lie down for a minute."

The men watched her leave, and Teves said, "I have known her a long time, and never known her like this. It's the strangest flu I ever came across. Anyway, we believe these to be pieces of a ceramic missile…"

Chapter 31 – A Dose of the Flu

Evelyn returned the next morning and discovered 3G had already provided a suitable office for her adjoining Redmond's. She settled in to work at once, and was surprised just how quickly things had moved on.

Perry Horner had also adapted well to his new surroundings, and was busy examining the ceramic pieces brought in the evening before.

April was feeling a bit better, and took time to assist him, hoping he could confirm they were parts of a ceramic missile. In due course, they developed an unusual bond, one that brought her youthful enthusiasm and his time-served experience to a new level of inquisitiveness. Perry was also anxious for test results, and soon the hits started coming. Johan Smidt was the first to be identified at the site of the train crash.

Perry brought with him a calming influence and a nose for priority, quickly linking previous incidents and slowly building a pattern. He took time to work with Nick Norton, moving him more centrally into the heart of their investigation. Without being officially asked, it appeared Perry had decided to stay for the duration. With a word from April, Evelyn put him on the books.

It did not take Rude long to hack into his copies of Rogers' hard drives, but it did take him a while to find all the related files and get past folder specific encryption. He assembled a full set of data in a hierarchy, before examining the individual components and comparing the information London had been given, with what was now available. The rocket was actually far more advanced than Rogers previously led them to believe.

Rude took his time with the tracking device, wanting to make certain he had all the pertinent facts and understood them. He began to revere Rogers increasingly. The man had devised a way to trace the invisible rocket when in flight. He had adapted a density modulator to identify the unique signature of the missile, it was very clever. Given he already had the frequency and density data, Rude thought it possible they could build a replica. He spent time working on it, and although the design was crude, it was a lot more than the nothing they had otherwise.

Redmond took Rude's report and thanked him for his efforts. He knew they could perhaps hash something together themselves, but that was highly impractical and amateurish, especially with the status of the nation at stake. Once alone Redmond placed a call to Vincent, and they agreed to meet in two hours' time.

Shackleton arrived before lunchtime and conferred with Redmond and London, April leaving moments later to lie down, to ease her recurring headache. They showed him Rogers' work and asked if he knew of anyone who could build the tracking device. Vincent asked for the room and use of the secure satellite phone. Once alone, he made several calls. He received a call back that a small team from Marine Corps Logistics, Barstow, would be on site that evening.

As Redmond saw Shackleton to the elevator, they passed April returning to her desk in ops. She appeared distracted. Redmond following her moments later, found her still feeling out of sorts.

She sat at her desk and Perry approached her. "April, great news, the ceramic is unlike anything I have ever seen before, except, it resembles Bob Rogers' design in greatest detail, and matches the samples London got from him earlier. The ingredients, are very strange, and a match to his, even the gases he said he incorporated.

"The best of it is, I found traces of burnt propellant on some of the samples. You found the rocket motor April!"

April rose with a big smile on her face, and went to hug Perry, but somehow tottered, and fell back into her seat, coughing badly. This time she wretched up a little sick into a tissue. Perry went to pat her back, but she reacted to his slight tap and pulled away. He stood back and stared at her, his mind working. This was not normal, and neither was it influenza.

He squatted down before her, even though it hurt his knees, and took her hands in his own. In a fatherly manner, he asked her to tell him when she had started feeling ill.

April was dismissive, saying it was just girl stuff, but Perry persisted. She revealed she was fine until a few evenings ago. Perry kept pressing, taking her back step by step, until he discovered that earlier on the night in question, she had rolled in a puddle of water under the decoy truck, lain on her back in it, and rolled out again.

Perry took a deep breath. "Do you mind... Could we take a look at your back?"

April nodded and started to pull up the back of her shirt. Perry found himself staring at a livid sunburn, peeling and in places cracked, fractures starting to seep a little blood. He called Redmond over at once, and spoke to him in whispers as April wretched once more.

Perry stormed into CSI demanding a Geiger counter. Darren, obsessed with his work, turned angrily to face him down. Jules went to a cupboard and got the device.

Perry turned his back, ignoring Yates' bluster, and went straight to the evidence lockers, and asked Siouxi for the water sample. He ran the counter over the outside of the bottle. It measured 12 Gy.

The others came behind him, and stopped to stare. Perry said, "Full quarantine now. This is radioactive, and everybody here needs immediate decontamination, and radiation badges. See to it, I have a young life to save. April lay in this shit for far too long! Excuse me, Darren."

Perry ran through to ops and shouted, "April, wash immediately, you have radiation poisoning. The water you rolled in was radioactive. Shower now. Move!"

Redmond swept her into his arms and ran for the bathroom, hollering for any female to join him. Bridger left her desk at once. Perry followed them, shouting; "Long shower, keep washing her, lots of soap. All her clothing needs to be disposed of. Have we got a radiation bag?"

Redmond grimaced, and glancing back as he ran, yelled, "See 3G, she will have what you need."

Less than a minute passed before 3G raced to them, carrying a large bag on her shoulder, a medic followed her with another. Redmond left the female bathroom with concern and relief, and asked, "Perry, how did you know?"

Perry looked up at the boss impishly and replied, "Let's just say I've been there, and it is not very pleasant." He smiled knowingly, and turning, walked away. Teves rushed up full of concern, having just received the news; Redmond filled him in.

3G came out a short while later and reported, "The radiation poisoning should not be too bad, once effectively treated. I have given her potassium iodide and DPTA, which should get rid of what is in her system. The thing is, her exposure was not too great, comparatively, but occurred over most of her body. She will need hospital treatment once she is cleansed."

Teves spoke up, "I know of an exceptional physician, leave this with me. I'll let Bill and Annaliese know at once."

Redmond said, "Excellent. See to it Teves, this is your top priority as of now. So, to hazard a prognosis, there is a lot of a slight contamination, rather than a large dose in one specific area. This is encouraging. Have your medic attend to CSI immediately, ops, all personnel even."

3G replied, "Here are your pills, take them now, just to be safe. I will issue radiation badges to all personnel, including visitors. The water and clothes will be put in separate sealed containers for storage, examination, and disposal."

Redmond said, "Great work 3G." His mind was working, and he spoke his thoughts aloud, "So, our truck was not actually a decoy after all. It was dumping radioactive water every day, but in small enough quantities scattered all over the region, so as not to be detected by any one sewage company. Clever. Teves, we will need a confirmation sample, but not today, see to April first. I'm gonna have a word with Nick, as this tells us a lot about our enemy."

Redmond went back into ops, looking for the profiler, but was sidetracked by Ronnie Spellman in his workshop. Intrigued, he went through, waving for London to join him. They found a very jubilant audio guy making progress, and he wasted no time in offering his latest. "I spent my initial time working on eight feeds that were easy to segregate from the mine audio. They are now recording each one for me independently. Some of these were for the prisoner area, and that continues to be of top priority.

"This morning I set out to try and identify other feeds, and used cross-channel Doppler sine curves to make extra gain—its all to do with time taken between differing inputs, before the source and related echo comes to another source: DST. Distance, Speed, Time, and simple math. By triangulating three sources, I can work out where a speaker is located. The results are heightened when I combine all the feeds. That's wicked, don't you think?"

Two pairs of eyes continued to stare blankly at him. Ronnie continued oblivious, "Anyway, the top-level information we have been trying to uncover was simply not forthcoming, so this was a means to circumvent background noise and detect other conversations.

"I concluded this was because of the highly protected area within the main facility. There has always been major interference in that area, and I set about trying to segregate it.

"I managed to isolate electrical signatures of some seriously large processing equipment, and later searched specifically for the tell-tale spikes of uranium two thirty-five and two thirty-eight. Eventually I isolated two thirty-five, and found they fluctuated over a twenty-four hour period. My conclusion is the yellow cake they are mining is being processed on site, and being refined to weapons-grade for onward transportation."

Redmond clenched his fist and shouted, "Excellent work Ronnie! Moments ago I discovered how they are dumping the coolant water, which is also radioactive. This confirms what they are up to, in my mind at least."

Ronnie enthused, and continued, "The signatures I have correspond to the Zippe Centrifuge, a device used for uranium enrichment. I believe this fits nicely with what you have already discovered. I cannot state the above with one hundred percent certainty, but it is highly likely.

"I took all these signatures and added them to my filters. By doing so, I was able to remove most of the background noise. I focused on a very narrow band appropriate to speech, and male pattern speech in particular. By triangulating on this specific point, I appear to have isolated some sort of inner control room, where information is beginning to flow. Here are some of the samples I have cleaned up so far …"

They listened and heard snatches of conversation concerning the refining process, and distribution. If Ronnie were correct, the decoy transfer vehicle, now known to be carrying radioactive water, would leave the hangar at 4:28 that evening, much earlier than usual. Redmond congratulated him, "Great progress Ronnie. Continue cleaning up the audio in that specific area. This, and that of the prisoners, remains top priority."

London stated as they left Ronnie's lab, "We need to prioritize."

Redmond acceded, "Indeed we do. You heard Perry identified Bob Rogers' ceramic missile as being the delivery device that started the firework warehouse blaze. We now have indicative proof of uranium enrichment. Put these two together, and we got serious problems. Let's talk this over with Nick."

Later that afternoon, the 'decoy' truck was loaded, and departed at precisely 4:28. Redmond made a point of congratulating Ronnie, and encouraged him to excel. April had already received treatment from the doctor in Rosa's town, and insisted on going to the water dumpsite with Teves.

Teves refused, and they had a war of words. April stated flatly, "I have already been exposed, so I am going in. I know the truck, I know the valve, I have my field kit, and I'll get a wind breaker made from radiation proof cloth off 3G. I promise never to roll in that shit again."

Reluctantly, Teves backed down. They tracked the overloaded vehicle, and both witnessed it appearing to dump water. April was again able to get residue water from the tank, this time filling two sterile bottles Darren had given her, sealing them in a radiation proof bag.

Yates later confirmed the contents were ordinary and local river water, but this time added that it was highly radioactive, and probably used as coolant during processing.

That was all the confirmation Redmond needed. He instantly cancelled all future observations of the truck, and insisted April take another fully cleansing shower.

Chapter 32 – Infiltrated

The crew from Barstow arrived just after 8 p.m. and set to work immediately. There were three of them, the Captain leaving the bulk of the work on the new radar detector to his Sergeant. The Corporal was there to run wiring and create a new monitoring station, which was set between and adjoining, both Laredo's and Lonely's workspaces.

The Sergeant was very interested in the design and asked for a copy, only to be denied by Redmond. Nonplussed by the rebuff, the soldiers did an excellent job, adapting an already state of the art radar system that had monitoring capability for the entire U.S. The Sergeant added an extra panel, purely for administering ceramic missile detection and allowing operator parameters to be preset, or input manually. He set the fields as specified in Rogers' notes, and switched it on. Everything checked out, except they were waiting for the second team to arrive with satellite dishes, and establish connectivity to the military grid.

The Captain was frustrated, and had made several calls to ask where the satellite fixing crew were. News came from the main gate, the team had finally arrived. They were shown into ops, and briefed by the Captain. One of them leaned casually against Laredo's desk, and she sent him away with a flea in his ear. They left moments later, and were shown upstairs.

The Corporal supervised setup on the roof for a few minutes, before watching his counterpart begin running cabling down the central core of the building. Routing would take forty minutes, but within the hour, the system was scheduled to be online and working.

Down in ops, they were unable to check the new software against a ceramic missile, but the Sergeant showed Laredo, Lonely, Rude, Bridger, and April, how to monitor for existing and known objects, such as aircraft and regular missiles. Effectively, he gave them a crash-course in how to be a modern radar specialist.

April did not need the depth of knowledge and sidled away, wondering why the fitting crew was taking so long to finish up. She reasoned they should have completed already, and be gone.

She went to find the men, but the roof was clear, and upon checking outside, everything appeared to have been put back in

183

their vehicle. However, there was no sign of them. She wandered through the lower levels, becoming more perturbed as seconds ticked by.

There were lights on in the computer room. She entered and found the two missing men working to either side of the stacked server array. "What the hell are you doing?" she bawled, stalking up to them.

The senior rose and greeted her casually; "Ma'am, we are simply being thorough and completing the installation. We should be done in a couple of minutes."

"Exactly what are you doing with those bundles?"

"Nothing to worry your pretty little head about, sweetheart." Her world went black.

She came to a minute later disorientated, with a throbbing head, her hands tied tightly behind her back. She had a strip of duct tape over her mouth that prevented her from calling out for help, and her headset had been removed.

Through slitted eyelids, April watched, monitoring everything the man nearest her was doing. He appeared to be placing charges. She knew this would be a major blow to the very heart of their operation.

The fitter across the other side asked for assistance with placing his explosives, and the leader cast a dismissive glance back at April, before going to assist. She rolled immediately he was out of sight, taking an electricians knife and cutting her bonds. She heard movement and rolled back to her former position just in time.

The man reached to his side and lifted a large amount of explosive, setting it within one of the lower housings. April rose silently and took him out with one blow to the back of his neck. She taped him and covered his mouth, searching his pockets to retrieve her headset, applying it, and turning it on.

She whispered into the mic, hoping Laredo was still monitoring comm. There was no reply. She crept quietly to the side of the server stack, and found the other man busy and in plain sight. She could not move against him without being seen and giving him warning. She waited until he turned to take a large block of explosive and place it against the backup array.

With his back to her, she crept forward and prepared to strike. Lonely came over comm. at that moment, and the man looked round. April struck, but he was forewarned and half parried her first blow. April shouted into the mic as they set for a fight, "Computer room compromised, bombs being set, two men, one down, one I am fighting. Assist now."

An alarm sounded as April closed on the man. He pulled a pistol and aimed to fire at her. She feinted and kicked the gun out of his hand, following with a blow to the head. He fell awkwardly, but near his pistol, and grabbing for his gun, rolled to fire at her again. April somersaulted for distraction. He lost target, twisting his body to try to get a new line of fire. The plaster cast in his face would be the last thing he remembered. April had him taped up by the time 3G rushed in with her security detail.

April left 3G to clear up the mess of men, and sauntered back to ops, ignoring the military, and headed for her workstation. She did not understand why it was always her that worked things out. She thought about a calming shot of Rebel Yell.

The Captain was full of apologies, which April dismissed at once as being irrelevant. Redmond asked him to make light of the deception in his report, since it would compromise their investigation. For now, they needed to keep it in-house, and on a severely restricted basis. The Barstow team left shortly after. The two fitters were conducted to the care of Salamander.

3G tasked Hershey to remove the explosive devices and add them to their arsenal. "You robbed me of my chocolate, April," he said, as he started to collect the plastique. "But I can't say I'm sorry you stopped them before the devices could be primed and armed."

§

Salamander continued with his interrogations of existing and newer captives. He was doing well, but all leads invariably came back to Del Fuego mine.

He received the new prisoners and wasted no time interrogating them. April reminded Redmond that the military Humvees they followed to Hoover Dam came from Twentynine Palms. Salamander became most interested in getting to the bottom of that fact. He swiftly moved to more intense forms of information extraction. The methods he used were borderline but the information soon flowed. They confirmed Twentynine Palms was a vast training base, mainly Navy, but also home to many arms and cliques of the military machine. One of the men revealed,

Chapter 32

"We're based at Twentynine Palms and work for Opus 3. Their civilian cover is ADF."

Salamander found the chain of command well hidden, and did not consider the men in custody to have access to higher information.

Chapter 33 – Anchorage Vista

Redmond went into ops early the next morning, having received a call from Ronnie. The sound tech had isolated more conversations from inside the secure area:

Clip 1:

Voice 1: "The processing is almost complete. All targets will be met on time."

Voice 2: "Good. What of Arizona?"

Voice 1: "That will be ready by tomorrow morning. You want me to arrange the rig?"

Voice 2: "No, there has been a complication on site. I need to defer. Prepare for transfer, but take no action. We will speak later."

Clip 2:

Voice 2: "There has been a change of plan. Contact Anchorage Vista and tell them this container will load as soon as possible. You better get on the documentation now. We will finish this with Arizona, and make good time, they may be on to us."

Voice 1: "Shit! You sure? OK, we are a go for tomorrow, I will inform the Captain, shipping, and port authorities at once."

Voice 2: "Good, the container will have to leave here by road. Contact Opus 3, tell them to get ADF to send a road train fit for the purpose. We will load tomorrow, as soon as it arrives."

Redmond wheeled out of the office to ops. "Skype me to the ridge. I want Bill, Annaliese, and Captain Williams in on this." Soon the screen filled with the faces of those watching from above.

Redmond hollered, "Get me what you can on something called 'Anchorage Vista'. I believe it to be a container ship now in dock hereabouts, and sailing late tomorrow."

Both Laredo and Bridger were on the task at once, competing as usual, Bridger beating her rival by a couple of seconds. "Anchorage Vista is docked at pier nine and due to sail with the morning tide, just after midnight tomorrow."

Not to be outdone Laredo added, "She is due to cast-off at 0415 hours, that is on the day after tomorrow, early morning."

The girls exchanged glances, both of esteem and contest. Redmond ignored the rivalry, "Thank you, both of you. Excellent work. Teves, April, I want eyes on, we need to learn a lot more about this operation. Laredo, do you have a destination?"

"Anchorage, Sir. It is the ship's home port."

Redmond stilled her enthusiasm, "I need to know where those containers are actually going. This should be stated on the cargo manifest. Teves, get eye's-on the paperwork, we need the final destination. April, you are convalescing but can join Manny for the ride. No more action until you are well and fully fit again, OK?

"Ridge Team, I need immediate confirmation of a tractor and trailer capable of hauling a forty-foot container. Expect this to appear sometime tomorrow. All eyes and audio on this please.

"Ladies and Gentlemen, I believe we are now entering the final sequences. While the mining operation may continue, the thrust we are seeking to understand will end in approximately twelve days time, according to information April obtained.

"Rude, please hone your future research to reflect this timetable, and look for any aggregation of potential occurrences over, say, the next three weeks at the outside. I am looking for a surge, and a drop-off point. That is when it will happen.

"What 'it' is remains to be identified, but we still go with a major threat and destabilization of the American system of government. The nuclear component can never be dismissed, but blowing up Washington with an atomic bomb simply does not do it for me, so look at what else could occur. Are we all clear on this? … Good, then let's get to it."

The next morning Redmond called everyone together for the morning briefing in ops. "Today we will at last be witness to some major developments, and perhaps begin to understand exactly what we are all up against. I know you will all give of your best. Just remain alert and notice anything that is unusual, or breaks the pattern we have so far established. Thank You."

Later that day, the crew on the ridge was the first to notice a large truck headed along the new road towards the mine. It was early afternoon, and the freight rig made slow progress over the rough trail. It entered through the large rear hangar doors nearest the mountains, and would presumably leave via similar doors at the other end. The team had good visuals and sound. The driver and the rig were from ADF, but little else was forthcoming.

The container loaded within forty minutes, but due to the angle of parking, hardly anything could be seen, apart from a forklift truck making twenty-one trips to the back. The rig departed a few minutes after the doors were sealed.

Redmond was frustrated, and asked the ridge team to get more cameras in situation for the next loading. He was untactfully curt, which manifested as mean. He took his concerns back to his office, where April eased his mind, before she left to find Teves.

April and Teves took watch on pier nine, and with live feed from Laredo, were able to follow when the container from the mine arrived, and entered the loading area. Paperwork was checked, and with sailing time approaching, it was only a few hours before it was loaded on board. Teves got binoculars on the container number, and it matched their information. He and April stayed to ensure the cargo was not off-loaded, and were happy when the ship finally left its berth at 0419 hours.

Teves wanted to complete the investigation, and headed for Shipping Control. He had the wrong badge and was stonewalled. He called Lonely for help, who woke Laredo, asking if she knew of anybody trustworthy to do with harbor police. Laredo offered a few names, before making a personal call, and going back to sleep.

Toby Raill met them some time later, and made it plain he was doing a personal favor for Laredo. It was very clear he and Teves came from opposing quarters of the police spectrum, but his help was greatly needed. Teves had hoped to make this a personable exchange, but Raill was all work and had no time for indulgences.

Teves said, "We need everything you got on this container;" The Undersheriff handed over a document, insisting, "The final destination is most important."

Raill left them in the Docklands Diner, a grand title for one of the worst eateries in the city of San Diego, and said, "I'll be back."

Teves smirked to April, "He'd be a shoe-in for a dumb-ball traffic cop, all bully bullshit, and no brains."

April laughed, but the waiting was hard. Come time, April opened up about her former life, and why she ran away from home. More was said with looks and touches, as their deeper understandings of each other's lives grew considerably. Teves' fatherly indulgence was that of counselor, and best friend.

A long time later, Raill came back. His attitude was perfunctory, but his report was excellent. "According to the sailing manifest, the Anchorage Vista will coastal hop, and reach Anchorage in six days' time. The container number you gave me is listed, and has no forwarding destination. That means it will be stored in the Anchorage container hub until somebody comes to collect it. This is normal practice for private shipping. The answers you now seek lie in Alaska.

"Please tell Laredo we miss her, but not too much. She will understand. Good day and bon voyage, as we mariners say."

The maritime cop sauntered away like a gunfighter looking for a new kid to kill, and without a backward glance. Teves said, "Mariner? I bet he's never even been to sea."

April laughed, and they wasted no time in getting out of the place, but they had the information they needed. April was quiet and Teves prompted her until she revealed, "I just want to go somewhere, anywhere they sell normal food and have normal patrons. Is that a big thing to ask?"

Teves chuckled, and on impulse, took her to his home to share early breakfast with his family. April was blown away by the change in dynamic, not only from the docks, but to be a part of a vibrant family unit—something long denied her. The visit restored her faith in humanity, especially when Teves called in a brief report, and Xochitl grabbed the phone, telling Redmond they would stay to sleep, and recover in her home.

Redmond gave them leave, knowing more was afoot than just a few hours downtime. He threw his energy into the tasks of the day. One concerned the exact location of the prisoners inside the hangar. This came when the rear doors were opened yesterday for the rig to enter. Existing triangulation was augmented with additional input from the ridge. This enabled Ronnie to fix the exact position and possible layout of the secure area. In turn, this meant that the plan for infiltration was updated.

By the time Teves and April returned to HQ, Redmond had discussed options with London. They concluded that the reference to Arizona had great bearing upon what they would do next. Their discussion was not conclusive.

Redmond made his way up for lunch a lot later than planned. In the canteen, he sat with Teves and April, bringing them up to speed on what had transpired. Although still sleepy, April could not let go of the mention of Arizona. She probed it with her mind, as her fork probed the food on her plate. Teves and Redmond talked quietly as she thought, neither of them wishing to interrupt any insight that might be forthcoming.

Eventually she took a mouthful of food, as she chewed over her words carefully, "The only thing, the only place we know of in

Arizona is the weird farm at Hoover Dam. The hotel in Phoenix was just a meeting place, agreed?

"We have supposed this is all to do with the diversion channels of the Hoover Dam. What if we're wrong? What if they are doing something completely different? I think we need to find out exactly what is going on in there, and quickly."

Redmond seized on her words, "This may or may not be the reference to Arizona mentioned at Del Fuego mine. But it remains something we should already have followed up. I'll see to it."

Redmond left immediately, his meal half-eaten, to find London and put a team in place. They needed to infiltrate Hoover Dam. The farm was so far off the beaten track, it simply wasn't a place to wander up to and ask for a job. A full tactical assault would show their hand, yet they needed information from the inside.

Redmond pulled up the satellite feed and was surprised to find the heavy trucks had now left the scene, and the conveyor belt and hopper feeding them had been dismantled.

He concluded that as digging had stopped, they must have moved on to the next phase. If this were not related to Hoover Dam, could they be commissioning the base for its true purpose? They had to be hiring, but how and where?

Redmond called Bridger into his office and they agreed that most likely any hiring would be done through ADF, although the names Coulson and DeMellor were not to be ignored. Redmond thought it likely most positions of any note would be filled internally, or via Twentynine Palms, but there were a raft of support services and manual labor that could be required, depending upon the nature of the site.

Bridger left with a new brief. It proved to be a painful, slow process. Leads appeared, but evaporated as quickly. She was searching ads in local newspapers when she got her first hit. An ad for kitchen staff in the Boulder City News, a weekly newspaper that had a local catchment area. The contact telephone number was Twentynine Palms. She called at once, unprepared for immediate interest and got an interview in the name of Maria Mendez.

She spoke to Redmond right away, and he authorized the action. Mendez was put out, but gathered herself for the greater good, and prepared to go undercover. She was given a suitable cover story, and references that were solid without being too good.

Chapter 33

Bridger was buoyed with success and found similar ads in other local newspapers in and around the Vegas area. The hits came, which she collated and presented four to Redmond. He assigned London the task of getting as many of their people inside as possible. This saw Walker, Hackenridge, and London himself being given interviews, again at Twentynine Palms.

Each of them was successful, and began work that day. London got a very brief message out, "Bridger, this is big. They need fitters. Who've we got? Gotta go."

Redmond knew London wanted more people on the inside if possible. Bill and Annaliese were recalled, the latter being taken on for general duties and table service. Her heart quailed, and she muttered to herself, "Is this all I'm good for? Being a busgirl?"

Bill was not successful, having failed the personality metric tests given him, since he had answered truthfully. However, two of 3G's security detail were employed as fitters hands. That gave them seven people on the inside, most with differing work schedules and areas of activity.

Time passed slowly, no word was forthcoming until late that night. Lonely was on comm. when London reported, "This place has nothing to do with the Hoover Dam. As far as we can ascertain, it appears to be a missile silo, and we are currently fitting it out. I cannot confirm missiles already on site, but suspect as much. These are probably very large missiles. Suggest options for ground assault are considered, with full-force capability. Do not attack until we find out more. London out."

Despite the late hour, Lonely found Redmond with April in the restaurant. She gave her report and took a large café a le Rude back to her desk. The pair followed her back down and listened to the replay of the message. Redmond turned to April with admiration in his eyes and said, "It looks like you were correct, again. If we were to put two and two together, we have a nuclear missile launch silo right in our own back yard."

April concluded, "Better here than somewhere far away, white with cold. You know, Alaska, the largest state in the Union, has exactly half the population of Hawaii."

They laughed at her reference to the most northerly U.S. outpost, and made their way to bed. Redmond courteously saw April to her room, before leaving for his own.

Chapter 34 – Test Flight

The next couple of days passed slowly. They were waiting to act, idling in anticipation. The frustration began to mount as small progress continued to be made, but nothing substantial came through. On the second afternoon, Laredo picked up an emergency call coming from Bob Rogers' landline. He managed to state he was being burgled, before the line went dead.

A police cruiser made a cursory inspection, but there was no sign of intrusion, or anyone at the address. The police left minutes before Bill and April arrived. Bill pried a window and let them in. The place was deserted, and all Bob's computers and peripherals were gone. April recorded on her cell. The living room displayed signs of a small struggle, but that was all. Bob Rogers had been taken.

Bridger was already tracking back satellite feed, spotting a beige sedan arriving, and two men entering the house. Within minutes, Bob Rogers was hauled out, apparently under restraint. All his computer gear was put in the trunk. The auto disappeared less than three minutes after it arrived.

Laredo tracked through traffic cam footage, isolating the license plate and following the trail in skip-frame. It was not long before all present knew Rogers was being taken to the mine. Teves' 'streetcam' picked up when the vehicle turned into the trail to the secure compound. Ronnie worked on audio preparation as the team on the ridge tracked the vehicle.

They had clear audio of Bob Rogers arrival. He insisted, "I am not going anywhere, or doing anything, until I see my mother and father."

A concession was made. He was given five minutes with his parents, allowing Ronnie to hone his parameters even more. Most of the conversation was as expected, but they did confirm the existence of five children also held in captivity.

Redmond was of two minds as to how long he could allow the parents of these kids to suffer, let alone the children themselves. He needed to act immediately, but how could he? The nation's fate lay in his hands.

He decided on safekeeping without taking decisive action. Nevertheless, they needed the information, and so as long as the children were not harmed, he decided to allow their imprisonment to continue.

Redmond told Ronnie and the rest of the team, to report to him immediately if the slightest threat was made against the hostages. He made it crystal-clear that rescuing them took priority over every other concern, barring only an imminent threat to national security.

Ronnie again came with critical information. The snatches of conversation when pieced together, made it plain Rogers was there to make the radar tracking device work. Computer professionals would ensure he no longer played for time.

There was a timeframe, but references to it were oblique. Redmond listened repeatedly to all extracts and concluded, Rogers' deadline to be within twenty-four hours. He called all stations to monitor.

Meanwhile, during his third afternoon at Hoover Dam, Gary Weinberg came through on his headset with a brief report. He was one of 3G's two fitters, and had finally been allowed into a secure area for a few minutes. "Laredo, copy to Redmond. I have visual confirmation of a missile silo and one ICBM. Nuclear warhead facility exists, but is highly secure. The missile is ceramic. Repeat, ceramic. Weinberg out."

No sooner had the revelation been relayed to Redmond, than the new radar tracking console came to life. It was set to monitor ceramic missiles only, and one had just been fired. Despite the range of controls, the best Laredo could offer was 75% tracking, but this was enough over time and distance, to define the missile's inherent trajectory. It launched from Homer, just south of Anchorage, and headed out south across the Pacific. The trajectory altered several times, meaning it was being guided.

April jumped in beside Laredo as Lonely made her sleepy way down to assist. Redmond was watching avidly as others gathered round, or followed at their own workstations. April asked, "Any idea where this thing will set down?"

Laredo could not respond at first, as manual guidance was still affecting the missile's path. However, given altitude and overall direction, she eventually answered, "Hawaii. Somewhere off the north coast of Hawaii is my best guess. Remember, this is a stab in the dark, OK Hon?"

April returned to her own station and brought up a satellite feed for Hawaii, and slowly trimmed Laredo's feed to reflect the missile's path. The minutes passed before the missile resumed a preset course. It appeared to be diving into the sea, but at one hundred feet, it leveled out and slowly descended to skim the surface of the ocean, as if searching for a target. April began projecting the flight path and isolated a small flotilla of ships, and nearby floating bales of debris.

The target identified she waited and zoomed her satellite feed in as the two came closer and closer. The missile hit the water and rode a cushion of surf, slowing and hitting the debris square. It was held at water level as six fishing vessels maneuvered to bring their shared net taut on the surface of the ocean. A much larger ship closed in to begin recovery. Satellite imagery caught everything, including the ship's name, Quasso Cruris out of Anchorage.

Redmond laughed. This was a Latin reference to the theatrical term, Break a Leg, meaning: Good Luck. He noticed the humor was lost in translation, and on all his team, except Bridger. It gave him an insight into the minds of his operators and adversaries, something he made profiler Nick Norton aware of a short time later.

The Information hit a chord with Nick. "Redmond, I'm sure there is a dominant overseer who had a sense of humor, although a warped one. I have spent time creating the entity for his personal and team profiles to work. My problem is, I can't put a name or face to this controller."

"Good work Nick, keep trying, and let me know as soon as you have anything."

The next report came from Ronnie, who called Redmond in to hear it, "I have celebration from a new area very near the controllers' station. Apparently, they tracked the missile also, and probably better than we did. The audio is confused, but this memorandum represents the jist of what they were saying..."

Redmond knew Rogers had been put to work, and his device had now been refined, his own parents the means to make him do this for people he loathed. Redmond took a moment to wonder why life was so unfair, especially to those who deserved recognition, respect, and reward. Instead, they were simply used by the rich and powerful for their own rewards. He settled to the knowledge there was a debt to be paid, and he would ensure full payment for Bob Rogers.

When April joined him, he accepted her presence without question. They studied the details provided by Ronnie, and discussed several points. In time, they agreed on a course of action.

Redmond took out the secure satellite phone and made a call to Euan. His message was received, and he was told to wait for a reply. 3G came in to update him on minor matters, and once done, he finally got round to asking her to provide a decent sofa he could sleep on.

3G was not sure what he meant until April, with great experience of her father, volunteered a resolution Grace could understand. Redmond was over six-feet tall, so April recommended a four-seater, leather sofa with deep and soft cushioning, full height back and low arms that were at the ideal height for a head to rest upon. 3G was just about with it when April whispered, "Get one with a massage function if you can, he needs that."

Grace did not even know such things existed, but was surprised when one was available and she ordered it immediately. This was the craziest job she ever had, and she loved it.

Agent 8 came back to Redmond, who was trying to eavesdrop on the girls plotting about his new sofa. They had not spoken directly before, but Redmond had no reason to distrust him, and stated, "This afternoon an Intercontinental Ballistic Missile was launched from American soil. It landed just over half an hour ago, hitting a small target just north of Hawaii. We followed it live on radar, supplemented by satellite visual. So did the enemy. I perceive you have no knowledge of this. Do you?"

There was silence on the other end of the line. Irritated, Redmond cut the connection. Time passed and Redmond's new sofa was being installed when the satellite phone finally rang. He cleared the room before he took the call. Euan stated, "We have no record of any missile delivery, although we do have a missile signature from Alaska. But no sign that anything launched. No one wants to pursue this. How good is your information?"

Redmond was surprised, but replied. "A missile was launched. We got visual once we knew where to look. It was ceramic and we tracked it. The enemy also monitored it, and celebrated a direct hit.

You want answers, you get your butt down here pronto. Redmond out."

Redmond knew he should have been more forgiving, but he had met this superior wall of better than thou before, and abhorred it. He left the crew fitting his new sofa, and went to share a southern dram with Bill. He found him in their new karaoke bar listening to 'Sweet Home Alabama', free-played on a Wurlitzer. Redmond pulled up a chair and poured.

Within the hour, Vincent was with him. His attitude was less than friendly. Redmond took him down to ops, showed him the recording of the missile, satellite feed of the hit, and audio from Ronnie. Redmond asked that a copy be made, and left Vincent to make his own road in this life. He was sickened by the petty politics, and bullshit.

He turned before leaving ops and stated, "Next time I ask for Euan to attend personally, I expect him to attend personally. Without him, this small team is all that stands between the status quo, and the annihilation of the America you and he purport to love so much.

"All this is Twentynine Palms, ADF, Opus 3, the Director of National Security, and Coulson, shoe-in Godfrey DeMellor. Whose side are they on? Certainly not America's. You can also tell Euan the Hoover Dam project is a missile silo, and they will deploy a nuclear warhead within the next few days, as will Homer. Our question is not if bombs will be deployed, because they will be. We are trying to define what type of nuclear bombs they will be.This could be critical to how we all proceed."

Redmond did not wait for a reply. Instead he opened the door and walked away. The door slammed shut behind him, violating the silence of his wake.

Vincent understood why Redmond was annoyed, and agreed with him. The evidence they had collated was way outside current military resources. Shackleton stopped by to have a word with Evelyn Steinbecker. He knew a storm was coming and wanted this team prepared and protected.

Later, Euan viewed the recordings and knew he had made a very big mistake. They had never imagined a ceramic and undetectable ICBM could be made so quickly, yet there it was.

Euan called Redmond to apologize in person.

The call went unanswered.

Chapter 35 – Slow Boat to Anchorage

The next morning Teves came to sit with April at her station, and said, "The only thing we have not covered is the passer-by report of the shooting star. Can you back-track satellite archives?"

April did as Teves asked, and was able to trace the path of a rocket. It had appeared coming out of a cloud in the night sky, and landed dead center in the middle of the firework warehouse. The immediate resulting explosion was massive. Hard as April tried, she could not identify any light plane in the area, or anything at all.

Teves called Redmond down to take a look, and they spoke about the implications. "I do not believe a fireworks warehouse was anything but a test target. Only we suspected a deliberate hit, everybody else wrote the incident off as being 'one of those things'. This was a test firing of a ceramic missile. So was yesterday's ICBM. Only this team knew these were test runs. Agreed?"

Teves nodded, but April asked, "Do you think there will be any others?"

Redmond replied quickly, "Not of the ICBM. As for the smaller missiles, I see no reason why not. This one was probably fired from an airplane. They could try sea and land delivery. If so, where would make good targets for a strike?"

Teves and Redmond swapped locations, but April kept her own counsel, until she had rehearsed various scenarios in her mind. She interjected, "We know the enemy. They have already tried to take one place out twice, and failed. They say third time lucky. What about this place?"

Redmond turned at once, and sprinted out of the room, hollering for 3G. She was with him moments later, and placed the base on highest alert. Redmond tasked her to initiate state of the art missile defenses, insisting they be put in place as soon as possible.

3G assembled a mobile anti-missile battery within six hours. Once in situ, Redmond insisted on having it interlinked with their ceramic missile detection facility. 3G saw the wisdom, although the experienced missile crew thought it a very strange addition to their perfect deployment.

§

London wondered if their time was being wasted at Hoover Dam. The two fitters had gained useful information, but otherwise the team had very low-level clearance. Mendez was confined to the kitchen most of the time, and while Annaliese did get to mix with the workforce, she was only working tables and cleaning garbage in the general mess.

He was considering reducing their numbers when Annaliese was promoted to the senior mess. The administrators were a chatty bunch, and once there, she was able to catch snatches of more important information.

Weinberg and Wiltshire proved to be good fitters, and were soon given more important work, at last gaining access to the restricted area. In time, they were able to confirm preparations were under way to launch a nuclear missile. The rocket was already in the final stages of assembly, but the atomic warhead would arrive later. They suspected the projectile would be fueled and armed quickly.

Most of their work was in the control room, where they were able to access systems and note priority codes. Everyone knew these were likely to change, especially when the unit was handed over for use. However, all information was recorded and sent back to headquarters whenever the opportunity arose.

Redmond insisted the team remain for as long as possible. They would come into their own once the decision was taken to invade the complex. London was appeased when Redmond turned his attention to assisting any invasionary force. He marked doors and access channels, priority corridors, and points of disruption. He identified several killing zones and gained access codes to specific doors.

Weinberg managed to get access to a plan of the entire base and quickly photographed the design. He was not able to send the details back until late that night, but the information was critically important. The next morning, Rude cleaned up the assorted images and produced a detailed, multi-dimensional map of the entire complex, adding London's reference points to his 3D computer model.

London was sent a copy and using it greatly improved his designs for ingress. He highlighted key points, updated all his previous information, adding door codes, and preferred routes. His mindset changed at once, now that he felt he was doing something useful.

§

On the second morning, Euan arrived and apologized, stating the timing of Redmond's call had been extremely awkward. He made a specific point of repairing bridges and enthused about what Redmond's team was accomplishing. He viewed all their information personally, spending much time going over the original footage of the local ceramic rocket and ICBM. The latter was a definitive threat to the security of the nation.

Redmond was mollified, nearly all wounds now healed by Euan's personal appearance. However, he did not trust Euan completely. They concluded with the two known nuclear silos, Hoover Dam and Homer. They agreed that a direct strike on Washington, D.C. was unlikely, since with the Capitol destroyed, there would be nothing left to take over. They reasoned the bomb would strike close to the Capitol, but not directly on it. Neither man particularly liked that scenario, but it was the best they had as a working hypothesis.

They surmised the first missile would likely be detonated in such a place to take out electrical services and communications, drawing in responders. Redmond reasoned the first warhead would likely explode around 4 a.m., finding most of the population still at home and cutting them off from effective communication, increasing fear and dis-information. But what of the second?

Euan stated, "To be effective and cause maximum destabilization, the second missile would probably detonate after the day was done and towards midnight, or let's say eighteen to twenty hours after the first strike."

Redmond acknowledged the wisdom, but countered, "I agree with you that this is the most likely scenario as things stand. However, I beg to differ with accepting this as a sure plan, for three reasons. First, we do not know which base will launch first. Second, as soon as we play our hand, the launch time of the second missile will be brought forward. According to our profiler, Nick Norton, this is a virtual certainty. Lastly, once we attack, the other base will prepare and take counter measures. It is imperative we hit both locations at the same time."

Euan saw the logic and agreed. Plans would be formulated for coordinated attacks on both. Euan stated he would supply any information they had on the Coulson base at Homer, although he cautioned it might be sparse and out of date. They parted in friendship, Redmond realizing the man had a lot more on his plate than he had imagined.

Redmond felt a lot better after their open discussion, and moved on to the next part of the plan. He called a group to him and laid out what needed to be done. "I need a small team to infiltrate Homer. I also need someone on site to follow the container after it leaves ship, and ensure it is not tampered with until it reaches its destination. Because of the recent missile launch, and an earlier recording, we believe this to be Homer, but be alert for anything."

Redmond was waiting for volunteers. Teves spoke up first. "I will check Anchorage docks, but I will not go undercover. Instead, I will ingratiate myself with local law enforcement and see what dirt I can dig up, especially concerning Coulson and their operation at Homer. I add that I believe it wise to have somebody floating on the outside, since this is not local territory for any of us."

Bill spoke next, "I will go and get a job at Coulson, Alaska. I will be less honest with my interview than I was at the Hoover Dam." He smiled and wagged his head as if in embarrassment.

"3G, perhaps I can go with a couple of your men and we can appear as soldiers of fortune on the trail together. The ruse is simple, and I doubt there are many casual workers in Homer. We are simply passing through on summer vacation, and looking to earn a few extra bucks."

3G responded, "That's good cover. I'll ask for volunteers, but I do not expect any difficulty."

All eyes turned to April, who was again lost deep within her thoughts, and had become active on her computer. She came back to the present and realized the others were looking at her expectantly. She spoke aloud, "Here's the thing. We need eyes on the container, and we ain't gonna get that unless somebody is on the inside.

"The Anchorage Vista has already arrived in Seattle, and will cast off for Vancouver tomorrow. I will go and work my passage up to Anchorage. Bill and I did something similar last summer, so I already know how Seattle docks are laid out. In addition, happily my cast came off this morning. Normally casual labor leaves as soon as the leg is complete, but there is always work to do, so I'm sure I can stay on board, at least until the container we are interested in is offloaded. With a little luck I will be able to follow where they store it, and perhaps find out when it is scheduled to leave. I will need to leave shortly. I presume midsummer is cold in Anchorage?"

Bill protested, but Redmond thought April's idea inspirational, and upheld it. Redmond authorized her use of the company jet. The meeting broke up, and within hours she was flying north. April slept well on the plane, and was greeted by local law enforcement in Seattle. They transferred her to the docks area, and stayed until the ship was identified. She was then on her own.

She wasted no time and immediately walked up the gangplank, telling a senior crew at the top, "I'd like to work my passage to Anchorage. I hope the Captain is in need of casual crew."

The man sent word to the Captain, who was not impressed, but decided to see her. He had been planning to charge her for passage, but she was young, attractive, and looked resourceful. She also said she had experience on board ship, and he spoke to the previous Captain on ship-to-ship radio. The girl checked out, and was recommended, so April was sent to work in the galley. She started immediately and both were happy with their deal.

The Captain checked on her several times that first day, but the Chef confirmed she knew the ropes and had not put a foot wrong. He added she was a very good worker, and so she was set for the voyage. She brought a little humor and female intrigue to service at the Captain's table, which went down very well with the crew. The Captain accepted her, but took her aside near the end of her watch to warn her to always lock her cabin door, and never let anyone inside.

April thanked him and stood on tip toes to give him a peck on the cheek. The man watched her leave and muttered under his breath, "Shit!"

The journey was short and soon it was coming time to leave. The Captain thanked her and offered her a little pay, telling her she had fit in really well. April was happy and accepted the money, but added, "Captain, I have nothing to do for a day or so, at least until my friend gets here. I don't know this place at all, and she is still on the road. A new city is always a little scary the first time, especially when you are on your own. Can I stay onboard until I meet up with my friend and help Chef prepare for the next leg."

Chef said, "That's fine with me Cap'n. Any chance of some shore leave?"

Chapter 35

They made a pact, and Chef left April with a long list of work to be carried out. He had twelve hours on shore, and April used her free time wisely.

Without being obvious, she managed to keep track of the offloading, conspiring to be on deck when the container she was interested in was due to be put ashore. The Captain noticed her and asked her if she should not be working. She smiled up at him and said, "I am well ahead of schedule and wanted to enjoy a few moments on deck. The air is so fresh up here, don't you think?

"Captain, what is happening here? I mean, how do they know where to put all these containers? It's fascinating."

She inveigled the Captain to explain the rudimentary working of the container hub. He liked her, and indulged her curiosity. He told her one section was bonded, and that related to international freight. There was a second bonded section on the internal side, for special goods like liquor.

The man pointed to a separate area and told her this was where standard internal U.S. containers were held. April was watching very carefully, and was lucky when the container she was following was offloaded next. She asked, "Take this container being offloaded now. Why is it being put way over there where there are hardly any others? It does not make any sense."

The Captain laughed and explained, "The containers in that area are private and internal U.S. That area is for quick release, so the container you are watching will be gone within twenty-four hours, and probably a lot sooner. I imagine the rig is already on its way to collect it."

April thanked him, before suddenly remembering something she had to do. She pecked him on the cheek again, and excused herself, leaving the Captain slightly bemused, but with a wry grin on his face. He watched her return to the galley, hoping she would come on board again.

April was worried she would still be on board when the container was collected. She sped through her remaining chores, cooked for midnight break, and made ready to leave at a moment's notice. She kept an eye on the container, but it remained where it had been put, on top of another one. The chef returned after midnight, having drunk well and greatly enjoyed his time on shore. April was relieved of duty at 3 a.m., and made her way out into the crisp bright cool of the Anchorage summer night.

Chapter 36 – The One Highway State

Teves flew up to Merrill Field, and arrived in Anchorage with Bill, Bert Singer, and Danny Schuler. They hired a battered old RV, and set off for Homer. Teves was provided with a rental, and introduced himself to the local PD. Evelyn had provided his cover, and he was well received by local law enforcement.

Teves drove across town and took watch on the container base. He had identified the container they were interested in. However, he had not heard from April and was becoming quite worried. He startled when she came over comm. "Teves, you here?"

His relief was palpable as he fought to control his emotions, "Yes, where are you?"

"I'm just walking out of exit 3A. You nearby?"

"I am waiting to pick you up. Thank God you're safe."

Teves watched April leave port, gunning the engine to get to her as quickly as possible. She hitched a ride as cover, and hopped in the passenger seat. Teves could not help himself, he simply had to give her a big hug. April was surprised, but knew the Mexican blood and love of family ran deep in his heart.

They broke quickly, Teves embarrassed and apologetic. April was more than happy, but acted as if nothing had happened. They talked about her adventures, and caught up. April had used her headset only in her cabin for sending messages out, not keeping track of the latest developments. She confirmed, "That container is bound for Coulson, Homer, and will be gone very soon."

Being so far north, the night was already lifting. A truck came for the container at first light, and once marked, April said, "Drive around … pull over at that stop sign."

She dove out and ran for the intersection, leaving Teves alone and wondering what she was up to. April had chosen her spot well. The truck would automatically slow, and it would be easy for it to pull over. She thumbed a lift, raising her arms to help flag the big rig down. The trucker pulled up, and asked her where she was headed. She said, "Homer," and was welcomed aboard.

Teves watched in astonishment, as April disappeared into the drab dawn. He had to laugh, because nobody could get closer to the container they were tracking, than to ride in the cab hauling it. He sent a report back to Lonely, marked for Redmond's first attention, and followed.

Chapter 36

April slept, as Highway 1 dragged on forever. They got stuck behind slow, and even slower trucks. They stopped twice for set driver breaks. Teves ignored them, but topped up with coffee.

During the second stop, another driver joined them. The men knew each other, both private haulers owning their own rigs. She learned he was also hauling a container bound for Coulson.

They made Homer a long nine hours later. As they neared town, Dek, the driver asked, "What're your plans?"

"I'm meeting a friend from college—an ecology project, but need to find work to fund my time up here."

After the container was offloaded, Dek took April to the reception area, where she was given an appointment with HR for 4:30 p.m. April was early, and HR was running late. She sold herself on her second year College status, and promoted her computer skills. The woman was all business and checked her bona fides, but skimmed through the coursework. The report was positive and she was hired, beginning work the next day. She took board and lodging as part of the deal, and was handed over to a secretary for processing.

That night she was able to call in, speaking at length to Lonely, passing on all the information she had. Lonely countered with information that Bill and the others were working on site, and that Teves was floating outside.

The next morning April reported early for her new job, and while she knew she was not that good at it, nobody else seemed to notice. She came up to speed quickly, helped by an experienced operator called Kensington who proved to be a great ally. She quickly learned the department had access to every part of Coulson's Homer computing resources. The only problem was, she did not have the security clearance.

Answering seemingly innocuous questions, Kensington filled her in on the basics. A typical male, he needed no encouragement to show off his vast knowledge to the new girl in the department.

She was the only girl as it turned out, and she knew he was casually hitting on her. April played him and discovered all she could as quickly as possible.

Kensington had far higher computer clearance than she did, so she set a plan in motion, sending a brief text to Teves. That evening as they finished work, April wandered out to get some fast food, and waited for Teves to pull up. Minutes later, Teves stood in the queue behind her, ignoring her. She felt him put something in her jeans pocket, and did not react, heading back to her room as soon as she had been served.

The next day she manufactured a pretext, and asked Kensington to explain. She knew he would need to login to her workstation to run through the problem, and he came quickly too close to her side. He said, "I'll need to login…"

April stood and turned her back on him before he completed his words, showing tech courtesy, ignoring his password. Her Smartphone was already active, and received a video of him logging in, from the bug she had placed underneath the monitor— the one Teves had given her the previous evening.

It was not until late on the second day that she was free to explore what this system could do, and replaying Kensington's keystrokes, got into the system at a much higher level. He had supervisory clearance, and she hoped that was enough for what she needed.

She worked late that night, pretending to need more time for work she had already completed. Instead, she brought up site schematics and focused upon the tactical area, which was separate from the main plan. She was stymied, as 'restricted information' flashed on screen.

There had to be a way around the problem. She knew Coulson from Nick's preliminary company profile, and he had stated they liked to keep eyes on their employees. April leaned back and asked herself, "In a large company, who knows all."

'Human Resources'. Her clearance allowed her into most HR systems. Instead of pursuing the main folders, she tried for access sideways, finding back doors to the information she needed, ones only HR personnel would normally think to access.

She followed her nose, and hit a seam of gold, a low level manager who had smelled a rat and reported his suspicions. His debriefing named files and folders, and he was summarily sacked. April now knew where to look.

The file search revealed the folders she needed, and she sat and gaped. She was looking at all the information they had been seeking. She pumped the air, knowing she had hacked the system, and blew Rude a kiss for giving her a brief hacking tutorial during quiet times during the last few days, when it felt like they were spinning their heels.

April stared, as the screen revealed plans for missile deployment. She downloaded all the schematics to her Smartphone, and followed with control systems. She caught sight of the words "Project: Old Lady Liberty" and focused on the folder.

There it was, the whole plan to take out the government of the U.S. She sent a copy to her Smartphone, and it bleeped to confirm the transfer complete, and started the next folder.

April continued to search the system, bringing other things into her send folder. She discovered a folder entirely related to ADF. She knew at once this information had to get back to headquarters. It seemed to list personnel and hierarchy, but she was distracted by a tannoy, "Intruder alert. Security lockdown. All gates and building to be secured at once."

April knew this was not related to her activities, how could it be? She reasoned it was a drill, but it compromised her situation. She immediately pulled up a schematic of the place, and transferred it as she looked for a way out.

She heard security enter the outer offices, they would be with her shortly. Her office was supposed to be empty. April closed her machine as soon as transfer was complete, after first wiping all traces of her activity. She knew computer experts could pull back her tracks, but not ordinary people, and right now, that was good enough for her. She removed the bug, and made her escape.

April found the air conditioning panel she needed and released the catches at the bottom. She slid through the top-hinged cover as security entered the room. She secured the grill, using a piece of gum to hold the lower part in place.

The ductwork was old and full of dust, and worse things. April knew most of it was dead skin, other people's skin, and pulled her turtle-neck up to use as a breathing mask. She made slow, if steady progress, at a delicate crawl to safety. Her hand fell on something furry, yielding, gruesome—something that smelled of purification. She wanted to scream, to be sick. She also wanted to use her cell as a light, but knew this would compromise her escape. She resolutely pressed onwards, silently, with darkness en-cloaking her every movement, slowly edging towards liberation.

She had a mental map and followed it. Redemption came when she reached a restroom that was vacant, and slid back into the real world. April scrubbed the decay and maggots off her hand, and used the hand dryer to dust herself clean. She knew she had to get the information back to HQ immediately, and strode out into a workers' mess. She spied her father sitting with a couple of men she knew. He almost rose, but with a flick of her head, April made it clear they were not to acknowledge each other.

She headed out through a side door, and saw the personnel gate was closed; security was already enhanced. She quickly ran to the truck park. Sirens sounded as she sought to make her escape; she knew she had to hide. She was alone among a fleet of tractors and trailers, and stopped to try to work out what was going on.

Rigs on the far side were dropping off cargo and leaving. There was no way she could reach one undetected. The nearest trailers had already loaded, and being released in an order, if only she could understand the pattern. She searched and followed a trucker back to his cab. The rig next to her fired its engine, and she dove on the rack behind the cab, buried herself three deep amongst the tarps and burrowed deeper.

Gate security was on high alert. The container was opened and examined. A cursory search was made for stowaways beneath the vehicle. April held fast, even when security lifted the top of the tarp, and thrust a metal rod deep and firmly into her stomach.

April wanted to cry out, but physically bit her tongue, knowing freedom was all but a cry away. The truck was passed through the gate and she was out of the Coulson maelstrom. It was freezing. Summer in Homer was worse than winter in San Diego. April wondered how people could even contemplate living in Alaska. It was so damned cold and perverse.

She made a call to Teves, requesting immediate extraction. Teves honed in on where she could jump the rig. Teves notified Redmond, who immediately initiated the team's jet to get April out of Alaska as soon as she arrived at Homer airport. They knew the crew would need to scramble, and fly down to Homer field.

April figured the rig would be headed for Highway 1, "As if this State had any other highways." She giggled, "A one highway State, not even an interstate, imagine, the largest State in the Union, and it only has one fucking road."

Chapter 36

She tittered about her personal view of Alaska, as it appeared to have more airports than schools. Giddy with adrenalin crash, she continued her mocking fun until the truck drew to a stop. She slithered out of her hidey-hole, and down onto the cold concrete road. She waited as the 6-wheel trailer passed over her, before making for the sidewalk. Teves recovered her minutes later, and they drove off in the opposite direction.

April was cold. It was a physical thing, and a mental thing. They grabbed some Alaskan fast food and copied her intel to Teves cell. In time, they were informed of the jets imminent arrival.

Homer Airport was a small field, yet security was unaccountably aggressive. Teves badged their way through the outer checkpoint, but the inner one became a problem, as the guards wanted to know what they were doing. Teves told them it was Sheriff's office business and none of theirs.

The situation was tense, but they were allowed through, although hands wandered to holsters. The tower tried to stall the jet, but it prepared for takeoff regardless and, having reached the runway, started to taxi for takeoff. The tower had no option but to clear them, and moments later the small plane rose into the night sky.

Chapter 37 – Defense of the Realm

The next morning, Rude processed all the information April had discovered. Most of it was critically important. Once filed properly, Rude sent a synopsis directly to the Chief. Redmond set the schematics and control systems aside, marking them for use when they took action against Coulson's Homer facility. The ADF folder threw up some surprising names, and Redmond knew at once, Euan needed to be made aware of the contents.

"Project Old Lady Liberty" was on an entirely different level. Redmond stared at the information, rereading just to make sure he was seeing correctly. They had the master plan, and it was horrendous. The only good news was, if the nuclear bombs were detonated, there would be little direct loss of life, although there would be widespread and ongoing contamination, for decades to come, across all of the U.S. and the world at large.

Opus 3 was referred to several times, the group playing a pivotal role in preparatory action. Redmond knew the names of some of the senior military involved, but did not know of more than a few of the corps and units mentioned. The enormity of what they were up against hit him.

Redmond asked Evelyn to come into his office, and with a heavy heart, picked up the one-ton satellite phone, and prepared to make his call. He was surprised to get through to Euan immediately, and told him he had intelligence of the utmost importance.

Euan probed, not wanting to make the same mistake as last time. Redmond replied, "Full details of a project called Old Lady Liberty, detailing the deployment plans for two nuclear bombs. Here is a catalog of what you will find…"

When he finished, the phone went silent. Redmond could hear a large intake of breath, and Euan breathed out resignedly. "I guess there is no way you can send it through to me?"

Redmond was quick to respond, "I could, Sir, but this information is much too encompassing, and so highly classified that I don't think there is a label for it yet. We need to discuss the implications here, where we have all intelligence readily available. I will have a copy waiting for you when you arrive. Redmond out."

Euan appeared to be fully committed to the greater America, as Redmond was. Yet, there was always some small detail, a response missing, like a sense of total loyalty that was lacking. He could not put his finger on what it was exactly, but he knew it was there all the same. Was it just busyness, politics, or not having time to spare? Redmond decided to dossier Euan, just in case his suspicions gained a foundation, however unlikely that should appear.

Early the next day, before the general briefing, Redmond called Rude, 3G, and Evelyn into his office. He had already spent time with April discussing the further implications of her discoveries.

Redmond began, "We now have excellent intelligence, but need to understand more. The military tech we face has never been deployed before, but it is a grave threat. I know the government has contingency plans for this event, but even with prior warning, I am sure they will effectively prove useless.

"Rude, I want you to dig up whatever you can on this, and translate the scientific jargon into plain English. I need to know what else may be special about these bombs.

"3G, be discreet, but see what you can find out via your contacts, both military, scientific, and professional. We need somebody who understands this stuff, and can explain it to a child.

"Evelyn, same for you, use your contacts and see if there is anybody useful to us. I am not looking for any more team members, we already have more than I anticipated. I am seeking information only. Any questions?" Redmond surveyed the faces. "Good, let's get to it."

Euan arrived later that morning, and was startled at the depth of information Redmond had amassed so quickly. Redmond laid it all down to April. They knew the twin launch sites, and now had a rough timetable. They had a handle on tracking the missiles and were working to improve that system.

They now knew the nuclear bombs would be detonated in such a way as to create an EMP effect. With the Capital, and virtually the entire country, electronically fried, the way was open for a new order to take control; they would have access to working electronics, communications.

The nightmare scenario settled heavily with the two men. Euan knew that to move against so many high-ranking military officers, politicians, and economic moguls would be an awesome undertaking, and yet that was what he was facing.

Redmond's phone rang. He put it on speaker, "I thought I asked not to be disturbed?"

Bridger replied, "Am I to presume you are not interested in the two missiles that are currently targeting our headquarters?"

Redmond raced down to ops, Euan a step behind him. The missiles were ceramic, and had only been picked up by Laredo's special console. Redmond commanded, "Send the missile tracking feed to the battery. They have obviously turned it off. Idiots! Tell them to act on it immediately and take those things out."

The Captain in charge of the battery was skeptical, since his equipment showed nothing. Yet, the feed from the control room showed a positive threat. He ordered the interception strike, and was amazed when two hits were recorded. Euan stared at the screen, knowing modern warfare had just moved to a new level.

Redmond came over comm., "Thank you for believing us Captain, you just saved our butts. Congratulations. Keep vigilant. There could be further strikes against us. Redmond out."

Redmond looked at Euan and stated, "That was a Coulson strike. I think you need this special radar at National Defense HQ."

Turning to his team he gave a series of orders. "Bridger, eyes on satellite for any possible fallout locations. Also, try to trace the source. Laredo, same with drones. 3G, take a team and see if you can find any debris from the missiles. Teves, April, you will make preliminary examination. Perry, get your bag, you are going with them."

With his instructions given, Redmond led the way back to his office. Euan was deceptively casual as he said, "I am coming to respect you Redmond. Your way of command is not excitable. You simply accomplish one job, and get on with the next."

Redmond thanked him, before getting back to their discussion. Their meeting finished as Euan tasked Redmond with stopping the ICBM's from being launched. He offered resources he trusted to back up the strikes. However, Euan elaborated, "Redmond, I need time. I need to put a wide net in place to catch all the powerbrokers before the silos are taken. That means hard evidence, not circumstantial, which is what barristers will reduce what we have at this moment, to. Our evidence needs to be watertight, like caught in the act."

Euan made good on his promise, calling Redmond to confirm combat units were being made available to him. Colonel Miles Aldridge contacted Redmond minutes later. Shortly afterwards, Redmond spoke in to Brigadier General Abram Salmond. He arranged a meeting with both at his headquarters for 10 a.m. the next morning.

April returned with 3G a few hours later, and she reported to Redmond, "We identified two locations. They were quite close to each other. There was a little media interest, but they have no leads. We pulled out so as not to encourage them, simply stating it was probably an event organizer test firing for July Fourth.

"Manny and Perry are working the scenes, but out of the way of the media. Perry will need to run lab tests when he gets back, but the early indications are, they were identical to the missile fragments we got from the fireworks warehouse. Bridger tells me they were fired from across the border, somewhere down in Mexico."

Redmond nodded, "Yes, they were. We will have an international incident if we follow this up. Good work in the field. Do you think this strike on us here could be because they know you were in Coulson Homer?"

April replied thoughtfully, "I guess it could be related, but they only have my name. I doubt anyone has gone through the computer thoroughly yet, why would they? Bill confirmed last night's security clamp-down was just a drill. It is just as likely we have a leak here. There are a lot of new people around."

Redmond asked Rude, 3G, and Evelyn to attend him at once. He began as soon as they settled. "I need to be sure we do not have a mole in this building. I do not think so, but I need full checks run on everybody that either works here, or comes here.

"I know we have all been positively vetted, and while there were a couple of minor issues, this is not what I am looking for. I need full background checks regarding any possible links to ADF, DeMellor, Coulson, and Opus 3. Pay particular attention to anyone out of Twentynine Palms.

"Rude, please check everybody, including the five of us in this room. Include all of 3G's men, plus any contract workers: janitors, the civilian cooks we now have, window cleaners, anybody that has ever set foot in this building. Include Euan and Shackleton also, I mean absolutely everybody.

"Evelyn, please liaise with Rude about all people that have been here, or are scheduled to come here, and check them out before they arrive. Tomorrow we have two military guys coming. You and 3G can compile a list to help Rude."

Rude responded, "That's quite some ask, Chief. I can do it, but what about the EMP stuff you wanted me to check out. I am doing well there, and should have something for you soon."

"Check out Bridger first, and she can check you. Get her working alongside you. She can do the research, and point you in the direction of which secure databases need to be accessed, a job only you can do. All of you, help Rude in any way you can, I need this dealt with and gone."

The day passed into the late afternoon before Redmond got his first answer, it came from Rude, "Chief, we've run full checks on all permanent staff, and everything appears to be in order. I got Bridger and the others working on the civilian personnel, all the contractors and that sort of stuff. She's becoming quite a good hacker you know."

Redmond dismissed Rude by saying, "With all our main staff cleared, I want you to focus only on the EMP, unless a red flag shows up."

Evelyn came to Redmond some time later. "Sir, I contacted an old associate, and in between gossip, managed to get a couple of leads, although I'm sure Rude has already found these. Please read my internal email, encryption key S5."

Redmond opened the newly arrived email, and read,
"Sir,

I have discovered a report by the United States EMP Commission dated 2008. It is regarded as the latest available EMP threat assessment, here's the link: http://www.empcommission.org/docs/A2473-EMP_Commission-7MB.pdf.
I have attached a copy.

My friend also mentioned something about Super-EMP's, and this threat is little understood. He gave me a reference to a publication called 'The Emerging EMP Threat to the United States' by Dr. Mark Schneider of National Institute for Public Policy (November 2007). Again, I attach a copy, but this information, although not classified, is not available to ordinary people. The link for confirmation is below:

http://www.nipp.org/Publication/Downloads/Publication Archive PDF/EMP Paper Final November07.pdf

Hope this helps.
Evelyn"

Redmond said, "Great work Evelyn, I need to study this. Send a copy to Rude, just in case."

Evelyn replied, "Already done, Sir."

Rude appeared in his office twenty minutes later, and was clearly looking very pleased with himself. Redmond knew it was good news, and enquired, "OK Rude, tell me what you got."

"Chief," Rude began, "You're not going to believe this. I was focused on April's research, until I got Evelyn's email. You see the parameters for standard nuclear bombs are irrelevant. If I presume three things, which I only have indications of, then I have this.

"One: The warhead container is made of ceramic, not the usual metal. I infer the ceramic is gamma-ray-transparent.

Two: The detonator is not a normal thermonuclear one, but something very old and special, and indicates a high-chemical detonator.

Three: The warhead is designed to explode as a nuclear fission explosion.

"Put all this together, and you have two Super-EMP bombs, ready to hit the U.S. The references are in my email of a moment ago, as is my full report."

Redmond pulled up the internal email and scanning, paused to read three excerpts:

"'Super-EMP Weapons for generating high-altitude E1 electromagnetic pulse:

http://www.futurescience.com/emp/super-EMP.html'

'An Introduction to Nuclear Electromagnetic Pulse by Jerry Emanuelson, BSEE.'

http://www.futurescience.com/emp.html'

'E1, E2, and E3 explained:
Nuclear EMP - E1,E2,E3 - Futurescience.com'"

Redmond looked up at Rude questioningly. The geek offered, "It's all about things called E1, E2, and E3, plus Earth's magnetic field, The Compton effect, and the atmosphere. I'll leave out the technical bits, so basically we have three pulses at nanosecond intervals.

"E1 is a Gamma ray. This is what decimates electrical devices. In a Super-EMP the effects of this are devastating. The three pulses occur virtually within one nanosecond, and are of far greater magnitude.

"E2 is a small problem, a bit like lightening, but not generally regarded as a threat.

"E3 is what takes out power transmission lines. Apart from anomalies like full wave induction and echo, like harmonics on a guitar string for instance, a feedback loop that self perpetuates at a set length and frequency. The main threat lies in control and monitoring devices called SCADA's, being disrupted.

"An ordinary E3 blast would cripple the grid, take out transformers, and cause a lot of physical damage. Because this is an old style fission reaction, the E3 component will likely, only cripple the control circuits, leaving the physical grid largely intact, but unusable. Bridger discovered Coulson Environmental Engineering specializes in manufacturing SCADA's.

"I am aware that our scientists have devised plans to build Super-EMP's. There is nothing official regarding production, you understand. Otherwise, only larger nations have the wherewithal to bring all this together. You can look for great bears and giant pandas if you like.

"Building the bomb appears simple, but it would be large, heavy. Delivering it to say, the stratosphere is the main problem. Ceramic casings seem to answer that issue. I would expect lower level and adjacent satellites in space to become inoperable also. Sounds like communications Armageddon to me, Chief."

Redmond scanned the document, finding the piece he required, and said, "The Soviet Union launched one of these things, in nineteen sixty-two? The only presumed deployment, the Arctic?"

Rude replied, "With fifty years of development since then, imagine what the physical effects would be now? If they unleash even one of these bombs, we're looking at smoke signals as our main form of communication. Permission to go gather wood, Chief?"

"Denied, but great work Rude." Redmond's mind was still scaling the impossibility of what confronted him, but there it was before him. He mused, "Add in all the disruption we have already catalogued, the main target, and all major cities already in a state of emergency, before the two EMP detonations, and what have you got?"

Redmond answered his own question, "A superpower in meltdown."

§

The next morning, Evelyn gave Redmond a brief on their expected guests, "Aldridge is clean, but Salmond has a couple of scabs—he wants to be a politician. It may be nothing, but be warned. Both Rude and Bridger think he is a small fish, but Bridger wondered if he was playing both sides. Politicians do that you know."

Redmond thanked her, and later welcomed the military personnel. They arrived punctually, and were shown through to his office. April was present, and Redmond asked Evelyn to stay. Both soldiers were sworn to total secrecy before the meeting began. The pair had a hard time believing in the invisible missiles. Redmond asked the Captain of the battery to come up. He, somewhat shamefacedly, gave his report, which was augmented by computer footage. The Captain dismissed, the two commanders were suddenly aware they were about to become operational in an entirely new battlefield scenario.

Redmond followed with details of the two missile silos and asked who would take which. The Brigadier chose the local option, and, being outranked, Aldridge was left with Homer. Hoover Dam appeared the easier target, as Redmond already had people on the inside, and in the right areas. The one star general accepted the intel from Redmond without any questions, and set about making brief outline for his battle plan. Redmond had to emphasize that no strike was to be made without his personal approval.

Salmond left moments later, full of bluster and treating the strike as a minor inconvenience. When he was gone, Aldridge looked at Redmond and stated, "He is younger than I am, but has been fast-tracked since leaving West Point. He wants to be a Senator. I am old school. I hope to gain a pip or two, and retire with a good pension, perhaps work in Army recruitment when I leave."

Redmond found his honesty reassuring. Together they worked to formulate a strategy of ingress at the Coulson compound way up in Alaska. Aldridge spoke at length to April, and was surprised by how much she knew. The Colonel was very interested in her escape from Homer, as it became evident to him that the entire town revolved around Coulson, their influence was ubiquitous.

This compromised a normal build-up strategy, and meant using a staging post. Aldridge said he would send up a scouting party in civilian clothes, and maybe try to get one or two working inside the company. They would make themselves known to Bill and his cohorts.

It was palpable that Colonel Aldridge took the assignment very seriously. In due course he departed, but kept in regular contact with Redmond. Salmond did not. Evelyn, April, and Redmond talked for a while after the military contingent had left. Evelyn knew her craft and was already erecting political firewalls, ones she knew would soon be required.

That evening headquarters was a hive of activity. A rig had arrived at the mine earlier that afternoon. Cooke had added several more cameras to their surveillance in the meantime, and on this occasion, everybody was able to see what was being loaded via live feed.

Down in ops, Redmond asked Bridger for an update. "The rig is being loaded with these spherical pods, you can see one there. They are about three feet in diameter, and you see the people wearing silver suits, yes? Those are radiation suits."

Redmond and April watched as twenty pods were loaded into the container. The final payload being four large wooden shipping boxes, and three smaller ones. They were larger than those from the train heist, but not by much. The last item was a small but very heavy box. Teves added, "That looks very similar to one I saw in Phoenix, and again at the container hub."

Redmond voiced what everyone was thinking, "It appears this is the payload for the second nuclear warhead. I will presume its destination is Hoover Dam. Comm., please monitor. This is the only thing I want you working on."

Lonely spoke up, "I will track it, and report when it arrives, whatever time that is."

Redmond spoke his concerns aloud, "I would like to take out this threat now, but the Secret Service have asked me to give them time to work on other angles of the greater project. I will call my contact at once."

Redmond spoke briefly to Euan, but the decision made by Washington, D.C. was to monitor, and only take the missile out once it was deployed, or the Secret Service net closed. Redmond hung up the secure phone, and knew that for the greater good, his operation was being compromised. He remembered his belief in his country, The American Dream, and thought about his options. There were few.

Lonely tracked the rig's progress, and called for Redmond when it passed through Boulder City, and turned off the main road heading for Hoover Dam. Redmond quickly finished his work and went down with April to confirm the warhead's arrival.

They were in good time and watched as the truck entered the large building at the rear and disappeared from view. Despite the late hour, he called London to advise him the nuclear material was now on site. London thanked him, although there was little he could do to get eyes on. However, the knowledge meant his plans were now a go.

When everything settled, Redmond congratulated Lonely on her good work, and asked her to monitor when the truck left, and where it was headed. They went through to check on the other permanent night staff. Sherry was working away in her own world. With Perry's arrival, she had become more structured in her approach, and archiving was coming along nicely. Both Redmond and April took genuine interest in her work. Neither of them was tired, but they knew they must sleep, as the new day would soon be upon them.

Chapter 38 – Bugged Out

Evelyn knocked on Redmond's door midway through the next morning. "Sir, I have confirmation from Rude, Bridger, and 3G. All personnel and visitors have proved clear. Most external calls that are not personal to team members come from this very office. I will of course continue to monitor your diary and liaise with Rude, but they are all clean as a whistle."

Redmond was very pleased everyone had passed examination, but this did not ease his concerns. He asked April to join him, and they talked the issue through. In summary he stated, "So, all personnel are clean. What else is there? What are we missing?"

April looked at him and replied, "Only the obvious, the two prisoners from Twentynine Palms. They work for the enemy, and were left unsupervised for the best part of forty minutes."

"Damn!" Redmond exclaimed. "They could have set bugs. Check for a transmitter on the roof, or hidden somewhere."

April was already heading for the door when she turned to say, "I'll check the base with 3G. We'll start at the top and work down."

One minute later, the girls were on the roof, aided by Cloverley, 3G's black-ops expert, and her surveillance specialist Tompkins. They discovered a medium range transmitter on the roof, just above the door leading outside. It was attached to a solar power pack, but the rest of the roof appeared clear, as were the satellite dishes.

Tompkins, cautious of other listening devices, drew them into a huddle in the middle of the helipad, and stated, "The transmitter has a range of ten miles or more, and could reach Del Fuego mine, for instance. This model has a modified receiving board, and can receive data using Wi-Fi. It is pretty well state of the art. Here's the part number, otherwise there are no markings. However, I happen to know it was made by Coulson Systems. We ordered some a few months back."

3G replied, "Excellent work. Run a full check of the entire building, everything. Check for video as well as audio. We are with you until this is done."

Tompkins went through the door and entered the building. He was using sophisticated tracking equipment, but stopped at once and pointed. He ushered the others outside and said, "There is a miniature camera mounted in the light fitting. I will presume it has sound capability. What exactly did these fitters have access to?"

3G rattled off a list: "First they were in ops for briefing, then up here on the roof. They had to run cabling down to ops, so had access to all the PBX closets on every floor. They fed the cables under the floor to Laredo's station. April found them in the computer room. Only one man did most of that, we presumed the other was working up here on the roof installing the satellite dish."

Cloverley remarked, "So ... that sealed cupboard over by the elevator head was also opened, to run cabling down, inside the building, and provide power for the dish. I need to see inside."

3G opened the panel, and they all stared at another transmitter. Tompkins checked the internals and spoke. "This sends information to the other transmitter. You see this cable attached to it. That is a computer cable. You said they were discovered in the computer room?"

She said, "Oh my God!" April began to run at once, but 3G shouted, "April! Wait."

Grace made her intention clear, "We are going to act normally, take our time, and pretend nothing is amiss. We have no idea how badly we are compromised. Everything we do or say, may be being monitored. You got that, all of you? Tompkins, do not wave that detector around, keep it close and out of sight.

"Priority, the central core, stairwell, and restrooms. We'll begin in the restaurant, and work through public and workspaces first. Bedrooms can wait, as can the basements. After ops, we'll check the computer room, and present an initial report."

The team worked through the building, finding the restaurant compromised by two audio bugs. They found a couple more in the bar area attached under tables. There was another camera bug on the first floor stairs, but CSI was clear.

There were two audio bugs stuck under desk edges in ops, and another under the new radar panel. The supervisory and secretarial offices were clear, much to Redmond's relief.

3G gave her initial report to Redmond, who reacted at once, "This could be extremely serious, or not. You say the computer room is clear of bugs? I want Rude in there to see what they may have hooked up to our system. What I really need to know is, what do they know? With all these electronics and concrete floors underneath the false ones, I need to know which bugs were able to transmit."

Tompkins spoke up, "That's not necessary sir. I'll monitor their transmission frequency and collect the data on our own receiver."

The team left, but April stayed with Redmond for a moment, before taking Rude for an unexpected walk. She set him to physically examine their computer arrays, and he motioned her to him, and pointed, whispering in her ear, "That's a USB Bluetooth wireless connector, and it is not one of ours. Fortunately, it is on the wrong server, but we have a serious problem. I'll check for others. Get 3G at once, there must be a transceiver in here, somewhere."

April left Rude scratching his head, and got 3G in there minutes later. Grace discovered the transmitter under the floor nearby, and it turned out to be hardwired to the roof. She said, "Want me to disconnect it?"

Rude said, "No, not yet. I need to trace where they have been first."

Redmond was seriously unhappy when he found out a few minutes later. His worry eased slightly when Rude talked about 'bots and spiders', and said, "The bottom line is, Chief, they were attached to the wrong drives, otherwise we would be fried by now."

Redmond replied, "Good. Isolate the two drives, I mean physically, and we'll start giving them misinformation. Well done. Full systems check, and separate double check, understood Rude? Our business revolves around secure information. Check they haven't planted anything in our systems either."

Rude answered at once, "Already done Chief, although I have a super-detailed scan running as well. There is nothing so far, and bots don't generally do that, although they can. My current check is for bots hiding as something else. Do not worry, this will all be sorted in a few hours time."

Cloverley came into Redmond's office just then, "Sir, we discovered there is only information from the top two floors, ops was not compromised. Your intuition was correct, too much concrete and interference. Want me to disable everything?"

Redmond said, "Remove all the bugs, but leave the transmitters on the roof, both of them. We are going to play some games with these wise-asses."

Redmond smiled for the first time that morning. A little later Rude confirmed their system was clean, Redmond's zest for the challenge returning, renewed by the inherently good news.

Regarding operations, another quiet day passed and it was clear the waiting was affecting everybody at headquarters. Ronnie let them know the Zippe centrifuges were being run down, and interference had diminished significantly as a result.

Redmond knew this was another clue that all processing of uranium was concluded. Now the focus of the enemy was turning to deployment.

More news came from Euan the next morning, but it was not the call to action they had been hoping for. Instead, he confided, "Our net is growing wider. It will be several days before we can close it. I believe it likely, Redmond, your team will be called to action before our Secret Service trap is sprung. With all our excellent intelligence, the only thing we do not have is a date for the missiles to launch.

"We consider it probable, invasionary forces are scattered around and outskirts of the continental U.S., concentrated perhaps in places like the Caribbean or Central America. Secret Service are monitoring selected sites for any sign of readiness. However, the likelihood is our teams will be reacting, and not on the preemptive offensive."

Redmond addressed Euan's concerns, and then his own. He asked that a missile battery be deployed at each launch site. He wanted to ensure that if the missiles were launched, they would be taken out before they got properly into the air. Euan thought the plan excellent and said, "Wait for a call from a trusted friend."

The conversation concluded and Redmond sat back with a mind full of uncertainties. He had expected Euan to be closing the net, not willfully growing it exponentially. He wondered for the second time, exactly which side Euan was working for. His only answer came echoing back the same as before, "the winning side." He briefly considered that Euan was playing him, but how could that be? They had to be on the same side, didn't they?

London managed to make contact after lunch, and spoke directly to Redmond. He had ascertained the missile control room would be finished within two days. London had spoken to Wiltshire briefly beforehand, and had confirmed they would all be out of the lower levels in three days' time. He also mentioned that Weinberg had told him that a missile was being primed, and that he thought the process would be completed within forty-eight hours. They surmised things were concluding for three days time, or possibly four.

No sooner had he finished the conversation than Lieutenant General Carl Bridgewater called. He had received a request from Euan and was about to action it. He asked specifically where Redmond needed the missile batteries located, requesting full details of the targets. The General finished by confirming the commanders of his two best units would be with him for briefing before the day was out.

Redmond breathed a huge sigh of relief. Now he had insurance in case anything went wrong. He knew, at worst, the missiles would be destroyed moments after they were launched. That was the best of his worst-case scenario. He called the Sergeant at Barstow at once, and asked for six more ceramic missile detectors to be available as soon as possible.

As evening approached, Redmond had been expecting two battery commanders to arrive. Instead, he found himself greeting Colonel Aldridge. He was surprised by the visit, welcome though it was. The men, with April present, discussed final deployment at Homer. Aldridge had already identified a suitable staging area. Redmond gave permission to proceed, and Aldridge gave the order for the advance party to begin operations at once.

3G interrupted them, stating that two battery commanders had arrived. Redmond had her show them up to his office. He asked the Colonel to stay, calling for Evelyn to attend. It was immediately obvious the men were eager to get set up.

Redmond took time to explain the situation. "You are likely to be our last line of defense. It is imperative that if the ICBM's are launched, they are taken out as soon as they reach fresh air. Destroy them as soon as they leave the silo, regardless of whether the warhead explodes. Do I make myself clear?"

All present considered nuclear detonation highly unlikely. Redmond surprised the commanders by telling them about the ceramic rocket that was undetectable with standard radar. He showed them video footage, before they spoke to his own battery commander. The commanders immediately identified the fix and lock problem, as Redmond's man spoke.

Redmond received word the Sergeant from Barstow was arriving by helicopter, and they all watched as the new detector was added to Redmond's missile battery. They were shown how to install the equipment, set parameters, and deploy it.

Once the installation was complete, Redmond saw his new troops to their vehicles. On the way he took a brief review. Aldridge said, The initial deployment will be in position by first light tomorrow. I will deploy my forces as soon as I leave.

Captain William DeWinter volunteered his missile battery for duty in Alaska, having had a little experience of arctic conditions. His opposite number was pleased. Captain Peter Winthrop gladly accepted the easier of the two assignments, nodding his deference to his friend and colleague. Redmond gave each battery commander one of the new ceramic missile detectors.

Redmond took the moment to speak openly, "Gentlemen, whatever happens in the field, remember you take your orders directly from me, on behalf of the President of the United States. Your only purpose is to prevent the successful launch of the missile. Do I make myself clear?"

Winthrop replied, "I have worked under Salmond before. Do not worry, your orders will not be countermanded by him, or anyone else."

The three military men left a short time later. Redmond returned to ops, where he found himself in company with April and 3G. He had a good feeling about Alaska, the more difficult of the two assignments. However, he remained worried about Hoover Dam. There was something in Salmond's attitude that simply did not fit the threat. He retreated to his office, accompanied by the girls. Evelyn interrupted and he asked her to stay.

April spoke into his thoughts, and told him she was going in with the first wave, and would take the best men 3G had to offer. She made the call because she too was nervous about how Salmond would perform. Redmond tried to dissuade her, and could have overruled. Her idea had great merit, but was this the best use of personnel? He asked, "Alternatives?" Waiting to see if anyone else had come to the conclusion he had.

3G spoke up and disagreed. "This is the wrong call, Sir. April is the only one of us who has experience of Homer, and I believe her insider knowledge to be vital to successful completion of that mission. Remember, we only have cursory information about the Alaskan complex, and perhaps if April could get to a computer terminal, she could learn a lot more. This information could be of instrumental importance to Aldridge. And besides, Bill will be there to watch her back." 3G looked knowingly at Redmond who nodded.

"At Hoover Dam we have many people on the inside. They already have a working knowledge of the place, and we know it is a far smaller operation. I would select somebody else to lead our team there, Sir."

Redmond spoke immediately, "That is the correct assessment. Thank you for your timely input, 3G. Who do you suggest for the role at Hoover Dam?"

3G replied at once, "I will go. It has been a while since I was on the front line. Nevertheless, I would really welcome the chance to prove myself to you, and the team in general. A woman of my age, doesn't get to be Sergeant First Class without being very good on the battlefield, Sir."

Eyes turned to look at her, and she answered them, "Israel. I was deep under cover in their army."

April immediately sided with her, adding, "It'll be great to see my father again." She started to cover her mistake, but no one present appeared to have heard the word she spoke. Instead she concluded by adding, "I must find Melissa and take her up for Bill, I am sure he has missed her."

Three pairs of eyes turned to stare at her. Redmond tentatively enquired, "Who is Melissa?"

April giggled and said, "That's the name of his shotgun. He calls her the only woman who will never break his heart."

Redmond acceded to their requests. He put the Cessna at April's disposal once more, and asked 3G to see to all requirements.

April leapt up and Redmond thought she was going to kiss him. Instead, she hugged him briefly, before she whirled away to find Melissa, and plan her mission. Redmond watched her leave, and looked over at Evelyn. She had remained quiet throughout, but had made copious notes. She said, "I thought she was going to kiss you."

Chapter 38

Redmond laughed it off as a stupid remark, stating, "Ours is an entirely platonic and professional relationship. She is simply a young and excitable girl. She reminds me so much of my own daughter."

"And your daughter is, what? Five? Hon, that ain't no first grader." Evelyn watched him for a moment, wondering how blind a man could be, for the truth was obvious to her. As he turned for his desk, she caught a look from Grace. It was affirmative. She stifled a chortle finding the situation so funny she had to make a weak excuse and leave, taking 3G with her.

Chapter 39 – Event Horizon

The following day during morning briefing, Nick Norton presented Redmond with a model team behavioral pattern, which indicated that Coulson would strike sooner rather than later. He had failed to identify the man in ultimate control, but had used Godfrey DeMellor as his archetype, and results from this fit the pattern exactly.

Redmond asked, "How certain are you that Godfrey DeMellor is the man behind all this?"

Nick took a moment to collect his words before speaking, "I have nothing directly attributable to the man, although Teves noted his son's presence in Phoenix. I did, however, manage to put together a personal profile from information mainly in the public domain, complimented by military and agency insight. He fits the character ninety-eight percent, meaning, if it is not him, it is somebody extremely similar, his son for instance."

"When will the strike start?" was Redmond's next question.

"Don't go putting words in my mouth Redmond, I don't work like that. DeMellor will strike at the first, best opportunity. That will be after both missiles are armed, and when his reserve is mobilized. With the information the team has, I would presume both missiles would be ready for firing some time tomorrow.

"DeMellor will not push the button immediately. Like I said, he will strike at his best opportunity. I would deduce this will be at night, and when his support forces are just outside the main blast radius. The ground disruption you have been tracking for months has not begun, so it is logical to presume this will begin on the morning of the strike, perhaps twenty-hours before the main threat is manifest. They will want maximum news coverage, maximum terror, maximum disruption, not only from their own sources, but also from inept people trying to help. From the profile, I would expect this to be Washington, D.C.

"This gives us another problem. The troop aircraft will need to be a safe distance outside of the EMP blast radius. Either that, or they will need to be safely hidden in a very secure place."

"Like under a mountain you mean," Redmond interrupted.

"I was not thinking of that exactly. But EMP shielding is possible, so yes, either that or a Faraday Cage."

229

"I doubt DeMellor would work that way, even if he had the resources. Secret underground hideouts large enough, and deep enough to shield several large aircraft would be very difficult to provide. EMP shielding is highly classified, and even if he has a line on it, prohibitively expensive on that scale. However, it would be cheap and economically viable to shield a cell phone or personal communicator.

"I also believe DeMellor likes his cash too much. I think the first strike teams have already been deployed, or are staging as we speak. This would be my best deduction, according to the profiles I have assembled.

"It would seem logical that support will come from off the Eastern seaboard, and link up with personnel already on the ground in Washington. They will bring with them new electronic systems and disperse them amongst the teams. When deployed, this would make the enemy virtually the only people with reliable communications in the whole of the Capital, and the East Coast U.S."

Perry spoke up, "I agree, and will add that as we understand it, there will be several hours delay between the Washington EMP, and the arrival of the second wave troops. Within this time, forces will be brought in from outside, that have working electronics and communication aids. Given the EMP blast radius, two hundred miles off the eastern seaboard fits the intrusion dynamic. The enemy would arrive within the hour if deployed by say, helicopter.

"In some ways it is like a typical terrorist strike, where the initial strike draws in crisis personnel, who are in turn taken out by a secondary, and larger explosion, the EMP. I feel sure this is DeMellor's objective, and opens the way for his invasionary forces."

Redmond brought up a map of North America, and put it on the main screen. He looked at Nick, but threw the question open to everyone in the ops room, "If you wanted to keep out of the blast radius, but have a large team ready to invade the U.S., where on this map would you put them. I already accept there will be a sea borne support, and possibly a tactical strike force off the East Coast. Bridger, try and locate the ship if you please."

Redmond left them to think it over. It was not a race. This question demanded the correct answer. His team suggested the eastern tip of Canada, Greenland, The Azores, and Florida? They knew that from any of these locations, the aircraft must already be preparing for takeoff.

Bridger had been working her own angle, and spoke up, "Sir, I have a hit on Coulson Maritime Exploration based in Bermuda, which is British of course. Satellite shows a secure compound, several large buildings, and small associated docks. I doubt this is a major staging post, but it could be where the supply of modern tech is stored and shipped from. It's about six hundred nautical miles from D.C."

Redmond replied at once, "Good work Bridger, I'll let Euan know immediately. I am sure Coulson would not risk an incident with the British government. But, as you pointed out, this is worth investigating, especially regards the stockpiling and supply side."

April was staring at the map, thoughts of Florida being quickly dismissed, whilst those of Alaska kept intruding, despite the fact she tried to swat them away. Subsequently something in her mind saw the obvious. She leaned forward in her seat and began zooming in. Others were aware she was onto something, but would wait for her to work it through. She spent some time panning around using the satellite feed, before she jumped up and pumped her fists in the air.

All eyes turned to her expectantly. She had a great smile on her face as she said, "Ketchikan, southern tip of Alaska, just north of Prince Rupert. There is a large buildup of militia northeast of the town."

Bridger and Laredo were on it immediately. They found there were dozens of vehicles hidden under camouflage canopies. There were almost as many billet huts, and moments later Laredo discovered the nearby airfield with almost eighty planes of all sizes and functions. Half of them appeared to be transport planes capable of transferring both men and equipment quickly to a drop zone.

They had the strike base identified. Redmond whirled to his office and called Euan again. "I request an all forces strike on an enemy base we have just identified near Ketchikan, Alaska. This threat is very real, video footage being sent now. The map and satellite coordinates are as follows…"

"If it is not possible to mount a strike, know we suspect that troops with full tactical and electronic capability will be sent to all parts of the U.S. Your previously identified task groups would augment this main strike capability.

"The final part of this report concerns tomorrow. The assault will begin with a concerted attack on the emergency infrastructure of Washington, D.C. I remind you, we may be one day out. When the attack deploys, expect explosions, bridge collapses, and strikes at malls. Hospitals will be subjected to viral outbreaks. The water mains will be blown, and fires will rage without dampening, drawing in all emergency services. These will become so stretched outside assistance will be called for. The Metrorail will be taken out, as will the railway. Power plants and the electricity grid will be targeted by cyber attacks, as will information services and landlines. I expect the internet to go down, and cell phone networks to cease functioning.

"Euan, what I am describing is an escalating state of emergency."

Euan kept his own counsel and said, "Go on."

"When, not if, Washington, D.C. is overrun with multiple local emergencies, out of state resources will be required. When the state of chaos is at maximum, the EMP bomb will be unleashed and everything that is electronic will cease to function. I suggest you get the President out of there, and to a safe place where he can continue to administer the nation's welfare.

"We also believe the second missile will detonate a second EMP wave several hours later, and after assistance has been sent in from outside the first blast radius."

Euan interrupted briefly, "Your theory makes sense. There are people I must inform as soon as we are done. Please continue."

"Euan, the very old pulse telephones, like the one Michael has. If the wiring is not fried, they will be about the only means of communication you have left. I suggest you log every single one that still works in the entire country as a contingency plan, beginning with the Capitol. I will install one here, your ability to contact Michael means we still have the mechanical analogue system at a local telephone exchange.

"We have plans in place to overrun both known missile launch sites, and we are confident of doing so. I also have artillery batteries equipped with ceramic missile detection. In the event of a missile being fired, we will take them out as they launch. Sir, I request interceptors patrol the skies above each location. I believe the threat, should even one of these missiles get out, to be that deadly."

Euan took his time to digest the information, and made a brief call. He stated, "You have your aircraft on standby. They will be in the air as soon as you have confirmation of launch time, or the silo doors open.

"I will inform the President, but know one of the Joint Chiefs' underlings remains under suspicion. The Director of National Security appears bona fide, but there are others—high-ranking officials in the department we are investigating. We need several more days to close our net, and it looks like time is running out before us. Let me know the moment you have news."

Redmond finished, "You will have your countdown clock begin whenever Washington, D.C. is hit. I would already be calling up the National Guard. I believe the threat is imminent. Our focus remains to stop the nuclear EMP's detonating in the atmosphere."

Euan seemed to choose his final words carefully, "I hope you are right Redmond. We will be monitoring and taking appropriate countermeasures of course. Regards Bermuda, that was an excellent call, Redmond, one we are diligently following up. Do your duty and we will all come through this thing together. I must speak with the President immediately. Please excuse me."

Invigorated once more, Redmond went down and spent time with ops. He could not fault their work. He was also aware that tomorrow night, or the next, he would need everybody on night shift. While he would monitor the situation, he encouraged them to devise their own shift systems as suited them best, ensuring one person of each team was always on duty and ready to respond to the first threat.

Rude joked that he needed a coffee machine in ops. Redmond saw the joke, but said to 3G with a wink askance, "You know those coffee machines they have at gas stations. They have many options and pour out something creamy that vaguely resembles coffee. Get one of those in here now, and put it over there. Any other requests?"

The calls for chocolate dispensers, snack machines, and even sandwich dispensers were quick in coming. Redmond smiled and said to 3G, "Do not over-indulge these children, but do what is reasonable regards increasing work efficiency." He smiled wistfully at her and walked away to catch up with CSI.

April followed him, and Evelyn watched, now certain her female intuition was correct. She chuckled to herself, wondering how this bizarre romance would play out in the round. She was already rooting for April.

The next day was a dud. Everyone was disappointed. April delayed her intrusion by twenty-four hours. Everybody was very aware they were at the event horizon. Redmond could not understand why he was worried, but he remained anxious. He knew something did not fit, but for the life of him, he could not work out what or who.

Redmond mused, "Waiting time is slow time; seconds pass like hours. Expectation of others quickly becomes as debilitating a handicap as hope, whilst useful things are left undone."

Redmond realized that hope and doubt were intertwined; expectation of others would be a while forthcoming. He deliberately switched focus, knowing Euan would eventually step-up, when it suited him.

April bounded in and said, "Nige, you're taking me out for a restaurant meal. I fancy curry, or Chinese."

He replied, "Italian, let's go."

They got back quite late, slightly drunk, and laughing. Evelyn noted that Redmond was already a lost cause, and pumped her fist in support of April. They ended up in their own bedrooms, and Evelyn thought that right. Their love would be a long time in the making. It would be all the sweeter when it bloomed.

But then, what did she know, with two failed marriages, and someone else's brat that insisted on calling her "Mother."

She almost turned away, yet her heart went out to this couple, even if they did not realize it yet. Redmond nodded to her as he passed by and went to his own bedroom, the ultimate gentleman, as always. Evelyn could not help but snicker quietly, a habit she used to hide her dreams of what could have been, should have been, and what could be.

In time, she accepted tomorrow was perhaps the biggest day for every living American. She knew she would be in the thick of a hoorah's nest of politics, and wound her weary way to her own room—and very lonesome bed. Alone again, naturally.

Chapter 40 – Under Siege

Lonely picked up on the first sign of trouble at 2 a.m. She had been monitoring all news concerning the U.S., and Washington, D.C. in particular. She began the log with the first entry using East Coast Time, "0502 hours ECT: 14th Street Bridge pontoon collapse, suspect concrete weakening agents used, local reports of a small detonation. Bridge closed to all traffic." She knew this was a main transit artery into the heart of Capitol Hill. Their target was identified.

Lonely logged several smaller incidents, before she made another entry at 0554 ECT: outbreak of Legionnaires disease, St. Elizabeth Hospital, now closed to all future admissions.

At 0605 ECT, Lonely began receiving reports from Union Station of people suffering from flu like symptoms. Within minutes, these escalated to breathing difficulties and muscle spasms. Reports came in from both upper and lower station levels, with heavy casualties being reported from the Metrorail.

Within ten-minutes Lonely updated: railway station assault had been summarily attributed to Sarin, and was a concerted attack with many sources within the complex. Air conditioning and internal fans shut down to slow dispersion, the entire station was closed.

Lonely informed Redmond, but urged him not to wake up. Redmond contacted the team on the ridge at once. "It has begun. I need your teams, and Cooke ready to go at 0615 hours PST."

Minutes later he was tightening his tie down in operations, monitoring activity. He spent a moment with Lonely and checked the log. He asked her to add columns for PST and Zulu Time. The pattern was clear, and as expected. From his office, he picked up the satellite phone and made a call. Agent 9 answered. Redmond said, "It has begun. This is simply a confirmation call that Washington, D.C. is the main target. I will speak to Euan later, although I expect you will be very busy today."

The call complete, Redmond stretched out on his sofa, and was asleep in moments. 3G woke him with a coffee at 6 a.m., and ran through his strategy for the day. His planning had been meticulous, yet he went through everything once again. Satisfied, his thoughts turned to their first action, freeing the hostages.

Shawn Cooke checked for thermals, but was little surprised when there was nothing of note. He hurried back to ensure Plan B was ready for takeoff.

Redmond knew timing was critical. Ronnie had established shift changeover at the mine was nominally 7 a.m., but this was like police and Army, the time they had to have transferred the watch and were actually on duty. Lonely had already moved the drone into position and was able to track when the day shift guards went for breakfast in the main canteen at 0620.

As soon as he received confirmation, Redmond actioned the SWAT and helicopters, and gave Cooke the go. He knew they were largely relying on the night shift being tired and getting ready to hand over duties to their opposite numbers, unprepared for a surprise attack.

With the helicopters airborne, attack dynamics rested with Cooke. He strapped himself into the powered paraglider and took to the air. He used the rear of the building to hide his approach, hoping no guards were on patrol, and slowing to a stall, landed gently on the roof.

Once in position, he cut a complete window out, using suction cups to set it to one side, and assembled his abseil gear. He fixed grappling hooks across the rooftop and brought them under tension. Once set, he spoke briefly to Lonely and entered the building. The message ensured two support helicopters would arrive within one minute.

Cooke landed on top of the central secure area, very near the rear of the building. Checking for foot patrols, he was pleased to note there were none nearby. Using a high-power nail gun, he secured a rope ladder and slid down to open the rear fire door. Seeing support abseil down outside, he propped the door open and set a charge on a twenty-second timer at the corner of the secure area holding the captives.

Meanwhile, the second helicopter at the opposite end of the building began firing, one missile taking out the guardhouse and main gate. This allowed ground forces to enter the compound in support. The chopper wheeled and fired again, demolishing a fire door set into the blast walls. Helicopter troops were already on the ground storming through the gap, and heavy fighting ensued at once. All defenders' attention immediately diverted to that end of the hangar.

The guard with the hostages was surprised when the door opened. He fell, firing his machine pistol at the doorway, as smoke grenades filled the corridor. The rear wall blew and, distracted, he turned around to confront the new threat. That was the only distraction the advancing team needed, and soon the sole guard was captive.

They used his keys to unlock all the cells, the prisoners scared stiff, but overjoyed to be rescued. There were eight of them, one more than expected. They were immediately shepherded out, and straight into the waiting helicopter that had since landed. Weapon fire came from the edge of the building, as incursive troops held firm to complete the extraction. Once the helicopter was out of range, word was sent to Redmond that they had also recovered Bob Rogers.

The crew dropped their precious cargo on the ridge and returned to the fight below. Laredo had already pulled in a favor, and a Police Department helicopter took the hostages directly to Headquarters. Redmond knew things were going their way and they would prevail. Although his words were very few, his smile was like the sun rising, and every single one of his team responded eagerly.

On the ground, the frontal attack was pinned down and taking casualties. The prisoners secured, Sergeant Raybold led his platoon up the rope ladder Cooke had provided. He set snipers to cover point, while his main force raced directly across the roof of the inner secure area to undermine defensive positions. As soon as they were in position, Raybold gave the order to fire. The enemy suffered many casualties, and fell back despite being reinforced by the day crew.

Under heavy assault, the defenders gave way and realized they were fighting on two fronts. Reinforcements swept through the main entrance of the mine to augment the attacking troops. Within minutes defenders were corralled. It was not long before they surrendered. Advancing forces were in control of all but the inner complex.

Captain Garth Brookes stepped forward as his men contained the compound and, under Rude's direction, entered the appropriate pin number to activate the electronic lock as he swiped their leader's security pass. Once inside, biohazards became his main concern. The few people inside were highly qualified nuclear scientists, who thought they were working on a secret project for the U.S. government. They were quickly disabused of that notion. The two guards with them were quickly dealt with.

The scientists were removed for debriefing as soon as machinery was safely shut down. All efforts inside became firmly fixed on the control room. It fell after an extended gun battle, the door was blown, and the occupants were soon en route to sample Salamander's generous hospitality.

No sooner was the hostage release confirmed than Redmond ordered the hospital orderly and his wife, plus the other parents, be brought to HQ. Their children would need to be debriefed, but this was a secondary issue to restoring their family unity, and finally easing their worries.

Redmond's team learned that all of the parent had been compromised, and had been forced to cooperate with Coulson's operation. Redmond left instructions for all the hostages to be returned to their homes just as soon as their debriefing had been completed. He tasked Evelyn with contacting Social Services regarding support and counseling.

His mood lightened when overjoyed parents began arriving to claim their children. Overdosed with gratitude, he returned to his office, seeking a cave to hide within. It was not to be, as April whirled in and changed his mindset within moments. Her youthful exuberance was contagious.

Soon their thoughts turned to Homer. As they spoke, his concern battled her fervor, and she skipped off as if to prepare for a school prom, ready to make up her face and choose her battle dress.

April streaked her face with dark, Army issue war paint, and donned camouflage for the intrusion. She took a final briefing with Redmond and 3G, before Grace reminded her she would not need the make up until late that night. April removed the face paint, and replaced it with her Goth. She needed to feel, to be herself. She slept a little, before making her final preparations, and attended her troops with 3G. Her men were waiting for her, and within the hour, the small team flew out of Gillespie Field.

Redmond was with ops, monitoring the latest developments in Washington; the fire department was the next to suffer, responding to a vehicle showroom attack very similar to the one in San Diego. As units were responding, a warehouse fire was reported in a commercial area close to Ronald Reagan Airport. A nearby water main blew; there was no water to douse the flames.

Redmond called Euan and told him that April and her team had departed for Alaska. They spoke only briefly, Euan telling him his forces were closing the net as quickly as possible. The President had already evacuated, and Congress had been closed for the duration.

The call finished, Redmond spoke to Darren. "Your team's work is far from complete, and yet I need everybody to man stations in ops. I know this is not what you signed up for, but this is the more imperative mandate. The final moves have begun."

Yates replied instantly, "Where do you need us?"

Redmond immediately relieved Lonely's vigil of Washington, D.C., which was taken over by Siouxi, thus freeing an experienced comm. operator.

Redmond spoke to Laredo, telling her he wanted her on comm. from 6 p.m. for a long shift. Laredo went back to bed for a few hours, took lunch as breakfast, and settled in for a long shift. Nearby, Bridger had done likewise. Rude took an afternoon nap, as did Lonely, but both were on the floor again before evening arrived.

Bridger set up a ticker feed that displayed the main strikes as they came in on the main screen. Darren and Jules worked together updating this, while Perry supported anyone in need. Redmond used April's workstation whenever he was in ops, needing to be aware of everything that went down.

Returning to her console, Laredo was surprised to find an old Bakelite rotary dial telephone had been installed at her comm., another was located in Redmond's office. She was about to query if this ancient technology had any worth, when she remembered about the EMP's.

She toyed with the dial, realizing the device was mechanical, and would still function even after all modern digital aides were fried. New respect grew within her for Redmond and the team. She asked Perry for his advice, before calling Redmond on it to congratulate him, also confirming that the device actually worked, and that she knew how to operate it. Unbeknownst to her, Redmond had already done likewise with Michael.

Redmond did not regard the three-hour time difference between Washington, D.C. and San Diego as being particularly significant to the team's operations. Time in Anchorage was one hour behind Pacific Time. Sunset was more than two hours behind. That was significantly more critical. Aldridge had kept his forces on Pacific Standard Time to ensure there would be no errors. He dismissed using Zulu Time as Redmond worried about his team, who were not used to working in what amounted to GMT.

Washington, D.C. continued to be hit with minor troubles. As the afternoon wore on, reports from other cities began to come in. Darren and Jules were being swamped with information before Nick brought himself and Ronnie to assist, and later Sherry joined them. The ticker-tape rolled swiftly:

1502: Pittsburgh lost all electricity.

1504: New York Stock Exchange down.

1505: Chicago, wildfire virus released on the internet.

1506: The Pentagon, extreme multi-bot attack, DDoS (Distributed Denial of Service).

1509: Rude: DDoS attack. Pentagon secure, internet capability compromised.

1512: Birmingham, Alabama; Communications blackout.

1534: Rude: Chicago virus identified as the first Super-virus ever released in the public domain.

1544: Under emergency session, Texas declares independence from The Union.

No one had expected the enemy would target more than one objective, but cyber attacks began to manifest in all major U.S. cities. The country buckled under the miasma of confusion, loss of functional power, and communications famine. Rude tried to trace the source, but each attack was routed differently; in spite of which, he persevered.

1606: Seattle IT hub disrupted.

1607: Silicon Valley IT hub disrupted. Major worldwide disruption of internet.

1609: Major cell phone relay stations swamped, data overload: D.C., N.Y., Chicago, LA, Miami.

Emergency services became increasingly stretched. The President called in the National Guard, and backup services arrived from neighboring States.

1713: Cascading explosions at storage facilities disrupt Washington Gas Energy Services.

1713: Cyber attacks and denial of service continue.

1713: Overload brownouts at Potomac Electric Power Company.

1716: Smartgrid failure. Northeast Megalopolis blackout.

1718: Water mains failure: D.C., Baltimore. Billions of gallons dumped from standing water towers.

The ancient Emergency Broadcast System was activated, and relayed a constant stream of information. Normal information channels became compromised, batteries failed and the few people who had hand crank radios, became one of the main sources of information.

This in turn started a stampede, as people took to their cars to escape the destruction of their known world, only to end up in endless traffic jams, roads having been sealed off due to other strikes. The scene replayed across the streets of America. Soon Washington was grid locked, preventing emergency services from reaching their targets.

The President made a nationwide broadcast, urging citizens to stay at home until the situation was normalized. His speech was effective, for those few who were able to receive it.

No one had counted on a hard core of agent provocateurs, apparently separate from the Coulson group, but taking advantage of the mayhem. They mixed with ordinary protestors, multiplying discontent, and urging groups to violence. As sunset arrived shortly before 8 p.m. Washington, the situation quickly became heated. From seemingly nowhere, crude weapons and Molotov cocktails came into the hands of the most agitated. Demonstrations quickly turned into riots. A state of emergency was declared and a curfew ordered.

Enemy explosions moved from targeting depots and mass storage sites, to sources within the gridlocked traffic. The first wave blew up fuel tankers caught in the traffic jams, causing panic as people fled their cars seeking safety. Many ran towards buildings, while others jumped into nearby rivers. The second wave targeted street-side gas stations. The explosions repeated in all major cities, intersections, and neighbourhoods.

Army reserves assisted the National Guard and local police, to begin returning some of the Capital's streets to law and order. They used cranes, bulldozers, snow ploughs, and brute force to clear streets for passage by emergency services, and opening escape corridors for ordinary people caught up in the civil unrest.

Riots created several no-go areas where looting was rife and numerous malls were overrun. Buildings were engulfed in flames. Emergency services fell back from the war zone and focused on containment. Insurgencies were reported across the length and breadth of America. The pattern repeated and multiplied. It was full dark in D.C. when Redmond noted the strikes appeared to be tapering off. He knew the citizens of his great country were being primed for the final assault, when even those who had prepared against 'Zombie Aocalypse' would be at a loss, as their generators, and supplies became useless and tainted.

3G called Redmond aside and stated she needed to prepare with her troops. They departed when a military helicopter arrived on the roof to extract them.San Diego had also become gridlocked as the evening wore on.

Redmond purposefully switched off the main screens, and called his teams together in order to focus their minds on the real work that lay ahead of them that night. "Everyone, gather round. What is happening in the Capital and across the country is horrendous, but it is also, exactly as we predicted. The situation is being brought under control. I remind you all, our only focus from now on is to stop the two nuclear missiles being launched.

"Ops, forget Washington, D.C.. There is nothing any of you can do to improve the current situation. You can each make a very big difference with our main objective. At all costs, we must prevent these ICBMs from being fired, and turning this nationwide disaster into Armageddon.

"I want focus brought down to your own desk, and your own work. Do whatever you can to prevent these rockets getting into the air. Every person in this great country is depending on you. So are April and 3G."

Redmond stopped speaking to look at everyone by turn, in the eye. Once he had reinforced his requirements, he finished, "The rest of you, please continue as you are. I need to know immediately of anything major that breaks the pattern. Let's do this and show our true worth. Thank you."

Immediately the atmosphere in ops was different. They knew April and 3G were leading raids, two of their own were going in. All minds focused on the danger zones. They were determined to support April and 3G to the best of their ability.

As darkness fell, first in California, and almost three hours later in Alaska, teams on the ground came to readiness and moved in to attack positions. They were held back for a while as sunset at Hoover Dam was at 1928 hours. Up at Homer it was scheduled for 2244 Pacific Standard Time. With the slow sunset in the north, full darkness could not be assured until 2315.

Redmond made the call, instructing both teams to begin their attacks at 2325 PST, precisely. He stipulated that he was to be informed immediately if the silo doors opened. Bridger was already monitoring both sites, but Redmond needed to state the fact as an order to his troops on the ground. He requested both pairs of interceptors to be flying over their target destinations by 2320 hours.

Time in Washington, D.C. was moving into the small hours. Siouxi updated Redmond at 11 p.m.. Washington time was 2 a.m. She reported, "The main streets are still chaotic, with gridlock persisting in these places. Otherwise, the suburban streets are relatively quiet, although a lot busier than normal. There are pockets of rioters, but the situation is largely under control. There is also similar news from other cities, and there have been no new cyber attacks for hours.

"In the Capital, power to hospitals and essential services has been restored, at the cost of rerouting from business and private buildings. This was to relieve pressure on fuel for their generators, although a little is getting through. Water is once more available to some domestic users with an order to boil, even if the supply is intermittent. There are standpipes on the streets, and not enough of them. Water tankers are beginning to arrive, where they can get through the mess left in the streets."

Chapter 41 – Hoover Dam

As Redmond worked with ops, 3G led her small group to the forefront of Salmond's attacking corps. She had been hoping to avoid the General, but knew enough about politics to become proactive when they accidentally came face to face. Grace was prepared and knew his type, "General Salmond, I was just looking for you. I have been sent in with a specialist platoon to liaise with our people on the inside and open the way for your main forces. We have orders to go in with the first wave and secure advanced bridgeheads. Where do I set up?"

"You don't set up. You go home." Salmond growled.

3G used her headset. Suddenly Salmond was receiving orders directly from Redmond. Begrudgingly, he accepted her presence, and instructed her to move in with Captain Delaney. The Captain proved to be an experienced soldier in battle conditions, having recently returned from duty in Afghanistan. 3G spoke openly about their ingress, asking for his dedicated support.

Delaney's orders had not been specific regarding ingress, and vague as to any quantifiable objective. His team was to make first penetration of quadrant A, and hold for further orders. The depth of first penetration had not been specified, and so he felt able to offer her his full support.

They moved within ten-minutes, and by 2315, were in advanced positions. London had at last been able to get into a tactical location where he could make radio contact.

London gave 3G the current code for an access door to the north of the compound, stating Annaliese would meet her once they were inside the complex. The seconds ticked by, and at 2324, the team made its dash toward the door. They were exposed and wasted no time. Grace tapped in the code and they were in.

London guided them through the outer corridors on his headset, the team taking out cameras as they progressed. Annaliese was waiting to lead them into the heart of the complex.

Mendez and Walker were running point on either side, while Hackenridge was waiting for them at a busy intersection on the far side of a large thoroughfare. At his signal, teams of four set off. Annaliese led the first, making three stops marking cover, before she reached safety on the other side. Other groups followed her lead in stages, and once across she took a lookout position.

Chapter 41

The whole team was almost across when Annaliese waved frantically. 3G, Delaney, and one other were left adrift in no man's land, sheltering behind a column and shrubby plant. Two men of higher management wandered down and took armchairs close to their position. Delaney signaled for radio silence. The men seemed in no hurry, chatting about baseball.

Only four minutes elapsed, but it felt more like ten to the trapped. In time, one of the managers looked at his watch and stated, "Thirty minutes to go, I better get back. You enjoy the evening and have one for me. I'll catch up with you in a couple of hours." The men stood and left, each going in a different direction.

Once safe again, 3G informed Laredo, "I have a clear indication that something important will happen in thirty-minutes time. I do not know what this will be. I presume it means either silo doors opening or the missile launch. I cannot be sure. The operation will be concluded in roughly two-hour's time."

Laredo passed the information directly to Redmond, who knew Alaska would now be working to a similar timeframe. He told Lonely to pass the information on to April and Aldridge at once.

Hackenridge led them deeper into the complex, and to a busy corridor they had to cross. Walker was at one end, and Mendez at the other. They signaled the all clear, and the team raced across the short divide, making safety in a little used stairwell, where London was waiting with a large smile. He said, "Past this point it is almost impossible to get a signal out. We have now entered the core area. Note the walls are three-feet thick, and block any signal. This doorway is the only access point for external communications. If any of you need to make a report, now is the time to do it."

3G and Delaney sent updates back, before following the others down below. Within moments, Laredo lost comm. All ops could do was wait and hope. Laredo just had time to get a coffee from the new machine in ops, before her station was busy again. She stopped to wonder how anyone could do such diverse things, with such aplomb, on the same day. She did not envy 3G her position.

3G and her companions rushed down the stairs to level eight, where London briefed everyone. "We have to descend one more level, where I will cross a passageway to the dogleg right, and open a secure door. Pay attention. Security cameras cover the corridor we will enter. We need to make our way through to a specific access passage, and at the end is the missile control room.

"Once we leave this stairwell and I have the door open, we must all run, since we will end up in a killing zone if we cannot reach control before they lock the place down. Fortunately, Weinberg is on the inside, and Wiltshire is waiting outside for our appearance. I am sure we will make it."

London was good to his word and led the team unerringly, taking out cameras as he went. Wiltshire was waiting at the other end of the last corridor. As soon as he saw them, he waved, taking out the camera at his end, and disappeared.

Meanwhile, inside the control room, Weinberg had been working on a supposed glitch. The controller was not happy with his presence, but apparently, a surge on one of the relay circuits might start a chain reaction that could prove critical. He had not bothered to confirm the story because Weinberg was one of the established crew.

With ten minutes to go, the controller opened the silo doors and checked missile trajectory. He initiated the final countdown sequence and looked across at the fitter. Weinberg received a message from Wiltshire, and went to use an internal telephone on an empty desk, "Hi, I need a VFC3-18R modulator relay immediately in control, this one has had it."

He appeared to receive a reply and thirty-seconds later Wiltshire was at the door holding up a device to the access door's camera. The controller let him in, as these two often worked together. He called out, "Get on with it and get your sorry butts out of my sight."

The controller's world went black when Weinberg chopped him on the neck and pulled him away from the control console. He ducked down as security brought their pistols to bear on him. Wiltshire held the door open and used it for cover. 3G burst through, rolling to take out one of the guards. Delaney was close behind her, and swiveled as he also rolled, firing at the other and badly wounding him.

They quickly took the three other operators prisoner and began to tie them up. The female among them complained, stating she was CIA and working deep under cover. She showed them her badge, which London confirmed was genuine. She was not tied up like the others, but was held with them in one corner of the room for debrief.

Chapter 41

Weinberg finished tying up the controller, as others did likewise with the hapless but still living guard. Annaliese was last in and closed the door, calling for people to help her barricade it. Wiltshire went round the room with a borrowed gun and shot out all the cameras.

Weinberg sat at the controller's console, and performed a quick review. The silo doors were open and the shed covering the launch shaft had been wheeled back. The missile was open to the air, the countdown registered 07:03 minutes, and dropping. He had to stop the missile from firing and brought up the abort screen. He was prompted to enter a password, and entered the original one, but it had been changed.

The countdown continued, with less than six-minutes until launch. With time running out, they tried to revive the controller, but he was out cold. Annaliese left the group to try to find a line out, hoping Rude would know what to do.

3G acted instinctively and began speaking with the operators. She demanded to know how to abort the countdown. They all replied it was impossible, that they were civilians and stated they had been brought in for this special task by the U.S. government. The CIA woman, Kerry Hearne was their liaison.

3G continued to debrief them, and discovered there was an executive office overlooking the console area, the hidden stairs leading up from the far side of the room. She turned to look as Hearne came up behind her and deftly placed a garrote around 3G's neck. In one swift move, Hearne yanked it taut and held a gun to 3G's head.

Using her as a human shield, she called out, "Stop what you are doing and move away from the consoles."

Everybody stopped to stare. She jerked the wire tighter, making 3G's eyes bug-out. People moved hesitantly away from the controls, but Hearne kept up the pressure on Grace's throat. She took control of the room, saying, "Good. Now throw your weapons to me. All of them."

It was clear to all that 3G was being strangled. Hearne glanced at the clock. There were only two minutes left until the missile launched. Hearne smiled and held her ground. She occupied the others by having them tie each other up. The seconds ticked by quickly.

3G heard noises outside the door and looked toward it. She knew she was expendable, and the only thing preventing the others reacting. She took a deep breath against her constricted throat, and sagged as if she was dead. Hearne had not been expecting this so soon, but had to react at once. The dead weight of 3G was dragging her off-balance. She was forced to let go of the garrote and bring her gun to bear on the invading forces.

Hearne had been unable to see that 3G was in fact only collapsing from the knees up. Her feet were in perfect balance and she was poised to strike back. She could still feel Hearne's body behind her, so knew her relative position. Opening her eyes to encourage her team, Grace sprang upwards violently.

There was a loud crunch as the top of her helmet crashed into the underside of Hearne's jaw. Both women fell awkwardly, 3G onto the floor semiconscious, while her antagonist went flying backward and bashed the back of her head into the wall.

Soldiers raced to them, quickly shedding their loose ties. Mendez was one of the few not to have been tied up. She ran, collecting her gun on the way, and stood over Hearne. She was willing her to react so she had an excuse to fire. The CIA Agent was out cold.

Mendez and Walker attended to 3G and Hearne, while Hackenridge took care of the operators. Both Weinberg and Wiltshire were already racing back to their consoles.

The access door was being repeatedly pounded with something heavy. Delaney gave his men orders to fire a few warning shots, the banging stopped. He set his men in defensive positions, next time he expected them to use explosives.

Meanwhile, Annaliese ran back to her call with Rude, who wanted to know what had happened. She ignored his question and looked at the countdown clock. It read 53 seconds until launch.

She reacted instinctively and yelled into the phone, "STOP! The missile will takeoff in fifty seconds. We have run out of time, thanks to the CIA. Tell Winthrop the missile will launch immediately, and get him to destroy it."

Redmond was on comm. to Winthrop at once, "We are out of time. The missile will launch in forty-five seconds. Take it out. I will speak to Salmond in a moment. Forget him. Do your job Captain. Save America."

Chapter 41

Redmond delayed his call to Salmond for another thirty seconds, leaving him no time to compromise their operation.

Back in the control room, Annaliese stayed on the line to give a short debrief to Evelyn. Rude kept trying to access the master control station, but too late. They all heard the roar.

The time was 0011. The first-ever, ceramic, nuclear Inter Continental Ballistic Missile had just been launched from American soil. It was intended to strike hundreds of miles above Cincinnati, and produce an EMP wave, that would take out all electrical devices over the entire Capitol District, and well as New York, Chicago, and Detroit.

Winthrop also heard the roar, having immediately brought his team to readiness for interception at source. The nose of the missile slowly emerged from the silo. With target locked via the device Redmond provided, Winthrop had set the acceleration compensator, aimed 100 feet high and directly vertical. The first missile winged the nose. They shattered the body to smithereens with their second missile just as it cleared the pod.

The nuclear warhead bounced within its casing, but did not explode. Specialist units recovered it a short time later from the ground nearby. Cheers of success filled the air, and Salmond called Redmond at once to confirm the threat was annihilated, praising Winthrop for his great work.

The great news from Hoover Dam buoyed the team. Redmond wasted no time in contacting Euan to tell him one threat had been eliminated. He had the call put on speaker, and was duly congratulated.

High praise continued to come through from Washington, D.C. and the military, but it was overstated and too soon. At Evelyn's direction, Redmond was prompted to say the right words, and he was very convincing.

Redmond left Evelyn to deal with all the unwanted praise. Another battle was still raging way up north, and the outcome was, at best, uncertain.

Redmond remembered one specific girl's eyes looking back at him from a doorway, and willed her to survive. His fist punched the air in front of him in frustration, and the other with rising determination, he set about his next objective, to focus everybody's efforts in support of April.

Chapter 42 – Homer

As 3G took her first steps in company with Delaney, Aldridge was giving final instructions to his field unit commanders. They were ostensibly playing "war games," and this had been highlighted by media leaks orchestrated by the Chiefs of Staff. There was already an ongoing war game in the South China Sea, which was drifting northwards. Aldridge knew Coulson would smell a rat, but hoped the enemy would not have the time, or resources to react.

Aldridge had already called up helicopter gunships to assist their initial strike, since Coulson Homer was a vast complex and they needed a diversion from their main strike thrust. He had made the standing order that no unarmed civilians were to be killed, but thereafter the brief was laid open to interpretation of the level of resistance offered.

April and her platoon had arrived a few hours before, and held an immediate but highly constructive briefing at the advanced staging area. Aldridge called for Captain Eric Van der Burden as soon as they concluded, and detailed her to join his advance force. He in turn assured her of the fullest support from his team. He assigned her to work with Master Sergeant McMillan.

April felt like she was a hot potato when, after a short briefing, McMillan in turn handed her over to somebody else. April waited for the next man to arrive, and rolled her eyes. Her platoon snickered in the background, which encouraged her. Sergeant First Class Melrose rushed in moments later and saluted.

McMillan saluted back and said, "Melrose, may I introduce Special Intelligence Analyst April Bekkons from the FBI. She is here under direct orders of the President. Give her whatever assistance she requires, and make sure she and her platoon come to no harm. Dismissed."

McMillan saluted again and left at once. Melrose's face fell when April asked him, "Whom are you going to pass me on to?"

Melrose saluted her, and stated plainly, "You look young and fragile, but I've heard a thing or two through the grapevine. I will be at your side until this situation is resolved, Ma'am."

"Ah!" said April. She dragged him by the hand to a nearby chair and briefed him more fully. They agreed to meet once more before they went in. Melrose hurried away, calling in a few favors owed, and bringing two men onto the team as April had requested, specialists in intrusion and explosives. Within the hour, Melrose checked his battledress, and went into the FBI tent. They talked about the mission, before he enquired about April.

Gerry Tavistock, one of the few regular men from headquarters, rose and said, "She may look like wisp of nothing, but you should know she is Fourth Dan Kung Fu. She was badly wounded, yet battered a brute of a man virtually to death with her bare hands. He had a gun and a knife. I hear she broke every single bone in his body. Don't let looks deceive you, she is one hell of a tough cookie"

Tavistock spoke into the stunned silence when they realized he was deadly serious. He related more of April's deeds, and all were in awe. April approached from the darkness, and could not help but pause momentarily to listen. Her heart swelled with pride, before the situation confronting them stilled her ego. She made a noise outside, waited a second, before marching in ready to give her parting words.

Everybody jumped up to salute her. She giggled, "Thank you. Now, if you ladies have all finished gossiping, we can get on with our mission. Here's how we play it. Sergeant Melrose…"

The attack on Homer also began at 2325 PST, and at first, they made great headway. Colonel Aldridge had tasked several small teams with taking out guard force and tactical positions. They secured the perimeter, allow nothing in, and only civilians out after duly processing them in a secure warehouse. Homer telephone exchange was already offline, as were all cell towers, a communications blackout in place, except for the military net.

Other teams under the direct control of Van der Burden went through the normal factory and warehouse levels, clearing civilians and forcing them to evacuate.

Bill was waiting with Bert Singer and Danny Schuler. They led McMillan's advance party deep into the complex, and to defensible areas, before they ran out of eyes-on, personal knowledge. Bill did offer them maps of the complex, upon which he had marked potential security positions, known cameras, and a route to a restricted area. He apologized for not being able to do more.

Aldridge was worried, and told Redmond of his concerns privately. They had not yet identified the missile silo, although it showed plainly on the separate section of the schematic. DeWinter was anxious, as he had nothing to target in readiness. Their only hope was to take the control center, and from there find the missile's location.

Otherwise, they relied on military drone operators to spot, within the darkening night, when the silo doors opened. This left them an estimated ten-minutes to react to the impending launch, and prevent the missile destroying the heartland of America.

Unlike Hoover Dam, Coulson Homer had evolved over many years, with layers of development, and although not premeditated, ensured an attack would be compromised. The complex was like a rabbit warren, with many renovations and dead ends.

Bill's information proved reliable at first, and guided them through the maze. They discovered a secure inner compound, but unlike Hoover, they had nobody on the inside and were stalled.

The military pressed ahead, blowing out walls, expecting to discover their goal around each corner. However, the expected control center never materialized. Instead of missiles, all they discovered was research and development, some areas being marked as bio-hazards.

Bill was unsure, as the map of the control center did not match what he was witnessing. All he had to go on was the intuition that something wasn't right. He spoke directly to his daughter. "Hon, the cookie ain't crumbling here, all we got is the back ass of a mule. There's ain't no place down here that feels big enough to be a silo."

"Any sign of control rooms, or large windowless areas that would be used by overseers keeping safe from radiation?"

"Nothing. There are research laboratories, and some computer banks, but nothing with enough display to control and guide a launch."

"Keep on looking," April replied. "It's got to be here somewhere. I'll see what else I can dig up"

§

April and Melrose had gone in with the first wave of attack. Melrose went, with their main platoon, directly to IT, while April rushed through to the canteen restrooms where she entered the Ladies Lounge with two male soldiers and one female. Everyone donned gas masks and gloves before entering the ventilation system.

As they crawled through the ductwork, Melrose headed for their rendezvous point, his ingress specialist leading the way. He was unaware of the source of the map that guided them, and was surprised when one of April's colleagues informed him the map was obtained by her infiltration. Melrose reviewed his initial assessment of the girl, and determined he would never underestimate her ability again.

April and her team made good progress and soon came to the outlet. She saw her chewing gum was still in place, pointed at it, then her mouth. The others understood. The room had low-level lighting, which meant it should be unoccupied. April moved to open the panel, but an arm restrained her. One of the troops had a miniature camera on a flexible tube, and indicated he wanted to put it through the slats and check.

April let him get on with it, and was shown two people still engaged at their consoles at the far end of the room. One of them was Dave the manager, and she whispered she needed access to his computer; they needed to restrain him before he had any chance to turn it off. The soldier made hand gestures, and they were set. She was unhappy at going in last, but saw the logic of it.

Her troops slid through without making a sound, and soon compromised the workers. April followed them, but stopped to listen as her father came over comm. "Hon, the cookie ain't crumbling here, all we got is the back ass of a mule …"

She noticed his worried tone, and said she would do whatever she could, her mind a quandary of possibilities and probabilities. Ignoring the lesser stations, April checked the Departmental Head's office first. He had already been hurried out, and had been prevented from turning off his computer.

April began working at Dave's computer, found a trail and followed it, ending up in a very secure part of Logistics. There she discovered a dedicated transport section labeled, "Inter Site Drivers." Dave's login gave her a better level of clearance and she could access specific information not available to her before.

April discovered a reference to a Military Firing Range, and asked Melrose to confirm. His reply came quickly, and was negative. Intrigued, she followed the lead where it took her, and made a startling discovery: they were in the wrong place. The missile was somewhere else. The complex they needed to target was situated close to east Bridge Creek reservoir.

She spoke to headquarters at once, "Lonely, this is urgent. There is a second site where the missile is located. It is not at this base, but close by. Rude, I need you into this network, look for inter site drivers, find out all you can, especially a subsidiary location.

"Bridger, I have references to a military firing range. Sergeant Melrose states categorically, that it is not on any map the military have. We think this is simply a ruse to keep people away and stop them poking around. I need immediate transfer. Locate the complex for us and send through the coordinates."

Redmond leapt into action, speaking to Aldridge first to divert the current attack to a nearby, but unknown location. Redmond came back to April before he gave the final order and simply asked, "How sure are you this is where the missile is?"

April did not hesitate, replying immediately and forcefully, "One hundred percent."

Within the computer, she was searching building services when she found another clue. She spoke into her mic, "Bridger, look to … just southeast of the reservoir, I have barracks and training halls mentioned in that location."

Redmond came over comm., "Excellent work April. I want you out of there now. Aldridge is preparing to ferry troops by helicopter as soon as we locate a silo. Head for the delivery yard nearest your current location, and get on the first chopper you can."

April stopped and thought for a second before saying, "The container I followed was offloaded here. Have somebody track down the inter-site drivers and they will tell you exactly where the other location is. We are leaving now."

Lonely locked on a spot using an Army drone, and identified a large circle, with a cluster of buildings half a mile distant. It was indistinct despite the night vision cameras, but it appeared they had identified a very large and secure compound. Presumably, most of the site was underground.

She informed Redmond of what she had discovered, and continued to monitor. Laredo beside her, glanced over and thought she could make out a couple of other similar circles, but the light was against them. Laredo told her they would inform Redmond as soon as their suspicions were proved correct. Bridger was bringing up a live satellite feed, but was still waiting for the objective to be reassigned.

Redmond confirmed the new orders with Aldridge, telling him to get DeWinter, April's team, and a strike force up to the reservoir as quickly as he could. Aldridge acted on the information immediately. He called Van der Burden to move out at once, but asked him to retain several platoons for ingress to hide their change of tactics.

Aldridge knew time was short. He spoke briefly to Military Transport, and commandeered several Chinooks, the first to take DeWinter and his crew, plus as many troops as they could, directly to the new location. He readied the mobile battery for new deployment at once, before charging Van der Burden with allocating troops to transport in other Chinook's on a need of ingress basis.

Chapter 43 – Bridge Creek

April and her small team raced to the nearest exit. She ran out into the delivery yard, and immediately saw the missile battery being coupled by wires to the underbelly of a Chinook. She waved her team to follow and sprinted hard to reach it in time. The Flight Sergeant stopped her and told her to join the other queues.

DeWinter saw her and hurried over, "Sergeant, Bekkons and her team are imperative to the success of this mission. They come with us. Let them inside."

The Sergeant counted the men and stated, "There are two men too many, we will fly heavy. I will inform the flight crew at once. Have a nice trip."

The flight was exhilarating, but nice it was not. They were crammed into two rows of hard seats set either side of the cargo bay, with their backs against the fuselage. The massive twin rotors managed to miss each other, but created a conflicting series of vibrations, as if the craft were trying to separate into two halves.

Despite this, April was able to update DeWinter during their short flight. With the clock firmly against them, they were both aware his crew's missile battery was vital to the success of the mission. Bridger relayed coordinates for them to set down. Coming in to land, the Chinook was dodging searchlights.

The whispering rushes of stealth-silenced helicopter gunships raced passed them as they exited the twin-rotor craft. Searchlights were taken out, and preparatory strikes initiated.

DeWinter moved his howitzer into firing position as soon as the last shackle had been removed. The Chinook took off at once, to be replaced by another dropping off Van der Burden and an advance force of U.S. Marines.

April ran for the nearest building entrance, her platoon one of the very first to arrive. They moved quickly and quietly, entering the building through a wall breached by a gunship's missile.

The dust of destruction billowed around them, the intermittent lighting making the scene appear more harrowing, macabre. Water dripped and electronics crackled in symphony, as human blood ran in rivulets across the deranged floor. People were groaning, bleeding, and dying.

April pointed for Melrose to move forwards with his men. She called for immediate medical aid and asked the attack helicopters to stop firing at the buildings. She was with a man bleeding badly from his arm. She made a tourniquet with a rip of cloth and stopped the blood loss.

She was just tying-off when the man wheezed, "Why are you attacking us? We are civilians working on a secret mission for the United States Government."

April rose and shouted; "Listen up. I know what you were told, but they lied to you. You have all been working against the interests of the U.S. I am FBI and here to stop a nuclear missile being launched on Washington, D.C. I am here under the direct, personal order of the President himself. Where is the control center?"

Medics, not troops, poured through the door and began to attend to the wounded. McMillan entered next with his elite corps. They ran ahead, and moments later, Melrose returned with their small force.

A medic was working on the man April had saved, although he was still in a very bad way. He spoke, realizing the truth of her words, "Ma'am, thank you for saving my life. I want to repay you the only way I can."

His words became whispers as his life ebbed. April knelt down close to hear his words. A few seconds later she stood with a large smile on her face and told the medics to take great care of him. She turned to Melrose and said, "Let's go."

As McMillan focused on penetrating the building they occupied, April surprised Melrose by leading them outside at the run, heading to the darkened rear of the clustered buildings. She led them unerringly to what appeared to be a guardhouse for an empty parking lot. There was a light on inside, but no one was visible. She ducked down close by in a hollow and stopped to brief her men. Partway through, a voice she had known all her life came over her comm., "April, where are you, you still alive? I'm coming to help. You bring Melissa with you by any chance?"

Her face broke out in joy and relief. She was smiling brightly, and close to tears. "Dad, I have her. We need you. We are here…"

A short time later, Bill finally laid his hands on his pump-action shotgun and some bear shot. He suddenly felt invincible and pumping the gun in the air, made his presence felt immediately by taking out the security stronghold single-handedly, while others planned. Direct action was his way. Melrose and the team ran to catch up with April, following the man. They all knew they now had a lion on their side.

§

McMillan's troops were being reinforced, and used explosives to break through a series of barriers. They encountered a mix of Coulson militia and civilians, who were either killed, captured, or evacuated. Everyone heard the noise and stopped what they were doing. A missile landed close by, taking out a helicopter. The airborne division quickly retreated, as missiles continued to rain down outside, before targeting the buildings.

Aldridge was already with his troops, having established an advanced HQ nearby. He was briefing Van der Burden when the first missile exploded. The briefing incomplete, he signaled the Captain to leave. He was straight on the radio, asking primarily for information about the new attack from the rear.

Before he was done, enemy helicopters arrived to hover nearby, delivering opposing forces to strategic locations, before relocating to fire missiles at Aldridge's troops. The Coulson foot soldiers were skilled in use of the local terrain, and were soon driving Aldridge's men back. The Colonel knew he needed reinforcements, and quickly. He turned back to the comm. and relayed a series of rapid-fire commands, determined he was not going to be overrun that easily. He ordered support be dropped behind and to the side of the enemy's new positions.

Coulson Homer's missile deployment schedule was behind that of Hoover Dam, but had been brought forward as Redmond predicted, by virtually twenty-four hours. At 0035 hours, the silo covering slid back to expose the missile to the cool Alaskan air. Presumably, countdown had been initiated, and the threat was live.

Taking stock, Aldridge knew they would not seize the control room in time. He prayed for a miracle, but knew it would not be forthcoming. He had a mission to complete, and would ensure they destroyed the ICBM.

Aldridge's discomfort was distracted when DeWinter fired a salvo. His team had no threat on radar, but within seconds, two missiles were taken out of the air. They were ceramic, and fired by opposing forces behind them. While information was collated and checked, Aldridge sent out a call to Redmond. "We predict the ICBM will fire within four minutes. We cannot get to the control room in time. DeWinter is briefed and ready to take it out.

"However, we are now coming under ceramic missile attack from the shore, and DeWinter has taken two of them out, saving many lives in the process. Know we are under attack from two sides. I will act accordingly and take steps to eradicate the external threat. Aldridge out."

§

As events in Homer unwound, Laredo called Redmond over, reporting, "Sir, Team Hoover Dam has requested permission to stay and assist with the clean-up operation."

Redmond took comm., "Congratulations 3G, this is a superb result. Your job is done. I want you, and all our troops on the first available chopper headed back to HQ. Understood?"

It was clear by her reply, 3G was not happy, but he knew most others would be grateful to get the hell out of there.

Words spoken at Redmond's side brought him to focus on the other concurrent threat, one still to be resolved. He wished April were nearby. That she was directly in harm's way only added to the nerves he was experiencing. His friends and staff committed to impossible action against even more impossible foes, he wondered if they would prevail. He felt like breaking, waiting on others' actions became a curse.

Redmond mused:

"Hapless worry time is slow time. It fires the mind's negativity, and distorts obtusely, mankind's true purpose and human conviction."

He knew he had to hold together, because the team— everybody was depending upon him to remain resolute. He unconsciously sat at April's station to monitor developments.

§

Back in the field, Aldridge felt the tables reverse. Missiles targeted his positions, and his forward thrust stalled. He picked up the comm., "McMillan, use your initiative to break through. Blow out the walls, use explosives and rocket launchers if you have to, but I need you to take the control room as quickly as you can. Stop this missile launch at all costs!"

The conversation hardly complete, Aldridge dove for cover as he heard the shrill whine of another missile approaching. It landed very close by and ripped the fabric of their command post to shreds. They were covered in mud, as a sense of mortality descended upon his operation.

Aldridge rose from the sludge with a new sense of purpose, grabbing the fallen mic and issuing a string of orders as he swiped dirt from his mouth and chin, flicking it away with grubby fingers. He asked one of the circling jets to identify their opponent's outer positions, ordering the other to come in close and prepare to fire.

He heard the explosions less than one-minute later, the pilot reporting, "Shore battery removed, Sir. Enemy support ship out at sea. It has a gun turret and missile batteries, permission to strike, Sir?"

Aldridge had the answer to his problem, a Coulson support ship with weapons capability. Now he understood the enemy forces, he could make constructive plans to prevail.

He desperately wanted to confirm the pilot's request, but he knew the interceptor aircraft represented their last line of defense against the much greater threat. A chopper would make a better tactical choice for offence against the ship's weaponry capability. "That is negative. Resume patrol to take out the ICBM if it gets through our battery. This is your top priority. Once we have dealt with the major, and most imminent threat, we will consider the ship at sea. Aldridge out."

Aldridge immediately spoke with the lead helicopter gunship, tasking them to disable the weapons of the vessel out at sea. "I need the gun turret disposed of by any means available. Try a pincer movement so at least one pilot gets a lock on it."

Good news came moments later. McMillan had used his initiative and blasted through to an inner area. Fighting was still heavy, but they had taken the defenders by surprise, and were once again moving forward and deeper into the complex. McMillan continued to take out walls when they became bogged down, stretching the defending forces, and eventually separating them from one another. The only thing his team did not do, was move downwards.

Chapter 44 – Into the Underworld

Meanwhile, April and her far smaller force were using intelligence rather than brute strength, and making swift inroads. They now controlled the direct access point to the control center many hundreds of feet below. Bill had killed one of the guards unintentionally, the others were now being interrogated. Melrose identified the Captain of the Guard and started to process. He was getting nowhere fast.

April interrupted him and held her revolver at the leading guard's head. He continued to refuse her enquiries, so she slowly pulled back the trigger. He watched the hammer rise with mounting dread. Suddenly, a bear of a man was gouging a shotgun under the guard's chin.

He stated, "Commander, now is the time to speak. If you want to live?"

The man said, "Twist, asshole." Bill pulled the shotgun away and rested it vertically along the crease of his chin. He looked deep into the man's eyes, and put his finger on the trigger.

April knew he would remove the man's face, and pushed her father aside. She took the guard in a wristlock, and quickly forced him to the ground. She had Bill sit on his back, and realigned so she could twist her captive's wrist, elbow, and shoulder, all against the joint.

The guard screamed with pain, and within seconds, they had the information they needed. Melrose called Aldridge directly and asked for backup. April confirmed as they swiped the commander's card and entered his pass code. The elevator doors opened and they went straight down with a dozen troops.

They braced for a firefight when the doors opened, Bill insisting on going first. Two surprised guards met them. They took one look at the invaders, and with a blast of encouragement from Melissa, laid down their weapons. Melrose took them prisoner, and after binding with click-lock cuffs, had one soldier return them to the surface. He came back down again a minute later with more troops.

April pushed past her father's bulk and led the way, deeper into the underground lair. They followed the short passageway directly ahead, which finished at a tee junction. The new corridor curved both right and left away from them, as if containing a central core. She beckoned four men to go paired in each direction.

They had only taken a dozen paces when they ran back dodging bullets. April knew the real battle had begun. As her men came back to them, grenades were hurled and they dove for cover, relinquishing the intersection as they did so. They took shelter in nearby rooms, grenades were thrown at them, and some were hurled back. They had a stalemate.

April called for Corditch, the explosives master, and spoke quickly. He handed her a large lump of C4 set with a 3-second timer. April called for short burst of weapons to fire, activated the timer, and threw it against the wall behind the defenders.

The explosion was deafening, and when the smoke cleared, the enemy bodies were a mush of blood and gore, not one enemy soldier was left alive. The wall opposing them had blown, and April was first across the gap, she did not look to the side. Others swarmed behind her; Melrose left men to build defensive positions, and take the curved corridor that presumably surrounded a central, circular core.

Fresh troops joined them from the rear, which Melrose immediately deployed, as they and others moved forward to follow April. They raced into the empty room, before slowly stopping in front of a very secure elevator located in the center. There was no way to open it. Troops spread out to cover the whole area.

The Guards card and pass code didn't work. Military men offered solutions, none of them practical. April took herself aside to think, as was her way. She knew they were so close, but just a whisker from the goal. She walked as she thought, and came around to stop beside a door that said "Sanitation. Keep Clear"

She thought the sign was very odd, before noting the door could only be opened from the inside. Her intrigue compounded when she looked around and saw a janitor's room beside the restrooms on the side wall. April realized she had almost walked around a rectangle, the elevator being set to the shorter front face. She was juxtaposition and tried the door, but it felt extremely secure.

Detecting a ruse, she ran the remaining few yards and interrupted the mighty genius of military planning. "Ladies, I need somebody to open the fire escape door, and I am sure the stairs behind lead directly to our objective. Come on!"

She turned at once and ran back. Elmer Corditch followed her at once, but he was low on C4 and wanted to keep the remainder for the final assault. She asked Melrose for a rocket launcher, but they were due in the next lift down. She tuned and punched her fist into the wall with frustrated power. To everyone's astonishment, a large chunk of plaster fell to the floor.

April mused aloud, "Aerated concrete blocks."

She stilled and found her center. She imagined the killing punch, and focused the blow in her mind and body. Using the heel of her hand, she punched with the whole force of her body behind the strike. The block stayed where it was. April was aware these things took time, the reaction was already at work within the composite brick.

She held up her other hand and counted to five. She knew the blow had to take full effect before she repeated it. Her next strike demolished the block, which crumbled to dust. Behind it was a second row of blocks. She kicked once and broke clean through the second layer, before using a fearsome foot barrage to enlarge the opening. As soon as it was big enough she dove through and opened the door from the inside, "Ladies, follow me if you will."

Sergeant Melrose bashed his fist into the wall, and only managed to crack the plaster. He looked forlornly after April as she disappeared, unsure why he had ever considered her fragile.

Several of his men also tried, only hurting their knuckles in the process. Their efforts hardly dented the plaster. Melrose swallowed hard and led his men into battle, following wholeheartedly to a man behind their extra-ordinary leader.

They went down a long way before reaching another fire door. Again, they were on the wrong side of it. Everyone expected April to put her fist through the wall, but Bill touched her arm and moved to the front. He stood far too close, and brought Melissa to bear. Grinning, he fired.

Concrete shrapnel exploded into the corridor they needed to access. Bill reached through immediately and hit the panic bar square on. The door opened and they were through. The leading troops walked into a hail of bullets, and several took serious injury. Bill shook the shotgun to reload, and blasted first left, and then right. The groans of the fallen encouraged others to flood through the bridgehead, and they commenced firing at once.

Chapter 44

Bill did not follow. Instead, he chucked the gun in the air, and sent a barrel of bear shot into the wall in front. It blew to dust, and afforded their troops a get out. Two men dove through for safety and immediately came under fire.

April was first to react, Melrose a step behind her. They somersaulted into the room intent on saving their men. Instead, they rolled and came up firing at guards in the main control center. Troops poured through after them, as first one guard, followed by the other, threw down their weapons and stood with hands high in dread of being killed.

Melrose took them away, as his corps surrounded the six other people in the room and motioned them away from their stations. April rushed to the controller's console, but knew too little time remained. She quickly spoke to Redmond, before rounding on the controller with her venom afire.

The roar of rocket engines was deafening.

They were too late: The missile launched.

Chapter 45 – Last Line of Defense

April huffed and walked away disconsolate. They had failed to stop the missile launch. She spoke at once, relaying the bad news to Redmond and Aldridge.

Her words were deafened by a series of very large explosions that obliterated her communication. Everyone except Bill, Melrose, and herself dove for cover. The controller reached for a panic button. April sprang at him, breaking his outstretched arm with a single blow. He recoiled in immense pain. She was no longer playing around.

At first, they thought DeWinter had taken out the ICBM, but the explosions continued and shook the whole complex. April requested immediate information. Bridger answered her, "Reports are unclear, but it appears your location is under heavy fire from several very large guns."

Above ground, DeWinter was targeting, waiting for the missile to appear above ground. Instead, a hail of large shells exploded, engulfing them in acrid smoke and alarm. The mobile defense unit was badly compromised. They worked quickly to try to repair the damage, racing against time to have it ready to fire. The unit was almost crippled, but not quite. Another shell landed too close and severely wounded the gunner.

DeWinter swore and ordered an immediate retreat. He realized the enemy was using spotters to fix their position for the long-range guns out at sea. The enemy had not hit anywhere near the silo opening, but was devastating their positions. His small force ran, but the driver insisted on trying to move the howitzer to safety. Moments later a shell landed on the cab, killing the valiant man instantly. The missile battery was completely wrecked. DeWinter reported the bad news to his Commanding Officer. His report received and relayed, Aldridge remained resolute. He pulled himself to attention, and continued to face the impossible situation.

Redmond interceded, thanking them for gallant work. He ordered the interceptor jets to take out the ICBM at all costs. They broke from holding pattern, but could no longer follow DeWinter's radar signature to get sighting and lock; it had disappeared. The threat was a ceramic missile.

As he dived to intercept, the air commander relayed the facts. "Red Wing, we do not have the new radar feed. Visual sighting only. We will have to fire manually, old school. Rely on your training.

"We have at best twenty-three seconds before the ICBM is faster than we are, and perhaps another eight seconds before it is faster than our missiles. From our current relative position, it will take us twenty-seven seconds to target our heat-seeking missiles, giving us only a four second window. Let's do this. Red Wing Leader out."

The strike aircraft dove and went to maximum thrust. The G-force was excruciating, but they came into target range, the ceramic missile dead ahead. They were above as Red Wing Commander closed, aimed and fired. His first two missiles fell low, as the ICBM continued to accelerate faster than he expected.

He would normally dive, but the air commander pulled up and climbed on a provisional collision course, one he constantly adjusted. To his wing, his number two aligned for attack. Mere seconds passed as two more missiles headed for their target.

One rocket missed, and the other clipped the propulsion outlet, shearing off an exhaust cone, but there was no explosion. His two heat-seeking missiles were locked on target, but due to their necessary trajectory to seek the heat source, ran out of fuel before they could get close enough.

The ICBM accelerating to match his aircraft's top rate of climb, Red Wing Commander aimed his remaining missiles to pass several hundred feet above the ceramic missile. It was already clear to him, this ICBM was accelerating faster than any threat he had ever faced before. He was working entirely on gut feeling. He had flown in the days before computers took over, and knew to trust his instincts.

He closed his eyes and made a momentary prayer. A split-second passed before he opened them, and saw his target surging from below. He judged their comparative speeds and acceleration, and knew he was a dead duck to take the missile out with his aircraft. This was a kamikaze mission, but one that would save his country. He knew what he had to do, and acted instinctively.

The distance between them closed too quickly, as the massive ICBM continued to accelerate, its speed now greater than his own warplane. However, he was still above it, and close enough to make out white lettering on the red, moonlit body and access panels beneath, as they came closer and closer together.

One way or another, he knew the beast would fall into the mighty Pacific Ocean.

Red Commander picked his mark in the sky, the tail of a wispy cloud just visible to the naked eye. He fired all four remaining missiles on board at one third of a second intervals. He was manually firing into the unknown.

The nose of the ICBM rose and passed him. He was so close to it, he thought he could reach out and touch it. His first missile was high, so was his second. His third caught the upper structure to the side, and almost spun the missile. The fourth missile hit dead center. The ceramic fuselage exploded in a ball of fractious flames.

He flung his aircraft starboard and down, hoping in vain to avoid the remains of the lower body that continued to target him. There was not enough time, and he knew it. The scrape of metal against shearing ceramic sounded like the wail of a banshee. He fought to control his interceptor, and flew on, the unearthly screech lessening as his fighter began to veer and sheer away.

Warning lights indicated his landing gear was crippled, but Red Wing Commander was jubilant. The fragments of wreckage were deadly, as shrapnel strafed his craft. He had holes in wings and fuselage, and a fuel tank rupture, but the old bird held together. He was wounded also, but still alive. He knew he would have taken the missile out with his fighter if the ultimate sacrifice had been called for. Soon he was clear and barreling tumbles through the air, his wingman following him in celebration.

Everyone watching heaved a great sigh of relief, including Redmond, who was first on comm. to congratulate the pilot. Helicopter gunship's came over the radio, reporting the enemy ship disabled and a support task force approaching to take the survivors into custody.

They were all rising to celebrate, when April came over the comm., instantly turning their overwhelming joy into despair.

She had just inspected the controller's console, and stated loudly, "There is another missile!"

Chapter 46 – Persephonê Rises

Everybody who heard her words froze on the spot. Mouths opened to gape, too shocked to utter a sound.

"There is another missile," April repeated. "It will launch in thirteen and a half minutes."

Redmond finally understood what had been worrying him so much over the last few days. He had failed to attach enough significance to the first container Teves and April discovered at the hub in San Diego.

Redmond castigated himself when he realized the second clue. April had identified two ICBM's when she was at Homer. Both were detailed to explode at the same altitude, one above Cincinnati, and the other over Salt Lake City. These would be the two missiles based at Homer. He deduced they did not have any information for the trajectory of the missile at Hoover Dam.

He considered, four large boxes and three smaller boxes. Divide twelve and nine by three respectively, equals one set for each of three missiles. There were also indications of three smaller, and extremely heavy boxes, one per container. Redmond cursed aloud. It was so obvious, once he knew what to look for.

Faces turned to look at him, unused to this manner of outburst. He explained briefly, "Homer had enough nuclear material for two atomic bombs. We all presumed these to be one missile each at Homer and Hoover Dam. By simply telling the container hub the cargo was going to Dallas, we presumed it did, and wrote it off as unrelated. It is now obvious this was a ruse, and that container was also loaded onto the Anchorage Vista. April stated the container she hitched a ride with, was one of two set aside for imminent collection.

"I missed the clues, and now we have virtually nothing to prevent this launch. That is, unless April can come up with something outside the box."

Redmond crumpled into the nearest chair, April's chair. He tried to focus on the present, not missed opportunities of greater understanding from the past. Finding a little resolve left within, he rose and spoke to each operator in turn, encouraging them to do their best, "All is lost, yet. Focus. Find a solution."

Up in Homer, the mood of premature celebration was sweeping all combatants, when Aldridge gave orders to fix for a second missile launch. Soldiers wasted valuable seconds to get their minds in focus. He had to wait moments longer for troops to answer his comm.

Aldridge received confirmation the missile battery was out of service. The fighter aircraft reported they had no missiles left and were returning to base. He thanked them genuinely for their great work, but asked if more interceptors could reach them in time for the second launch. The answer was immediate, and negative.

Aldridge and Redmond both tried other military channels, but there was simply not enough time to get any assistance to them. The Colonel spoke to the helicopter gunships. The pilots reported in turn, each having used up their supply of missiles on the ship at sea. Even if missiles remained, Aldridge knew they needed a missile lock to fire, and there wasn't one.

With a heavy heart, Aldridge briefly considered crazy options: deflecting the missile, but where would it land? Bombing the silo, but to what effect, he only had small arms in advanced position, RPG's and C4. He opened a secure channel to April, Melrose, and Redmond. His report was chilling and brief. He began, "Melrose, The only chance of preventing the third ICBM launch lays with Agent Bekkons and her team. I am sending reinforcements down to you, April. What do you need?"

She replied without thinking, "Rocket launchers."

April suddenly realized what she had said, and wondered as her subconscious mind worked in advance of her reality. She had been at the controller's console for a very short time, but was unable to bring up the abort screen. At her order, the controller was dragged to her and she sat him down in his chair.

She shouted at him with menace, "I need this launch aborted, now."

The controller replied that it was impossible. April pulled her revolver and aimed it at his head, and asked him again. He gave the same reply. She snatched the weapon down and fired a bullet between his thighs, very near his genitals, ripping both legs badly, but knowing she had not hit anything vital.

She grabbed him by the throat stating, "You may consider me a bad shot, or you could consider me an extremely good shot. I will demolish your limbs, one by one, until you type in the code to abort the launch. Do I make myself understood?"

He nodded and flopped down into his chair, but failed to react. April spun him back to his console, placing her revolver aimed at his left hand. Bill was there to hold his hand outstretched. April placed the barrel to his wrist, and began pulling back the trigger, as she looked him in the eye.

The controller visibly wilted and attended to his console, bringing up the abort sequence, typing in the access code, before highlighting "yes", and hitting the enter key. The screen went blank, and moments later came back up. The clock continued to count down.

April had him do it all again, before smelling a rat. He had glanced back at an office set above that appeared to be empty. April reasoned this was the manager's station. She spoke quickly, "I need into that office up there at once."

The controller stated he did not have a key, and nods from other operators told her this was likely. At her gesture, Sergeant First Class Melrose stormed up the stairs and found a high quality lock set in a maximum-security door. It would take hours to get past this. The rocket launchers had been recalled to repel the surface invasion. They were waiting for replacements to make their way down, which would take several minutes, time they did not have.

Melrose took the butt of his machine gun and bashed the wall next to the top of the stairs. It gave instantly and revealed another plasterboard skin on the inside, sandwiching a 4 x 3 wooden frame. He stood outside the metal staircase and first made a foothold. Once set, he bashed the temporary plasterboard walls with his rifle butt. They gave quickly and with enough of an opening, he dove through. There were sounds of a scuffle before the door opened and Melrose stood aside, the manager lying unconscious on the floor. He held the door open for April, and as she came to him, he saluted, smiled, and stated, "As you wish, Ma'am."

April stopped to looked at him. She took his rugged jowl between finger and thumb, and shook it playfully, "Ma'am?"

She let go with a big smirk on her face, and waltzed inside still muttering, "Ma'am … Ma'am?"

The Sergeant was beetroot red and offered a magnanimous grin, as it took over his entire face. Captain Van der Burden, who had just arrived with reinforcements, came up the stairs next and shook his hand, "Thank you, Master Sergeant Melrose. Yes, a field promotion. What's the critical situation this moment?"

April was beginning to settle into the new console when McMillan rushed up. "Ma'am, I have just received information we have captured the head of IT section. My men are working on him now and I am sure he will break quickly."

April glared at him. Neither did she believe anyone would break within the time remaining, even if they had the knowledge. It was a diversion; she focused solely upon what difference she alone could make. The console had not been turned off. She took her time and realized a second silo door had been opened, and the missile was set to automatic countdown.

She almost called for the controller, but she did not trust him. She glanced back at the manager, but he remained lifeless, spread-eagled on the floor. She closed her eyes and with her eidetic memory, recalled the keys the controller had pressed. She ran over them again to be sure in her mind, guaranteeing there could be no mistake.

She watched as her fingers flew across the keyboard, one eye on the monitor, and the other on her excellent recall. She pulled up the screen she needed, and reached the abort prompt. She highlighted, "Yes," and hit enter. The screen dulled and she glanced at the countdown clock in the main room below, seeing it change from 8 minutes to 07:59. Mere seconds passed, but each one felt like minutes. She stared at the screen willing it to life. Around her voices murmured, all watching the computer intently.

The normal screen returned, the countdown continued. The manager was still out cold. She rifled through his drawers, pockets, checking his wallet and personal items carefully. She tried two other codes, but neither would abort the launch.

April knew she was wasting valuable seconds. She brought up the abort screen and rushed to the stairs, leaving orders in her wake, "Get someone computer literate to sit in that chair. As soon as you get the abort password, enter it. If it is successful, inform me immediately. Van der Burden, McMillan; do we have rocket launchers down here yet?"

The Master Sergeant confirmed, and she took one wistful look at the countdown clock, which had subsequently ticked down to 06:52. She cursed like a trooper, and left at the run. Melrose followed her instantly without waiting for orders.

She needed a new plan, and fast. She noticed Teves had joined them, and she had no idea how he had managed that feat. Her memory jogged, and she remembered how he always thought about the bigger picture. Immediately a new tactic bubbled up from her subconscious mind, as she repeated the mantra, missile launchers.

She climbed on the controllers station and stomped her foot hard, shouting for silence. "I ask every rocket launch crew to volunteer now. Our mission is more than dangerous, it is extreme. We will all probably die."

Six men rushed forward, three carrying launchers, and thee carrying ammunition packs. April said, "Thank you. I need the manager's and controller's keys and swipes. Now!"

Melrose took the controller's keys and handed them to April. She glanced at them and shook her head, dropping them on the desk. From above came a shout. McMillan threw down another set of keys. Bill intercepted them just short of April's grasp, and held up a peculiar, circular barrel of a key, saying, "I presume this is what you are looking for, Ma'am?"

She felt like hitting him, but his wide grin made her leap down to hug him instead. She broke quickly and asked for the keys. Her father said, "No. I am going with you."

He appeared to be the only person who knew what her plan was, until Melrose stood before her with the manager's swipe card, and stated flatly, "So am I, Ma'am." Teves immediately appeared on her other side and stated, "So am I, Ma'am. You are not going anywhere without me!"

April cursed, but did not wait, she said, "Let's go!"

She ran out of the control room, and back toward the elevator. Reaching it, she left the outer lock open, and gathered her men inside. Melrose, Bill, and Teves followed her. April put the strange round key in a special access override, and turned it. The descend panel glowed, showing two new subterranean levels. April punched the button for the very lowest level. They were headed directly for the launch bay.

The descent took longer than April expected, but she used the time wisely to brief her men. The door opened and they were in the bowels of the pit. They heard the whish of steam as the ICBM prepared to launch. Using the noise to locate it, they came to a great round bay.

In the center was an impossibly tall missile that seemed to reach into the heavens themselves. Teves shouted above the noise, "Three-minutes till lift-off."

April and Melrose were discussing the best place to hit. Once agreed she gave the order, "Gentlemen, align square and bombard the exact-same spot of the engine housing, just where it meets the main body. Reload and keep hitting the same mark, over, and over, and over again. Does everybody understand?"

Teves called out, "Two-minutes."

The new Master Sergeant gave a short series of commands, his men running immediately to gain strike positions. Their orders were simple, 'Keep firing until the fuselage explodes'.

To a man—they all knew, and accepted, they would not survive the resultant fireball. Corporal Hogs Hogan, a cheeky youth aligned and fired the first marker, laying a bet with his comrades that he would topple the beast first. The others responded in kind, their camaraderie, their public mask, being the effusive and light-hearted banter of men knowing they were about to do and die.

As his aide reloaded, Hogs pulled out a stogie and lit it with practiced ease, casually flicking the still burning match at a "No Smoking" sign. The match went out, his joke not being lost on any man nor woman present. Teves called out, "Ninety-seconds."

As Teves spoke, April looked around and noticed a strange low concrete structure set to the far wall. Curious, she moved away with increasing pace. She made out an access door and began to run toward it, as her mind tried to work out why such a strange construction should be present at the back of a launch bay.

April reasoned it must be the real command station. As the thought became her focus, her strides took on urgency. With mounting belief, she sprinted, coming to a door with camera above. Reaching instinctively for the buzzer, her hand stalled, and tried the handle instead. The door opened.

There was one man inside, who she took by surprise and quickly overpowered. He had been looking only at his monitor readout. She had already accessed the secure terminal when Bill and Teves came to support her.

April stated, "I need the launch abort code, NOW!"

Teves said, "Fifty seconds."

April knew there was little time, and not a lot they could do to make the man break, although both Teves and Bill tried numerous threats.

April knew she was now in the real missile control, and she quickly scanned the monitor. Time passed quickly as she brought up the abort screen and tried the controller's code. Nothing happened. She brought up the screen again and stared at it. She closed the silo doors, as anything might help prevent the launch.

Rocket launchers fired regularly outside, but their power was not enough to bring the missile down. They fell silent, all ammunition spent. Teves called out ten-seconds.

April was not fazed, and reasoned this control already had the password preset, or perhaps there wasn't one. She left the password field blank, moved the mouse, and pressed "Abort". She reasoned this was the ultimate secure area, access denied to all those, except of the highest security level. She also knew she had nothing to lose.

The screen went blank.

Her heart sank, knowing their last chance had gone already. Her eyes were glued to the monitor … time slowed once more. Behind her, two paired eyes never blinked; they waited and willed for a miracle.

The display came back up, flashing: "Launch Aborted"

A cheer erupted as she stood in triumph, pumping the air before pounding her fist into the desk, and almost breaking it in two. She wheeled in celebration and hugged her men, but cursed herself for being such a dummy. Big arms enwrapped her, before she broke away. She still had a job to finish.

She stood the missile down, and in short time, spoke to Van der Burden, who relayed the good news to Aldridge and Redmond. Jubilation erupted within the control room as people rushed to congratulate each other, but everybody knew that April deserved the real plaudits.

Some time later, she reappeared from the underworld with her father at one side, and Teves the other. She received great applause, but deferred, stating, "I could have done nothing without my team. I was just the girl sitting at the console." This time her words had no effect. Everybody knew what she had accomplished.

In the underworld, the rocket launchers were empty as their troops returned. Melrose met them at the elevator door, and they conceived a plan as they rode up. April was not getting away with it that easily. When they reached the control center, Melrose and his men surrounded her. Hogs distracted her by saying, "Ma'am?" Meanwhile his troops grabbed her arms and legs.

They sang, "Hip, Hip, Hurrah!" as they formed a mosh pit, surfing their hero from hand to hand overhead.

"Who's our hero?
She's our Ma'am!
Bustin' walls down,
with a slam.

Extra missile
She don't slack
When we're spent
She got our back

Followed her to
Hell and back
Third one still
Is in its rack

Sound off
One, two
Sound off
Three, four

Count 'em on down,
Four, three, two, one.
Four, three, two, one,
Zero!"

From that moment on, everybody insisted on calling her "Ma'am." April needed action to get rid of the unwanted congratulations, that was if they would ever stop throwing her high into the air?

Chapter 47 – Homeland

Moments later, Colonel Aldridge marched into the Homer control center and declared victory for their troops. He was a little premature. Mopping-up operations took several days, but eventually Homer was cleansed of the nightmarish Coulson stain, and in time, began to recover.

Redmond was greatly comforted to know April was OK, and that she had again achieved the impossible, by aborting the missile launch. It was the only ICBM to be terminated before lift-off, the only one still intact.

Redmond already knew the people who fought alongside April were calling her "Ma'am." His face cracked into a broad smile. He knew how the team would play that one, once she came home safely. Feeling accomplished and content, Redmond strode purposefully back into the main arena, his professional destiny fulfilled. Three nuclear bombs all prevented from reaching their target destinations. He was proud of the team, and told them so as a group, before personally praising their individual efforts.

He did not tarry, but spoke to Euan as soon as he was finished. The Agent asked him to hold, The President came on the line immediately, thanking him, and all of his team. He asked about "The Girl."

Redmond told him truthfully, "She prevented the last missile from launching, when all our other options were exhausted."

The President reflected for a moment before saying, "She is such a young thing to prevail against such enormous odds, and prevent the tragic destruction of our great nation and all its aspirations. The country owes her a debt of deepest gratitude.

"You both deserve the highest Honors, and in time, I will see to it. Thank you, Redmond. You have achieved the impossible and protected the American people and their way of life. Thank you again. Goodbye. God Speed, and God's Blessing."

April returned as the sun melded into the San Diego night. Redmond was waiting for her especially, although he spent more of his time congratulating the greater team. April saw through his protective shield, quickly reading his schoolboy ruse for what it was.

Between times, a day disappeared with praise from people they had never heard of, nor likely would again. As things quieted,

Chapter 47

Redmond called for a full debrief, handing over the bulk of the legwork to London.

Meanwhile, celebrations continued at headquarters. After a while, Redmond walked away, knowing he had won the first battle, but worried that by this victory he had lost the war. He reasoned his team would be disbanded at the first opportunity.

He was astounded, when he received a secure call late that afternoon. The President spoke to him personally, "Redmond, I have used my personal discretion and made your team a bona fide member of the security community and intelligence network of the United States of America. Congratulations my boy, keep up the good fight."

Redmond was elated, and went down at once to tell the team the good news. He was somewhat startled when a large, black, pit bull raced across the room, and bounded directly for April. He reached for his Glock, but stalled when she let out a whoop of joy, and caught the monster in her arms.

He turned as a Texan voice said, "We figured on including the whole team."

Beside Bill, Teves added, "Allow me to introduce Satan, Michael, and John to the team. Without them, we would never have begun all this."

As the sun moved into late afternoon skies, the messages from well-wishers slowed, and life began to resume an air of normality. That dissipated as soon as Redmond announced there would be a celebration party that evening on the top floor.

In due course, Redmond announced, "Celebrations commence in five minutes." The rest of his words were cut off, as people cheered, moving quickly to the lift and stairs. Redmond called April aside stating, "I need one minute with you, please, and then we are done."

April knew she would give Redmond one hell of a lot more than one-minute, all he had to do was ask. Instead of taking her libido in his palms, he handed her a fax that read, "Military Appointment. April Bekkons, Honorary Lieutenant 1st Class, 23rd Marine Corps, Homer." Captain Aldridge and Master Sergeant Melrose signed it. The citation read, "For extreme courage and valor on the field of battle."

She was stunned. First Annaliese, followed by Evelyn and 3G hugged her. Redmond tried to, but somehow he did not seem to know what to do, or where to put his hands. April hugged him instead, and jumped up to peck him on the lips. He blushed, and immediately turned, heading directly for the safety of the corridor.

Minutes later, April walked into the Karaoke bar, and mighty cheers erupted. A chorus of "Happy Birthday" was followed by "I'm twenty-one today", as the party became a double celebration. April was the star of both.

The next morning, Redmond called a long weekend break for all staff. They had Friday through Monday for personal matters. 3G and a small team offered to stay and staff HQ, in exchange for a five-day break when everyone else returned. Redmond chuckled and agreed; he alone knew she had an ulterior motive.

Evelyn waited for her moment, eventually shepherding Bill and Annaliese to where April and Redmond were relaxing alone. They knew she was up to something, all waiting on her words.

"All this," Evelyn waved her arms around, "Would not exist but for one person. I have given Manny, Teves and his family, two weeks at my villa in Acapulco. All you need to do, Boss, is sign the vacation award."

Redmond signed immediately, as their job was done. However, he became distracted, because his PA did not leave, but hovered expectantly, as if choosing her moment to strike.

"Here are six tickets for a VIP, all-expenses paid, weekend at Caesar's Palace, Las Vegas; gambling excepted of course. I have one each for Michael and John, so these four are going begging, any offers? All you have to do is take them and turn up tonight."

Bill rose at once to take two, followed by the second pair, and handed one each to his daughter and Redmond. "Time to put the wheels on the road, no looking back."

All but Redmond were elated, until Evelyn whispered in his ear. She turned to leave before Redmond could protest, and grabbed Annaliese by the arm. Taking her out of earshot, she said, "Make the most of it."

She pecked Annaliese on the cheek. It was most unlike her self-perceived true nature, but she felt devilish and so proud of these people. Annaliese turned immediately to look at April.

April flicked her head and said, "Let's get the hell out of here and have some fun at last!"

Chapter 47

At the doorway, the girls turned to look at their special men and giggled, entreating them with mysterious and forbidden feminine wiles to follow.

The girls locked arms, skipping and laughing, leading the way, deep within whispered intrigues of conspiratorial female plotting.

Each of them knew her chosen man was a work in progress.

The End

Epilogus

Redmond

Redmond debriefed all personnel, in order to formulate a full report for the powers that remained. However, it was several months before most of the picture emerged. As he put the finishing touches to his final review, he added specific incidents to his personal log:

Ketchikan

Lieutenant General Bridgewater sent a large force from Fort Lewis, JBLC, to Ketchikan, the strike beginning at 2330 hours, PST. The sprawling Ketchikan base was designed as a staging post, and offered little resistance. The enemy base was under full-scale assault before they became aware of intrusion.

The base commander was in custody before he could destroy the invasion plans. This information could have proved of vital importance in determining the number and deployment of the ceramic warheads, but was not discovered until it was too late. By the time details were relayed back to HQ in San Diego, the nightmare scenario had already come to pass.

Before the raid on Ketchikan began, several aircraft had already left for Washington, D.C., their arrival timed so the large transport planes would be outside the effective EMP blast radius when the first nuclear bomb exploded. That missile was due to be launched from Hoover Dam, but enemy troops would be boots on the ground while Washington was still trying to figure out what had happened. A fighter squadron was scrambled and escorted the aircraft to a secure military base where they were taken into custody.

On a ship off the east coast in International waters, registered in Bermuda, they located and arrested the secondary force poised to bring working electronics, after the secondary EMP waves had passed. American warships surrounded the ship and brought it to harbor for purposes of containment of the situation, and incarceration of hostile forces.

The operation was deemed a great success, and enormous intelligence was gathered over the weeks that followed. Investigations are not yet concluded. It will take months, if not years, to reveal the larger extent of the Coulson-DeMellor web of intrigue.

Euan's great net was never closed. The Secret Service and their allies did swoop, ridding Capitol Hill of DeMellor's malign influence. However, investigations are set to continue, and, likewise, may last for a long time.

The ICBM's

Experts discovered the Hoover Damn missile was designed to take out Washington, D.C. and the electronics surrounding 600 miles, at an explosion altitude of 40 miles. This was not part of the information TIA Bekkons got from Homer, but was discovered by Rude when he ran a computer check of the base near Las Vegas. The missile was programmed to explode above Mount Union, Pennsylvania, and would also have also brought New York, Chicago, and Detroit to their knees. As it was, the mayhem created by the build up of small disasters has left those cities crippled.

(NB: Authorities are taking this as an opportunity to improve secure infrastructure in all levels of transit communications.)

The two Homer missiles were set for higher altitude strikes, designed to cripple the entirety of the U.S. One was due to explode in the atmosphere above Cincinnati, and the other above Salt Lake City, taking out all digital electronics, communications, and computers used across America. The detonation height was set for 60 miles, and the area of significant disruption estimated to be about 1500 miles in diameter, being the physical event horizon.

Regarding the surviving missile, government scientists continue to work on it, and plan to replicate it. This will give the United States of America a significant tactical advantage in modern warfare.

Decoration

The President was true to his word. After deliberating for several months, he created a new Medal of Honor, arguing with his advisors that such bravery in the face of impossible odds demanded recognition higher than the current civilian mix of Congressional Gold Medal, and The Presidential Medal of Freedom with Distinction.

This new award was open to both military, and civilians, and ranked above all previous accolades. It will become the de facto measure of an Americans' ultimate and truest worth.

TIA April Bekkons was selected personally by the President to receive the first, highest accolade, The United States Medal of Outstanding Valor. I, Redmond am the second recipient. I wonder how rarely it will be awarded in the future.

Tactical Awareness Bureau

It gives me great satisfaction to know our team is now confirmed as a semi-autonomous member of the U.S. security community. Our brief is simple, to keep tabs on any threat to the security of our nation. Our acronym, 'TAB', defines our purpose better than any mission statement could ever do.

The first mission, initiated days after the celebratory party returned from Vegas, was delivered in person to our HQ by the Director of the FBI. The primary task was to assist Euan with tracking down all people who had evaded his net. The secondary mandate was to discover, how they escaped detection.

Redmond concluded his report, with the annotation:

The President was noted to remark publicly: "Without them [Redmond and his team], this great country would no longer exist in its present form. However, the threat persists, and we must remain ever vigilant."

www.ingramcontent.com/pod-product-compliance
Lightning Source LLC
Chambersburg PA
CBHW061545170626
46811CB00001B/92